NO
GREATER
LOSS

NO GREATER LOSS

A Faith Clarke Mystery

Julie Bates

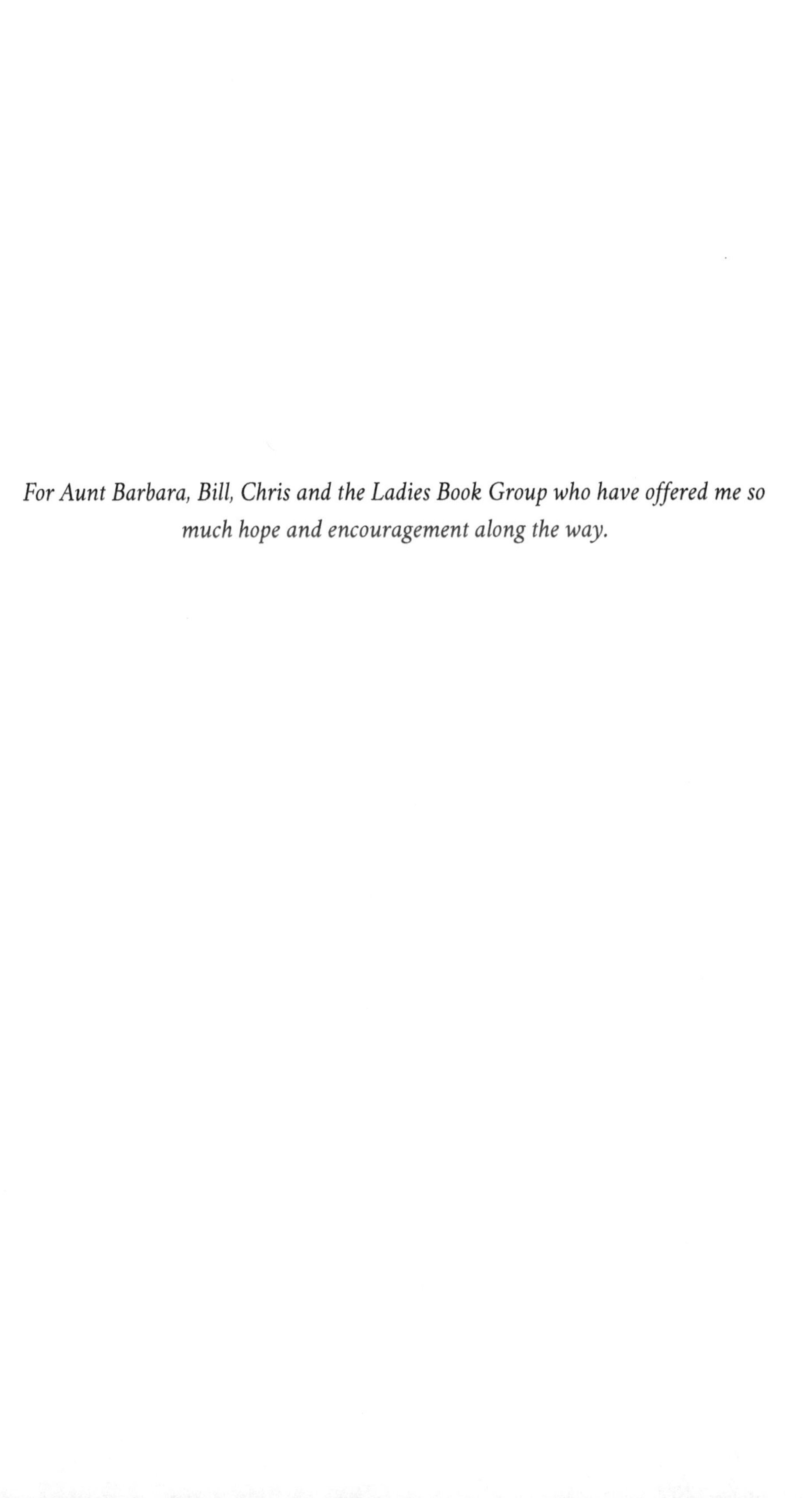

For Aunt Barbara, Bill, Chris and the Ladies Book Group who have offered me so much hope and encouragement along the way.

Praise for No Greater Loss

"With *No Greater Loss*, Julie Bates continues the saga of Faith Clarke, a widow who manages a tavern in colonial Williamsburg while trying to discover who has murdered or abused three women and a soldier. Walk the streets of Williamsburg with Faith. You'll smell bread baking in fireplaces, hear noises that could reveal a spy, and worry that the British are approaching. This riveting, fast-paced mystery evokes a time of fear and anxiety in American history."—Marlie Parker Wasserman, author of *Inferno on Fifth*

"Full of conflicts and dilemmas, *No Greater Loss* is a tale of family drama and murder, so richly woven I felt I'd gone back in time to the Revolutionary War."—M.A. Monin, author of The Intrepid Traveler mysteries

Chapter One

Faith shivered as she left the warmth of the stand-alone kitchen to head back into the tavern. Icy wind blew across the yard, and through the heavy layers of clothing she wore. She wrapped her heavy woolen shawl tighter around her shoulders as she scurried up the path to the relative warmth of the tavern. Frost killed grass colored the yard in shades of brown and yellow. A few dead plants waved as the breeze blew their dried limbs about, animating them into a spectral semblance of life. Mournful lowing sounded from the barn. The cows didn't care much for the weather either. Titus had fed them at dawn along with the few horses that boarded with them for when couriers from the Sons of Liberty rode in. Her father-in-law's spy network continued even after his passing a few years ago. It had been weeks since a messenger had come through with a letter from Jeremy Butler, Washington's spy, and now her brother-in-law. After the General's victory at Princeton, the army had settled for the winter. Faith had replied, although there was little to add. Winter slowed all activity as everyone sought to avoid the cold.

Her shoes clattered as she went up the steps of the back porch. Faith paused, to look about the home she had worked so hard to own. Frost dappled the yard and sparkled off the dead grass. Rough ground lay churned up from where the garden had been. The frozen earth held little but a few dead corn stalks and dried up squash vines which cast a desolate air about the place. She watched a few leaves fall from the oak that took up a corner in her back yard. Beneath it sat an abandoned bench where, a few years ago, a man had professed his love, only to retract it weeks later. The pain had faded to a dull ache. Although she still saw him in town, selling newspapers and at the print shop where he was indentured, they didn't speak. After his abrupt ending of their relationship, Faith spent weeks wondering what had happened and weeping at night when no one could see. His near death from arsenic had left him fearful of relationships, and there was nothing she could do about that. Faith was still angry, but she had moved on. She had no need of any man in her life. Will McKay might still haunt her dreams some nights, but he was no longer in her thoughts every day. The doorknob slipped in her gloved hands as she tried to open the door. The wind blew the scent of wood smoke across the yard, bringing with it the scent of cooking meat. After a few seconds of twisting, the door swung open, allowing her to go in and cut off the breeze that ran chilly fingers up her dress.

Faith enjoyed keeping a tavern. After her husband's sudden death a few years ago, she had become the owner of a business. It had been frightening at first, but as time passed, she found she enjoyed making her own decisions. Taking care of her guests kept her busy and informed on all that went on in town. People from every walk of life stopped in for food, drink, or simply to catch up on news. As she looked out over the taproom, Faith was relieved to see that a handful of men occupied some of the tables that filled the room. During the slow winter months, when few people traveled, the local populace made up most of the tavern's business. She was grateful for those who came in and kept the tavern running.

A fire crackled in the hearth, providing both light and heat to the room. Its bright orange and yellow flames chased away the shadows left in areas where light from the windows did not reach. Her younger brother Seth stood behind the bar pouring drinks and keeping anyone from helping themselves.

A pair of soldiers played cards at a table in the center of the room. In the months following the Declaration of Independence in Philadelphia, Virginia's various militias had become an increased presence. Soldiers in their hunter's shirts and breeches drilled regularly on the green near the armory. Their presence had become a regular part of daily life in Williamsburg. Her main news regarding the war came in her sister's letters from Philadelphia. Faith worried about Hannah being so close to the fight, but her older sister was of no mind to flee. She wondered what her sister knew about Butler's clandestine activities. The smile dropped off her face. She hoped Hannah knew what she was getting into. It was a dangerous game, one that kept her up nights, when contemplating her own involvement even though the British fought their battles far north of Virginia these days. Her father's farm lay on the outskirts of Philadelphia, although her younger sister Charity had said they hadn't seen any trouble.

Faith knew only too well that trouble came when least expected. The past few years had been turbulent. She longed for a day when she did not have to worry about having enough money to pay her debts and keep her business solvent. She had no husband to share the load and no desire to find one. Her brief experience with Will McKay had made her leery of romantic entanglements. Even now, when she saw him in town, a brief stab of hurt resounded in her heart. No brief period of joy was worth the long pain of regret.

Out back, the steady thwack of an axe resonated through the walls and inside, where fires had to be kept going. Titus York kept busy chopping wood. They went through it quickly in the winter months. Faith was grateful that both he and his wife Olivia had agreed to stay as employees after their manumission. She would not have been able to run the tavern without them, even if there was little to do currently. No guests currently inhabited the rooms upstairs, which meant they did not bother kindling those fires. She walked over to the woodpile by the fireplace and stirred the coals with the poker before adding another log. Her younger brother Seth spoke from behind her, "I was going to do that."

Faith looked over at him and smiled. "I've gotten used to doing things myself. I prefer to stay busy."

Seth nodded. "Me too." He looked out at the room where only a few tables were occupied. "It's been a slow day."

She was aware. Not many people traveled in the winter, preferring to stay close to home unless they had business in the capital. So much had changed in the past few years. The royal governor had fled a few years ago, and now the immense mansion he once lived in was occupied by the fiery attorney Patrick Henry, now acting as governor. Every day, she saw men in uniform headed toward the Capitol building down the road from her tavern. She saw them leave as well but had no idea where they went.

Faith left the main room to slip back to her bedroom, where the tile stove provided a reasonable degree of comfort. Her ledger waited. Its meager entries told their own tale. She tried to ignore the quiet. Eugenia had arranged for Andrew to stay with George Wythe in his large brick mansion near the governor's palace. She had argued that there was no better man to study law within the entire colony, and Faith could not disagree. Yet she missed her son terribly and thought thirteen was too young to leave home.

Out in the kitchen, Olivia baked bread for the week. She had her own loss to deal with. Her son Joshua, a few years older than Andrew, now worked and lived as an apprentice with an apothecary, carefully measuring out herbs and tonics under the supervision of the two men who ran the business and visited various homes in Williamsburg treating ailments. His visits home were few. Faith hoped he had found happiness in his new trade.

Titus entered through the back door carrying a large armload of wood, which he stacked near the fireplace. He went back down the hall and out back. Faith already knew he would be taking another load to his wife in the kitchen. Olivia stayed busy preparing meals for both family and guests. Titus would go in and sit down to spend a few precious moments with his wife as he slaked his thirst with a mug a cider and a few biscuits left from breakfast.

Within a few hours, men would come into the main room for a drink and a hot meal. It was then Faith would discover what was going on in town. There had been little information to share with her spymaster. Jeremy Butler had not been in Williamsburg in months. From what little Hannah had said, she gathered that he stayed close to General Washington these days providing what help he could.

Not many people traveled in the winter. Whether it was snow, rain, or the ever-present chill, very few people left their homes, which meant Faith's business rested with the townspeople who came in to drink and get a hot meal. With the fighting in the north and the British blockading the coast, her business had dropped. She was holding on by a hair. Faith tried not to worry, but the lack of money coming in frightened her.

The main door opened, letting in cold air. Faith shivered. Her quilted petticoat, a Christmas gift from her mother-in-law Eugenia, kept out a great deal of chill, but where it stopped, the icy touch of winter penetrated through her wool stockings. She stretched her legs out toward the stove, shivering as a blast of heat drove the chill from her ankles and feet.

Faith looked to see who had entered the tavern. She recognized the uniform as one of those worn by the various militias in town. Most days, they trained on one of the green spaces in town. She had become accustomed to the sound of their muskets firing along with the faint call of the men in charge. Men in uniform could be seen throughout the town as they prepared for the enemy to invade.

This man's uniform varied from what she had seen. Instead of breeches, he wore long gaiters made of navy blue wool. The soldier was of medium height with a stocky build and thick sandy hair. His tanned features indicated he spent a moderate amount of time outdoors. He wore a deep blue jacket with red facings along with a red vest accompanied by a small round blue hat turned up on the left, the uniform of the Virginia militia. He was an officer used to commanding men.

He made a short bow and met her gaze with bright blue eyes. "Greetings, mistress, are you the proprietress of this place?"

Faith nodded. "Yes, I am Faith Clarke. I own Clarke Tavern. How can I assist you?"

He looked about the interior before sketching a brief bow. "I am Captain Gregory Hoag of Fredericksburg. I will need your tavern as lodging for me and my officers."

She raised an eyebrow. "How long will you be renting rooms?"

He smiled, revealing a full set of teeth. A few were slightly crooked, which added to the craggy handsomeness he already possessed. "I will need your rooms for the length of my regiment's stay in the capital. The governor will pay you each month for room and board for me and my men."

Faith chewed her lip. Steady income would be a blessing through the winter and in the coming months. She quickly did calculations in her head. "That would be two pounds, forty-five pence for the use of my tavern per month."

He nodded. "I will request a warrant from Governor Henry in your name. Once the council approves it, you will receive your funds."

It still jarred Faith that the hot-headed lawyer Patrick Henry resided in the Governor's Palace and held the office formerly held by an appointee of the King of England. He managed the business of the colony along with his council. In some ways, there was little difference than when the House of Burgesses met just a stone's throw away from her small tavern.

The captain watched her for a moment before asking. "How many rooms do you have upstairs?"

"Four, two large and two small. There are two large beds in the large rooms with hooks for clothes. The small rooms contain one bed. The beds are large enough to accommodate four comfortably. There are pallets for the floor that can be pulled out as well."

Captain Hoag looked to the left at the taproom was and its roaring fire. Her brother Seth had stepped up to the bar in her absence. He chatted with an older gentleman as he filled his tankard.

Hoag's head turned to the other side of the hall where Faith maintained her office and her bedroom in the back. "How many sleep there?"

"That is my room," Faith replied. "I conduct my business there as well. It is not open to guests." She watched Hoag's gaze circle the room again. His booted foot tapped as he contemplated her space.

He offered her a charming smile. "I imagine it's hard for a woman to run a business on her own without a man to guide and protect her."

Faith's voice chilled. "I manage. My staff assists me in ensuring my guests are tended, and no one acts in an untoward manner. I assume you will inform your men that no ill behavior will be tolerated within these walls."

"Ill behavior? Certainly not, Mistress Clarke." His tone was faintly mocking. "But you cannot blame men far away from home for admiring an attractive woman who serves their ale.

Faith's eyes narrowed. She had dealt with plenty of drunks and men who thought she provided more than food and housing. "No, I would blame their commanding officer for being unable to control his own men."

The captain straightened as the smile vanished from his face. "Message received, Mistress Clarke. I would warn you that I expect civility from those serving my men as well."

"And they shall have it," Faith replied, meeting his gaze squarely. "As you noted, I am a woman alone. I have to be careful. These are dangerous times. I would hate for the Virginia Militia to lose a soldier foolish enough to attack a woman in her own home."

Hoag stared at her for a long moment before replying. "Very well," he said as he replaced his hat. "I will report to the governor that I and a dozen of my men will be lodging here in the shadows of the capitol. We will move in later today. I bid you good day." He opened the front door and shut it firmly behind him. The sound of his boots echoed on the boards of the porch and down the steps.

Faith watched him through the window as he was joined by two other men in similar uniforms. Apparently, they were all engaged in arranging lodging for their men. They spoke in low voices as they walked toward the wide brick walls of the Capitol Building, kicking up dust as they went.

Faith's heart beat rapidly in her chest. Her tavern would soon be full of militia from wherever in the colony they had been pulled. While she was grateful for the income, she disliked being forced into anything. There was nothing she could do once he had chosen the tavern for his men. They were expected to support the militias that came into town. Faith had heard of other taverns in the colony that the provincial government paid to house soldiers. She wondered if the women there felt threatened. She hoped not.

Seth watched her from across the room, concern on his face. Despite the fact he tried to be the man of the house, he was still her little brother. She couldn't see him any other way.

Faith forced a smile on her face as she walked over, mindful of being watched by the curious eyes of the men who had come in for a drink, a meal, or both.

"Is thou well?" Seth whispered as he wiped down the bar with a rag.

"Well enough," she answered. "We be hosting a dozen militia officers, paid for by our governor." She nodded as a man held up a tankard for a refill. Faith picked up a pitcher of ale and went about refilling drinks for her guests. So many men had become soldiers. They had begun to outnumber the farmers and tradespeople who had once been her stock and trade. A log popped in the fire, making her jump. She wasn't the only one. A few of the men had started to rise out of their chairs, checking for threats.

Faith drew in a breath. "More ale?" she asked as she moved about filling steins. Titus appeared in the doorway, carrying the first course of the afternoon meal. Within moments, the men's minds and hands were engaged in spooning down her cook's fine beef stew. Seeing that Seth and Titus had the room well in hand, Faith moved down the hall and out back to see if Olivia needed her assistance.

A steady plume of smoke rose from the chimney of the small building out back that housed the kitchen and the rooms above where Olivia and Titus lived. Faith walked down the pathway, eager to be out of the cold. Nonetheless, her eyes took in the dull grey sky above. Would it bring rain or snow? She wasn't crazy about the prospect of either. The dull brown grass could be very slippery after a cold rain, especially if there was sleet mixed in. Her foot wobbled on a stone, causing her to wobble a few moments before she regained her balance.

Faith straightened. Now was not the time to wrench an ankle by not paying attention. With both Andrew and Joshua gone, everyone needed to stay moving. She walked more carefully, listening to the crunch of the broken shells that lined the walkway as she made her way to the kitchen.

A welcome wave of heat greeted her as she pushed open the door. Olivia used a large wooden spoon to stir the stew simmering in the iron pot hanging inside the fireplace, where she prepared all the tavern's meals. A bright red cloth covered her hair, although a few dark curls escaped at the nape of her neck. Her gray-striped skirt was tucked up to avoid the flames coming up from the logs in the belly of the fireplace. As was the pink apron that protected it from stains. She had pushed up the arms of her shift to work; its neckline was visible just above the floral print of her bodice. The scars on her neck, from a long-ago fire, had faded to a tone a few shades paler than the surrounding skin. Olivia never spoke of it, although Faith was aware that it had nearly killed her. It explained the caution she exercised around the roaring flames.

She turned to look at Faith, her cat-like eyes narrowing as she analyzed her employer's expression. "Is everything going well inside?"

Faith shrugged. "Well enough. We will be bedding a dozen new tenants soon."

Olivia raised an eyebrow, waiting for her to elaborate.

"A group of militia officers are taking up residence. The governor's council will pay their room and board."

Olivia nodded. "You know they will pay in continental currency."

Faith nodded. "It's all anyone has these days. I don't even remember when I last handled English or French Coins. Regardless, it is income we need."

Olivia knew that. She haggled ruthlessly for meat and vegetables at the market. What little there was looked pitiful but still filled a belly. She was already planning to plant seeds as soon as the earth was warm enough. She longed for fresh greens and fruit. She met Faith's eyes. "You need to ask about provisions."

"What?" Faith replied, startled.

Olivia waved an arm around the space, noticing the bare rafters where ropes of onion and garlic had once hung. "There is barely enough food for us, much less a bunch of soldiers. They have been contracting with taverns and grocers all over Williamsburg the past few days. They will provide money or supplies to you to feed their men."

Faith nodded. She should have realized that. "Captain Hoag should be back later today. I will take up the issue with him. "Is there anything else I should request?"

Olivia paused, her nimble brain calculating. "Blankets, pork, beans, flour, sugar. We're going to need supplies if we're to keep them comfortable. You may also want to see if they have horses to stable. We will need supplies for them, too. Ask Titus. He will know what we need."

Faith nodded. Titus managed the stables, although since Seth had come down from her father's farm, he had taken on many of those tasks as well. She wondered how her family fared up where there was so much turmoil. Her father had returned to Pennsylvania after spending a few months with her after his wife's passing. Isaac Payne was not a writer, so Faith's only news came from her sisters.

Olivia's voice broke into her thoughts. "There's food to be served in the main room. Men will want their dinner." She gestured to platters of boiled potatoes and ham.

Faith balanced the large tray as Olivia opened the door. The chill took her breath away as she retraced her steps into the back of Clarke Tavern. She paused for a moment to let her eyes adjust to the shadowed interior. The voices from the main room seemed louder. As she entered, she heard a loud "Huzzah," which made her jump. Titus had come in behind her. He hastily retrieved the tray and began passing out food. More militia had entered. Seth was busy filling tankards with ale to men lined up at the bar.

Faith's eyes widened slightly as she realized the number of men in the room had tripled. Turning about, she ran into Captain Hoag.

"Easy, Mistress Clarke," he said. "I would hate for anything to happen to our fair hostess."

Faith shot him a look but restrained her tongue. This was more than a dozen men, and he knew it. She had business to discuss with him. "Let us retire to my office so we can better arrange for the care and feeding of your men."

He followed her willingly across the hall. Faith propped the door open and stood where Seth could see her from the bar. Hoag remained standing as well. He looked over at her tile stove, and his eyes widened. "What is that?"

"A gift from my father," Faith replied. "He got it from a Moravian in the North Carolina Colony."

Hoag stood in front of it, holding out his hands to the steady heat. "This would be a nice prize for any home. Your father is a thoughtful man."

Faith picked up her ledger. "Yes, he is. He was here not long ago before returning to his farm." She flipped to a blank page. "We will have to make arrangements for food and blankets for your men. I don't have a lot on hand at this moment. We will also have to make sure there is room for everyone to sleep." She shot him a look. "There are more than a dozen men out there."

Hoag held up a hand. "Do not fret, Mistress Clarke. I have made arrangements for a line of credit for you at the local stores. We will find places for all the men. Even a barn loft is comfortable after sleeping in open fields. The bills will be approved by me, and I will submit them to Governor Henry's council for payment." He met her eyes, smiling as he warned her. "I will check to make sure your purchases line up with what is provided to me and my men."

"Understood," she answered, raising her chin to stare back at him. "I have never defrauded anyone."

"That's a good thing," Hoag said. "I would hate to be the first to apply a whip to that delicate ivory skin. You should begin receiving deliveries of rations tomorrow." With that, he left, leaving Faith to stare after him, wondering what she had gotten herself into.

Chapter Two

The pale sun cast comforting warmth on Olivia's shoulders as she strode into town. A large basket hung on her arm, almost empty for the moment. Even in the dead of winter she took pleasure in the walk up Duke of Gloucester Street. Two or three days a week, she left breakfast in the hands of Faith and the assistant cook Dorcas and left to go to the market. The streets were quiet in the early hours, just after dawn, with the exception of other cooks and maids headed to the market and people preparing to open their businesses for the day. She paused by the gate to the apothecary's yard, hoping for a glimpse of Joshua. Like any mother, she knew he had to leave the nest, but his absence created an empty space in her heart that no amount of work could fill.

The side door opened, and her heart leapt as she recognized a familiar dark head. Joshua York was tall like his father, but he had her rich, coppery skin and faintly tilted eyes. He was halfway to the small herb garden that filled close to half of the narrow yard before he realized he was not alone. Whirling about quickly, he took a defensive pose before recognizing his mother and relaxing slightly. "What brings you here?"

Olivia lifted her basket slightly before letting it settle back into the crook of her arm. "I'm headed to the market before it gets too busy." Her eyes drank him in, from his neatly braided queue to the apron that covered his shirt and breeches. His sleeves were rolled to just below the elbow, exposing lightly muscled forearms. He wore deep blue stockings she had knit for him during a slow period at the tavern. "How are you?"

She shouldn't have asked. His body stiffened.

"Why do you ask?" He shivered in the cool air as he stared at her.

Olivia felt a chill from more than the air. Joshua was seventeen now and of an age not to want his mother hanging around. She shrugged. "No reason. I haven't seen you lately, and I wondered what you were doing."

He ran a hand through his hair. "I stay busy here at the apothecary. I have many jobs to perform, and Dr. Galt expects me to excel at all of them." He looked at her. "I need to gather herbs for a remedy he is taking to a family in town. You had best get to market or all the best things will be gone."

Olivia dropped her eyes from his, sadness welling up at the dismissal. His voice softened. "I will drop by Sunday after church. I have a few hours then that I can call my own."

She nodded and turned back to continue her journey down the street. In winter, the market's offerings were far smaller than in the warmer months when people brought the bounty of their gardens to sell. Nonetheless, Olivia still found saltfish and game. A flash of orange in a corner alerted her that someone had pumpkins to sell. Eager to have something to add variety to the stew she planned, Olivia moved toward the table, making her way through the other men and women intent on filling their baskets as well. Something hooked her ankle, causing her to fall. She looked in dismay as her hard-gotten goods spilled across the floor. She heard laughter as she scrambled to pick up her purchases. A man who tended a stall of leather goods stooped down to help her.

Olivia thanked him as he grasped a trio of onions and dropped them back into her basket.

He leaned back on his heels and looked up at her. "Those women are mean."

"What do you mean?" Olivia asked as she rescued a bunch of turnips from being stomped.

"One of them tripped you so the other could get to that stall first." He gestured at the two women, both in brightly colored skirts underneath snowy aprons. "Those two are part of the Randolph Household. Their mistress expects the best there is to offer, so they work together to get it. The one on the left is Marianna, the shorter one is Jane. I've seen what they do." He helped her up. "You're better off avoiding them."

The pair of women stood in front of her. Olivia tried to move around them, but one of them slid over, blocking the way. "Excuse me," she said loudly, trying to get around. The woman didn't respond, instead turning to keep her back to her and block her from the table. The other slid over to the table. She talked in a loud voice, exclaiming over the pumpkins as she picked out the largest one. "These look amazing. I know you have been storing them in your cellar, but I swear they look like you just pulled them off the vine. My mistress will be so pleased to see these served at her table."

The woman behind the table beamed as her husband put more of them on the table. Some still had a few green spots on them; a few were wrinkled slightly with age. Olivia tried to get past, but the shorter woman moved closer to the table, keeping her away. Finally, Olivia moved to the outside and stomped on the foot of her opponent.

The woman yelped as she hopped away.

"Excuse me," Olivia said as she went to the table to check the available produce. She watched the freshest and best go into the basket of the other woman, who kept talking as she grabbed up radishes and cabbage as well. As she turned to go, she smirked at Olivia. "You can have what's left."

Anger burned in her belly as she heard them cackling as they went to leave the market. The woman smiled at Olivia apologetically. "I'm sorry I didn't see you standing there. How can I help you?" Olivia worked to keep her smile from turning into a snarl as she picked up two smaller pumpkins to add to her basket, grateful that the cellar at Clarke Tavern still contained dried apples among the herbs that they had bundled and hung to dry. She felt fortunate that the garden had been productive over the summer so that the cellar still held a variety of vegetables. But it wouldn't last long with a house full of hungry men. There was no telling when they would receive rations from the militia to feed the men who would be staying at the tavern.

Olivia knew who had an abundance of what. As a cook for a small tavern, she had forged connections with other cooks throughout the town. She knew the apothecaries' cook kept an abundance of culinary herbs and that cooks for places such as the Wythe House had large supplies of meat and grain from the plantations their families owned. Olivia had homebrewed ciders and ales from the abundance of fruit they had picked and preserved throughout the warmer months.

Olivia left the market and walked to the large brick tenement on Duke of Gloucester Street, where Georgia Clements published her Virginia Gazette with the help of her son and the indentured servant Will McKay. She spotted them at work through the window as she passed by to go to the separate kitchen behind the house. Will and her employer, Faith Clarke, had been betrothed once. Now, they barely spoke. Part of her wondered what had driven them apart, but her wiser self knew it was better to stay out of it. She had far more important business to attend.

Smoke rose from the tall brick chimney of the tidy one-and-a-half-story frame house that was the kitchen and home of the cook. As Olivia approached, she spotted her quarry stepping outside to pour water out of a big bowl while keeping the contents from coming out with it with one hand. She recognized the process. Olivia had spent plenty of time soaking the excess salt from salt pork to make it edible.

Without looking up, Athena said, "What brings you here, Olivia York?" Taller than most men, the regal dark-skinned woman dominated any space she was in. Rich dark hair peeked out from a snowy white kerchief that set off her clear skin and the shells she wore in her ears. She finished draining the water before going back inside.

Olivia followed and set her basket down on the table. Athena eyed it but said nothing. "I have some news to share," Olivia said as she stepped closer to the fire to warm herself. "A group of officers has moved into the tavern. There's talk of British warships in the Chesapeake."

"That rumor has been going around for a few weeks now. I haven't heard it confirmed by anyone." Athena ran the patriot spy network in Williamsburg in the absence of her partner, Jeremy Butler, who she regarded as a son. He remained up north gathering intelligence for Washington. She undoubtedly had someone keeping eyes on the York and James Rivers looking for the enemy.

Olivia nodded. "That's true, but no one expected our former governor to raid the coast last year either." She looked about, always curious how other women ran their kitchens. Athena kept her space well organized, with crocks lining shelves on one side of the room. Within the fireplace behind her, a huge iron pot steamed as water boiled inside.

Athena put a small amount of lard into an iron skillet she had heating on a spider over the fire. It hissed as it melted, leaving a shiny coating on the interior. From there, she put the meat inside, browning it before adding it to her pot.

Olivia watched her in silence and waited until she had completed her task. Once Athena had finished adding the pork to her pot, she added a bay leaf from her spice box and looked up at Olivia with an inquiring eye.

"The militia is using our tavern for some of its men," she said. "They are working out arrangements with Faith over the pay and what they will provide for use of the rooms It sounds like more troops are coming into town."

Athena nodded. "They expect the British to launch an attack on the capital and we are close to the coast. Ships sail up and down the rivers all the time. It would not be difficult to land troops and march in before we could muster much of a defense."

"When will the British come?" Olivia said. "Have you heard?"

Athena shook her head. " I have not. But we can't rely on messages to tell us what to do. We have to keep our eyes open. There are still plenty of people in this town who would welcome the return of the British to our capital and our colony." Her face turned grim. "They would help them any way they could."

Olivia nodded. She knew that as well. Servants talked about the goings on in the homes they served. Both she and Athena knew which homes held loyalists and that some of the affluent homes near the governor's palace kept in correspondence with their allies in other colonies.

Outside, they both heard the steady chop of an axe. Olivia wondered if it was Will McKay. The young Scot came in a few minutes later to drop a load of wood in the rack next to the fireplace. He paused briefly to warm his hands before heading out. Athena offered him a cup of coffee which he refused with a brief apology. Avoiding eye contact with Olivia, he headed back out.

Athena shook her head. "He hasn't forgotten her." She took up a large knife and began chopping carrots with quick strokes to add to the pot on the fire.

Olivia offered her a pumpkin. Although it was slightly shriveled, the flesh inside would still be good. Athena thanked her and offered her a bunch of parsnips in return. Athena returned to her table as Olivia let herself out of the warm kitchen and into the chilly air.

Her breath created a smoky cloud as she exhaled. She would have to hurry to make it back to the tavern in time to get the rest of dinner cooking. Olivia wondered if the soldiers had arrived. She was uneasy about the situation, but in truth, there was nothing either of them could do. No one could refuse the militia room, board, or supplies. They had no way of knowing what sort of men they were or how well their captain could control them. She prayed they were an orderly lot. Young men away from home dealt with loneliness in a variety of ways: liquor, dice, and willing women. God only knew how they would occupy their time when not drilling on the field. Yet they were the men who would engage the British in battle. Who knew how many would make it home unscathed? Olivia was glad Joshua remained busy with his apprenticeship. She quickened her pace, certain the tavern was filling up with men who had agreed to battle against the greatest military force in the world. The governor would pay their receipts, but it would be up to them to make use of what they were provided to care for the men.

Titus would have to mind the liquor cabinet. If they weren't careful their stock would disappear in the night. Olivia shuddered. She disliked dealing with drunkards. They presumed everything and everyone was available. This was one of the reasons she always kept a knife on her person.

As she looked down the street, she saw a crowd gathering not far from the market. A ship had come in with a load of human cargo. Olivia's stomach turned as she saw them, wrapped in chains and shivering in the cold air. She wanted to scream at the inhumanity that drove people to sell other human beings no less valued in the eyes of God. As she watched them shuffle forward, dragging their shackles, rage rose until her eyes blurred. She took deep breaths, aware that if she did as she wished, she would accomplish nothing and likely be thrown into the gaol. She couldn't watch. It was too painful to see those with skin like hers treated like animals. It was unbearable.

Olivia turned off of Duke of Gloucester Street and crossed down past the guardhouse and magazine to the farm fields that stretched out behind the small homes that lined Queen Street. In the distance, she could hear the firing of muskets as the militia trained on the Palace Green. The breeze picked up, chilling the exposed parts of her face. Olivia turned her head down and picked up her steps. The sooner she was back in her warm kitchen, the better. Clouds scurried overhead, warning that inclement weather approached.

Branches from the trees slapped against one another, creating an eerie clatter as she hurried home. Their skeletal limbs cast long shadows across the path, reminding her that it was not many hours past dawn. Her foot slithered on a slick patch of ground. Olivia caught her breath as she recovered, relieved not to have fallen one more time this morning.

A stray dog crossed the road in front of her, no doubt heading back to his home. Looking about, Olivia realized she was the only person on the road. No horses or wagons trotted by on the way to and from town. With the cold, no one lingered out in the yard. No cows had come out to pasture yet to chew on the partially frozen grass. Clouds gathered overhead, painting eerie shadows over the landscape. She hurried on, eager to return to the tavern. Olivia longed to hear the familiar sound of her husband Titus singing as he worked in the stable or chopped wood for her fire. It was too quiet and isolated out here, even though she could see houses not a stone's throw away from the fallow fields on either side. Eager to get home, Olivia left the road to cut across the broad stretch of land, hoping to cut her travel time.

The partially frozen ground was rough with broken weeds and clods of dirt. She stumbled over a rock protruding from the earth. As she paused to regain her footing, a bright splash of color caught her eye. Half hidden by weeds a large piece of deep red fabric lay on the ground contrasting sharply with the surrounding dead grass. As she moved more closely, she realized the fabric covered something bulky. By now, curiosity outweighed the winter chill. Olivia wondered why someone would leave such a large piece of cloth and whatever goods lay beneath. It made no sense. She wondered if she had inadvertently come upon some smuggler's cache. The sky rumbled low overhead. If she didn't hurry, she would be caught out in cold, wet rain. On the other hand, it was good quality fabric, which meant something even more valuable might be underneath. As Olivia looked down, a shiver ran down her spine that had nothing to do with the cold. A woman lay curled up on the ground, her skirt over her head and torso like the windblown blossom of a flower torn apart by a storm.

A sick knot of dread formed in Olivia's throat. She knew the look of death. Dark-skinned legs rose above the ties around hand-knitted stockings and a bare bottom. The skirt flapped in the breeze, covering the woman's head. Olivia reached down and pulled it back, Hair spread out over the ground in a dark wave obscuring the woman's face. She swept it back to reveal a face stiffened into a mask of agonized death, darkened blood coating the lower half. Olivia fell back with a shocked cry. Her own breath huffed in the chilly wind as she looked down at a woman broken and discarded on the cold, barren ground.

Chapter Three

Olivia shuddered as she drank the brandy Titus poured. Her graphic account of what she had seen galvanized everyone into action. Even surrounded by the solid form of her husband and the blazing heat of the kitchen's fire, she shivered as her mind went back to the corpse lying in the field. Her eyes went to the fire where Faith stirred the stew she had started earlier that morning in preparation for the midday meal. Dripping fat from meat on the spit hissed as it hit the hot logs, sending up tiny puffs of smoke.

"I need to finish dinner," she said, rising from her seat at the worktable. The kitchen was her kingdom, and everywhere she looked, she could see things that needed to be done. She wobbled as a gray haze filled her eyes for a few seconds. Olivia moved to the table, determined not to let shock overwhelm her.

Titus put a hand on her shoulder. His sherry-colored eyes filled with protective love as he spoke. "You've had a shock. You need to take a moment." He rubbed her shoulders as she sat back down. His hands dug into tight muscles, trying to ease the fear that filled her.

Olivia shook her head. "I'm not the one who's dead. The best thing for me to do is focus on the here and now. I have over a dozen men to feed in a short time, and I still need to put biscuits on to bake." She looked down at the table where she would normally be at work. Stacks of vegetables waited to be chopped. A large bowl sat on one side with flour in it for beaten biscuits. She had planned to get the butter and milk once she had returned. On the fire, a pot bubbled with apples from the stock of dried ones she had put on to soak the day before. The rich scent of nutmeg and apple perfumed the air, along with the heady scent of meat roasting. She needed to return to her normal routine. The image in her mind remained vivid and horrible. Olivia willed it to go away.

Faith spoke from where she stood near the fire. "I can do it, if you need some time. Most everything should be ready shortly. There is very little left to do." She looked in the stone oven built into the side of the kitchen wall. The large ceramic crock of beans and pork stood deep inside, along with the Cheshire pork pies filled with the salt pork they had soaked overnight and potatoes from the cellar. It would not be difficult to complete what Olivia had started. "I am sure Dorcas and I can manage one meal without you."

Just then, the chubby little junior cook came in, her cheeks flushed from the outdoors. She started chattering as soon as she saw Faith. "Ellen and I got all the beds upstairs made and laid fires ready to light," she began. "I made sure there were candles in the rooms while she put in clean chamber pots." She paused to take a breath. Her eyes gleamed with excitement as she smoothed her tidy white apron that covered the bright stripes of her skirt. "The soldiers are already coming in. Our main room is the fullest it's been in months!" As she stopped to draw a breath, she took in the expressions in the room, before her gaze stopped on Olivia. "Has something happened?" she asked slowly, the joy fading from her face.

Faith spoke. "Olivia has had a nasty shock. Can you help me make sure everything is ready? It sounds like we will have a lot of hungry men to feed." She stood by the fire, soaking in the heat as she cast a watchful eye on all the cooking food.

Dorcas nodded before walking over to join her. "Dinner should be ready soon. Ellen and Seth are getting the officers settled. They were pouring drinks when I left. I can get biscuits ready to bake and put them in after I check the meat on the spit."

Olivia rose from the table. "I'm not an invalid." She went to her beloved knives, kept sharp enough to split hair. "I can chop these vegetables while you make bread." She looked at Faith. "Go make sure all is well with our guests; we will be fine." Her gaze went out to all the people trying to care for her. A knot formed in her throat at the knowledge of all the protective love about her. "I will be fine."

Faith wasn't sure about that, but she went back into the tavern. Olivia was a stubborn woman. She would not let a shock slow her down. Faith didn't blame her. She, too, had found balm in following the regular routines of the day. She hurried to the taproom. The maid, Ellen, was shy around people and avoided crowds whenever possible. If Seth forgot to lock the liquor cabinet before he left, her supplies would be cleaned out in short order. She really did not fancy dealing with a bunch of militia well-lubricated with the contents of her bar.

She was pleasantly surprised to discover her main room in reasonably good order when she arrived. Seth was pouring tankards of homebrewed ale at the bar as men stood waiting to be served. Faith was surprised at the orderliness of it all until she saw Captain Hoag standing just to the side watching his men. Tension lined his body, and there were shadows under his eyes. Despite his obvious exhaustion, his uniform was meticulously neat, and his boots polished to a glossy finish. His hat rested on the table next to him.

When he saw Faith, his focus turned to her. He softened his gaze with a smile that showed beautiful white teeth briefly before his lips closed. "Mistress Clarke, it is nice to see you once again." He offered her a brief bow.

Faith responded with a smile of her own. "I see your men have found their way here." Her gaze circled the room, taking in the men sitting in small groups at tables, their chatter filling the room with sound.

He nodded. "Yes, most of them have arrived. I will have a few more men arriving later tonight. We have just come from drill practice on the green. I appreciate that your staff has prepared the rooms. I saw your girl, Ellen, lighting fires, it's appreciated on a chilly day like this."

Faith nodded. "I am fortunate to have her here."'

Hoag looked about the room. "I assume a meal will be served before long?" His men had taken most of the tables. She spotted a pair of tradespeople at a small one near the window, but otherwise, the occupants were members of the militia.

Turning, she met Hoag's glance with a nod. "We're waiting for the sheriff, but that should not delay serving dinner."

"Why do you need the sheriff?"

Faith turned to look at him. "My cook found a dead body in the field behind the armory. We have sent for the sheriff to handle the matter."

The captain's face stilled. "I'm sorry to hear that. It cannot have been a pleasant experience." He looked around at the men drinking and talking in the room. "Do I need to send some men to assist?"

Faith shook her head. "I will let the sheriff decide what he needs." She looked about the taproom. Seth minded the bar as Ellen went back and forth carrying drinks for the men seated at the tables scattered across the broad room. Despite light from the windows and the crackling fire, parts of the room remained in shadow. As the day progressed, she would have to light the tin lanterns they kept on the wall.

In one corner, a man softly blew on a fife, sending forth a plaintive tune. A hum of chatter, almost like the buzzing of bees, drifted throughout the room, offering noise but few distinctive words. A chair scraped across the bare wooden floor as a man rose to get a drink. Some men sat near the fire playing a game of dice. While others held cards or talked. At one table, a man read the Virginia Gazette to three companions who sat listening to his words.

"The men are hungry after training in the cold," Captain Hoag said in her ear. "When can we expect to be served?"

"Within the hour," Faith replied. "Dorcas should be here shortly with the first course." She looked at the busyness of the room. These militia were mostly men ranging in years from late teens to possibly thirty years of age. They had likely come from farms and towns throughout the district. Despite the hours of training, they seemed in good spirits.

Dorcas and Titus entered carrying trays loaded with bowls. Upon their entrance, the men cheered as steaming bowls of beans were set before them. Faith walked around to ensure everyone had a spoon and to reassure them that they would be returning with more. Soon, plates with wedges of meat pie, stewed apples, and biscuits were in front of the men who dug into the food with enthusiasm. Within minutes, other activities had been abandoned in favor of nourishment. Faith felt the nervous energy that had filled the room with ease. She turned to the captain, who had not moved.

"Would you like to join them?" Captain Hoag still stood just inside the doorway of the main room. Although he faced the taproom, he looked as if he was focused on another time and place. Faith touched his arm, and he startled slightly before catching her gaze. She repeated her question.

Hoag shook his head. "I have a few things to take care of before I eat. Thank you for the care of my men." He looked about the room. A faint smile curved at one corner of his lips. "They appear well pleased at the moment." He bowed before slipping out the front door. The heels of his boots sounded against the boards of the porch as he stepped down into the yard before heading toward the road.

Faith watched him for a moment before turning toward her guests. She wondered where he was heading. She wanted to ask if he had any news concerning the British. Faith paused to let her gaze take in the busy taproom. The men were rapidly cleaning their plates. She had been mildly startled as the enormous quantities of food they had prepared disappeared. Her eyes circled the room, checking to make sure cups were filled and no one was waiting for food. Titus had come in to take charge of the bar while Seth went about refilling drinks. Ellen collected empty plates and put them into a large tub that would be taken back to the kitchen for washing. The men cheered as Dorcas brought in small bowls of bread pudding. By the flush of pleasure on her face, Faith guessed she had made it herself. She had worried about adding extra help when Olivia had first suggested it, but the two women had more than proven their worth in the past year. She turned and looked about the room. The master sergeant leaned against the bar, talking idly with Seth, who had returned while Titus went to get another keg of cider. He was older than most of the men, with a receding hairline that emphasized a long face darkened by the sun. A wide-brimmed wool hat covered most of his head. His thinning hair was caught back in a business-like queue that tapered down to between his shoulder blades. He squinted as he talked, which made Faith wonder if he was a touch short-sighted. His tankard stood near his elbow at the bar.

As Faith came closer, she could see it was nearly full. Her nose had developed enough that she knew he was drinking rum rather than the short beer they had been serving the men. She looked at Seth, who shrugged.

"Greetings, Mistress," the Sergeant said. His accent suggested he had spent most of his life somewhere in the New England Colonies.

"Greetings, Sergeant," Faith said with a smile. "Welcome to Clarke Tavern. I hope you enjoy your stay."

"Septimus Paige at your service, Mistress," He doffed his hat as he made a faint bow. "This is far better than making camp in the woods. I like sleeping in a bed at night."

Their conversation was interrupted by Titus' entrance into the taproom. He went straight to Faith. "Mistress, you are needed in the kitchen."

Faith went with him down the long hallway. Once they left the taproom with its row of windows, shadows fell over them. Voices and the thump of moving chairs faded as they walked to the back of the house. Titus said nothing as he led her out the door. He shut it firmly behind them and paused on the narrow back porch.

"The sheriff is here along with one of his men." Titus' lips tightened as if he fought to prevent further words from escaping.

Faith nodded. She knew neither Olivia nor Titus cared much for the sheriff or his men. Few of the freed or enslaved community did. There were too many memories of those captured trying to find their freedom. She didn't blame them, although she realized Johnson was only doing his job no matter how unpleasant.

"He probably needs additional information from her," Faith said as they descended the steps. "I'm sure there's nothing to worry about."

Titus snorted. "There are some things you could not begin to understand." He let her take the lead as they went toward the small building that housed both the tavern kitchen and Olivia and Titus's private living quarters upstairs. The muted sound of voices could be heard through the closed door. Titus opened it and stood aside as Faith entered.

Flames crackled from the fireplace, providing both heat and light. Steam rose from the black iron pot hanging just inside the hearth. Olivia stood facing the two men inside. One hand was hidden by her apron. The other rested on the table where a partially cut squash lay.

The sheriff nodded to Faith. "Good afternoon, Mistress Clarke."

"Good afternoon," Faith said cordially. "How can I assist you?"

The sheriff nodded. "I was trying to get the facts from your cook here. If you could persuade her to tell me the truth, I can be on my way."

Faith frowned. Olivia was no liar. From the tenseness of her body, the past few moments had not been friendly. She knew the other woman was angry from the set of her jaw and downcast eyes. If she had looked up, the sheriff would have seen the fire in her eyes. "Olivia is a woman of integrity. She was clear about what she saw. Surely, that poor woman's body should be evidence of that."

From the sheriff's expression, Faith knew something was wrong. The sarcasm in his tone left no doubt.

"There is no body, nor any sign there was one there," he said. "Mistress Randolph has not seen her household slave Marianna since she went to the market this morning. I just came from their house, which is in an uproar over the disappearance. I realize that as a recently freed woman, you might have sympathy for a slave and want to help her escape, but under the law, an enslaved person is considered property with no rights." He sighed tiredly. "Mistress Randolph is greatly upset and wants Marianna returned." As he leaned forward, Olivia tensed. "No matter what tale you spin, I will find her. Her punishment will be much worse the longer she is gone. If you could tell me where she is hiding, I can fetch her back, and we can forget this ever happened. I have no desire to disturb another household."

Silence fell in the kitchen, broken only by the faint bubbling from the large cookpot. Olivia's face was bleak. "I didn't lie. I didn't know that was Marianna although I now realize I had seen her wearing a brightly colored skirt like the woman I saw lying in the field. She was dead and covered in blood. Marianna didn't run away; she was murdered. I don't know what happened, but it was horrible." A shudder went through her body. "No one should be treated like that. She was abandoned like trash."

The sheriff went quiet for a moment. His homespun trousers were stained with mud. His boots had pieces of grass sticking to them. He pushed his tricorn back on his head, revealing a pale half-moon of forehead over a tanned face. Exasperation filled his voice. "I and my men searched all over that part of town. In the fields, the woods, and every barn, smokehouse, and pig lot nearby. We found no body. There was some blood on the ground, but that could have come from an animal, and there wasn't much. I don't know what you think you saw, but there was no body in that field." Johnson gestured to his man, and they both went to the door. The Sheriff turned just before heading out into the cold. "If you decide to tell me where she went, send a message to the courthouse or Chowning's Tavern, and I will come as soon as I'm able." With that, he strode out. Faith watched him leave, walking swiftly around the tavern to the fence gate on the other side of the yard.

She turned back to Olivia, who had not moved. "Olivia," she began before the other woman cut her off with a swift chopping motion from her hand. The other hand emerged from under her apron, holding a formidable-looking knife, which she sat down on the table as she took several deep breaths.

"I know what I saw." Olivia's voice resonated throughout the room. "They can say what they want, but that woman is dead. I saw her body; I saw what was done to her." She shook her head angrily as she picked up the knife to continue cutting the squash before her. She looked up at Faith. "You know I'm telling the truth. You should after all these years." She continued chopping, her knife hitting the wood-cutting board in a steady rhythm born of long practice.

Faith's voice was soft as she answered. "I know."

Chapter Four

Darkness fell early, leaving Olivia no choice but to light a few candles to help her finish her work before walking upstairs to the room above the kitchen where she and Titus lived. The space was small, but it contained all they needed. There was the rope bed that Titus had made. Over it was a coverlet she had stitched from leftover fabric from various sewing jobs. They had a secondhand chest for their clothes and a small table and two chairs that Faith had let them have after it became clear they would not fit in the taproom. Soon, they would have a rug once she finished braiding all the pieces and stitching them together. She was too tired tonight. Olivia stripped down quickly, feeling the air raise goose bumps on her flesh. Downstairs, the door creaked closed as Titus came in for the night after chopping one last load of kindling. She didn't wait for him despite hearing his feet on the stairs.

One lone candle lit the room as Titus got ready for bed. Olivia lay swathed in a comforter, watching him strip down. It never ceased to amaze her that she was wed to such an attractive man. A few silvery threads of gray had begun to make their way through his scalp. There were a few white hairs on his chest as well. He still looked as hale and strong as when she had first met him. The crinkles around his eyes from sun and laughter were a little deeper than they had been, but time left marks on everyone in one way or another. His hands were slightly gnarly, but she didn't care. She recognized the marks of time on her own body as well.

Olivia remained troubled about the events of that morning. It chilled her to think that someone had come back to remove the dead body after she had found it. Even in winter, the trees were thick enough to hide someone from view. Titus had gone back to the field with Will after the sheriff had left. It had been as he had said. There was no body on the broken ground or any sign that one had ever been there.

"Are you sure you checked everywhere?" she asked.

Titus looked over at her. "Will and I turned over every blade of grass out there, and then we checked where each other had been. It was as the sheriff said. There was some dried blood on the ground but no body." He signed. "The ground was churned up where we found the blood, but that could have been from an animal. There are foxes and bears in those woods."

"Not this time of year," Olivia retorted. "Most every creature is holed up in a den until the weather gets warm, you know that." Tears gathered at the corners of her eyes. She angrily brushed them away. Weeping did no good. Frustrated, she glared at her husband, unable to find words to express the fear and rage boiling inside.

He reached out a hand and stroked her face. "What frightens me is that you nearly walked up on a murder. I don't know how to keep you safe, and you matter more to me than my own life." Titus shook his head. "I can't think of any reason someone would leave a dead body out in the open like that and then just haul it away. It makes no sense." His eyes met hers. "I believe you, Olivia. I do, but I can see why the sheriff has a hard time. No one likes to feel foolish, and Mistress Randolph likely chewed his ears off when he couldn't find her slave alive or dead." After doffing his breeches, he sat on the opposite side of the bed from her. "We live in strange times, and I'm not sure when or if things will get any better. You would think people would be concerned about a young woman missing, rather than getting mad about missing property." Sadness laced his tone. "That's all we are here, property. Sometimes, I think we'd be better off somewhere else."

"Where?" Olivia said. "No matter where you go in these colonies, people judge us by our color, not our character. At least Faith stands up for us. She is a rare person. It's a pity that man you call friend didn't see that."

Titus caught her gaze. "Will hasn't forgotten her. He won't admit it, but he feels the loss. I see how he works himself half to death all day trying to get her out of his mind. Arsenic may have half killed him, but heartbreak is what ails him now."

Olivia sighed in exasperation. "He's the one who abandoned her." Although Faith had told her little beyond that Will no longer wished to marry her, she could see the pain it caused. She wanted to take him by the scruff and shake some sense into him, but her own husband intervened.

Titus worked closely with Will to send intelligence to the Sons of Liberty. He managed the horses in the stable behind the tavern. He also took care to hide messages in the saddles and retrieve them from riders coming into town to trade goods in the market. "Stay out of it," he said as he ran his fingers through her long black curls as they prepared for bed. "They need to find their own way, just as we did."

She growled softly as she thumped her pillow. "How can a man be so stupid? He nearly died. You would think he would want to embrace life after that."

Titus looked over at her. "Will has his pride. The poison left him feeling weak and helpless, and he did not want to be a burden. No one does." He shook his head. "He should have waited out his indenture before declaring himself. Will is not free to make a life with anyone for three or four years. There is no point making promises when you can't keep them for a long time to come."

Olivia looked up at him. "We did." She ran her fingers down his muscled thighs, watching how the muscles jumped at her touch.

Titus admired his was as the firelight burnished her skin and reflected in her dark eyes. "But I knew Master Moore supported my courtship of you. He told me so."

"Did he?" Olivia was piqued. "Was our marriage his idea too?"

Titus shook his head. "Woman, you know better. I loved you from the moment I saw you. There was no one else for me. Master Moore chose not to get in the way. Then Mistress Clarke, Faith," he amended. "She decided to free us, which made life even better. We are blessed to be where we are." He captured Olivia's hand as she started to tickle his more sensitive areas. He growled, which made her giggle.

Titus blew out the light before pulling off his shirt and slipping under the blankets with her. Coals glowed from where he had banked the fire to keep through the night. "Move over, woman; it's cold out here," he growled as he ducked under the blankets.

"Then why did you take all your clothes off?" She asked with a sly grin.

"Because," he said as he raised her shift. "It's warmer when we lay to skin."

Olivia snorted. "I don't think that's the only reason."

Later, Olivia found herself awake and unable to fall back asleep. Beside her, Titus' soft snore assured her that he was deeply asleep. Her husband rose every day before dawn to stir the fires, and she had no intention of waking him. Outside, an owl hooted as it hunted for food amidst the bare winter trees. It would be difficult to find anything on these cold winter nights when all creatures burrowed in warm hollows waiting for the kiss of spring.

Her mind refused to settle into the rhythm of sleep. Her dreams had been a series of pictures from her day, all ending with images of a young woman's body on the ground covered in blood. Although she didn't think there had been that much blood, in reality her imagination turned the bright floral print of her skirt and kerchief into a bloody horror. Olivia lay with her body tight and heart pounding. Images from her dream left her filled with terror. Unable to dismiss the images, she endeavored to focus on something else. She listened to the comforting rumble of Titus's snores as she made mental lists of her plans for the next day. Olivia catalogued what was left in the root cellar and what she could do with it. They still had some potatoes as well as beans and small amounts of other vegetables and herbs. They were nearly through the last of the garlic she had braided and hung from the rafters. She would have to be careful with it.

Through the window, she could see the waning moon, a narrow sickle that glowed against the deep blue of the night sky. A few graying coals remained of the fire that Titus had banked for the night. Otherwise, the room remained wrapped in the enveloping cocoon of night.

A soft scratching sound followed by a rattle chased all thought of sleep from her body. Olivia lay in bed with her eyes wide open, trying to determine whether wind or animal was causing the noise. The noise stopped and then picked up. Her heartbeat raced as she kept telling herself it was only an animal attracted by lingering food smells from supper, which had been served and cleaned up hours ago. Her mind was having none of it. Whatever caused the noise downstairs was not normal.

Downstairs, the kitchen door rasped against the floorboards. Olivia sat up, shivering in the chilled room as terror flooded her from head to toe. Someone was downstairs in her kitchen. She was sure of it. As if to confirm her thoughts, soft steps made the slightest of noises as a stranger prowled below. Something rattled as if an unwary arm had brushed against it. Her mind raced through several possibilities. It could be that Dorcas had come from her room in the cellar to retrieve something she accidentally left behind, but Dorcas hated the cold. She didn't go out if she could avoid it. Ellen, her roommate, had no reason to be out and about at this hour. There was no reason to rob the kitchen. Other than dried herbs and cooking tools, there was nothing to steal. Definitely nothing that was worth risking spending a few months in the gaol until the circuit judge arrived to pass sentence. As the surreptitious noise continued below, Olivia's fear turned to anger. Someone dared to come into her home in the middle of the night to steal food that she had worked hard to provide and planned to prepare. They had no right to it. It was past time she put a stop to this foolishness. Olivia was petite in stature, but she didn't suffer fools. Decision made, she rose to deal with the problem. Whoever had slipped in below was going to regret it.

Olivia considered waking Titus but hesitated. The last time someone had broken into the kitchen, Titus had tackled the darkened figure only to discover Faith's younger brother, Seth. The young man had come seeking leftover pie and ended up with a multitude of bumps and bruises from the encounter. She did not want to rouse her husband over nothing. Although if Seth had come to raid her kitchen again, Olivia intended to give him a tongue-lashing he would never forget.

She donned her shift before heading to the steps leading down to her domain. Moonlight gleamed on the blade of the small knife Titus kept for trimming candle wicks. It lay on the table. Olivia paused. All of her knives were downstairs in her kitchen, waiting for her to start the day. She gazed over at Titus, sound asleep in bed, and a wave of protective love flooded over her. He and Joshua were her world, and she would do anything to protect them. While she believed her visitor downstairs was likely harmless, Olivia didn't believe in leaving things to chance. She grabbed the knife before going down carefully, her bare feet feeling the way.

Olivia looked around as she came to the end of the stairs. A blur of motion was her only warning as a figure shoved into her as he rushed past, out the door into the night. She tried to scream, but the noise caught in her throat, leaving her with a squeak. She caught herself as she stumbled into the table and her knife clattered on the floor. The door slammed, echoing throughout the building. Upstairs Titus stirred. Their bed creaked as he moved.

"Olivia?" He called. "Olivia!"

She heard the thump of his feet as he hurried across the floor and down to her. His feet thundered down the steps as he ran, bellowing her name.

"I'm here," she called. "I'm alright." She went where candles were stored. She took one and lit it by touching the wick to a tiny flame that lingered in the fireplace. Titus went to her like a moth drawn to light.

"I heard you cry out," he said, touching her face. Titus stood stark naked in the darkened room, holding a length of wood in his hand long and heavy enough to do significant damage. Tension tightened the muscles of his body, and his eyes swept the room.

The door stood wide open, filling the room with cold air. Titus shivered as goose bumps rose on his arms. He strode over and shut the door, pulling the latch firmly in place before returning to her side. "What happened?"

"Someone broke in," Olivia replied. "They ran out when I came down."

Titus swore softly. "Why didn't you wake me? I would have dealt with it. You could have been hurt." He glared at her as both anger and fear filled his expression.

Olivia let out a pent-up breath. "I thought it was Seth raiding the pantry. You scared him half to death the last time he came in."

Titus looked over at her. "He should have known better than to knock around the kitchen after midnight." He took a deep breath and moved closer to the fire. "Is anything missing?"

Olivia looked about the shadowed room. "It's too dark to tell." She went to the grate and added a few smaller sticks of wood from the firebox on the side. After a bit of poking a small fire emerged providing illumination to the space.

Placing her candle in one of the tin lanterns, she cast its light about the room. She walked around the room, looking at her table and shelves as the light fell on them. Olivia paused as she came to the window and set the lantern on the floor. Outside, all she could see was darkness and the skeletal limbs of the trees outlined against the sky. Nothing stirred. She smiled as she caught Titus in the reflection of the glass backed up close to the fire. "If you get much closer, you will roast your behind."

"It's cold in here, woman." Titus wrapped his arms around himself dramatically. "A man could freeze in this weather."

Olivia snorted. "I'm sure you will survive."

Titus turned to warm his front, leaning forward until a pop from a log made him jump back.

Olivia snickered. "Not afraid of damaging something important, are you?"

"You would regret that." Titus came up close to her back and wrapped his arms around her. His warm lips caressed her ear. "If you are done looking around, we could get warm together upstairs."

"Hmmm," Olivia said. "My feet are kind of chilly."

Titus groaned. "Not the feet. They're like blocks of ice. I don't know how many times you've put those close to my tender parts."

"It's the warmest part of your body," she pointed out.

"That's not what God made that for, and you know it," he grumbled. "I wrap up a hot brick for your feet every night and put it in the bed."

Olivia leaned back into his comforting warmth. "That you do." She looked over her shoulder at him. "You are a good man, Titus York. I am blessed to have you."

His teeth flashed white in the darkness. "Yes, you are." His gaze sharpened as her body stiffened when looked over his shoulder, as something caught her attention. "What is it?" Titus turned swiftly, ready to defend his wife.

"There," she pointed as she shone the light on her worktable. They walked together to where Olivia worked most of the day. Weighted beneath her mortar and pestle lay a rectangle of cloth that had not been there when she went up to bed. As the lantern's light fell on it, she could see it was a brightly colored kerchief darkened with dried blood. She had last seen it on the dead woman's head. Her pulse raced at the sight of it.

Titus saw her expression, and his darkened. "Someone knows you're telling the truth."

Olivia shivered at the thought of someone watching, biding their time.

Titus swore and went to pick it up. Olivia stopped him. "It's a warning," she said. "As if a bloody piece of cloth would keep my mouth shut." Angrily, she threw it into the fire.

"Do you think that was wise?" Titus watched as the bit of cloth turned to ash.

"I don't care," Olivia's eyes welled with tears. "No one believes me anyway."

"I do," Titus said, taking her into his arms.

Chapter Five

Will McKay glanced over the type he had just set. The press was ready to run the next few pages of the latest edition of the Virginia Gazette. He despised the advertisements for runaways, but as an indentured servant, he had no say in the matter. His mistress had pointed out that the money from these and other announcements kept the newspaper in business. Georgia Clements's husband had bought his indenture shortly before his death from a sudden fever. She had taken over the press and done well with it. Other sheets hung in the shop, drying before they would be assembled together to complete the newspaper. He was meticulous in his work. It mattered to him that every entry was correct and spaced for optimal readability.

His mistress's son walked about, checking to see if the previous page's sheets were dry enough to take down. One day, eighteen-year-old Marcus would inherit the business, although he didn't seem to take a great deal of interest in it. He did what he was told, but Will had learned not to leave detailed jobs like typesetting to him. The boy lacked the patience for the job. He would rather be out with his friends. His sixteen-year-old sister Rebecca had a better head for business. The war had brought her back home from the school her mother had been sending her to up north. He could hear her voice at the other end of the shop as she sold a gentleman some stationary.

Rebecca was too pretty for her own good with honey gold curls and cornflower blue eyes that many men liked, and she was well aware of it. He had watched her go out with ribbon rosettes in her hair and a determined look on her face. She had tried flirting with Will, but he ignored her. She was too young to interest him, and he had no desire to stir up the kind of trouble involvement with his mistress' daughter would cause. Will treated her like he would one of his sisters. His heart still belonged to a stubborn Quaker on the far side of town. No matter how he tried, he couldn't forget Faith, or the hurt look on her face when he had broken their engagement. Some nights, that last meeting played out in his dreams, and he wanted to kick himself for the sheer cowardice that had caused him to do that. There was no changing the past, and he doubted she would ever forgive him.

Paul came in from the back, where he had been mixing up a fresh batch of ink. The faintly sweet metallic scent clung to his clothes as he brushed by Will carrying the results of his labor. The liquid was heavy, and he walked carefully to avoid any of it slopping onto the floor.

"That should last us through this printing," Will observed as he took in the pot filled with combination of crushed, and strained oak galls, green vitriol, gum arabic and water. The smell always made him think of slightly off Madeira. The thought of which made him queasy, so he passed off the job to the other man who had no traumatic memories to stir such a physical reaction. After his poisoning two years ago, Will no longer touched fortified wines. The occasional aches in his bones and bouts of tiredness he blamed on the arsenic he had accidentally imbibed. He had become far more cautious about what he ate or drank as a result.

Paul set the pot down carefully. "I hope so. Ma like to of skinned me when she saw what I was mixing in one of her soup pots. She told me not to touch anything in her kitchen ever again without asking, or she would tan my hide."

Will grinned. Paul and his twin Silas had a formidable mother. Athena Wise had taken over the role of cook for the Clements household a few years ago. The nearly six-foot-tall woman used it as a front to hide her work as a spy for Washington. For all that, she was an excellent cook and territorial about her kitchen, even with her beloved boys who worked as handymen and informants throughout the town of Williamsburg.

Paul shot him a look. "It's not funny." He stepped back and began working on inking the type Will had just set. The inking balls made a sucking sound as the bottom made contact with the metal type and released ink onto the surface. Holding one ball by the handle in each hand, he laid ink across the surface with a speed born of long practice. Once he was done, he stepped back to let Will complete setting up the press.

As Will attached paper to the board and closed it down over the inked type, Paul asked, "Did you find that woman?"

Will completed turning the press down to ink the sheet. As he pulled it out and opened it, he paused to check his work. He nodded as he saw it had printed cleanly across the page. This was only one of several pages to be printed. He shot a look over at the younger man. "Titus and I combed through that field and found nothing." He handed the sheet over to Paul, who hung it to dry on a line stretched across the room while Will placed a fresh sheet of paper in the press. "The sheriff's men had already gone through there and made a right mess of things, so it was hard to tell where to look." He sighed. "I'm sure Olivia saw something, but there was no body there to be found."

"Maybe you weren't looking in the right place," Athena strode into the print shop. Although technically she was Georgia Clements's cook, she dominated the room like a queen. Her dark eyes swept through the shop and took in what the men were doing. Stepping carefully to avoid hanging sheets of printed paper, she walked over to Will and her son. A bright blue cloth covered her hair. It matched her skirt, which was a few shades darker than the jacket she wore over her shift. A checked apron completed the ensemble. A few inches taller than both men, she looked down at them with a serious expression. "Olivia saw a dead woman, someone's slave. As to what was done with the body, only God knows. Our people are given little respect in this world. Don't belittle a woman you know, to be honest. You know she would never make this up."

Will flushed. "That's not what I meant. But you have to admit it is strange. Why would someone leave a dead body in the middle of a field? And how could it just disappear? Mistress Randolph is certain Marianna escaped, and Olivia is covering for her. I just set the type for an advertisement offering a reward for her return."

"Mistress Randolph," Athena's disgust was clear. "That woman does not treat her people well, and everyone knows it. No one cares because they are people of color. She's rich enough to dispose of a body if that's what she wanted."

Will shot her an incredulous look. "Do you truly believe Elizabeth Randolph, one of the most prominent women in the colony, killed one of her slaves and hid the body? Why in the world would she offer a reward for Marianna's return?"

Athena's deep voice resonated through the shop. "Money does not equal morals. That woman can pay to have her dirty work done just like most people born into privilege. An advertisement proves nothing other than she knows to cover her tracks." The door into the shop opened and slammed shut as her other son, Silas, entered carrying a crate.

"A shipment of paper and books came in from France. Where do you want it?" He huffed as he walked the box to the back of the store before setting it down on the floor behind the press.

Will looked at the large square crate. "I wonder what Georgia ordered. We will open it after we finish printing. The Gazette needs to go out." He returned to the press. Putting together an edition of the newspaper took hours, from setting the type to printing to assembling it and taking it out for distribution. He had very little spare time for which he was glad. Thinking about the past only caused him grief.

It took most of the day to complete the paper. By the time they had printed and assembled every copy, it was nearly supper time, and Will was starving. Marcus helped him stack up issues of their edition of the Virginia Gazette. "When will it go out?" The younger man asked curiously. He was only just beginning to comprehend all the work that went into the family business.

"Tomorrow," Will answered, "You will go out with either Paul or Silas and sell papers along with Eduard and Henrik." Georgia had purchased two additional indentures last fall. Will shared space, in the cellar with them. He appreciated that his mistress avoided purchasing slaves, although he considered indenture only a few steps above it. Will had signed away his freedom for seven years to escape across the Atlantic. Sometimes, the bond chafed, but he knew one day he would be free. Those poor souls from Africa or the Caribbean had no such hope. Georgia Clements treated him fairly, and he was grateful. He tried to be kind to both men, Eduard, who had escaped France for religious reasons, and Henrik, a German who spoke little English and shared little beyond his name. The young man wept sometimes in his sleep, which made Will wonder if a matter of the heart was involved. Will had learned German from spending months on a ship to the new world with a large group of them. He kept it up, dealing with some of the Germans who came to Williamsburg from the Shenandoah to trade throughout the year.

He gestured to Marcus. "You lock up. I need to get this ink off my hands before it stains everything in sight." He sighed in relief as the bolt slid shut without anyone running in, at the last minute. He was looking forward to a good meal without interruption. Lunch had been a hurried affair. Will hadn't even gotten to enjoy the apple dumplings he'd smelled Athena cooking. He hoped she had saved him one.

It took him a few minutes to straighten up the store so that it was ready for opening in the morning. He could hear Georgia and her son in the small dining room eating. His stomach growled as he finished putting away the tools of his trade and made sure the blinds were drawn for the night.

After removing his leather apron and washing his hands, Will went to the kitchen. Paul and Silas were already sitting at the table as were Eduard and Henrik. Without a word, Athena served an earthenware bowl and set it in front of him. The rich scent of beans with pork rose up to tickle his nose. A wedge of bread with jam followed it, along with some pickled vegetables. After offering a blessing over the food, they dug in. Athena joined them after she poured ale for all of them.

No one spoke at first. They were all hungry after a long day of work. Athena took ladylike bites as she watched them. A faint smile curved her lips, as she looked over her boys. Although Will wasn't her son, she treated him like he was. The Scot was only a few years older than Paul and Silas. He was likely the same age as Rosie. The smile left her face. It had been ten years since she had last seen her daughter, who had been sold away and ripped from her arms to profit the man who had owned her and said he loved her.

Athena would never stop looking even as she despaired seeing her on this side of heaven. Jeremy Butler, her other fosterling, checked his contacts up and down the coast for any information about an auburn-haired slave named Rosie or Rosalind. Ten years had passed with nothing. She wondered if she was even still alive.

The faint scent of burning warned her to check the fire. Paul beat her to it, moving over the pot full of sweetened apples with a tool to a cooler spot on the hearth. "I've got it, Ma," he said. "Sit down and finish your meal. You've been over that fire all day." Athena sat down. Her boys liked to fuss over her from time to time, and she let them. She was not surprised when Paul and Silas took charge of serving the apples with their pillowy dumplings to everyone there.

"I'll take these to the family," Silas said as he slid three bowls onto a wooden tray. The door swung shut behind him, as he went up to where the Clements lived behind the print shop.

Will watched him go. No one commented on the fact that he had been welcome to eat at the family table until Georgia Clements's daughter returned home. Rebecca Clements enjoyed attention, especially from men. He had found her attempts to engage him in conversation annoying but had remained polite for his Mistress' sake. Georgia Clements had not commented, but within a few days of her daughter's return from Baltimore, she had informed him he would now take his meals with the other servants.

After supper he returned to the print shop to make use of what little light was left to finish his work on the Gazette. Together, Paul, Henrik, and he finished assembling the last round of dried sheets into completed editions for distribution in the morning. He could hear the voices of the women upstairs as they prepared for bed before night fell.

Darkness came early in the winter months, emphasizing the cold that crept in through every hole and crack in the wall. Nightfall had its uses as well. It made it much simpler for Will to accomplish his tasks as part of the patriot spy ring in town. Few people chose to brave both cold and darkness, which meant he could slip out without drawing attention to himself.

Tonight, he planned to check one of the dead drops that Jeremy Butler had set up when he had first come to Williamsburg to collect information as the colonies headed toward war with Britain. Will didn't know who left notes in it; his task was to check it regularly. He was glad he didn't know. It was safer, should their activities be discovered. Sometimes, he had gazed at the handwriting, wondering whose hand it was; a merchant, a farmer, someone in trade. Whoever it was, he passed by the James River frequently. The notes frequently contained observations on the activity on that waterfront.

As Will went out into the yard, he looked up. The curtain in the upstairs window moved. The faint glow of a candle revealed golden hair and the white of a shift. Rebecca waved at him. He ignored her, irritated. The window scraped as she cracked it.

"Where are you going?" She repeated her question more loudly when he continued without stopping.

Will said, "I'm checking on the animals before I turn in. You'll catch a chill like that. It's not the weather for opening windows."

She pouted. "Ma kept me busy with mending, so I didn't get a chance to see you. Will you be in the shop tomorrow?"

Will shook his head. "I have to deliver papers. You need to listen to your ma. Young girls like you need to watch their reputations."

"I'm a woman now. I will turn seventeen in June. Most of my friends are already wed with children. Her face looked sad for a moment. "I thought I would be by now, too."

Georgia Clements came in behind her and shut the window. Will could not see the older woman's face in the darkness, but he knew she was not pleased. He shrugged before heading back to the barn to make good his excuse. There was little he could do beyond avoiding her daughter as much as possible.

After killing a few minutes listening to the cow as she bedded down in the loose stall next to the horses, Will slipped out. His dark jacket helped him blend in with the shadows. In the few minutes he had delayed full dark had fallen. As he paused to let his eyes adjust, he cursed Georgia's daughter and her need for attention. Avoiding her was getting increasingly difficult. He hoped Georgia made a match for her soon, somewhere far away from Williamsburg.

The streetlights were being lit on Duke of Gloucester Street as he stepped out. Will paused, considering the best way to access the dead drop without drawing attention. People didn't like it when strangers cut through their yards in the dead of night, and then there were the dogs. Will had learned the hard way that some people in town left their dogs out to roam. Fortunately, in the dead of winter, a lot of them bedded down with their families inside or in a nearby barn or shed. He couldn't rely on that, though.

He pulled his collar up to protect his neck. The cap he wore covered his hair and helped keep his ears from freezing. Faith had knitted it for him. The wool had come from her father's farm in Pennsylvania. When he touched the soft gray hat, he remembered her busy hands knitting it as they had talked by the fire in the tavern. That had been over two years ago. He shivered as a breeze picked up and blew against his face.

He headed east toward the Capitol Building, although that was not his destination. Will had sometimes wondered if the man who left messages there worked there. Many people traveled in and out either as part of the General Assembly or one of the individuals attached to the new governor, Patrick Henry. Will kept to the shadows cast by the closed shops facing the street. As he passed the Raleigh Tavern, he could hear the faint murmur of voices as people continued their drinking into the night.

His business was further down behind the old Coffee House. It had been closed for a few years now. Its once gaily papered walls shut tight until someone else decided to rent the building. With a war on, no one had taken much interest in the building, which meant no one paid it much attention. Will waited in the shadows for the night watch to pass, not that they were much of a threat. On cold nights like this, they tended to go from tavern to tavern, taking some libation before stumbling down to their next stop. Nonetheless, he wasn't tempting fate. There might be a new recruit feeling frisky and sharp-eyed, and he had no desire to have to come up with an excuse for being out in the middle of the night.

Limbs from nearby trees rasped against each other as a faint wind stirred them. He wondered if rain was coming. The thought of a cold winter rain mixed with sleet made him shiver. At last, the watch passed, and the faint light from their torches faded, leaving pitch blackness in their wake.

The wooden gate that led to the level below opened easily. Despite the deserted air of the place, someone kept things in good repair. The box built into the side of the back wall was barely detectable in daylight; he would have to rely on his fingers to locate it in the pitch black of night. The path led down to the lower level. Out from it, the ground declined to where a creek ran. It gurgled as it moved over the rocks that covered its narrow banks.

Clouds filled the sky, making it more difficult to navigate in the darkness. The breeze picked u,p bringing the smell of the coming rain. Will hurried down the gravel pat,h desiring to complete his mission and return to his room where he could have a small fire and be dry.

Mist began to fall from the sky, sending icy fingers of water down his spine where his collar did not cover his neck. Will broke into a run for the shelter of the roof where it overhung the building. As he turned, his foot hit a large stone lying on the ground. His ankle turned, throwing him to the side. Time seemed to stop as he fought to keep his balance. Gravity won. He hit the ground hard and rolled down the embankment. He grabbed frantically for a handhold to stop his headlong tumble. The icy wet tussocks of grass slid right out of his grasp. His back hit something solid, stopping his fall and knocking the breath clean out of him.

Will lay on the wet grass, catching his breath as the chilly rain enveloped him. His heart pounded in his throat. The creek burbled loudly behind him. It was too close for comfort. Once he caught his breath, he sat up, trying to orient himself. Up the hill sat the deserted coffee house waiting for him to complete his mission. He sat up and started checking himself for injury. Aside from the stinging of his hands and the ache in his back, nothing hurt. As he inhaled again, his nose caught a whiff of decay. It grew stronger, strong enough to make him gag. Something dead was close.

He looked to see what had stopped his fall. A heavy bundle lay on the ground when he pushed against it, it squished, and the origin of the smell became obvious. Will crab walked back, unsure of what he was seeing, until his eyes picked out a foot sticking out from what he now realized was a skirt. He'd found a dead woman far away from where Olivia had reported seeing her. Only God knew how it came to rest here.

Chapter Six

Faith heard voices outside her door. She raised her head cautiously. It was way too early for anyone to be about. Soft thumps of people stumbling in the darkness confirmed her suspicions. Someone was about while the household slept. It was times like these she wished there was someone else who could deal with things, but a widow had no such luxury. It was up to her to defend her home. Shivering as the warm covers fell away, she grabbed a heavy wool shawl from on top of her clothes chest. Picking up a poker she used for her room's tile stove, she tiptoed to the door and put her ear to it. Two voices whispered in the hall. Once she recognized them, she opened her door and stared out at Titus and Seth. Both showed signs of hasty dress. Titus' stockings hung down, and his shirt was untucked. Seth's hair stuck out all over, and he was missing his breeches. Goosebumps rose on his bare, hairy legs.

She stared at them. "What is going on? 'Tis the middle of the night." She at least had enough sense to wrap up before heading out where there was no fire burning. The tavern was chilly this time of night. She had pushed her feet into a pair of moccasins she had traded for with one of the natives, but her feet were still cold.

Titus looked at her, his face grave. "Will is in the kitchen with Olivia. You need to hear what he has to say." He turned to Seth. "Get dressed. Once we verify the body is still there, you can get the night watch while I stand guard."

"What body?" Faith said. Her heart began to race as the words chased all remaining sleepiness from her brain. Something had happened. It was the only explanation for Will to be across town in the middle of the night. "Is Will hurt?"

"Shhhh," Titus frowned at her. "We have a house full of militia." He shook his head as he whispered. "Will is fine, just chilled and wet."

Faith dropped her voice. "What body?" Titus pointed toward the back door. His other hand held a punched metal lantern. Its light cast shadows on the wall as it provided faint slivers of light in the dark tavern.

"Go talk to Will. He's in the kitchen with Olivia and Dorcas. I think he found Marianna." He looked at Seth. "I'll see you in the kitchen in a few minutes." He strode out. For such a big man he walked with the silence of a cat. Faith and Seth stared after him, their eyes following the light of his lantern.

Faith didn't like being in the dark, even with her little brother. She hugged the wool shawl even closer, wishing this was all a bad dream. Moonlight streamed through the narrow window by the front door, barely illuminating the front of the hall.

"Do you think it's true?" Seth whispered. His eyes looked huge in the shadowy darkness.

"I do not know," she replied. "But I intend to find out." Faith turned and went back to her room. She could hear Seth heading back to the small room he occupied behind the bar. She threw on the first clothes she could find. Enough light came from the stove for her to find a skirt, stockings, and jacket. Her stays took a minute to tie. Faith ran a comb through her hair and pinned it up before donning a cap. If she had to meet with Will McKay in the middle of the night, she was going to be as prepared as possible.

Her breath made white clouds of air as she closed the back door behind her gently so as not to rouse her guests. Her ears tingled in the cold air as she hurried down the path to the kitchen, where she could see tendrils of smoke rising from the chimney of the brick fireplace. The door opened easily under her hand, although the cold metal made her wish she had used a corner of her shawl to grasp it.

The fire blazed in the hearth sending out a welcome blast of heat as well as light. Will McKay sat on a chair in front of it, shivering. Clad only in an oversized shirt that had to belong to Titus, he stretched his legs out to the heat. The firelight picked up the strands of red that curled on his shins. His soaking wet hair hung in snaky tendrils down his shoulders. Olivia handed him a cloth which he used to dry his hair.

Faith stared at him. "What happened to thee?" When upset, her Quaker speech came back, although even she recognized that it was fading away, much like a lot of the things she had held to in childhood.

He looked at her, then away for a moment before answering. The silence between them lay heavy as it did whenever they encountered each other. "I was out walking when I stumbled and fell near the creek that runs by the old Coffee House. She was lying there in the grass." He shuddered at the recollection. "I don't know where she's been, but she's been dead a bit. The body has already begun to decay."

Faith was incredulous. "Thou were just out walking in the middle of the night in the rain and cold. Thou will need to do better than that. I have a good idea what thou were about but it's nothing to be shared with the sheriff. Why come here?"

Olivia intervened. "He couldn't stay out in the cold soaked to the skin. It would be the death of him. We are close by, and we can concoct a way for the body to be discovered without revealing what we do to support the cause."

Faith nodded. They all knew that even though the British were not currently in town, their supporters were. Unfriendly eyes could be anywhere watching for those who collected information for the patriots. She looked over at him. "Are you alright?"

Will nodded. Now that he had finished toweling it, his hair stood out in a wild tangle. He began running his fingers through it as he leaned into the fire.

Olivia handed Faith a wide-toothed comb and nodded toward him. "I'll get some coffee brewing while his clothes dry." Will's shirt and breeches hung in front of the fire. Water dripped from his stockings, which lay draped over the spit. She approached him as if he were some wild creature caught in a trap. He saw the wooden comb in her hand and said nothing. His eyes were large and dark. This close, she could see the stubble on his cheeks. He half closed his eyes as she drew closer, the dark fan of his lashes spread across his cheeks. "I'll try not to pull," she said softly as she picked up a lock of hair.

His wet hair lay dark and sleek in her hand. Faith gently teased out the tangles in the ends before moving up the strands toward his scalp. As she combed a deep breath came out of him as he surrendered. He leaned forward, submitting to her care. As she gained confidence she combed more deeply, rhythmically going up and down until his hair looked like a length of silk. As it dried, the locks began to curl at his nape and alongside his ears, their dark red color becoming more apparent as they dried. He smelled of damp and the faint musky scent of man. His body relaxed as his muscles warmed in the heat of the fire. His breath moved in and out softly, causing his chest to rise. A few auburn curls rose from the opening of his shirt. Faith tried to ignore the flutter in her own chest. She was not getting tangled up in this man again. Her heart still bore the scars.

The silence was broken by a rapping on the door. Faith jumped. Her gaze met Olivia's before the other woman took a knife and went to the door. Will's eyes opened wide, he rose looking around the room. Olivia gestured for him to go upstairs as she spoke. "Who's there?"

"It's Captain Hoag. Is everything alright? I saw people moving about in the yard and wondered why at such a late hour."

Olivia paused to let Will creep up the stairs before slipping the knife into her pocket and cracking open the door. Hoag stepped in and looked about. He nodded to Faith, who remained by the fire. Seeing him glance at the stool, she slid it over under the nearby table. The captain walked over to join her by the roaring blaze. His polished boots reflected the flames. Despite the hour, he was fully dressed, his hair neatly queued. Water droplets sparkled on his tricorn hat.

"Tis an odd time to be up and about, my lady," he murmured softly. "I would think you would need your rest for the coming day."

Faith's mind raced to think of a palatable excuse. She was saved by her younger brother coming into the kitchen. Hoag looked at him, taking in the fact that he was dressed and carrying a lantern.

Seth ignored Faith's warning glance and said. "We found the body. I am on my way to the sheriff's. It may take a bit in this weather." The rain had lightened to a drizzle. Droplets sparkled on the brim of his hat and dripped down onto the floor. He looked at the fire wistfully for a few minutes before he suddenly realized his sister and Olivia were not alone. He took in a quick breath, surprise plain on his face.

Hoag looked over at the young man. "What body?"Although his tone was mild, his blue eyes took on a silvery gleam as they focused on Seth, who stood frozen in place. The wooden heels of the captain's boots made a light tapping sound against the floorboards as he stepped to where he could look at all three of them in the flickering light of the fire.

A shiver went down Faith's spine as she contemplated the man before her. This was not someone to be trifled with. Looking at his grim expression, she wondered what they could say that wouldn't cause trouble.

"I suggest you tell me what in Hell is going on before I send someone to drag Sheriff Johnson out of bed in the middle of the night." He looked at Faith. "Death requires explanations. Think carefully about what you say."

Faith exhaled, mentally cursing whatever had roused the militia captain out of bed. As she glanced over, she realized his vest was misbuttoned. She bit her lip to keep from showing amusement at the anomaly. It was no time for humor.

Faith opened her mouth to speak before Seth interrupted. "I found a dead woman at the edge of the stream that runs by Charlton's old coffee house. I ran here to get help." His words tumbled out as he glanced at Hoag before sliding his eyes away to examine the roaring fire. A log broke apart just then, sending sparks flying up in the hearth.

Hoag held out his hands toward the heat. The shifting flames cast shadows on his face and emphasized the creases around his eyes and the sides of his mouth. On his left pinkie, he wore a gold signet ring. It gleamed in the light. Hoag appeared to be speaking to the hearth. "It is a few hours short of midnight in the dead of winter. If that weren't enough it is raining. No one goes out in such weather unless circumstances compel it. Since I assume you didn't know she was there, some other reason must have sent you out."

Seth gulped and looked over at Faith. Nineteen was too young to be playing mind games. Hoag looked to be in his early thirties. As a military captain, he managed men every day. Seth was no match for him.

Hoag let him stew a moment before continuing. "Were I to guess, I would speculate that a young buck like you might have slipped out to meet with a young lady. There are many fair flowers in Williamsburg. Perhaps one of them has caught your eye?"

Seth flushed and looked down. Hoag laughed softly. "So you went out to meet a girl and were on your way back from your assignation." The smile left his face. "And you found someone dead in the creek. Do you have any idea who it might be?"

Seth shook his head violently. "I couldn't tell. It's too dark."

"I imagine so and too wet for a torch to stay lit. It is very smart of you to gather a lantern for your return. Allow me to go with you." He glanced at Faith. "Mistress, could I trouble you for another lantern? I would hate for us to become separated in the dark and wet."

Faith looked at him before she spoke. She could not tell what he was planning. "I've already sent my assistant Titus to watch over the body. This is a matter for the sheriff to handle."

"These are not the times for anyone to be about alone at night. We have no way of knowing how the young lady met her fate. She could have slipped or met with foul play. Either way, I think it best we go together."

Faith couldn't disagree with the logic. A sideways glance revealed her brother looking miserable and more than a little scared. There was no helping that. The captain had them neatly boxed in with no choice but to accede to his wishes. She reached up and took a lantern down from its hook on the wall. Faith stuck a taper in the fire and used it to light the candle in the lantern. After she shut the lantern, she handed it to Hoag.

Hoag gestured to Seth. "Let's go, son. The sooner we get the sheriff, the sooner we can return to our beds." They headed out into the grey, dark night, their lanterns creating a faint glow as they traveled back toward town.

"I wish he hadn't woken," Faith said as she stared after him. "There is no telling what is on his mind."

Olivia added a log to the fire. "He was already awake. It takes time to get that uniform on, much less pull on those boots. I bet if you go up to his room, you'll find the fire is burning from where he's fed it." She returned the poker she had been using to stir the fire. "He's militia, supposedly on our side, but there is no telling what he does when he's not leading drills. These days, people are in turmoil, and what they support changes from day to day. We're all trying to survive this conflict, and only the Good Lord knows if we will."

Faith stared at her. "I always thought you supported revolution."

Olivia shrugged. "I support freedom, for all people. Patrick Henry, Jefferson, and Washington all talk about liberty, but I don't hear anyone offering it to my people. Governor Dunmore, before he fled, offered manumission to anyone who supported him."

Faith stared at her. "Surely you didn't believe him?"

Olivia met her with a hard gaze. "I haven't heard anyone else address the issue. Not that it matters. He and his family fled across the sea to England. All we can do is support the revolution and hope more men like George Wythe continue to advocate for us."

Faith nodded. She knew that Wythe was an attorney respected by Washington and Jefferson and he had put forth suggestions to free slaves. She also knew that his words had been met with opposition by the majority of the men in government. Wealthy planters did not want to give up their workforce, no matter the suffering it caused. It filled her with anger. "Heavenly Father, she prayed silently. "When will this end?" There was no answer, and sadness filled her heart at the fate of so many who had done nothing to be treated so ill.

She accepted a cup of coffee that Olivia offered her and sweetened it with honey. It was too early for there to be cream for it. The cows were fast asleep. Faith sipped the dark liquid and waited for the men to return. Tiredness swamped her, but she was determined to wait. She sat down at the table and put the cup down in front of her. Her head felt heavy. In what felt like minutes, Olivia shook her awake.

"They're back." She went to open the door, letting in the cold, wet air.

The icy blast erased sleep from Faith's body. She stood up just as Titus and her brother entered the room, shaking off the water at the doorway. They stood together at the fire. Neither spoke as they held cold, reddened hands to the blaze.

Titus spoke first. "The Sheriff has her loaded on a wagon. They are taking her back to the Randolph House for them to bury." His face was lined with exhaustion. "Animals have been at the body. They will get her in the ground quick."

Olivia spoke. "Does Gowan know?" Both she and Titus went to the church on Nassau Street led by Gowan Pamphlet, who served as minister when he was not working for his mistress Jane Vobe at her tavern.

He shook his head. "I doubt it. I will get word to him later this morning so there can at least be a memorial for the poor girl."

Olivia's face tightened. "I doubt the Randolphs will let anyone off for the service."

Titus looked over at his wife. "We'll find a way, love. We always do."

"Where's Captain Hoag?" Faith asked.

Seth looked over at her. "He stayed to talk with the sheriff about having his men patrol the city."

Faith nodded. "I guess it makes sense to help keep the streets safe."

Seth's expression turned bleak. "That's not the reason they were discussing increasing patrols. They want to prevent more slaves from escaping."

Faith shot him a shocked glance. "There is a murderer loose in this city. Surely, they want to catch who did this?"

Olivia's tone was laced with bitterness. "Do you really believe they will waste valuable resources on the death of a slave? The enslaved are not considered people; they are property in the eyes of the law. Don't be so naïve. You've lived this, you've owned people."

"Not anymore," Faith said quietly. "I freed you."

Olivia wiped away angry tears. "Yes, you did, but look at all the others in this town who will never have that option. Too many die frightened and alone, never having a free breath."

Faith knew she was thinking about her sister Stella, who had died in the gaol a few years ago. They never spoke of it, but she knew the death haunted Olivia.

Titus spoke. "Folk from the Randolph House say she didn't run away. She just disappeared when she was out running errands for her mistress." He grew quiet for a moment. "Something terrible happened to that girl no matter what the law says. With all these soldiers in town, there's no telling what could have happened. The taverns are full, and the men are on edge waiting for the British to invade." He shook his head. "No one is going to take time to find out how one slave died. It's not worth their time. Not enough people care."

"Does she have family here?" Faith asked.

Olivia snorted. "I doubt it."

Titus replied. "The enslaved at the Randolph House will take care of that. They are probably the only family she had." He shook his head. "My heart goes out to them."

Faith nodded. "God rest her soul."

Olivia said. "There will be no rest when violent death is swept under the rug as if it didn't matter."

"It matters," Faith said. "Believe me, it always matters. If not here, then in heaven."

"Then may God avenge her." Olivia's hands were clenched at her sides.

"May He avenge her indeed," Titus said.

Chapter Seven

Faith had never been to the small church on Nassau Street. One of the local gentry had offered his carriage house after he had discovered a group of enslaved and freed people worshiping under the trees near his estate. She knew that Olivia and Titus attended it and that many people of color went there. She felt faintly embarrassed by her own spotty worship attendance since leaving the Quaker faith. While she loved the organ music at Bruton Parish, she longed for something less formal and more personal. Faith wasn't sure where to find it.

The building stood two stories high with wide doors for vehicles facing the street and a narrow door on the side for people. Narrow windows let in light, although sconces on the brick walls held candles that had been lit. The floor was solidly packed earth. No hearth graced this building, so everyone remained bundled against the chilly air. Faith could see her own breath and that of others as well. She stood next to Olivia. Titus was on his wife's other side along with their son Joshua, who still wore his apron from his work at the apothecary.

Behind her, Faith heard a few coughs and the cries of a young child. Despite the light streaming in through the tall, narrow windows, she could see very little in the room except it was crowded with people of color. She stuck out because of her pale skin, as did Will, who she had spotted as they had entered through the carriage doors. From her limited viewpoint she could not determine where he was now. In front of her, separated by three rows of people, a woman sobbed, accompanied by others. It cast a mournful pall on the gathering. Faith shivered with more than cold. All these people gathered to mourn the loss of one of their own who had been brutally taken away.

Voices hushed as their shepherd Gowan Pamphlet entered the room. He was a man of middle years, medium height and broad of frame. His dark, intelligent eyes rested on Faith briefly before moving on to acknowledge other members of the congregation. In his hands he held a well-worn copy of scriptures from which he began to read. His rich baritone reached the far corners of the room as he read from what Faith recognized as the book of Ecclesiastes. Over the muted sobs and murmured prayers, his voice covered them like a warm blanket as he said.

"To everything, there is a season, and a time to every purpose under the heaven: a time to be born, and a time to die;" His voice continued until he ended the reading with *"a time to keep silence and a time to speak; a time to love, and a time to hate; a time of war, and time of peace."*

When he finished, the silence continued as he led them in prayer. Then, to Faith's surprise, a few people spoke. An elderly woman talked of Marianna's hard work and cheery spirit in the Randolph House. A boy mentioned how she liked to sing to the chickens as she fed them and how beautiful her voice was, and then a young woman moved to the front and turned to face the crowd.

Olivia's voice at her ear breathed. "That's Joanna."

The short woman could barely be seen in the room. Someone helped her onto a wooden block so she could stand taller. Her face was swollen from crying. "Marianna was like a sister to me. She was my family, my dearest friend, and now she's dead!" She drew in a ragged breath. "Somebody took her and left her poor body to rot like she was an animal. She deserved more; we deserve more! White folks treat us like livestock, but we are God's children just like them. Marianna desires justice. Do you hear me—justice!"

"Justice!" The crowd picked up her cry. It echoed through the room, taking a life of its own. Her voice was drowned out in hearty amens and cries of agreement. Voices from within the crowd wailed and moaned. Faith could not see where Joanna went in the crowd. The cries emanating from the dimly lit room, along with the packed crowd, filled Faith with unease. She had never experienced anything like this. People around them swayed as they sang and called out for mercy on the deceased. Raw emotion filled the enclosure. She felt as if she couldn't get enough air. The gathering had grown increasingly restless after Joanna's words, and Faith noticed that more than a few angry looks were being cast at her.

A rich alto began singing from somewhere in the room. It was an old familiar hymn comforting in its familiarity. Other voices joined in until the building was filled with the sound. A lump rose in Faith's throat at both the beauty and sadness of the music. She watched as people sang, some with tears streaming down their faces as they mourned. Faith looked at all those gathered and wondered how much was it grief at the loss of a compatriot or grief because fate had treated them all so cruelly.

As the singing continued, some people swayed in rhythm. Others moved through the crowd, circulating and murmuring. An angry undercurrent was building. Feet were stamping now in rhythm as the music died out. Uneasiness ran down Faith's spine. Titus started moving them toward the door. His big frame blocked anyone from interfering. Silas and Paul brought up the rear.

Faith heard Reverend Pamphlet speaking to the crowd but could not catch his words. There was too much noise from all the people in the small building. As they exited through the side door, she heard raised voices. Pamphlet's deep voice responded. Titus picked up the pace as they walked back toward town. "What is happening?" she asked.

Titus responded. "You don't want to know." And kept walking.

Faith stared at his back in frustration.

One of Athena's sons leaned over and whispered. "Folks are angry over how she was treated."

"How all our people are treated," Olivia said. "This world treats us like property, not people, and it's not right."

"And if the wrong people hear you talk about it, it will get worse," Titus said grimly as he looked around them. "We have to be careful."

Olivia quieted but the flashing of her eyes warned that her thoughts were anything but silent.

Faith pondered what to say. She knew all too well how hard it was to manumit slaves. It had taken quite a bit of work and not a few favors to free Olivia and Titus. She could not imagine what it would take to free everyone, although she knew it needed to happen. Rather than offer useless platitudes, she continued walking with them back toward Duke of Gloucester Street. When she looked back, she saw that Will had joined them. Like the rest of them, he wore a black band of mourning on his arm.

One of Athena's sons spoke. Faith could never tell the twins apart. "Mom expects us to come back to see her. She wants to have a meeting."

His brother looked over at him. "Si, you forgot to tell them she's going to feed them, or maybe you just want more of her pecan pie."

Silas smacked his brother in the arm. "You like it too, little brother." He turned back to the others. "Mom does put on quite a spread. Mistress Clements said it was okay as long as someone was working on setting type for the next edition of the Gazette. She's has some new advertisements to place."

The group walked in silence. As they drew close to Duke of Gloucester Street, traffic picked up around them as a few men rode by on horseback. Faith pulled her wool cloak closer around her as a wagon rattled past. Although the cold she felt came from deep inside, fueled by the horror of violent death.

Olivia said little as they continued onto Duke of Gloucester and down to where the printing shop and the Clements' home lay. Titus caught her gloved hand with his as they walked, offering silent comfort for whatever painful thoughts circulated in her head. Even in winter, the main street of Williamsburg stayed busy. People moved about conducting their business bundled up against the cold. They turned down a side street to enter through the gate to where the separate kitchen lay. White smoke billowed from the chimney before dispersing into the skeletal limbs of naked trees.

Athena looked up as they entered. "Come in, get warm. I have coffee ready, and you can eat." She went back to the fire where a large black pot hung. On the coals, a cooking spider rested. Faith spotted the iron pan sitting on the table. From the aroma of bacon in the air, she knew what had been in it. She joined the others around the table upon which rested a large pea pudding with bacon and pecan pie still uncut. Athena's sons stood at the corner nearest the pie. She looked over at them. "Don't get any ideas. We will bless the food and serve our guests first, and then you can get some pie." One rolled his eyes; the other grinned and stuck his hands in his pockets. She looked over at them. "Make yourselves useful and serve the food. It's not long before we will all need to get back to work. The world waits for no one."

Olivia shook her head. "I'll take coffee then I need to head back. We have a tavern load of men to feed before long. Dorcas will need my help." She held her hands toward the fire. Titus looked at her with concern.

His voice was soft. "There was nothing you could do. She was dead when you first found her. At least now she has been decently buried and prayed over."

"It's not enough," She hissed. "No one cares about what happened to her. It wouldn't be any different if it was you or me." Olivia looked over at Faith. "I know you would cry, but you would replace us. You would have to in order to stay in business."

Faith sat down her cup on the table. "All lives matter, Olivia. We were all created in the image of our Father. I never knew Marianna, but no one deserves that kind of death. I am so sorry you were the one to discover her body. I wish I knew what happened. She deserves justice as much as anyone else."

Athena joined them at the table. "What I want to know is why her body was moved. First, it was in the field where Olivia came across it, and then a few days later, it turned up across town. That doesn't make sense."

"No, it doesn't, but neither does killing a young woman and leaving her in a field." Will McKay's face was grim. "There are a lot of strangers in town, brought in to serve in the militia. Men away from home get lonely and drink too much. They go off and do things they normally would not do. We all need to be more careful."

He looked around at the women in the room. "None of you should go out alone anymore. Not to market, not to see your family or friends. These are dangerous times we live in, and there is no telling when things will return to normal or if they will. We can all make time to escort you ladies about." He looked at Titus. "You and Seth can look after Olivia and Faith. Paul, Silas, and I can look after our people."

Titus nodded. "It's for the best." He dug into the food before him and chewed thoughtfully. "You make a fine pie, ma'am. I appreciate it." He picked up his coffee, blowing on it gently before taking a sip. "I've seen some of the militia out late at night. They slip out and get into mischief. More than a few can't handle their liquor. I'll have a word with the other men at the taverns to keep a sharp eye out. I don't know what happened to that girl, but our ladies need to take care."

Faith protested. "I have business to attend. I do not need an escort to go down Duke of Gloucester Street in broad daylight. Titus and Seth are needed at the tavern, especially with it being full of militiamen." Faith was tired of men telling her what to do. As she glanced about, she tamped down her irritation. Their well-intentioned orders didn't sit well with her. "I have taken care of myself for some time now. I don't need a man to watch over me."

Will started to speak, but Titus shook his head before speaking in a gentle tone. "No one is belittling you, Miss Faith. But these are dangerous times, and many of these men the militia has taken on are ruffians. They have no respect for a lady. Most of these lads are bigger than either of you, and they hang about in groups. You're a strong woman, no doubt. You've handled a lot in the past few years. None of us want anything to happen to you. Let us help until things settle down here in town."

Faith objected. "And how will you accomplish your chores if you're escorting me?"

Titus spoke. "There's always wood to be cut, that's for sure, and it's good to have a man at the bar. You women can go in twos if it's daylight. One of us can go with them on market days. Mistress Genia wants to send Old Malachi over to us. He's too old to do much, but he could manage the bar and keep an eye on things while we're out."

Faith looked over at him. She had had very little contact with her former mother-in-law since she had helped clear her of the accusation of killing her own husband. She wondered how Titus had connected with her. But he was a free man and what he chose to do in his off hours was his business. Pushing those thoughts aside, she glanced over at him. "Who is paying his wages? We're stretched tight as it is."

Titus replied. "He's not free. Mistress Genia knows he's too old to do much work and not worth selling. She knows if he's here, you will feed and clothe him and save her the trouble."

Faith felt a spark of helpless anger. She couldn't free the man, he belonged to Eugenia, but she could give him his dignity and allow him to end his days useful and well cared for. Titus waited for her reply. "Let him come. We can find a place for him."

Titus nodded. "I will go over there and let the housekeeper know." He polished off the last piece of his pie and rose. "Thanks, Athena, that was mighty fine."

Olivia rose to go with him. "I need to get back to the tavern." She shot her husband a look. "No one is likely to bother me on Duke of Gloucester Street."

"I'm still walking you to the gate," he replied, giving her a look.

Olivia said nothing but waited for him at the door.

Faith rose as well, dusting crumbs off her skirt. Athena was a fine cook, but she had had little appetite. Her mind was still trying to piece together what had happened to Marianna. What could have precipitated such a cruel and violent death? It made no sense. "I need to head home too. We have a large group of men to feed."

Athena rose as well. "I need to speak with you before you leave." She waved them off. "Will can walk you home once we're done." Olivia and Titus left, followed by the twins, who laughed as they scarfed up the last few biscuits to take with them. She sighed as they exited. "Those boys eat like it's their last supper." She stirred the coals in the fire before turning to Faith.

"There's a few things you need to know about Marianna." She dusted her hands on her apron which was spotless. "She was no wide-eyed innocent no matter what her friend says about her. Those two sneaked out at night, often by all accounts."

"But they are enslaved," Faith protested. "Surely their mistress kept an eye on them."

Athena shook her head. "Mistress Randolph assumes everyone is where they are supposed to be. That doesn't mean they are. She can be harsh, so no one in the servant quarters is going to tell on anyone else."

Faith pondered that. "So what was Marianna doing?"

Athena's eyes looked off in the distance. "That I am not sure. She was young and pretty and foolish. If I was to guess, I would say she was meeting someone."

"A man?"

"Hard to say," Athena answered. "Her friend isn't likely to say, although I'm sure she knows. Joanna has a reputation for slipping in and out of the house. Their cook thinks she takes things to sell on the side, but then Flora also thinks they may be selling themselves on occasion as well."

Faith's eyebrows shot up. "That's a pretty harsh accusation."

Athena shrugged. "There aren't many ways to make money if you belong to someone else. Their overseer is willing to look the other way for part of the money. They are attractive, and men notice that. These men are far from their families. They get lonely. Some probably pay for a few hours of companionship."

"Companionship?" Faith looked skeptical.

Athena continued. "If we're lucky, she just picked the wrong man to step out with. Someone got drunk and angry and went too far."

"And if we're not?"

Her face turned grim. "Then we have a cold-blooded killer in town who may strike again."

Chapter Eight

Will placed a bundle of Virginia Gazettes into the wagon. Once he had them loaded, he would deliver them throughout Williamsburg to the shops and individuals who had paid for a subscription. Marcus should be out here helping, but as had become the usual, he was not. That boy would arrive late, rubbing the sleep out of his eyes, and apologize profusely before doing the exact same thing the following week when it was time to deliver papers. His mother knew, but Marcus paid little attention to her scolding. He knew the paper's schedule as well as anyone but apparently was not concerned about the work that kept them in business.

Silas brought out another stack of newspapers. They made a solid thump as they landed inside the wagon. "That's a lot of papers to load by yourself. Where's my brother?" He looked about before looking at Will with a disgusted expression. "Someone should be out here helping you."

Will shrugged as he went back for another load. "The job still has to be done." He grunted as he lifted another load bound with twine and walked it out to the wagon. Not too many people were out in the cold. A few women were headed to market, bundled up in cloaks and scarves against the chill. He didn't mind being out. The sky was a clear blue, and activity kept him warm enough. Will enjoyed the opportunity to go around and talk to people as he delivered and sold papers throughout town. It also allowed him a chance to pick up any useful information to share with his fellow patriots although not much was happening since the last royal governor had fled two years ago. Will longed to join the fight but his indenture kept him bound to

Williamsburg and to the memory of the girl he had abandoned.

Will spotted a lanky figure on a horse headed east. Their new governor, Patrick Henry, now occupied the palace at the northwestern edge of town. He rode to the capitol every day, greeting people as he went down Duke of Gloucester Street. He tipped his hat at Will as he headed by going slowly down the road.

Someone was cutting wood nearby. The steady chop of the axe carried across the yards. Figures moved about Chowning's tavern nearby, undoubtedly getting ready for the day. Noise filled the air with the rumble of carts as they rolled over the cobblestones headed to the market. Even in winter there were goods to be traded and sold. Once they passed, Will could hear voices from people calling out their wares as they headed into the market. From his vantage in front of the print shop, Will could see a variety of people making their way there. He suspected Athena had someone going to see what was available to put in one of her many cookpots.

Out back, the rooster crowed, reminding everyone that it was morning and past time for breakfast for him and his harem. Athena must have heard them; Will heard the low hum of her singing as she took food out for her precious birds. She treated her birds like beloved pets, even if the occasional cockerel was sacrificed for dinner. His stomach grumbled.

Silas looked over at him. "Ma has some ham and corn cakes ready. Go get some breakfast while I finish up."

"Are you sure?" Will eyed the stacks of newspapers waiting to be loaded. In truth, there was not a huge number left.

Silas nodded. "Little brother will come out once he finishes braiding his hair." He rolled his eyes good-naturedly. Both boys had beautiful black curls that they usually braided into a que to keep out of the way and slicked back with whatever pomade their mom made in the still room. Paul's vanity was a source of amusement to both men.

Will gave an exaggerated sigh. "Very well. I will not turn down your mother's cooking any day." He walked around the house toward the separate kitchen in the back, not wanting to disturb the Clements family sleeping upstairs, although he wouldn't have minded waking Marcus. He was old enough to accept the responsibility that came with work. If he wanted to keep the print shop running after his mother retired, he'd better start acting like an adult.

Will opened the gate to the white picket fence that separated the public from the private part of the house. Closing it gently, he looked up at the windows, hoping not to see a certain blonde head stirring. He really did not want to deal with Rebecca this early. Although he was glad she helped her mother in the shop, it worried him when she came over to watch him work. She liked attention, and it irritated her that he chose to ignore her. Will had noticed early on that she loved to flirt with the men who came into the shop. In a town brimming full of young bucks in the militia, she was a flame to dozens of entranced moths. Trouble was bound to break out soon if she didn't stop.

As he neared the barn, he heard the horses nicker. They knew what time it was. Paul had fed them earlier, and they were ready for a jaunt about town. He smiled as he heard them in their warm barn. He enjoyed working with animal,s and Georgia Clements kept a magnificent pair of bays. They responded to the reins with the gentlest of touches. One day, he wanted a pair of horses of his own when he was no longer indentured and could make his own choices.

Athena put a plate in front of him as soon as he entered the room. "Make sure you wash all that ink off your hands," she admonished. Turning away, she picked up the coffee pot with a thick cloth and poured him a large cup.

Following orders, Will washed up at a basin set up along the far wall near the door. When he finished, he dumped the dirty water out where it would not form an icy puddle in the path. He sat down and began to eat quickly.

"Did your mother not teach you to say grace?" Athena frowned at him.

"I didn't want the horses to wait in the cold," he said as he put down his fork. After he offered a quick blessing, he picked up his fork again and took a bite of warm corncake.

Athena glanced over at him. "Paul hasn't brought the horses out yet. He'll wait until everything is loaded before he brings his girls out into the cold."

"He is protective of those mares," Will acknowledged. Paul was an excellent hand with most animals. He was the quieter twin and preferred the company of animals to people.

Athena looked thoughtful. "I hope that the militia doesn't get any ideas about them. I've seen some of them wandering around town, going into barns and sheds." She shook her head. "There's too many of them. Young men with little to do after drilling are going to get into trouble."

Will nodded as he chewed. She was not wrong. He'd seen the soldiers in the taverns and on the street. Boredom and loneliness were the devil's tools. He wondered if that was what had happened to the enslaved girl, Marianna. Images of her body had woken him in the small hours of the night, leaving him covered in sweat and unable to settle back. He gulped some of the coffee, gasping at the heat. She had sweetened it with honey for him which Will appreciated. "I need to get those papers delivered," he said as he put his empty plate with the other dirty dishes that one of them would wash later.

Paul had finished hitching up the horses as Will approached. He nodded to the younger man as he wrapped a wool scarf around his neck. "Have you seen Marcus?"

Paul shook his head. "Not since last night. He got in pretty late. From what he was saying, I think there must have been a dog race on the outskirts of town."

Will frowned. "That's a good way to lose money."

"I think he found that out. His language was not what you would expect a church-going young man to use." Paul checked over the harness carefully as he stroked the mares.

Will pretended not to see him feeding bits of carrot to them as he sweet-talked his girls. "I'll take the run to the capitol if you want to go up toward the palace."

Paul nodded. "There's not as much to deliver there. I can probably do it with the cart and the mule. I'll see you back here in a bit." He trotted off back toward the barn.

Will climbed aboard and set off east toward the capitol, which stood at the end of Duke of Gloucester Street. He clucked to the horses and started off. After five years of indenture, this was routine for him. After a brief stop to drop off papers at a nearby tavern, he hopped back up into the seat. A shout made him turn his head.

Marcus Clements trotted up to the wagon and pulled himself up, huffing. He had dressed in haste. His breeches were partially buttoned, and his shirt tails hung out from under his coat. His hair flowed loosely from under his hat. He was also in need of a shave.

Will stared at him before clucking to the horses to continue. "Pull yourself together, man. You look a fright." He focused his eyes on the road as Marcus righted his clothes and pulled his hair back before tying it with a leather strap.

"I'm sorry, Will. I overslept." Marcus yawned. "It's too early to be working. I haven't eaten breakfast yet."

"You would if you had gotten up," Will replied ruthlessly. "Paul and Silas helped load the wagon." He glanced at the young man. Marcus looked the worse for wear with a puffy face and bags under his eyes. "I'll swing by the market to let you off with a load of papers. You can sell them at a table. You can probably find coffee and some bread there. Mistress Swartz makes some huge rolls."

Marcus smiled. "That would be great." Then his face fell. "I forgot my purse."

Will handed him a few coins that Georgia had given him in case he needed them. "Here, go get food." He pulled up outside the Market Building and watched Marcus hop down.

"Don't forget the papers," he called out as Marcus made to leave. The young man returned and took a bundle out of the wagon. "I expect you to sell all of those. Don't' waste the work."

"I won't," Marcus promised as he walked slowly, balancing the heavy bundle as he walked into the long wooden building that served as the town's market.

Will watched him hoping he had made a wise decision in letting him go. Marcus had to learn how to run the business; it was his future. He turned the horses and continued east. He stopped at the taverns that lined the road along the way, chatting with the servants who were busy getting ready to open.

It was quiet this early. Within a few hours, the city would wake, and the streets would become busy with people about their business. He turned north to catch a few businesses off of the main road, planning to pass by the gaol before swinging past the Presbyterian Meeting House and back toward Duke of Gloucester Street. Faith's tavern lay that way, although he tried to tell himself that wasn't the reason he chose that route. She would be busy tending to her guests. Clarke Tavern had a load of militia occupying it now, which meant she would stay busy cooking and tending the men, or so he hoped. She had a talent for finding trouble.

Will pulled up in front of a local cooper. He knew the man enjoyed reading the headlines. He was a fellow Scot, which meant Will did not have to explain to him about why he had felt obligated to leave. "Hello, Malcolm," he called as he applied the brake and stepped down. The older man stepped out, took a paper, and paid with Virginia currency.

"Would you like to come in? Peggy has just taken some scones off the fire."

Will shook his head regretfully. "I have to get these papers out. Send my regrets to your wife. Perhaps another time."

The cooper nodded and turned to go just in time to grab his son as he shot out the door. "Whoa there Jaime, it's too cold to be running about without a coat." His voice became inaudible as he herded the boy back inside.

Will smiled. Malcolm McBride had all a man could want: a thriving business, a loving wife, and a large family of children. Was it five or six children he had now? Will was not sure. It was a house full. Every time he entered the business, the voices of children could be heard.

As he entered Nicholson Street, he spotted a familiar figure trotting swiftly down the road. Faith's younger brother worked at the tavern doing a little bit of everything. He was best with the animals and took good care of the horses that stayed in the barn out back. Faith didn't let him handle the large platters because of his tendency to drop them. Both she and Olivia kept him busy with tasks that didn't involve breakable goods, such as tending animals, the bar, or peeling potatoes. All of which he did without grumbling. Seth seemed happy to be in Williamsburg and showed no interest in returning to Pennsylvania, for which Will was glad. No matter what she thought, Faith could use a man around the tavern, even one as young as Seth. Will appreciated that he kept the tack and animals ready to go at a moment's notice without asking why.

"Hey, what are you doing out so early?"

Seth Payne stopped and turned around, replacing his startled expression with a smile. "I had an errand to run. Faith prefers me to get things done before it gets too busy." He shrugged. "I'm used to early hours. The cows expect to be milked early and all the animals need to be fed and their stalls mucked."

Will nodded. "I'm heading down that way; I can give you a ride. It will get you home a bit sooner."

Seth climbed aboard, and they set off down the road. He had the same blue eyes and reddish-brown hair as his sister, but without her strong chin. His hair was cut short but curled around his ears, giving him a boyish look. He said nothing more as they continued down the road.

Will pulled up to the gaol and hopped down. "I give last week's papers to the gaoler to pass out to the prisoners. It gives them a way to pass the time." He hefted the bundle over his shoulder and headed to the side door by the prison wall. "Mind the horses. I'll be back shortly."

He didn't stop to see if Seth heard, although he thought he saw him nod from the corner of his eye as he went up the steps to the house. One of the gaoler's sons took the papers and thanked Will.

Faith's brother had not moved from his seat on the wagon. Will hopped up and took the reins. "I'll head to Mistress Campbell's residence next," he said. "You can get off there, or I can drop you off on my way to the Capitol Building."

Seth paused before replying. "I can get off at Mistress Campbell's tavern. I don't wish to trouble you." He looked about as they turned on Waller, where the large white building gleamed in the morning sun. He hopped down and made to cross the street.

"Seth," Will called.

Payne looked back at him but kept edging away.

"Be careful. These are dangerous times."

Seth nodded before turning and running across the street toward his sister's business.

Will looked after him thoughtfully. "Whatever errand you were running, I'm sure it had nothing to do with your sister's tavern." Hefting a stack of newspapers, he walked around to the back entrance to deliver his load and collect money for it. As he delivered papers, he wondered what Seth was doing out so early. It was none of his business. He had broken the connections he had with Faith and her family, but it was no good telling his heart that.

Faith Clarke filled his dreams. No matter how hard he tried, he couldn't forget her heartbroken face when he had ended their engagement two years ago. Back then, he had been an impertinent indentured servant who had envisioned the last four years of his bondage flying by. He knew better now. Arsenic had taught him the bitterness of endless days of aches and pains with an uncooperative body. Will had recovered for the most part. He still felt the cold most mornings and moved more slowly than he had, but he could work. What he could not do was repair the damage he had caused when the fear of being a crippled invalid had ruled his life. He had cut off everyone who mattered to him, and it had taken time to repair the damage, except with Faith. She would barely talk to him.

His mind turned back to last night when he had nearly frozen in the cold rain. She had come when Olivia and Titus had summoned her and said nothing when he had hidden upstairs from the sheriff. He remembered her hands in his hair, combing it and smoothing it with her touch. It had warmed him in places he hadn't even realized had grown cold. He didn't know what would have happened if they had not been interrupted. Maybe she didn't hate him as much as he thought. Will pushed the thought aside. Faith deserved more than a man with two more years of servitude who had already betrayed her trust. At least, that was what he told himself.

Chapter Nine

Faith walked around the taproom refilling tankards with the short beer she and Olivia had brewed over the summer. Behind the bar, the older man, Malachi, poured drinks and kept an eye on their stock. The men had just come in from drilling on the field behind the armory. The boisterous sound of many voices filled the space. She went from table to table as quickly as she could, avoiding the ones where she knew the men might be apt to become a bit too friendly. She didn't appreciate having her bottom smacked or pinched as she served tables, which was why she had started leaving a few sections of the room for Seth or Titus to manage.

As she sat down a tankard, she felt a tug on her skirt. Faith whirled around to see a Sergeant grinning at her. She glared in return.

"Now, there's no need to be unfriendly," he said. "A pretty thing like you should appreciate some attention." He slid his eyes down her. "These nights must be cold for a widow woman with no man to keep her warm"

"That's enough, Phillips," Captain Hoag rose from where he had been sitting near one of the windows. "Mistress Clarke is to be treated with respect. Anyone who breaks that rule will feel the lash." His boot heels thudded on the oak floor as he walked over to stand in front of the sergeant. "Make sure the men understand and yourself as well." Hoag's face had darkened with anger. His hand still held the quill he had been writing with. He jabbed it into the table, splashing ink onto the pale wood as the reed split. Voices in the room fell silent as the two men stared at each other. All eyes in the room were on them.

Titus slipped from behind the bar, waiting to see if a fight would break out. His eyes swept the room, looking for signs that the man's friends might jump in to defend him. Faith moved off to the side, setting her tray of drinks down on the bar. She looked for something she could use to fend off combatants before grabbing a short piece of wood usually used to prop open a window. Malachi moved bottles and other breakable items from the bar to the shelves below out of easy reach. Tension filled the room, sharp as a blade, as everyone waited for the next move.

The sergeant's eyes searched the room, seeking support. His companions looked away, unwilling to get caught up in something that could end with painful consequences. His face paled as he realized no one was jumping in to support him. "It was just a bit of fun, sir. No harm meant. Sorry Mistress. It won't happen again." He looked like he might be sick.

"See that it doesn't." Captain Hoag stalked back to his table holding his body ramrod straight. The papers he'd been dealing with crackled as he brushed them aside. Eyeing the broken quill, he shoved it away in disgust. Gesturing for Malachi to move aside, Faith stepped behind the bar and reached for a bottle she kept far from her main supplies. The older man said nothing as he watched her pour a drink and put the bottle away, although he raised an eyebrow as his nose caught the scent of cognac. Despite having arrived the evening before, he had fit in easily with their way of doing things.

Faith brought the goblet to Hoag. He took a sip before looking up at her in surprise. "Very nice."

Faith shrugged "I only have a few bottles, so I keep it in reserve for certain occasions." It had been a gift from Daniel Moore, her late father-in-law's son from an earlier marriage. It had been a peace offering after all the acrimony following Ezra Moore's death. She still missed him. He had been the voice of reason in the family. and they all suffered from his untimely death. Daniel had taken over most of his father's shipping concerns, but as far as she knew, he had no knowledge of his father's support of the rebellion against the English King. She had no intention of informing him of it either.

Captain Hoag gestured for her to join him. She demurred. "I'm afraid I'm needed in the kitchen, among other places. Running a tavern is constant work." Faith smiled at him. "I appreciate the offer. I will see if I can locate a fresh quill for you to use."

He sighed. "It is very difficult to focus on the business of the army with all this distraction going on."

"Perhaps you would be better served in the private room." She gestured for him to follow her down the hall and out back. "I also own space across the alley. Sometimes groups like to meet away from the general crowd." Faith grabbed a warm wool shawl off the hook where it hung by the back door and wrapped it around herself before she opened the door. Grass crinkled underneath their feet as they walked the short distance to her private meeting room. She fished the key out of her pocket and unlocked the door.

Hoag looked about. "I thought I had examined every space in this tavern. I didn't realize you also owned this space."

Sun streamed in from the window, providing light to the room. Frost remained etched on the panes since no fire had been lit in the hearth to melt it away. Faith moved aside to let the captain enter.

Hoag ducked his head under the low door frame and stood inside, looking about at the simple table and chairs. He walked about, taking it in, looking at the bare, dark walls and barren space. The cold hearth had a fire laid and ready to kindle for which Faith silently blessed Titus for his thoughtfulness. Hoag said little as he checked that there were candles in the sconces and wood lying in the unlit firebox. His gloved fingers drummed lightly on the table. "This will work. If you don't mind me kindling the fire, I will inform my men that this will be my command center. If you do not mind, I may put a bed in here as well for my own use. It will ease the crowding in the tavern."

Faith nodded. She had expected as much. Although she liked having the freedom to rent the room, she realized that her tavern now housed men from the militia. She had no idea how long it would last, but at least she knew Governor Henry would be paying the bill.

They fell in step as they walked back to the main tavern, each of them immersed in their own thoughts. Once they reentered the building, Faith hung up her shawl and headed back toward her office. He followed. She reached over where she kept fresh quills for writing, the feathers of each felt like silk as they brushed her hand. Handing one to Hoag, she offered him a smile. "One quill, as promised." Although he took the quill, he didn't move from where he stood. Faith's eyes met his. "Is there anything you need, Captain Hoag?"

He removed his hat and held it in his hands as he looked down at her. He was a tall man, somewhere over six feet. His upright stance made him feel even taller. A faint, embarrassed smile crossed his face. "Mistress Clarke, forgive my forwardness, but I have a favor to ask."

Faith folded her arms and waited, eyebrows raised. Something in his tone told her this was more of a personal than professional request.

"I've been asked to supper at a well-respected home here in town later this week. The lady of the house is the widow of a man whose family is quite prominent in Virginia. Her niece lives with her as well as other family." He smiled disarmingly. "I requested that you and your mother-in-law be invited as well since I have no family here. I have heard that your late father-in-law was a well-respected man in this town. I beg your forgiveness, but it is difficult for me to sup with complete strangers. Since I have come to stay in your tavern, I feel a certain familiarity with your presence. It helps me feel less of a stranger. I hope you will accept the invitation. It would mean a great deal to me to have the opportunity to form acquaintances with the families who call Williamsburg home."

He looked at her, waiting for her response. A few strands of hair had escaped being tied back with the rest; they lay across his forehead until he pushed them back with an impatient hand.

Faith chose her words with care. "I assume you are speaking about Elizabeth Randolph, whose husband was Peyton Randolph, formerly head of the House of Burgesses and a prominent delegate to the Congressional Congress before his passing." She paused. "That is one of the most prominent families in town. They sup with people such as Governor Henry, Thomas Jefferson, and George Wythe. I doubt Mistress Randolph will be keen to invite a tavern keeper into her home. I imagine she would like you to become better acquainted with Betsy Randolph, her niece."

A pained expression crossed his face. "That's what concerns me. I have no intention of encouraging a relationship with any woman. I have men to train for battle. My focus is on what lies ahead." He rubbed his temple. Faith doubted he was getting much sleep. "We are engaged in a war with the greatest army in the world. Anyone engaged in the patriot cause faces long, hard battles and a high likelihood of death. I refuse to contemplate subjecting a lady to such heartbreak."

"I take it you are not married."

He didn't answer. For a moment, Faith thought he would turn away without a word, but at last, he spoke. "Not anymore. She died a few years ago. My daughter now stays with my sister's family in Norfolk."

"I'm sorry. That must have been terrible." She didn't know what else to say. Silence fell between them for a brief span of time. Across the hall, the men of his unit's voices rumbled up and down in volume as feet moved across the floor. Within the confines of her office, fire crackling in the tile stove was the only sound except for their breathing.

Hoag looked up with a faraway expression on his face. "You remind me of her a little. Her hair was the same color, and she also had freckles across her nose." He straightened and turned. "Sometimes I imagine she's still here even though I know she is not." He turned to walk away and then turned his head. "I would be grateful for the company, Mistress Clarke. It makes these kinds of events much more bearable."

Faith listened to his footsteps as he returned to the taproom. His life must be lonely far away from his family. She had never considered the cost of bearing arms against Great Britain. Hoag and those like him spent months far away from family and friends, practicing for battles that all knew would come soon. She wondered if joining the militia simplified things by keeping him focused on other matters. Her heart ached for the little girl, left to relatives, while her father chose to bury his heartache in fighting a war. Faith's mind turned to the other problem: supper at the Randolph home. They were one of the most prominent families in town. Many times, she had passed the extensive house and grounds on Nicholson Street, but she had never entered the property. She knew better than to believe Elizabeth Randolph would welcome a tavern keeper to eat supper at her table.

Later, when she went to check on the status of dinner, she mentioned the invitation to Olivia. It was baking day. While Olivia worked on making the loaves that would carry them through the week, her assistant worked on the mid-day meal. Dorcas was carving a ham while a pot of beans bubbled over the fire. Smaller pieces of meat she gathered to drop into the pot. Faith's nose picked up the scent of cabbage cooking. After a moment, she spotted it at the edge of the fire, simmering in a pot of water on top of the metal spider.

Olivia's sleeves were rolled to her elbows as she worked to shape yet another loaf. The door to the brick oven built into the mantle was closed, but Faith could smell bread already baking inside. Once she had finished and put a cloth over the dough to rise, she looked over at Faith.

"The bread smells wonderful," Faith complimented as she met the other woman's eyes.

"Thank you," Olivia said. "Dinner should be ready in another half hour."

Faith watched her work. "You make the best bread."

Olivia smiled. "It takes a little time to do it right. I will need to do more later this week with all these men here, but this should take us through the next few days." She paused to check on the bread in the oven, releasing a rich, yeasty aroma. Taking a pair of heavy folded cloths, she pulled out a few loaves and set them on the table to cool. Without pausing, she pulled a cloth off some loaves that were sitting on the side. Using a baker's peel, she loaded these into the oven and closed the metal door set into the brick. She took a deep breath and used the edge of her apron to wipe the sweat off her face.

Faith walked over to the nearby keg of cider and filled a mug before handing it to the other woman. "Here."

Olivia swallowed thirstily. "Thanks." She set the mug down on the table and looked over at Dorcas. The small woman had finished slicing ham and was getting ready to put it into a greased pan before placing it on another spider resting over hot coals from the fire. "I can take care of that. Why don't you see if there are any apples left in the cellar? If there are, we can stew them to go with supper."

Dorcas looked from one woman to the other. "I can take some time to do that." The door creaked as she shut it behind her, cutting off the cold air.

Olivia watched her go. "She's pretty smart. I bet she will stay a good half hour."

Faith shivered as the chill goosed her neck before dissipating into the room.

"So what is it you want to talk about?" Olivia's dark eyes gleamed with amusement at Faith's start of surprise. "I can tell from the expression on your face. You are not good at hiding your feelings at all, but then you've never had to."

Faith's laugh was rueful. "There are times it would have been useful." Without a preamble, she told her about Captain Hoag's invitation. "I don't know what to do. Mistress Randolph will not welcome a tavern keeper to supper, but he begged me to come to keep her niece from getting the wrong idea."

Olivia snorted. "You're forgetting who you are. Master Ezra may be gone, but he was a dear friend of her husband. He and Ms. Genia supped there many times and the Randolphs at their house. You are part of the Moore family, albeit by marriage. What you need to worry about is finding a proper dress."

Faith paused. She was correct about that. There was nothing fancy enough in her clothes' chest to cover such an occasion. "I haven't received the first payment from the Captain, and there is no time to go to the milliner."

"Go to your mother-in-law and ask for her help." Olivia went over to put the skillet on the spider and watched the hog fat melt. When it began to sizzle, she added the meat and stepped back far enough that the hot grease would not burn her hands or get on her skirt. Picking up a long-handled spatula, she waited for the meat to brown. "Her own pride will compel her to help you, and since she's no longer in mourning, she probably has a lot to choose from."

"I'm a good five inches taller than her," Faith protested.

"You have a few very nice petticoats. All we have to do is add some embellishment, and they will make a nice underskirt." Olivia caught her gaze. "I'll take a look at what she lends you and make a trip to the milliner. She can get those alterations done in no time. With that contract with the militia, Mistress Hunter will extend you credit."

Faith mulled that idea. "Maybe, although I doubt Mistress Randolph will deign to send me an invitation to her house. I'm not part of her social circle."

"Eugenia is, and they have the bond of both having lost men to the revolutionary cause. Her year of mourning has passed, and she has been accepting some invitations. It would do her good to get out and about." Pots clanked as Olivia moved things around to cook evenly over the fire. She moved with the ease of one who had done it for years and knew how to get the best out of the flames. Once everything was where she wanted she stepped back and looked at Faith. "You will probably hear from Mistress Randolph or Eugenia later today or early tomorrow."

Faith thought that unlikely. Still, the thought drifted in and out of her thoughts despite her best attempts to quell it. Before long she was caught up in the business of running her tavern. Dinner was served with Seth and Titus ferrying trays of food back and forth while she served the drinks Malachi poured. Ellen, the household maid, had gone upstairs earlier to clean while the men were out drilling. After the men had been fed, they drifted out, some to patrol the town, others to find other means to occupy their time.

Faith went to her desk to the growing piles of correspondence, messages, and bills that awaited her. On top, where she suspected it had been placed deliberately, was an invitation to supper from Elizabeth Randolph. No sooner had a shiver of dread gone down her spine than George, her mother-in-law's doorman and delegated messenger, stepped into the entryway.

As soon as he spotted her, he walked over and bowed. "Mistress Clarke, good afternoon. I trust you are well."

Faith smiled in spite of herself. George's formality always amused her, although she would never wound his dignity by saying so. She admired his loyalty to Eugenia. When offered a choice of going to the home of Ezra's older son, Daniel, or staying with his widow, he opted to stay with Eugenia. In her widowhood, she needed staff she could rely on even more than when she had been a prominent matron of the capital. "I am fine, George. What brings you here?"

"Mistress Moore wishes you to join her for tea tomorrow afternoon. Nothing formal," he added when he saw her face. "It will be only family. It has been a while since she has seen you."

Faith was tempted to retort that she had been unaware that her former mother-in-law had desired her company, but decided it was wiser to keep her mouth shut. She knew why Eugenia had invited her, and for once, practicality outweighed her pride. "Certainly, it has been some weeks since we last spoke." That wasn't due to any acrimony, but Eugenia didn't go to the market for food, and Faith didn't go to many supper parties. They orbited different worlds. She had no time to take tea with the local gentry, not if she wanted to make a living. "When would she like me to come?" Mentally, she was sorting through her clothes chest for something appropriate.

"She expects you at two," George said almost apologetically. He visited the tavern from time to time and knew that it was perilously close to the end of dinner.

Faith sighed. Eugenia was Eugenia. "Tell her I will be there." She turned, to go tell Olivia she would not be there to help at the midday meal tomorrow when she heard George cough. She looked back, raising her eyebrows in query.

George offered a shy smile. "We at the Moore House have missed you, Mistress Clarke. We have always regarded you to be a steadying influence. It will be most pleasant to have you in the house again." With that, he turned and went out the door.

Mystified, Faith stared where he had been. "I wonder what that is about." She had little time to ponder his words. Voices from the taproom propelled her forward back into the world in which she lived.

Chapter Ten

"Stand still!" The milliner spoke through a mouthful of pins. Faith froze on the stool upon which she was perched. Her stockinged feet had noted the smooth wood and its lack of purchase from which to dig in her toes. She would just have to hope she didn't overbalance when she stepped down.

Eugenia made a wide circle around Faith and the milliner, watching the work being done. Olivia had been correct; Eugenia did have a gown to lend which only needed minor alterations to fit. She clucked as Mistress Hunter's apprentice carefully made adjustments around the waist and bust. Her mother-in-law looked well in a blue wool dress with imported lace at the neck and sleeves. Her cap was delicate linen with dark blue ribbon accenting it. Her ears displayed pearl earrings that Faith had not seen before. Eugenia appeared excited to be invited to the Randolph House and was determined not to be embarrassed by her former daughter-in-law.

Faith felt like a chicken circled by foxes. She had submitted to having her stays pulled in and stripping down to her shift. She kept her thoughts to herself, knowing they would not be appreciated. Mistress Hunter chatted animatedly with Eugenia about trims for the gown that would make it current.

"You are fortunate that this fabric is still popular this season. We can dress it up with the ivory lace and ruffles I have received recently from Belgium." She walked about Faith, her dark eyes taking in the fit and length of the gown. She made a few suggestions to her apprentice, an enslaved woman named Alicia.

Faith eyed herself in the mirror. The steely blue of the fabric shimmered with silk threads that had been woven with wool to create the fabric. Delicate embroidery framed the low scooped neckline and elbow-length sleeves. The old lace had been removed as had the serpentine ruffles about the bottom edge. The milliner had pinned gold-toned rosettes at the elbow just where the sleeve ended and added ruffles in a warm ivory that matched what she planned, putting around the neckline. Despite the sun illuminating the room and the roaring fire, she shivered, eliciting a martyred expression from Alicia, who waited until she stilled before continuing to pin the hem.

Eugenia stared at Faith's legs. "You need silk stockings. Woolen ones are too common for being entertained by Elizabeth Randolph."

"They keep my legs warm," Faith protested, although she realized she might as well have tried arguing with the delicate pink roses printed on the wallpaper.

Eugenia snorted. Her lip curled back, revealing even white teeth, an expression that made her appear somewhat canine. "This isn't about comfort. This is about making an impression. This could be your introduction to a better sort of company. You will have to make sure that the captain does not pay you too much attention at this gathering. Elizabeth will want him to socialize with her niece. With the rebellion, Betsy has had limited opportunity to meet men of good standing. Mistress Randolph knows his family. He could use a good wife to manage his land and mind his daughter."

Faith wondered if they had taken any time to consider Captain Hoag's feelings. Given his desire not to attend supper alone, she knew he was aware of the impending snare and determined to evade it. She wondered if Betsy Randolph knew what her aunt was planning. Undoubtedly, she did. Marriage was a game of chess in the upper classes where everyone was trying to win increased wealth and privilege. She was glad that, as a widow, she didn't have to consider such things.

"Faith," Eugenia called. "You can step down now. Please do not waste Mistress Hunter's time or mine."

Faith hesitated as she contemplated the best way to get down. The stool wobbled as she leaned to hop down. Alicia saw her hesitation and offered a hand. Faith took it and stepped down quickly, thanking the other woman. Getting out of the dress took help from the milliner and her assistant. Not only was it fashionably tight around the chest and bosom, it had enough pins in it to intimidate a porcupine. Faith was relieved to get back in her own clothes although, her stays still felt tight.

The week flew by on wings. The day of the supper party opened with gray rain that darkened the sky and turned the streets into a watery mess. Ellen stayed busy sweeping mud out of the entryway despite the boot scraper they kept on the front porch. She muttered something under her breath as she once again worked to remove muddy tracks off the floor. Faith picked up the sand bucket and began sprinkling white sand on the floorboards to pick up any more mud that was tracked in.

Ellen looked over at her. "I sanded the floor last night before I went to bed. I copied the pattern from one I had seen in the Capitol Building. She sighed. "I came upstairs early to stir the fire and discovered someone had already tracked it all up in the middle of the night. Who wanders about at that hour?"

Faith offered a sympathetic smile. "I have no idea. I did see it before I turned in. It was pretty. I'm sorry your work was destroyed before anyone got to appreciate it."

Ellen rolled her eyes before returning to work. Her quick, energetic movements made short work of the task. When she looked in later, she could see Ellen making another design in the sand. She smiled and left her to her art.

Her dress arrived before dinner. Since she was busy collecting money to pay for a few tabs that men in town had run up, Faith gestured for the delivery person to lay the dress and petticoats on the bed where they would not get dirty. She went back to the kitchen where Olivia was frying potatoes. Steam rose from the pan as lard popped and sizzled among the thick-cut slices.

Faith murmured appreciatively. "Those smell wonderful."

Olivia put the black iron spatula aside as she backed away from the fire. "Better to use them before they go bad. I saw that these had started growing eyes, so I cut them up quickly while we could still use them."

Another iron pan sat on the edge of the fire, a heavy lid covering the contents. Olivia left it alone as she moved the hot and graying coals to where she wanted them. Off to the side Dorcas brought in a stack of plates in preparation for dinner. A clean ivory cloth covered her hair and emphasized the smooth copper brown of her skin. She was a few shades paler than Olivia, with a small snub nose and a perfect cupid bow mouth. Her small hands displayed strength as she arranged the heavy wooden trays on the long table in preparation for feeding the men inside.

Faith nodded. "Another hour, then?"

"Half an hour," Olivia corrected. "Most everything is ready. These potatoes should be ready soon. As long as our men are ready to help serve, we will have the food ready to go."

Faith nodded. The militia would be back from drilling soon. She had seen Captain Hoag slip into the private room not long ago with some of his staff. The other men would be along shortly.

They all had gotten used to the routine of feeding the men early in the morning and watching them go out. When they returned for dinner, they were tired and hungry. In the latter part of the day, the men drank and played games of dice and went into town to entertain themselves. Captain Hoag spent much of his time in her private room meeting with his fellow officers, going over dispatches and maps as the men discussed the best way to defend the town from the enemy. Faith brought drinks to them as he and his lieutenants gathered around one of the tables discussing strategy.

Knowing she had a brief span of time, Faith brought a pot of coffee that Olivia had brewed along with a half dozen of her good china cups. Hoag nodded at her as she poured and offered cups to the men. Once he had decided to take the private room as his office, he had asked for her to be the only one to serve them when he met with his men. Not even Titus was allowed entrance to feed the fire. Hoag or one of his men tended it while Titus left kindling at the door. When he made the request he had emphasized the need for discretion. "Servants can talk; I know I can trust you not to gossip." Faith had nodded. No one at the house supported the British but as

Jeremy Butler had explained long ago, sometimes a careless comment was all the information he needed to confirm an action of the enemy.

The sun was sinking in the sky as she went to prepare for supper at the Randolph House. Shadows darkened the room enough for her to light a few tapers to see what she was doing. Olivia came in with a pitcher to refill the basin. She helped Faith out of her work clothes down to her shift.

While Faith washed her face, Olivia laid out the garments for the party. Sitting on the other side of the bed, Faith removed her shoes and woolen stockings and put on the thin silk ones blended with wool that Eugenia had given her. She shivered as she stepped into her shoes, missing the solid warmth of the thick wool. "Is it necessary to freeze for fashion?'

Olivia laughed. "Would you prefer to be doing this in August?" She handed Faith a petticoat, the first of many layers. After she adjusted her stays and stomacher, Olivia handed Faith the split rump padding that lifted the skirt up. Faith felt a bit ridiculous but knew that this was now the fashion. Next, she tied a pocket at her waist where it would line up with an opening in her skirt. After that came a quilted under petticoat and a full-length linen one over it.

Finally, the top petticoat that matched the gown went over Faith's head. She then pulled on the rest of what Eugenia had called a robe a la polonaise. After adjusting the sleeves, Faith began pinning the false waistcoat in place while Olivia adjusted the ruffles and tucks that embellished the back. The décolletage revealed more than Faith was accustomed to. She took a snow-white neckerchief and tucked it around her neckline to alleviate the feeling her breasts were about to escape.

Olivia looked at her critically. "It needs a bow." She reached over to the bed where the milliner had sent a light and a dark-colored bow that would coordinate with the gown. She picked the silvery blue one and pinned it at the center of the neckline. "It matches the ribbon we threaded through your hair." She shook out Faith's dark wool cloak. "The coach will be here soon. Miss Genia will be itching to get to the party."

Faith rolled her eyes. She had no doubt of that. Eugenia had been delighted to be invited to the Randolph House for supper. She had offered to share her coach with Faith and Captain Hoag so that they could arrive in style. They were fortunate that Eugenia had been able to hang onto a conveyance after Ezra's sudden death. She and his adult children had spent weeks negotiating every item not covered by Ezra's will. Fortunately, he had been a man who considered the details, which meant Eugenia had kept the house, staff, and many other items. His businesses he had divided among his sons, leaving money and some household items to his two daughters. Despite the fact Faith was not a blood relation, he had chosen to provide for her as well, setting aside money for her son's education and ensuring the tavern was clear of debt. He had also left her the responsibility of his network of informants surrounding Williamsburg, a fact that kept her up some nights.

Captain Hoag waited in the main room. His eyes brightened when he caught sight of her. "You look exceptionally well this evening, Mistress Clarke." He bowed. The captain had taken time to work on his appearance as well. His uniform had been pressed, and his boots shined to a high gloss.

Outside, the carriage pulled up. The footman hopped down and put out the step for them to enter. As Hoag handed her up into the carriage, he said. "I hope this is a pleasant evening for us all."

"I do, too," she replied as she took a seat next to her former mother-in-law. Eugenia's eyes gleamed in the dim light. Like Faith, she wore a heavy woolen cloak that covered her gown. Her hair was dressed high in a pouf that Faith suspected had been amended with a pad. It rose up like a tower to where a jeweled headpiece rested. There was just enough light for Faith to see the sparkle of jewelry at her ears and throat. As she settled her skirts, Eugenia frowned as she placed a protective hand over her own skirts, which took a generous portion of the seat. Hoag wisely kept his legs in the narrow opening between the two billows of skirts as he settled on the opposite side.

The streetlights were being lit as they passed down Waller Street before turning onto Nicholson. A few horses passed by as people headed home for the day. The only sound besides the creaking of the carriage was the steady clop of horses' hooves on the road. As they came to the Randolph property, the sounds of other horses could be heard across the frosty air. Within moments, the door of the carriage swung open, and the footman held out his hand for her to disembark. Hoag offered his arm to Eugenia. Faith fell in behind them as they walked down the path to the home of Elizabeth Randolph.

An enslaved man in livery opened the door. As they entered, Mistress Randolph spoke. "Let Roger and Phillip take your cloaks while you warm yourselves by the fire in the parlor. We will be ready to retire to the dining room shortly."

Faith looked around the room, taking in the elaborate wallpaper and the elegant marble mantel surrounding the fireplace. Hoag migrated over to another officer and spoke with him. In addition to Faith and Eugenia, another woman stood near the fire. Her hair was pulled up into a high roll with a few curls streaming down her shoulders. A long feather curled back from her headdress and dangled above her left ear. A younger woman, presumably her daughter, stood next to her. This woman wore a robe de polonaise similar to Faith's, except it was in a rosy pink shade. Pearls glimmered in her ears and at her throat. Her dark hair was held back from her face by a broad rose ribbon tied in a bow on one side. Behind it, a profusion of curls tumbled down her back.

Soon, they were all in the spacious dining room, seated around a long table covered with a snowy linen cloth. Faith listened to the conversation around her and tried to show interest. The lady to her right, Mistress Kindle, chattered gaily about the difference between a gown in the French style and a gown in the English style. Faith nodded politely and tried to keep her eyes from darting around the table. Not surprisingly, Captain Hoag was seated next to Mistress Randolph's niece, Betsy Harrison. Eugenia was seated next to an older Frenchman in uniform.

After being served a potato soup, rich with cream, the servants brought in several meat dishes. Steam rose from platters that had been kept warm by the fire. Faith recognized one servant from the funeral. Joanna went around the table helping serve guests. She stumbled as she drew near to Miss Harrison and the Captain, slopping gravy on the floor.

Mistress Randolph hissed. "Clumsy fool. Clean that up immediately and go to the kitchen. Send Little Aggy to take your place." Joanna looked down at the floor as her mistress scolded. A faint flush rose in her cheeks as her lips pressed tightly shut. Once Elizabeth Randolph quit speaking, she turned away. A tear streaked down one side of her face as she left the room.

The tablecloth and dishes were removed for dessert. A petite woman, who Faith presumed was Little Aggy, came in with a platter of small cakes while a man followed with a wine bottle that he held with a cloth wrapped around it. Another followed with clean plates that were set down in front of each guest. Conversation continued as the staff served the dessert moving silently around the table with an efficiency born of long years of service.

Faith stayed busy answering questions about her opinion regarding the best colors for the season, her son's studies, and whether she believed the British would come to Williamsburg.

Mistress Kindle brushed that idea aside. "People have been worrying about that for months." She waved a hand languidly. "It is plain they have no plans to come here. Their hands are full fighting our men up North."

Faith eyed her. "That's no guarantee that they won't come down eventually. We don't know, but that we might wake one day to see a British warship on the river. It's not been that long since our former governor was raiding our coastline."

Master Kindle snorted. "Dunmore turned tail and left and took all his foolish promises with him." He looked over at Captain Hoag and the other officer. "Our men are spoiling for a fight. They will run the British back into the river and across the sea to England."

Hoag raised an eyebrow at that remark. "Our men train hard, that is true, but let us not forget that the British have been a respected fighting force for hundreds of years, whereas our men have come in from their homes only in the past few months to train in the art of war."

"Art," snorted Kindle. "How hard can it be to hold a gun?"

"They all know how to hold a gun. Most learn to hunt for game not long after they've gotten into breeches. Very few of our men are used to following orders or know how to engage an army." Hoag's patient tone spoke of long hours on the field training men for a fight they were ill-prepared to handle. "The winter gives us time to prepare, and for that, I am grateful. I am sure one day we will be called to engage the enemy whether here or in one of our colonies to the north. Washington will need all our men in order to win this war. They need to be ready for what they will face." Hoag tried but failed to keep an edge of irritation out of his voice.

Kindle started to speak again before being nudged by his wife. He shot her an irritated look before taking a sip of his wine.

Mistress Randolph took control of the table. "Let us find a more pleasant topic to discuss. All this talk of battle is upsetting to the stomach."

Hoag smiled at her. "Here, here. There are far more pleasant topics to attend. Tell me, madam, where is the best place to find silk ribbon in Williamsburg? I can tell that you are a lady of discriminating taste. I have a younger sister and a daughter that I would like to send something pretty."

Elizabeth Randolph smiled gratefully at the captain before suggesting a milliner she went to and the wide selection of trims they had in stock. Hoag leaned in to listen, his focus entirely on his hostess.

Kindle turned to a neighbor. The older gentleman began a story about one of his dogs that soon had those surrounding him dissolving into laughter.

Faith's thoughts remained on Joanna. She wanted to speak to the enslaved woman about her friend, but there was no chance she could slip out and go to the servant's quarters without causing a stir. Olivia would be the best person to speak to her. Still, she wondered. What had Marianna done to merit such an end? But the enslaved woman never returned to the public side of the house.

As the evening ended and their carriage pulled up, Faith looked back at the house. A faint mist rose from the damp ground, casting a spectral air about the area. The moon was nearly full and cast its luminous gaze on the ground, yet did nothing to dissipate the dark shadow cast by the house on the side. In the dim light, Faith spotted a figure watching them as they mounted the steps to enter into the carriage. Her white cap stood out from the darkness, as did the kerchief around her neck. Although the darkness concealed her face, she felt certain the woman was Joanna. Concealed by darkness, she watched as the carriages were loaded and people headed away from the place she was never free to leave.

Chapter Eleven

Olivia rose early to start the day. The fire in the upstairs fireplace was already blazing as she threw back the covers and began to get dressed. A smile crossed her face as she noticed that her clothes had been placed on a chair not far from the hearth to warm. She knew who was responsible for that. His whistle could be heard downstairs as he headed out to tend the animals in the barn. She rolled out of bed and tried not to shriek as her feet made contact with the icy floor. Her breath came in white puffs as she hurried to add layers of clothes between herself and the chilly air. Staying near the fire helped a little, but this time of year, the cold air crept in constantly. It took a moment to locate her shoes. Finally, she spotted them just under the edge of the bed where she had removed them the night before. Covering her hair with a sky-blue cloth she had bartered the milliner for, she headed down the steps. Titus had already kindled the kitchen fire so that the room was warming up as she entered. He had filled the kettle with water for her as well. Olivia smiled as she set it on the fire to heat. That man was always doing little things like that. He had a way of making her feel treasured without words.

As the water heated, she fried some ham left over from the day before. Her nose warned her that the meat was done. Olivia removed the pan long enough to set the smoking ham on a platter on the table. Once she finished with the ham, she put in some corncakes. They hissed as they hit the hot fat in the pan. While they cooked, she fried a few eggs left from those gathered yesterday. Just as the coffee boiled, Titus came in with a bucket of milk from the cow in the barn. Setting it down carefully, he washed his hands in the nearby basin and sat down at the table. Within minutes, Seth, Dorcas, Ellen, Malachi, and Faith joined them around the large wooden table.

Faith asked Malachi to offer grace. The elderly man started to demur before Titus nodded encouragement, followed by the others. He bowed his head and offered a short but reverent blessing. Afterwards, they dug in, drowning out the morning's chill with hot food and warm company. No one spoke as they passed the platters about along with the salt.

Neither Seth nor Malachi cared much for coffee, so they drank mugs of cider with their meal. The older man seemed to fit in well with life at the tavern. He spent most of his time behind the bar where he had already developed a good memory for what regular customers preferred to drink. Although he was still enslaved, Faith insisted on paying him along with the others. Olivia was certain that she had not informed Eugenia of that. Everyone knew Malachi would likely spend the rest of his life with them, whether or not he would be manumitted remained to be seen.

After the meal, everyone left to perform their morning chores. Dorcas prepared to feed the chickens and retrieve eggs while Ellen went to the cellar with Malachi to retrieve fresh supplies of cider and short beer for the bar. Outside, Solomon had begun to crow.

"I'm coming," Dorcas huffed as she wrapped a heavy shawl over her body before taking the bucket of feed for the hungry rooster and his harem. "Crazy old rooster can't wait to eat." She snorted. "You would think he ran the place."

Titus laughed. "He thinks he does." Pulling a cap over his head, he went out to chop more wood for the very hungry fire. Within minutes, the steady sound of chopping could be heard outside.

Seth entered the kitchen. A few strands of hay stuck to his coat from where he had cleaned out stalls in the early dawn hours before breakfast. "Has the cream been skimmed off from yesterday's milk?"

Olivia answered. "Dorcas will tend to that after she deals with the chickens. There are still a few clean pans down there. The cows don't produce as much in the cold weather."

He nodded. "Give them another month when the grass and clover come out, and we will be blessed with it." He looked over at the kitchen. "Could you make pancakes one day? My ma used to make them sometimes." His expression was wistful.

Olivia's gaze softened. It hadn't been a year since Faith and Seth's mother had passed. Neither spoke of it, but she knew from her own life that grief lingered and welled up at unexpected moments to bleed anew. "I think I could do that in the next day or two. There will be buttermilk left from churning to make some."

"That would be nice." Seth headed to the small barn out back, where Titus had already gone out to feed the animals. Olivia cleared away the dishes and prepared to fix breakfast for the soldiers staying at the tavern. In addition to slicing more ham, she beat eggs to scramble in the fat left from cooking the meat. In the pot over the fire, apples simmered, releasing a sweet, fruity odor that perfumed the kitchen.

Faith returned from the main tavern, where she had gone to check the fires and make sure the bar was stocked. She looked over at Olivia. "Would you like me to roast more coffee beans or make biscuits?"

"Make biscuits," Olivia said. "I don't think these men are ready to face your coffee."

Faith made a face. "It's not that bad."

Olivia chuckled. "I guess it depends on what you are accustomed to drinking. Some of them may like the flavor of charred beans."

Faith rolled her eyes and got out a dough bowl. As she mixed flour, salt, and other ingredients, she started humming. Once she added buttermilk, she kneaded the dough gently on a board before cutting out the biscuits and putting them into a Dutch oven, which would then be put on the hearth with coals on top, where they would bake for breakfast.

Olivia noted the dark circles under Faith's eyes. She wasn't surprised. Once her employer had arrived home and gotten undressed and her hair undone, it had been late. She doubted she had slept well. Although they had never discussed it, she was aware that her mistress got up in the night from time to time and wandered through the lower levels of the tavern. Titus had seen her up and about when he rose to kindle fires before dawn. She did as her husband recommended and did not mention it. As Titus had noted, it was not their business.

Olivia disliked interfering in other people's affairs, but she was certain Faith was unaware of some things that were occurring in her own family. They had a few moments before they would be interrupted as they prepared to feed the men inside the tavern. She couldn't let the opportunity pass. "Have you spoken with Seth lately?"

Faith looked puzzled. "Not really. He seems to have settled in well enough. There's no meeting house, but I think he's been visiting the Presbyterian Church nearby."

"That's not all he's been doing."

Faith's eyes narrowed. "What do you mean?"

"He's been hanging around the Randolph's property. There's a girl he's been seeing."

Faith relaxed as she went over to stir the pot, which continued to bubble gently. "It's been over a year since he relocated here. I guess it's only natural he would seek company. Who is the young lady? Does she come from a good family?"

"Tabitha has worked at the Randolph House since she was a small child. Her mother was one of the housemaids before she was sold away."

The smile left her face as the other woman's words penetrated. "Are you telling me he is seeing an enslaved woman?"

Olivia nodded. "I've seen them at the market. He's helped her carry things back to the house. At first, I thought he was just being kind, but there's more to it than that. He's been seen on the property, and she slips out to meet him. If they are caught, there will be trouble."

Faith looked thoughtful. "There are many free people of color in Pennsylvania. I wonder if he is unaware of her position."

Olivia shot her an incredulous look. "This is Virginia. How could he not know? Not just because of her skin tone, although I hear she's pretty fair-skinned, but also because of the tight reign that family keeps on their people. If the enslaved community knows, it won't be long before the family figures it out. Then they will punish everyone they feel is responsible."

Faith paled. "Seth is accustomed to having freed people around him. My father did not believe in owning slaves. He thought it was the devil's work."

"Your father is wiser than most," Olivia responded. "But that changes nothing. You need to speak to him and make sure he understands the danger of what he's doing. The Randolphs could have him arrested for trespassing. They could accuse him of interfering with their property." She paused to let that sink in before continuing. "The worst punishment will fall on Tabitha and anyone they believe to be aiding and abetting them. She will be punished, beaten, sent away to some awful place."

"Surely not," Faith protested. "They are young and foolish. This will probably pass by spring. I doubt much will come of it."

"Then you are naïve," Olivia said bluntly. "Slaves are not considered people. They are treated like livestock to be trained, bred and sold to increase the herd. They are property." Her voice turned rough. "Ignored until someone shows interest, then they move to protect their investment. Your brother's actions will cause immense pain and grief to people who have no voice and no recourse from the anger of those whom the law says owns them."

Faith paused to put a lid on the Dutch oven and slide it just inside the hearth. Taking a small shovel, she put a small stack of hot coals on top to make sure the top and bottom cooked evenly. When she was done, she turned to Olivia. "Seth is one of the kindest people I know. He would not deliberately harm anyone." She sighed. "I will tell him to be careful and make sure he realizes the young lady is under stricter rules than he may realize." Faith paused. "Titus said someone broke in the other night. Was anything taken?"

Olivia shook her head. "I think it was a warning. He left Marianna's head cloth on the table but took nothing."

Faith stiffened. "We need to tell the sheriff. Where is it?"

"I threw it in the fire." Olivia's voice was expressionless.

"That was foolish. It's proof that you told the truth," Faith stared at her like she had lost her mind.

Olivia shot her an angry look. "He has his mind made up already. That is clear. All that cloth would do is make him suspect I killed her, and I have no interest in being shut up in the gaol for the remainder of the winter."

Faith spoke slowly. "I think he is as fair a man as any here in Williamsburg."

"If you are white." Olivia banged a pot as she moved it to the side of the fire. "People of color are treated differently by the law. You should know that. You've seen it.

Faith bit her lip. "I have, but I cannot believe—"

"Believe what you want. It changes nothing." Olivia turned away to tend the fire. There was nothing more to be said.

Faith moved toward the door. Picking up the shawl she had dropped when entering, she wrapped it around herself. "I need to bring up some butter from the cellar." With that, she left.

Olivia stared after her, frustrated and angry. Faith didn't understand how dangerous it was to be enslaved. Her ignorance mirrored that of her brother, and it could cause a great deal of harm to families within the Randolph household. Olivia knew from personal experience that one's family could be broken up and sold on a whim, never to see one another again. Her hand clenched into a fist so tight her nails made painful indents in her palm. She could not, would not allow that to happen to anyone she knew.

Outside, the steady chop of an axe told her wood was being cut for the fire. Cutting wood was a daily task, one that required more and more attention as the weather grew colder. The men in the household worked throughout the day to keep the fires stoked. Olivia had even cut some kindling when needed. Seth helped Titus keep the many fires stoked throughout the day and into the night. The two men still had some parts of a log from a tree that fell during a storm a few weeks ago. All the limbs had been used, and now they were sectioning off the trunk to split into lengths suitable to feed the fires. Olivia heard the door rattle and moved to open it.

Seth entered. His arms were filled with wood. Olivia caught his eye as he turned to leave after depositing his load. "You need to stop going over to the Randolph property. It will only cause trouble."

His gaze skittered away from her to focus on the opposite wall. "I don't know what you mean." A flush rose up his neck.

"Yes, you do. Your sister may not know what you're doing, but I do." She moved until inches separated them. "Tabitha may be young and pretty, but she is enslaved. There is nothing you can do to change that."

Seth shot her a stubborn look. "She should be free. No one deserves to be treated like a horse or cow."

Olivia laughed bitterly. "You have no idea what it means to be enslaved. At a moment's notice, you can be beaten, sold, and sent to do a nasty task you would never choose to do on your own. Once Mistress Randolph realizes you are interfering with her property, that girl will be punished and quite possibly sent away."

"No!" Agitation made his voice go up. One look at Olivia's face, and it dropped. "That can't happen. I love her." His breathing went up and down in short gasps. He shook his head violently. "Tabby deserves better. I want to do what is best for her."

"Then let her go," Olivia said softly. "Elizabeth Randolph sells people who she perceives as trouble. You don't want that to happen. This is the only home she's ever known."

"I've been taking extra work to earn the money to buy her freedom."

Olivia sighed. "What makes you think she would sell her to you?" Torn between pity and irritation, she reached out a hand to his chin and forced him to meet her eyes. "Listen to me. You have to let her go. No matter what you think, no matter what you feel, this will never be. She is enslaved."

Frustration laced his tone. "How can you say that? You know what it's like. I'm going to free her and give her a far better life than she's ever known."

Olivia shook her head. "I'm free because your sister is different from most folks around here. Even at that, Jeremy had to call in a favor to get our manumission." Her voice roughened. "It is virtually impossible to free a slave even when the owner is willing to do so. Elizabeth Randolph is not. All your interference will do is lead to tragedy for that poor girl."

Seth's eyes glittered. "There has to be a way."

Olivia's voice was unyielding. "Let her go."

"I can't accept that." Seth strode to the door and slammed it behind him.

Olivia spoke to the closed door. "Unfortunately, you have no choice."

Chapter Twelve

Faith dropped off her receipt for expenses for housing and feeding the militia troops at the Capitol. Soldiers stood outside the building, stomping their feet to keep the blood circulating. These days, the city bustled even in winter as the governor and the House of Delegates prepared for the eventual invasion of the British Army. She hoped they were ready, but doubted anything could prepare them for fighting a war on their own doorstep.

After speaking to Olivia, she felt somewhat embattled herself. Knowing her little brother's love of animals, she had gone to the small barn behind the tavern and found him currying a horse. She hadn't seen the elegant black before. Faith presumed that someone had come in to relay a message using the network set up by her late father-in-law, Ezra Moore.

Seth sang a familiar tune as he stood with the mare inside the roomy stall. Faith recognized it as one their father had sung often in the mornings as he went about his work.

"Hey said the black bird sitting in a chair
Once I courted a lady fair.
She turned fickle and turned her back.
Ever since then I'm dressed in black.
Hey said the blue jay as she flew.
If I were a young man I'd have two.
If one proved fickle and chanced to go,
I'd have a new string to my bow."

He stopped when he saw Faith watching him. "Hey there, are you needing me for something? I'll be done with Clara soon enough. He ran the brush down her sleek hide one more time. The horse nickered softly as he ran a few fingers down her muzzle. "That's a girl. There will be oats for you tonight." He rubbed her glossy back before turning toward his sister. "Do you need help inside?" He stepped out of the stall and closed the door behind him. He placed the brush on the shelf where it rested. He shifted his feet back and forth restlessly as if called by an unseen voice. As he turned, Faith saw a line of scratches that extended from the lower edge of his cheek to his jaw.

"What is that?" Faith exclaimed. She reached out to get a better look, but Set shoved her hand away.

"It's nothing," he muttered.

"That's not how it looks." She stared at him. A shiver of unease went down her spine. He wore the same look he had when he was small and was hiding something."

"Tell me what happened."

Seth shrugged. "I got too close to some briars, that's all."

He was lying. From the stubborn set of his chin, Faith knew she would get nothing out of him. "if you won't let me tend it, go see Olivia. It needs to be cleaned so it will heal quickly."

"It's just a few scratches," he muttered. "I don't need to bother Olivia."

"Olivia is concerned about you," Faith began.

Seth's head whipped around. "Olivia should mind her own business. What I do on my own time is no one's concern but mine." His left hand clenched before he carefully released it.

Faith remembered their mother tried for years to train him out of his left-handedness, but nothing worked. Their father had finally told her to leave the boy alone. It had left Seth able to write with both hands, but in times of stress, he went back to the dominant hand he'd been born with. "I'm not here to judge. I'm here to tell you to be careful."

Seth looked at her. His long, dark lashes made his eyes look even bluer than they were. His expression was furious. "Tabitha deserves better than to be regarded as little more than livestock. She is a woman with hopes and dreams, just like you. She is a skilled seamstress and can look at a dress and know how to recreate it. If it were not for Mistress Randolph, she could earn a good living at the milliners."

"Unfortunately, the law regards her as Mistress Randolph's property, and there is nothing we can do about it." Faith kept her expression neutral. Such a skill could enable the Randolphs to have much clothing made in-house, costing them nothing but cloth and thread. They wouldn't willingly surrender those abilities.

Seth shot her a stubborn look. "She's afraid to ask. Tabitha is terrified of what her mistress might do if she thinks she wants to go somewhere else if only to work a few hours."

"It is her decision," Faith pointed out. "You cannot tell Tabitha what to do."

He took a deep breath. "I can buy her freedom."

Faith's eyebrows shot up.

"I've been seeking extra work. Hopefully, within a year, I will have enough to make an offer. Once she's free, she can make her own choices."

"It's not that easy," Faith said softly. "I wish it were. Elizabeth Randolph has never manumitted a slave. She's known to be possessive. She's been tough with those who have been recaptured after escaping. I would tread carefully were I you."

"You are not me, although I thought you might be more sympathetic. You were willing to leave Pennsylvania and the Quaker Faith for Jon. This is not much different."

"Do you love this girl? You barely know her."

Seth looked down for a moment before meeting his sister's gaze. "She's the best thing that has happened to me since I arrived."

Faith let out a deep sigh. "You know there is almost no hope for the two of you, don't you?" She hated to say it, hated to think it, but she knew that free and enslaved people did not mix. Even if the girl were free, no one in Williamsburg would accept them as a couple.

Seth offered a sad smile. "I know what you're thinking." With that, he went out the door and broke into a run across the yard and out down a side street far from the judgmental glances of his friends and family.

Faith had just finished cleaning up after supper when trouble arrived at her door. She was helping Malachi restock the bar when she heard the front door open and shut. The older man stiffened as he looked out into the entryway. Faith whirled around to see the Sheriff standing in the doorway to the taproom with two of his men. They all looked grim.

"Mistress Clarke," the sheriff strode forward. "Where is your brother, Seth Payne?"

Faith had been wondering that herself. He had not come in to help serve the soldiers, which meant more work for the rest of them. Ellen had left off skimming milk pans to help fill tankards and carry trays of food to the hungry men. They had only just finished the task and her brother remained absent. "I'm not sure," she answered as she wiped her hands on her apron. "Is there something wrong?"

The sheriff raked her with angry eyes. "Another of Mistress Randolph's slaves has disappeared. He was seen on the property just before the girl was discovered missing. I would like to speak to him about it."

Faith's mind raced. She hoped her brother had not done anything stupid. She hid her shaking hands under her apron and worked to keep her voice calm. "I'm sure there is a reasonable explanation. My brother has been doing odd jobs around town to earn some extra cash. While he has at times worked with enslaved and freed people, I cannot imagine him doing anything against the law." As she spoke, she mentally prayed she was telling the truth.

The sheriff snorted. "He's a young buck with his blood up. He's the hottest-headed Quaker I've ever met, not that I've known many." He cast his eyes around the room. "I've spoken to him once or twice. He doesn't get drunk, mind you, but he does like to get into arguments with men anyone with sense would leave be. Slavery is an institution in Virginia. It has always been this way."

"That doesn't make it right," Faith retorted.

They were interrupted by one of the sheriff's deputies who ran in. "They found her on Botetourt Street. We'll need a wagon to bring her in.

The sheriff frowned. "Just tie her up and make her walk."

The deputy shook his head. "She can't."

"Did she break a leg or something? You need to explain yourself before I go authorize a wagon for one escaped slave."

"She's dead, sir," The deputy said. "Someone cut her head almost all the way off." His face turned pale. "I've never seen anything like this. There is blood all over her body and clothes like someone slaughtered a pig."

Silence fell over the room as an image planted itself in everyone's mind. Even the few men who had lingered near the fire playing cards had quit talking. Faith was surprised when Malachi came from behind the bar to join them.

"Sir," the older man said. "Let me get you a blanket to wrap her up in. Let us provide her with a dignity in death she did not receive in life." His eyes met Faith's in a wordless plea. She nodded her consent.

The sheriff turned to Faith. "Where is your brother? He was the last one seen with her. From what I hear there was quite an argument over at the Randolph house. Mistress Randolph wanted him arrested for disrupting her household. Then Joanna disappeared and all hell broke loose."

"Joanna?" Faith said, surprised. "Is that who disappeared?"

The sheriff sighed impatiently. "Who did you think I meant, Elizabeth Randolph? Your brother got into an argument with her when he went over there. Joanna told him to leave, and he got mad about it. From what I hear she raked his face good when he tried to force his way past. I was going to take him to the gaol to cool off for a day or two. But now it looks like he may have gone too far. We were looking for him when Mistress Randolph let us know that another of her slaves had disappeared." He shook his head. "She's going to have to keep a better watch on her place. This is twice I've been out this week for one thing or another. There was no trouble whatsoever when Peyton Randolph was alive." His cold gray eyes met hers. "I need to see your brother. Where would he be likely to hide?"

"What are you accusing him of?"

He shot her an incredulous look. "Isn't it obvious? Your brother murdered her and likely the other enslaved woman as well. We have to catch him before he strikes again."

Chapter Thirteen

Faith couldn't sleep. After the sheriff had authorized a wagon to collect the dead woman's body, he searched the tavern from top to bottom. He had turned the room where Seth slept inside out and unstuffed the straw from his mattress. His deputies had gone through the barn. At the end of the day she had collapsed in bed exhausted, too tired to hang up her own clothes.

When pebbles rattled her window, she wasn't terribly surprised. Faith doubted anyone at the tavern was getting much sleep. A quick look out her bedroom window revealed a pale blonde head in the darkness. Cold air brushed her ankles as she stepped into her shoes and grabbed a blanket to keep out the chill before heading to the door. She paused to look out the front window to confirm her visitor before drawing back the latch.

She let Jeremy Butler inside. Doffing his hat, he strode into her office and stirred the coals in the tile stove before adding more wood from the nearby stack. He turned to face her, remaining close to the heat.

"What are you doing here?"

"Keep your voice down," he hissed. "You have a load of Virginia militia upstairs, and I have no intention of explaining myself to them."

Faith whispered. "Why are you here?" She still hadn't quite adjusted to him being her brother-in-law. It felt strange. She lit a taper from the fire and used it to light a sconce on the wall. In its wavering beam, she took a good look at him. He was thinner than when he had visited in the fall and looked tired. Dark circles accented lines that had deepened at the corners of his eyes.

He took a moment to sit down gesturing for her to do likewise. He stretched his feet toward the fire with a sigh. "I wanted to see how everyone was doing before the fighting started again." He cut a glance her way. "Hannah says you're not exactly a prolific letter writer."

Faith flushed. "I answered her last message. Not a lot is happening here."

"I wouldn't say that. This town teems with activity. It never ceases to amaze me how such a modestly sized city as this can have so much happening in it. Your little brother is a hunted man." He hesitated. "I don't know him well, so I will ask. Do you think he killed those women? Athena told me he's been hanging about the Randolph House moony-eyed over a girl. The Randolphs are a powerful family. They have no tolerance for anyone getting into their business. They will deal with him one way or another. He would be wise to stay away." He paused and pinched his nose. "As I recall, he left the Pennsylvania Colony over trouble with a woman."

Faith hesitated. Seth had been a small boy when she had married Jon. Once Jon and she had relocated to Virginia, she had lost track of most of her siblings until her return to Pennsylvania last year. She didn't really know the young man who had shown up on her doorstep after so many years. Faith chose her words carefully. "I have seen nothing to indicate he would do such a thing. He is infatuated with a young lady at the Randolph estate."

"An enslaved woman," Jeremy shook his head. "Quakers. Do any of you accept reality? I loathe the practice as well, but it's a way of life in these colonies. There is no hope that the Randolphs will free her. Surely, he knows that."

Faith sighed. "I really don't know what is going on in his head. He left Pennsylvania after the girl he loved chose another. He was heartbroken. I hoped coming here would give him a fresh start." In truth, having him here had been good for her, too. She missed her family, although she had no intention of ever going back to Pennsylvania. Her home was in Virginia. Her visit back to the place of her birth had only made her realize how much she had changed. She was no longer Isaac Payne's daughter but a grown woman. She would not give up that independence, no matter how lonely she felt at times. She wondered if her brother felt the same way. Being a younger son could not be easy.

Jeremy looked at her. His voice was gentle. "He's quite young in the ways of the world, isn't he? I imagine he spent most of his life on your father's farm before he came here. Has he reached the age of twenty-one?"

Faith nodded. "He would have reached his majority in November."

Jeremy's expression turned grim. "Then he's no boy, not in the eyes of the law. If they believe he killed those women, he'll hang. Even if he didn't kill them, he's made a reputation for himself as a troublemaker." He looked out of a front window into the street. Down near the Capitol Building, a streetlight flickered. It provided the briefest sliver of light, enough for them to be aware of the man patrolling around the Capitol's exterior wall. He backed away into the shadows of the room. She shivered. The blanket she had wrapped about her was not enough to stave away the cold she felt inside and out. The fire crackled. Jeremy had kept it small so as not to disturb the men upstairs. Edging closer, she felt a little better.

Faith looked at him. "He may be naïve and foolish, but he's not a killer." She remembered his hands gentling a sick colt, his patience with a frightened sheep caught in a bush, his kindness to the women who worked at the tavern. He carried heavy loads for them and protected them from unruly guests. "Is there no hope for him and the young lady?"

Jeremy thought. "I've seen him with her. In another place, no one would realize she was a slave. The frontier is far less restrictive regarding such things. Athena has heard she was fathered by one of the Randolphs's distant relations and sent here to be rid of the reminder."

"Poor child."

Outside, a rooster crowed, followed by another a short distance away. Upstairs a floorboard creaked before silence fell back over the house. Before long, people would be stirring about in their homes, preparing for the day.

"I'd best be going," Jeremy said. "I'll be here a few more days before I head back north. Athena knows how to reach me." He looked her in the eyes. "If you hear from Seth, send word. He's not going to get out of this mess without help. People are frightened, and the law will want a quick solution to the problem." With that, he slipped out the door, closing it softly behind him.

Faith snuffed the candle and stood in the darkness, thinking. Jeremy Butler was correct. Seth had gotten himself in trouble once again. Blaming someone new to town who had already stirred up a prominent family would be an easy solution to a pressing problem, whether it was true or not. Experience had taught her that getting to the truth was not often the highest priority. Her mind turned to the brutal deaths of the two enslaved women. Why were they killed? What possible benefit could there be in it? She could not believe her brother was a killer. It didn't fit with what she knew of him. Although a dark corner of her mind reminded her, she barely knew him at all.

Her mind turned to Hannah up north in Philadelphia. It wasn't a safe place to be right now. Washington had been battling the British and not doing well. The Continental Congress had abandoned Philadelphia in favor of York, where the Susquehanna river separated them from the British. Hannah's husband was engaged in a dangerous game. Nathan Hale's death was proof of that. The poor man had been discovered, convicted, and hanged within days. Were Butler discovered, the enemy would show no mercy on either of them. Faith shuddered and pushed away the thought. Although Williamsburg was held by patriots, it could change should the British push south or their navy come ashore in Virginia.

Butler undoubtedly knew that General Washington and the Continental Army were struggling. It was probably why he was down in Virginia in the winter, sneaking about in the dead of night. The patriot cause could use every crumb of intelligence to be found. If the tide of battle didn't turn soon, the cause of independence might soon be lost.

Faith sighed as Solomon, the rooster, sounded his call. There was no use returning to bed. It was time to start the day. She walked back to her room to prepare. Dropping the blanket she had wrapped about herself, she grabbed her stockings and began to dress for the day.

Out in the kitchen, Titus had just stirred the kitchen fire to a roaring blaze. It cast a warm orange light as it chased the long, dark shadows of night from the room. The faint scent of coffee lingered from the beans he had roasted and ground last night. Smiling, he mixed the ground coffee and water and set it down on a shelf just inside the fireplace.

Olivia came down the steps. She covered a yawn as she entered the room before taking in the roaring fire and the metal pot inside. "Is that coffee?"

He smiled. "Yes, it is. I just put it on so it will be a few minutes before it's hot enough to drink. I'll go check on the animals, and it should be ready when I return." He walked to the doo,r stopping to kiss her cheek before putting on a jacket and woolen cap and slipping outside. As he left, he heard her say. "I'll have breakfast ready for you."

He smiled as he left, the warmth he felt was from far more than the fire he'd built. Life with Olivia just kept getting better. They butted heads from time to time, but he knew deep in his soul that she loved him, and that centered him and kept him whole. That their son was free, and only a stone's throw away was a blessing he thanked God for every day.

The cold air chilled his face and made him glad for the thick wool hat Olivia had knitted for him. It kept his ears from getting frostbitten. He broke into a whistle as he trotted out to the barn, eager to be out of the wind.

Steam rose in wisps from the noses of the livestock as he entered. The cow mooed plaintively, eager to have her milk taken to relieve the pressure on her udder. The horses snorted and tossed their heads as they watched him with bright, intelligent eyes. Their stalls smelled of fresh hay, which surprised him until he spotted a pale blonde head in the back.

"Jeremy! When did you get into town?" He reached out and hugged the smaller man, happy to see his friend in one piece.

"I'll tell you once you put me down," Butler gasped, kicking his dangling feet for emphasis. Once he regained his footing. He grinned back at Titus. "I see Olivia is treating you well. I just got in last night. It was a good time to see what was happening in Virginia. You never know where the enemy will strike next."

"It's not going well. Is it?"

Butler shook his head tiredly. "Winning this war was never going to be easy. But Washington is a canny man. Not many men would have crossed the Delaware in the dead of night on Christmas Day." He smiled briefly. "I'm sure he surprised the hell out of the Hessians at Trenton. We needed that victory and the one at Princeton as well. Despair is not our ally. I've risked too much, gone too far to surrender now. We have to fight, and we have to win. There is no other option. None of us can afford to be captured."

Titus knew he was thinking of Nathan Hale. He wondered if Butler knew him. The espionage world could not be that large, especially not in the colonies. He changed the topic. "If you'll finish the stalls, I'll milk Daisy, and you can join us for breakfast. I know Olivia will be glad to see you."

Butler lifted the rake he had in his hand and went back to removing old bedding and putting down new. Given the small number of livestock, it didn't take long. Butler looked down the rows of horses. "I thought I had sent a black mare this way."

Titus whirled around. "You did. I put her in that stall on the end." He walked over to look. "I swear she was here when I bedded them down last night."

Butler walked over to him. "Someone got her last night. Not many people knew she was here. I'll keep an eye out. She's pretty distinctive." His tone was mild, but Titus could hear the anger underneath. Jeremy had a nasty temper when roused. He'd hate to be the man on the receiving end of it.

The men walked together into the kitchen, which had warmed up considerably. They both removed coats and hats and stood near the fire, but not so close as to disturb Olivia, who was frying eggs.

"Wash up in the basin," she said. "You both smell like livestock. Then you can sit at the table. "We're almost ready. Faith and the girls should be here soon, along with Malachi."

"We're here," Faith said as she entered, followed by Ellen, Dorcas, and the elderly bartender. All four were shivering. Faith said nothing when she spotted Butler at one end of the table. They all took seats on the hard wooden benches on either side. After a brief invocation, platters were passed around. Titus stood and poured coffee, taking time to serve his wife first, followed by the others. The sugar cone stood where everyone could reach it to pinch off enough to sweeten their cups.

Once the meal was complete, everyone hurried to their chores. Dorcas thanked Titus for doing the milking. She picked up the pail in a gloved hand and took it to the cellar to separate. Once the cream could be skimmed off, churning butter would begin. Titus helped Ellen clear the table before going out to chop more wood. Between cooking and warming the house, they went through it at a tremendous rate.

Faith paused and looked over at Jeremy. "Is there anything I need to know before I go?"

He shook his head. "We're good. Let me know if you hear from your brother."

Faith left without answering.

"Do you really believe she will do that?" Olivia asked as she heated her skillet to fry more meat

"If she wants him to get out of this mess alive." His tone was grim. "His infatuation with that girl makes him a convenient patsy for all concerned. If he's not careful, he will end up on the end of a rope."

Olivia continued her preparations. Hungry men did not wait well. She took a long iron spoon and stirred the large pot of mush. There was plenty there to fill an empty stomach. Looking around, she frowned. "I need more meat."

"I can get it," Jeremy offered. He knew where all the meat was that they had dried, pickled, and salted for the winter. Pulling on his hat and coat, he trotted to the side of the house where the outside cellar doors lay. He carried a lantern to help him find his way in the darkness. His woolen mittens made the latch a little tricky to pull aside, but he managed. The hinges shrieked in protest as he opened one of the doors and went down the ladder inside. In the winter predawn, there was not enough light to guide his steps. Although his light provided some illumination, long shadows shrouded most of the space in darkness. Barrels lined the floor while meat that had been dried and salted hung like large lumpy ghosts from the rafters, along with braids of onion and garlic, which faintly scented the air.

It took him a moment to find what he wanted, and then he had to find a ladder so that he could get it down from the rafters. The pale, dangling masses made him uneasy, although he knew there was nothing to fear. As he worked to get the meat down, he realized he was not alone. Despite the deep silence, the hyperawareness he had developed over years of being a spy kicked in.

He kept his voice soft. "I'm not hunting you, boy. But the first place the sheriff will look for you will be your sister's home and business, and they will leave no stone unturned."

Seth stepped out from the shadows where he had hidden behind a couple of stacked barrels. "I have committed no crime." He looked about him within the confines of the narrow room. "Where would I go anyhow? I'm a stranger here to everyone but Faith."

Butler sighed. Marrying Hannah had given him responsibilities he could do without, including advising her younger brother. "You've been seen at the Randolph House frequently, which is enough to rouse suspicions. It's also easy to blame a stranger when something bad happens rather than consider one of your neighbors could be a killer."

Seth stared at him. "I didn't know those two women. I had no reason to kill them. I was only there to see Tabby."

"An enslaved woman," Butler reminded.

"A human being with the same hopes and dreams as you or I," Seth propelled himself forward until he was within inches of Butler's face. "It's not right the way they treat her or other people of color. Who are we to say these people are less because their skin is a different color?"

Butler's tone was gentle. "I agree, but unfortunately, the law does not. That girl is controlled by the Randolph's who are powerful, especially here in Virginia."

"I don't care who they are." Seth ran nervous fingers through his hair. A few strands fell loose into his face.

Butler suppressed a sign. Had he ever been this young? "How does Tabitha feel?"

"She loves me," Seth answered. "We want to get far away from here, marry, and start a life of our own where no one knows or cares where we came from."

Butler's eyes widened. "And where do you think this could be?"

"The frontier. From what I've heard, people can make a new life for themselves there without being bothered by the government or stupid laws that benefit only a few."

"Have you been on the frontier? I have. It is a wild place. The land is owned by the natives who don't take kindly to strangers taking it away from them. There are no doctors, no sheriffs and supplies are limited. It's a hard life all around." He didn't add that he had enjoyed the camaraderie of friends, both native and not. His time on the frontier had given him the space he needed to sort out his life after a heart-rending loss.

"It's the only chance we have," Seth said. From the stubborn look on his face, Butler knew his mind was made up.

"First, we have to get you out of Williamsburg alive," Butler said. "Tabitha cannot marry a dead man, and if they catch you, you will be on the short end of a rope before you know it."

"I'm not leaving without her." Seth folded his arms and stared at Butler defiantly.

Jeremy met his gaze. "First, let's get you away from your sister's tavern, and then we'll figure the rest out."

Seth looked at him suspiciously. "Why would you help me?"

Butler sighed. "Hannah and Faith would expect it of me, and I'm not so old that I cannot remember what it was like to be young and in love. God help me." He shook his head.

A shadow fell over them as Titus peered down. "Olivia was wondering what was taking you so long. I guess I see why."

"Take Olivia her meat," Butler said, handing it up to him. "I have another issue to deal with." After the other man left, he turned to Seth. "Let's get you out of here."

They emerged from the cellar. Seth helped Butler latch the door back. Butler extinguished the lantern before setting it down on the edge of the back porch.

"Why did you do that?" Irritation radiated from Seth's voice.

"Light attracts attention," Butler explained. "Your eyes will adjust to the dark shortly. We don't need to be stopped by anyone on our way. You need to be quiet and follow me. The fewer people who see you, the better."

"Where am I going?"

Butler smiled. "It's time you met my friend and associate, Athena Wise. If anyone can figure a way out of your current dilemma, it is she."

With that, they sped through the darkness, avoiding the center of town and instead cutting through backyard gardens and paths that led around town, through dark stands of trees that hid them from the road. By the time they had made it to the print shop, the sky had turned from darkest blue to a deep gray, warning them the sun would rise before too long.

Smoke rose from the separate kitchen behind Georgia Clements's print shop and home. Butler gestured to the small building. "Let's get you inside."

Seth's anxious face looked from Butler to the small building. "Can you trust her?"

"I trust her with my life every day." Butler opened the door, taking in the blazing fire and looking at the tall figure he had loved like a mother since his childhood.

Chapter Fourteen

Will rolled his shoulders. He was stiff from running the press. There had been a lot of news to print of late. Reports of battles far north of Virginia, land sales, announcements of persons leaving, and advertisements for work all had to be carefully laid out to fit on the four pages that comprised each edition. His least favorite were the advertisements for the sale or escape of slaves. He had no choice in the matter since he was under indenture to Mistress Clements, but he didn't like it. His heart went out to the poor devils facing sale with an estate or who had mustered the courage to run away. His only choice was to place each advertisement where it would not be easily seen by the casual scanner of headlines.

Will stood stretching his back, which ached from all the leaning over to set the type. It was a laborious task, but one he took pride in doing right. He had learned to read from his mother. The fact he was literate had been a deciding factor in Georgia's husband taking him into indenture. Within a few years, he would be free and have the skills to be a printer on his own if he had the money or patronage to afford a press. It was a dream he longed to have come true, even if he had not figured out how to make it happen.

Out in the streets, he heard the happy sound of children running down the walk outside. He smiled as his eyes went to the window. A pale sun lit the sky and illuminated Duke of Gloucester Street. A pair of boys chased a chicken down the street. The bird, intent on avoiding a grisly fate, stayed well ahead of them. Will lost sight of them as they turned a corner and went down an alley. His sympathies were with the bird.

Seeing children caused a wave of sadness to well up inside him. His parents had wed far younger than his current age and had already started their family. Will wondered if he ever would. Faith Clarke's face rose in his mind. Once again, he bitterly regretted breaking away from her. Being poisoned, then facing a seemingly endless recovery had sent him into a deep depression. Fearing being a helpless invalid had driven him to spurn her. Will didn't blame her for avoiding him. He had hurt her badly and had no idea how to heal the wound. Even if they never got back together, he at least wanted her friendship. He feared that would never happen.

Outside the press room, a door slammed, followed by the sound of feminine laughter. His mistress, Georgia Clements, and her daughter Rebecca entered through the front door. They had been to the milliner. Marcus followed, carrying boxes and bundles. Will offered him a sympathetic look. He'd had that task himself a time or two. It was amazing how much all that female frippery weighed.

Rebecca offered him a flirtatious smile before her mother herded her through the print shop. She had added pink rosettes of ribbon to her hair, woven among her curls designed to attract attention. Will hoped she stayed back there. She made him nervous. The easy relationship he'd had with Georgia faded with the arrival of her daughter. He hoped she knew that he was doing nothing to encourage her. Rebecca enjoyed male attention and was used to getting it. Will's lack of reaction piqued her. He had the uncomfortable feeling she took it as a challenge.

Silas came in with a load of wood. As he fed the fire, he glanced over at Will. "Got that next sheet of type set?" He knelt down to stir the coals. The flames responded by leaping up and licking the fresh fuel. Will felt the rush of warmth and moved over to warm his hands. They had taken to cramping if he got too cold.

"Third page is ready to run," He replied. "The first two pages should be dry."

Silas rose and checked one of the sheets hanging to dry. "I can run the press if you would like to take these down."

"Thanks," He straightened up, easing the crick in his neck. "It would feel good to move around." He stretched, letting the knots work out of his shoulders. Stepping out from the press, Will began taking down previously printed sheets and stacking them where they would be assembled with the remaining pages after they had been printed and dried. Once all four pages had been completed, the newspaper would be ready to sell.

Silas picked up the ink balls and began the process of beating or inking the type. He fell into an easy rhythm as he moved the padded balls up and down before setting them aside, taking a sheet of paper, and attaching it to the frame. Although he had only come to them last summer, he and his twin Paul had adapted to life at the Printers easily. Will was grateful for the extra hands, which made the shop run much more smoothly. Eventually, the new indentures, Henrik and Eduard would learn the press. Currently, Georgia has put them to more basic tasks such as chopping wood and tending stock. Already, Will knew that Henrik was good with stock, and Eduard had an interest in plants and herbs. He helped Athena make her medicines. She had speculated he had been or worked for an apothecary in his past.

The door to the back opened and shut as Marcus and Georgia entered the shop. Marcus walked over and began speaking to a man who had just entered and was eyeing the stationary. Georgia watched her son for a moment before going over and checking on their progress. She nodded as she watched Silas hang up a freshly printed sheet.

"The paper should be ready to go out after dinner." She helped Will take down dried sheets. "Marcus can help you deliver papers to the local taverns. It will do him good to see our subscribers."

Will said nothing. He had been out with Marcus before and knew that he had little interest in learning the business. He wasn't sure what the young man wanted to do with his life. At his age, Will had been struggling to survive the enclosure of the land his family had farmed for generations. He doubted Marcus had missed a meal in his life.

For the next few moments, they worked in silence. The front door opened again, admitting someone in a militia uniform. Will recognized Captain Hoag. He had seen him drilling his troops on the green. That the captain had chosen to house his men in Clarke Tavern left him with mixed feelings.

On one hand, he was glad she had a steady income from housing and feeding the men. On the other hand, she was associated with an attractive officer in the Continental Army. Will rubbed the back of his neck. He didn't like it although he had no right to an opinion. Jealousy was not an emotion he should be feeling. Faith deserved to be happy and cared for, but his heart said something else altogether. He sighed. He didn't even know if she and the captain were anything beyond cordial associates. It was never wise to make assumptions. While he might find Faith impossible to ignore, Hoag might well have a wife or sweetheart elsewhere. He hoped so.

No one had moved to wait on the Captain. Feeling ashamed of his woolgathering, Will wiped his hands on a cloth and moved behind the counter. As Hoag walked among the books and made his way to the post office. Will met him with a polite smile. "Can I help you, Captain Hoag?"

Hoag shot him a glance. "I don't believe we've met."

"My name is William McKay. I am one of the printers who works for Mistress Clemons."

"I see." Hoag paused. "I would like to post a letter to my sister. Can you help me?"

Will nodded. He calculated postage and took the Captain's coin. As Hoag turned to go, Will asked. "Do you think the British will be coming anytime soon?"

The other man paused before replying wearily. "Only God knows. I am sure that when the time is right, they will come. Our men keep watch every day, so you can be sure when they set foot in the colony, we will know, and we will be ready." He turned to go when a feminine voice spoke behind him.

"It is good to know that our militia works so hard to keep us safe."

Hoag turned to see Rebecca Clements positioned so that the sun coming through the window bathed her in golden light. The effect was dazzling, and his face broke into a smile as he beheld her. "Greetings, mistress. I do not believe we have been introduced."

She giggled as her mother moved to join her. "This is my daughter Rebecca, Captain Hoag. She has recently rejoined us after a stay at one of our fine academies for young ladies here in the colony."

Captain Hoag bowed. "Welcome home, Mistress Clements. I hope you are enjoying your return to your family."

Rebecca curtsied in return. "It is good to be home, although I miss the dances that we had each week at the academy. It is much quieter here in Williamsburg."

Hoag smiled down at her. Rebecca Clements was several inches shorter than the captain and looked small and delicate in comparison. She smiled back at him, basking in his admiration. "There are still teas and suppers in our fair capital, mistress. All you need is an invitation or two to join. I will have a word with Governor Henry. He is hosting a supper at the Governor's mansion in a few weeks. I am sure there is room for your mother, brother, and yourself."

Rebecca squealed in delight. "That would be marvelous. Oh, Mama, we must visit the milliner. This will require something quite special."

Georgia Clements looked alarmed. "We normally do not move in those circles. I know the governor is a good, godly man, but surely his table is for the elite of town."

"Nonsense," Hoag said. "You are a business owner in this town. You have a stake in this war. Your son is of an age to serve in the militia. Every house will soon surrender its sons and servants for this war. Before it ends, we will all have sacrificed to the cause."

Silence fell over the room. Hoag made a quick bow. "Now, I must return to my men. We will be drilling most of the day." He exited swiftly. The door swung shut behind him with a bang.

Georgia Clement had gone ghostly pale. Rebecca took her hand. "He didn't mean it, Ma," she said. "Marcus is a boy they can't take him."

Her mother did not answer but stood still, her eyes fixed on the door that Captain Hoag had just gone through. She drew in shallow breaths as her eyes tracked his progress down the street. Around her, the conversation continued.

Silas shook his head. "Don't believe that. I've seen boys younger than him sounding the drum as they march. Washington needs every man and boy for the fight. "It won't be long before we are all enmeshed in battle. If we don't go, the British will come here." He sighed. "And there's a good many of us who will never make it back home."

Will knew Silas spoke the truth. They both had skirted the edges of the war, doing their work in stealth, knowing capture meant death. The battle was more brutal, and death more immediate. He knew that, at some point, he would have to join the fray. The only thing holding him here was his contract with Georgia Clements. He couldn't legally leave for two more years. Some days, it felt like forever.

Georgia Clements moved forward toward her private residence at the back. "Come, Rebecca; we have work to do. You have yet to finish your embroidery."

The younger woman rolled her eyes. "Surely I could be more use in the shop." She fluttered her eyelashes at Will, who backed away. Rebecca looked like she meant to stay put, but her mother grasped her arm firmly and took her through the door at the back. Marcus picked up their packages with a grunt and followed.

He paused before going through the back door. "Am I really old enough to be a soldier?" He began whistling as he continued back, the strains of "Yankee Doodle" fading as the door shut behind him.

"That young man has no idea what fighting means,' Silas noted as he began inking the type in preparation for another round of printing.

Will's response was swift. "I hope he never does."

Chapter Fifteen

Faith stood outside her tavern, looking down the road. The broom in her hands made short work of the leaves and dirt that had gathered on her porch. With the men going in and out, the porch needed regular tending to look decent. Ellen was busily airing the linens. It was a rare mild day which meant they could do many chores the cold prevented. Her fingers still felt chilly, even with the open-fingered mitts she wore for warmth inside and out.

Since the trees that lined the road all the way to the brick walls that encircled the Capitol were mostly bare, her view had expanded greatly. In addition to people going about their business, she could see groups of militia on patrol. These days, they were everywhere.

She wondered where Seth was. She had heard nothing from her brother since he had escaped the sheriff, who was certain he was a killer. Faith could not believe that. It went against everything she knew about him. Yet there had been no additional bodies found since he had fled. It was a damning thought to have.

The porch was now free from debris, so she stepped back inside. The taproom only held a few local men who had lingered after dinner to read the latest issue of the *Virginia Gazette*. Will had dropped it off a few hours ago. She had seen the wagon pull up and watched him hop out. He had forgotten his hat which made the afternoon sun turn his hair to a blaze of autumn fire. Faith let Titus handle the transaction. Although the initial pain had faded, she didn't feel comfortable speaking to him. Faith was sure he felt the same. She had noted how he managed to be busy whenever she stopped to place an advertisement at Georgia Clements' shop.

As she warmed her hands, her mind turned to her son Andrew. The thirteen-year-old remained busy with his studies with George Wythe in the large brick mansion just off the palace green. Wythe had extended an invitation for her to visit at any time, but she had hesitated to take him up on it. She missed Andrew terribly. She wondered what she would do when he married and started a home of his own. Theirs was a small household, and it felt empty all too soon with both Olivia's son Joshua and Andrew living elsewhere.

Faith glanced about the tavern. Malachi stood behind the bar, as usual, his dark eyes keeping an eye on everything. He wiped down the wooden counter where men came to get their drinks. The elderly man paused when he felt Faith's stare.

"Can I help you, Mistress?" His voice was deep and cultured. At some point in his life, he had been among the upper class to speak in such a way.

Faith shook her head. "I am fine, Malachi. I think I may step out to visit my son. I will let Titus know to check on you before I go."

"Thank you, Mistress Clarke, that is thoughtful." Malachi went back to his polishing. He didn't speak a lot. Titus had told her how pleased he was with his own room in the cellar, next to the one Ellen and Dorcas shared. That section of the cellar boasted a huge fireplace to help keep out the chill. Moving him to the inn had taken little persuasion. Her mother-in-law had seemed relieved that Faith wanted to keep the elderly man close by. Technically, he was still Eugenia Moore's property, a thought which grated on Faith.

"No one should ever be property," she muttered as she went down the hallway and out back to the separate kitchen. Perhaps it was time to have a discussion with Eugenia about that. Given his age, her mother-in-law might not argue too much about manumission, and maybe the new governor, Patrick Henry, would be easier to deal with than his predecessor. One could only hope.

Smoke rose from the kitchen's chimney, sending a plume of white into the clear blue sky. For once, the weather was mild, which explained why

Ellen sat on a bench outside sorting through the dried peas. The chickens were enjoying a rare outside venture as they scratched about the yard. Faith enjoyed hearing her girls cluck as they trotted about. They were much quieter when shut in their henhouse. The solid thwack of an axe split the air. Titus stood before the chopping block in his shirtsleeves, cutting more fuel for the always-hungry fires. Since Seth had fled, the burden had fallen on Titus to keep the fires fed. She looked over where dead weeds were all that remained of last year's garden. Within a number of weeks, it would be time to turn the ground and plant. She would be glad when that happened. The rough ground looked abandoned.

Faith knew there was little point in worrying, but concern about her brother's fate drifted across her mind during quieter moments of the day. She didn't know where he was or what he planned to do. The sheriff dropped by from time to time to inquire if she had heard from him. He probably kept the house under watch. It wouldn't surprise her.

While the chickens scratched about the yard, Faith ducked into their cozy abode to seek eggs. Her girls had been productive thus far and she hoped it continued. Although Dorcas checked every morning, Faith knew sometimes the girls left a surprise or two by afternoon. It was a good excuse to get out of the tavern. Olivia was a fine baker, and the smell of baking bread and cakes lifted her spirits. Solomon, the rooster, cast a beady eye at her as she emerged from the henhouse. "You have nothing to worry about," she scolded. "I have no plans to cook you or any of your harem."

The stocky rooster strode off in majestic splendor, no doubt to seek more food before the hens gobbled it up. Faith headed to the kitchen to surrender her prize to Olivia. She was busy this time of day. Although dinner would not be served for hours, it took time to prepare all the food over an open hearth even with Dorcas to assist.

She opened the door to a welcome wave of heat from the fireplace. Olivia stood over the long wooden table, chopping vegetables. Her knife made short work of the carrots and potatoes before her. Faith eyed the loaded spit rotating over the fire. "Pigeon pie?"

Olivia nodded. "Silas dropped them off yesterday. He had more than his momma could use, so they thought of us. We still have some onions and garlic hanging in the cellar, so these will cook up nicely for dinner."

Faith nodded. Olivia made excellent meals out of what they had to work with. "Is there anything you need me to do? I thought I might go see Andrew." She moved closer to the fire to warm her cold feet and hands. As she held out her hands, the rapid-fire sound of hooves sounded outside, followed by the sound of a voice calling out. She didn't hesitate but ran toward the door and out into the yard.

A black horse stood in front of the barn. Jeremy Butler stood there, reins in hand. Titus reached him before Faith. "I found her wandering in a field on the edge of town." His hands ran over the glossy dark hide of the mare. "She seems in good shape. I'm not sure how she got where she was, but now she is home."

Faith nodded as her eyes took in the empty saddle. "Let's get her into the barn. She's probably hungry and thirsty." She followed as Titus took her bridle and led her inside. The mare stood quietly as he removed the saddle and tack. While he brushed her coat and tended her needs, Faith examined the saddle, hoping for clues. "Seth wouldn't leave a horse like this," She said aloud. Butler started to speak, then turned his attention back to the horse.

The well-worn leather looked like it always did until Faith leaned in closer. A few smudges of dirt were on the pommel and seat. A scrap of fabric was hanging onto the stirrup. Before she could retrieve it, Butler reached it.

He held the light-colored scrap in his hands. "It feels like wool," he said as he touched it lightly with his fingers.

"Like from a jacket?" Faith hazarded as she squinted at the frayed bit.

"Or a blanket," Butler said. "It's hard to tell. I found her not far from the Randolph Estate."

"What would she be doing over there? It's less than a mile away. Anybody could walk over there."

Butler examined the fabric. "Not if you were trying to move a body." The other two stared at him. Butler continued. "Sheba is as dark as night, and she's strong. A man could wrap a body in a blanket and put it over her back with little comment."

"Joanna," Titus breathed. "You think that's how she ended up in that barn on the edge of town."

Butler's face was grim. "It would be easy to do if you already knew you were going to kill her."

Faith paused as her fingertips detected something dried on the saddle. She leaned in for a closer look. The dark brown of the saddle made it difficult to detect. As her fingers slid around the edge of the saddle, down toward the stirrup, she encountered something sticky. She lifted up her hand to see the brownish smudge and smelled the faint coppery tang. Faith shot Butler a glance. "It's blood."

Butler grabbed her hand to examine it himself, before running his hands down the saddle himself. "So it is. Not much, though." His lips twisted. "A dead body wouldn't bleed much."

"Seth didn't do this." Faith blinked back tears. "We have to find him."

"And do what?" Butler asked gently. "There's a warrant for his arrest. Sheltering him would get you into trouble as well."

"They're going to kill him," she said, trying not to sniffle. "You know how these men get when they are hunting down someone. They are more likely to shoot him than arrest him."

Butler sighed. "You're not wrong. But he's in no immediate danger. He's with Athena until we figure out what to do with him." He looked at Faith. "Quit fretting."

Faith swallowed hard. She wanted to go see him, but she would attract too much attention. She had little doubt her absence would be noted. Captain Hoag and his men spent a great deal of time at the tavern. She was grateful that they were drilling on the green at this time of day. "So be it," she said at last. "Take care of him. I pray he doesn't do anything stupid."

"A bit late for that," Butler replied as he slapped on his hat. "Let's pray the young fool doesn't get himself into deeper trouble." He went over to the mare that Titus was brushing. Her dark coat gleamed in the shadowy light of the barn. "If only you could talk," Butler strode out into the yard, leaving the other three inside.

Faith went back to the tavern. Hoag met her as she approached the back steps.

He nodded as their eyes met. "I wondered where you might be."

Faith smiled. "I stopped to check on the stock. The winter weather tends to expose all our vulnerabilities, even on a day as mild as this. She looked over at the chickens clucking in their pen. "Today is a good day to let them out to graze and get some exercise."

Hoag nodded. "It is a good day for some fresh air for all of us. The winter months can leave us all longing to escape the walls within which we live." He walked beside her back toward the inn. His cheeks had a faint flush in them that added some color to his face. The captain was an attractive man, if a little distant, on most occasions.

"It is a good day for a walk," Faith agreed. "After dinner, I may post a letter to my sister in the Pennsylvania colony. I don't hear from her often, but I pray she is well."

"After Washington's recent victories in Princeton and Trenton, the front has quieted for winter. One hopes the British are considering their losses." Hoag looked down at her. "It is quite likely that they will try for Philadelphia in the spring. It would be a prize hard to resist."

Faith swallowed. She didn't want him to know Hannah still resided there, too stubborn to flee the danger. She could only pray her older sister remained safe and no one knew she had wed one of Washington's spies.

They took the steps together, the wood creaking under their feet. Hoag held open the door to allow her inside first. Faith smiled her thanks as she went toward the taproom. She could hear the voices of men inside. She wondered how Malachi was handling them. After sticking her head in, it was clear there was no reason for concern.

A fire crackled within the fireplace, lending a cheery glow to the room. Malachi stood at the bar, filling one of their redware steins with some of the beer they had brewed from apples last fall. Roughly a dozen men filled the taproom; most had drinks at hand. A pair of Hoag's men played chess near one of the front windows, making use of the sunlight. Three men sat at a table listening to the fourth read from the latest issue of the *Virginia Gazette*. Hoag looked about the room, his face grave.

"Most of my men are practicing their musket skills. These few have mastered it. Once they have finished their drinks, I will gather my officers in my room to discuss strategy. If you could bring our meal to us when dinner time arrives, I would be in your debt."

Faith nodded. Her private meeting room had been rebuilt by her late father-in-law after a fire had gutted it. The income she received from renting it was a continuing gift from him. She still missed him, still felt angry at a life cut short by greed, but she continued onward. The whole reason she had become enmeshed in the patriot cause was due to his influence. Faith sent a thought upward. "I hope we win." She had no doubt Ezra looked down from heaven to cheer them on. He had never been one to sit on the sidelines of life. She couldn't imagine him doing it in death.

The door creaked as it admitted another man. Faith recognized the militia uniform even if she did not recognize the man.

Hoag did. "Sergeant Graves, what brings you here?" He appeared mildly curious, but not concerned. That changed when he saw his sergeant's expression.

"A local farmer rode in. He received word from a neighbor who lives not far from the York River. He swears he spotted a British Warship sailing this way."

Hoag stiffened. "We have to check it out. The risk to the capital is too great. Has word been sent to Governor Henry? "

"That is my next stop," Graves replied. "I wanted to give you time to muster your men and send word to the other officers."

"Well done. Go to Governor Henry. I will gather my men." Hoag turned to the men sitting in silence at their tables. "We will send scouts to confirm while we prepare to engage the enemy. Our native allies will be the swiftest and most discrete." He gestured to a man nearby. "Private Smith. Go to the men on the green. Tell them we march within the hour."

The man left his drink and rushed out the door. His boots pounded against the wooden floor as he jogged toward the green. Hoag gestured to the other men. "Go reinforce the Capitol. There is little doubt they will try to capture the governor before they sack the town." He turned to Faith. "I will treat this threat as real until it's proven otherwise. You may want to prepare to flee, given your proximity to the capitol."

Faith shook her head. "I have nowhere to go, and I cannot abandon my only source of income. I will stay until the news is confirmed. Then I and my staff will decide what to do."

Hoag's lips thinned. "There will be no time once they hit the ground. We will do our best to keep them out of Williamsburg, but should we fail, the British will swarm the town like savages. There is no guarantee they will treat you or your staff with any respect." He drew in a short breath. "When the fighting commences, it becomes a game of kill or be killed. There is no grace or mercy in any of us. You would do well to keep that in mind."

Faith met his gaze, hoping she looked braver than she felt. "I will." She nodded to the front door. "You have responsibilities to attend, as do I. It is best we use the time we have to prepare." Her hands clenched into fists beneath her apron, hiding the fear and anxiety she dared not show.

Hoag looked at her. "Be careful. These are wicked times." He turned on his heel and headed out the door. As he left the porch, he picked up speed, running toward his men, no doubt hoping they had time to prepare for battle before the enemy came.

Faith turned back to the taproom, where she met Malachi's eyes. He had heard everything. "Do you know how to fire a weapon?" she asked bluntly. There was no need to whisper. The room had cleared out when word of a possible British invasion had come.

He shook his head. "I'm not raising a gun to anyone. I've seen enough lives taken in my time."

Faith's tone softened. "You are a pacifist, then."

Malachi caught her gaze ruefully. "Call it what you will. I know better than to point a gun at a white man. That is guaranteed death no matter what you believe."

Faith sighed. "You're not wrong, although I wish it were not so. You are a man like any other." She walked over to him noting the wariness he tried to hide. She didn't blame him; Malachi had not had time to get to know her or anyone else. "I don't know if the British are truly coming or not. I respect your decision not to bear arms; therefore, I will offer you a choice. If you wish to return to Mistress Moore's home, which is deeper in town and probably safer, I can cover the bar."

Malachi shook his head. "If you permit, Mistress Clarke, I prefer to remain here. I may not fight, but I do know how to hide, and I would prefer not to leave you or the other ladies with no one to protect them." He lifted his arm to show a cudgel he had apparently been keeping under the bar. "I can defend myself and others if the need comes. Soldiers can be brutal to women. It doesn't take a gun for that."

Touched, Faith swallowed a lump in her throat. "I am grateful for your concern, Malachi. Please be careful. I would hate for you to come to harm."

Malachi went back to wiping down the counter. His knuckles were beginning to get gnarly with rheumatism. He was not a tall man, but he stood straight and walked like someone much younger than he likely was. She wondered what his story was. Regardless, he had made his feelings known. He was not going anywhere.

Faith walked down the hall and out back. Olivia and Titus needed to know, as did Ellen and Dorcas. When she entered the kitchen, she was surprised to see all of them gathered there. She looked at them. "You've heard the news."

Olivia nodded. "There's been militia running all over the place. Everyone knows." She nodded at the girls. "It would be best if they went over to the Clements. Will's mistress is in the center of town. It will be better defended should the British come."

Faith nodded. This was no place for teenaged girls. They both looked scared. "You will be safer there. Athena will look after you. I'm sure Georgia won't mind." She looked at Olivia and Titus. "What about you two?"

Titus stared at her. "I think you are in more danger than us. We can watch the tavern. Malachi will mind the taproom. You need to go to your mother-in-law's or with the girls to the Clements."

"It's my tavern," she protested. "How can I leave you in danger while I take shelter?"

"They're not going to be as interested in us as they will in a pretty white woman."

Faith rolled her eyes. "I'm not all that young anymore."

"You're still very pretty," Will McKay entered the kitchen. His hair was tousled with ends coming out of his que. He still wore his leather printer's apron under his coat and his fingers remained stained with ink.

Faith stared at him. They hadn't spoken in ages.

"Come with me to Georgia's, at least until we know if this threat is genuine or not. You are on the edge of town, right where the British are bound to enter. They won't care that you are a respectable widow. Many of them haven't been around a woman in months. They will be on you before their officers have a chance to rein them in."

Faith took a breath. He was doing a good job of scaring her. She looked over at Titus and Olivia. Olivia nodded.

"I have plenty of knives at my disposal, should it come to that. Go while you still can."

Faith exhaled slowly. "I need to get a few things from my room."

"Hurry," Will said. "If you are not back in a few minutes, I'm coming in to get you."

She shot him a look before trotting out and up the back steps. Seeing Will McKay never ceased to rattle her. At one time, she had thought he loved her. She was irritated that he had barged in and started issuing orders, even if everyone else was in agreement with him.

Faith went and grabbed her warmest shawl. Opening her clothing chest, she grabbed the knotted handkerchief that contained her only jewelry, a gold ring, and a simple pearl necklace from Jon, her late husband. She intended to pass them on when Andrew grew up and took a wife. Stuffing them in her pocket, she raced out back where the others waited.

As they walked away, past the Capitol, militia marched past them toward the York River, preparing to meet the enemy. Officers on horseback rode past toward the shouts of men spoiling for a fight.

Will said nothing as he guided the three women into town. People scurried past, heading home. Horses and wagons clattered down Duke of Gloucester Street, fleeing the pending invasion. Merchants locked their doors despite it being midday, their faces grim. No one had forgotten the horrible few weeks that Earl Dunmore, their former governor, had raided along the coastline, destroying what he could.

Within minutes, they reached the print shop. Georgia Clements met them at the door and locked it behind them. "We'll know before nightfall if the rumors are true," she said. "Until then, we will continue getting our paper printed." She looked at the women. "You two can join Athena in the kitchen. She will appreciate the help and my other two indentures are nearby with the stock if any trouble arises. She looked at Faith. "Do you have any experience with printing?"

Faith shook her head. "Then you can help me fold newspapers while the men print. My daughter Rebecca is catching up on the mending down the hall."

Faith nodded. It was definitely better to have something to do. The newspapers were four pages long. It didn't take long for her to catch on to how it worked. Georgia offered her a leather printer's apron to keep the ink from smudging her skirts. It didn't help her hands, though. Soon, her fingertips were smoky gray from ink.

They folded in silence, stacking the finished papers to be distributed once it was safe to do so. Light shone through the windows, revealing dust motes that floated in the air. Faith sneezed.

"Bless you," Georgia said never pausing in her task.

"Thank you," Faith replied. Behind her, the men continued their work. Will passed by them to hang up more sheets to dry. After the initial panic the streets cleared out. A few horses rode past, their riders headed out of town, but no people strolled down the cobblestones to shop or socialize. Faith wondered what was going on. She expected to hear gunfire or see men in the streets as the British Army approached. The stillness unnerved her. Beside her, Georgia stopped. They had folded the last of the dry sheets of newspaper.

"It's as good a time as any for a break," Georgia Clements straightened her back and rolled her shoulders. "Rebecca should be done with the mending so she can join us." She walked slowly to the door that separated the print shop from her family's private living space. As she cleared the door, she looked about.

The room was quiet and tidy. A chair had been placed near the fire which crackled in the hearth. Sun from the window on the other side spread across the seat and onto the basket by it. A partially darned sock rested on top of what looked like a stack of clothes. Lines down either side of Georgia Clements's mouth indicated her displeasure.

"Rebecca!" She picked up her pace and looked into the other rooms. "Where is that girl? This is no time to be wandering away."

The rooms were deserted. She stuck her head back into the print shop. "Marcus, have you seen your sister?"

Marcus paused from where he had been sorting statinery. "I'm not sure," he said, his eyes darting around the room.

His mother was not fooled in the least. She marched over to him and put a finger under his chin. "Tell me the truth this time. The British could be at our door at any moment."

"I tried to stop her," he began. "She wouldn't listen."

"Why didn't you tell me?"

Marcus paused, a deep red flush spreading up his neck.

"She threatened to tell your ma about the gambling, didn't she?" Will said.

Marcus looked down at the floor. "Rebecca saw me getting some coins out of the cash box—not many!" he added defensively.

"I thought it looked a bit light," Will said grimly. "You've been robbing your own mother, haven't you?"

A look of shame crossed the young man's face. "I was going to pay it back."

"Where did she go?" Georgia asked.

"She said something about going to the milliners for some new ribbon." He shot an angry glance at Will. "I'm not the only one who dipped into the coins. Rebecca didn't like how you ignored her. She's used to getting her way."

Will frowned. "She's little more than a child."

Marcus shrugged. "She doesn't see it that way. All her friends are getting married, and she's still at home doing chores. There aren't many eligible men left in town. Many of my friends have joined the militia."

"Are you thinking of doing that?" Will watched Georgia's face go pale.

Marcus shrugged. "I'm not much for marching and taking orders. Not that I am against the revolution," he added quickly. He frowned. "But I have been approached by the militia."

"You are too young," Georgia exclaimed. "They have no right to press you." She paused to look at him. "I lost your father. I won't lose you."

Marcus put his hand over hers. "I am here, Mother. Fear not. Even if I join the Virginia militia, as you can see, there is little conflict here. The British are far north of here."

Georgia shook her head. "An eighteen-year-old boy has no need to join the militia. You have no way of knowing where you could be ordered to march. General Washington is from Virginia, and he's now head of the entire Continental Army."

The back door slammed. Rebecca Clements walked in, swinging her bonnet by its strings. She paused as she saw everyone gathered in the parlor. Her eyes darted from one face to another before she went toward them. "Are we gathering for tea?" Her tone was light.

"Where have you been?" Georgia Clements walked to her daughter. "I have been out of my mind with worry." Her voice choked. "The British army could be running through these streets at any moment. What were you thinking?"

Rebecca bit her lip. "I didn't mean to worry you," she said at last. "Waiting for something to happen grew tiresome, so I stepped out for a breath of air. Since I saw and heard nothing, I thought it was safe to go get a bit of ribbon for one of my caps." She reached out and took her mother's hand, which was shaking. "I'm sorry mother. I won't do it again."

Georgia Clements's eyes filled with tears. "I couldn't bear it if you should come to harm."

"I'm here, Mother. Why don't I see about getting us some of your peppermint tea and some of Athena's scones? I won't be a moment." With that, Rebecca headed out to the kitchen, leaving her bonnet on a nearby chair.

Faith walked over and picked it up. It smelled faintly of tobacco and lavender. Wherever she had been, someone had been smoking a pipe. She looked out the window to watch the younger woman enter the small outdoor kitchen. Faith watched her, certain that Rebecca Clements was a liar.

Chapter Sixteen

fter several hours, Faith went back to the tavern. There had been no invasion of British Troops, and she suspected it was not going to happen. She was not going to live her life based on rumors of what the British planned. The streets were gradually filling with like-minded people who were also determined to go about their regular business.

As she entered the gate, a faint murmur of voices greeted her. She followed the sound around to the entrance to the root cellar, whose doors lay spread open. Titus stood at the side. Next to him stood her brother.

"Seth!" she cried before grabbing him into a hug. "I've been so worried."

Seth squeezed her tight before releasing her. "I've missed you."

Faith dropped her voice. "Are you hungry? Do you need anything?"

He shook his head. "Olivia fed me well. I came to pick up a few things before I go." He nodded to the open door. "I can slip up the steps to my room without anyone seeing me from the front."

"Be careful," she spoke softly. Being out in the open increased the chances of him being seen. "Everyone is looking for you."

He shook his head at Faith's expression. "I can't stay. I didn't lay a hand on either of those women, but no one believes me. I'm not waiting for them to hang me. It's time to go."

Faith exhaled slowly. He wasn't wrong. The war had worn people out and made them intolerant and quick to judge. "Write to me when you're safe. You don't have to tell me where you are, just that you are safe. I will let Pa know." She hugged him again. "You'd best go quickly before you are discovered."

"A little late for that." Captain Hoag stepped around the corner of the house, his expression grim. "Seth Payne, I am placing you under arrest for the destruction of the property of Elizabeth Randolph. I will let the sheriff know you have been located. You will stay in the gaol until the next district court convenes to decide your fate."

"I didn't have anything to do with the murder of those women," he protested. His eyes darted about nervously, looking for a place to run. Hope died when he saw three of Hoag's militia men surround them from behind.

Faith protested. "There is no evidence he committed a crime. Surely you see that."

Hoag's voice was flat. "That is for a judge to decide. He has already shown his willingness to run, so I must take him into custody. It's what the law demands." He gestured to his men. "Take him to the gaol."

Faith stifled a cry as Seth darted past her, only to be tackled to the ground by the militia. They dragged him up roughly before tying his hands behind his back with rope and marching him away. She turned to stare at Hoag. "The court will not convene until June. That is months away from now."

Hoag shrugged. "He made his choice, and you were more than willing to help him. The gaoler will keep him from starving. The cells were cleaned out recently, and fresh straw laid out." He looked at her. "Time will tell whether or not he's an innocent man. Now I have other business to attend." With that, he turned and walked away. His boots echoed on the wooden steps that led to the front porch. The door banged shut behind him.

Faith shivered as the breeze picked up, pulling strands of hair from her cap. "Now, what do I do?" She said to no one in particular. She stared up at the gray sky, its dullness only adding to her depression.

"Find out who really killed those girls," Titus said.

Faith stared at him.

"You've done it before. You can do this." His sherry-colored eyes took in her distraught expression. "He's your brother. He has no one else to clear his name."

"You're right," Faith swallowed the knot in her throat. "I need to talk to

Tabitha and find out what he was doing on both occasions. They can't argue with a solid alibi."

Titus shook his head. "Mistress Randolph is not going to let you talk to her slaves. You know better. Regardless, no court will listen to the testimony of a woman of color. Our words have no value under the law. Go see Athena. I bet one of her sons can get a job over there if they haven't already and find out what's been going on."

Faith nodded. "Can you and Olivia manage for a little while?"

He smiled. "We always have." He looked about. "She's probably already got a meal ready for the men. Everything will be fine. Do what you must." He turned to walk back toward the kitchen. Within moments, the sound of an axe chopping into wood filled the air.

Faith shivered. The air was chilly but not bitter. She wrapped her heavy wool shawl around tighter and set off down the road to where she was sure to find Athena. She could hear the shouts of militia men returning to town in small groups, no doubt desiring to get out of the cold and relax before resuming their duties around town. Rather than take the main road where she would undoubtedly run into them, Faith took the footpath that led to Nicholson Street. She averted her gaze as she spotted the gaol in the distance. Thinking about her brother in her cell was too painful to contemplate. Later, she would come with blankets and food for him. Thinking about what he faced made her shudder.

Birds darted across the sky, looking for food. She admired the brilliant red flash of a cardinal as it sped off into the woods. Other than the occasional cry of a bird, the forest and fields stayed silent. This time of year, all the fields were fallow, covered in the stubble of grass or grain that had been harvested months past. A few cows wandered about outside of a barn, their breath creating faint clouds of steam as they exhaled. Something crashed through the bush. Faith nearly jumped out of her skin. She drew in a few shaky breaths. "Silly goose," she said aloud. "It's probably a deer or some other wild creature." Her heart beat rapidly for a space of seconds as she continued down the path toward the road.

Her boots crunched on the ground. Despite her dismissal of the noise, she kept a close watch on her, searching for anything out of place. Two women had died. Her hands gripped into fists. It would have been wise to bring a weapon, even a walking stick had its uses. Faith intended to avoid the Clements's home altogether in hopes of avoiding any further drama. She had enough troubles of her own.

Faint moaning caught her attention. At first, she dismissed it as the wind, but the faint tickles of breeze that had been blowing died down, the noise did not. It was becoming louder as Faith continued down the path. She looked around, trying to determine where it was coming from. Perhaps it was a stray animal. She would hate to think of a stray calf or dog out in the cold.

Clumps of brush lay on one side of the path, bushes waiting for spring to put forth leaves to cover their tangled branches with green. Faith picked up a stick. Wounded animals could attack without warning, and she had no intention of being mauled. The distant sound of breaking branches made her heart pound. She approached slowly, her eyes darting back and forth.

A sob followed by a faint cry told her this was no animal in the bush.

"Who's out there?" Faith continued to move forward, straining to see.

"Help me," Hoarse gasps followed.

Faith recognized the woman's voice. Seeing the movement of brush, she rushed toward her, dropping her stick to the ground as she stumbled toward the figure she now saw sprawled on the ground. "Ellen," she cried. "What has happened to thee?"

Ellen's clothes were torn. Her neck cloth lay on the ground, spotted with blood. Her stockings sagged at her ankles. Her skirts were hiked up, revealing scratched and bloody legs.

Shocked, Faith knelt by her. "I'm here."

Ellen gasped as she endeavored to push herself up off the ground. Her eyes were wide and shocked. "Don't leave me."

Faith shook her head. "I won't. Let's get thee home. Can you walk if I help?" Taking off her shawl, she wrapped it around the shivering woman."

The girl staggered as Faith helped her. "It hurts," she whimpered. "It hurts." She leaned heavily against her. Faith wrapped an arm around her, shivering as the cold air bit through her jacket.

"Olivia and I will take care of thee, whatever has happened." Stress brought back the Quaker speech she had mostly abandoned. Burning anger filled her as she noted marks on the other woman's face. She tamped it down. Her focus had to be on getting her home where she could be cared for properly. The walk felt incredibly long, although the tavern was only a stone's throw away. Faith huffed under the weight of the other woman as they staggered back home. Ellen's lip bled from where she bit it. She shuffled her feet to move forward„ her breath coming in short pants.

Titus spotted them from the yard. He dropped the ax and ran toward them. "What has happened?" He cried as he met them on the path. He reached to take Ellen's other side.

"Careful, she's hurt," Faith said as she sought to catch her breath.

"Let me take her," Titus bent down and scooped her up, hurrying toward the kitchen, bellowing Olivia's name.

Her head popped out the kitchen door. Her eyes widened as she saw them. "What in God's name?" She exclaimed. "Ellen? I sent her to the store a few hours ago." She looked at the woman's bruised face. "Take her to her room in the cellar. I'll be right there."

Faith followed, stirring up the fire as Titus laid her gently on the bed. He spread a blanket over the shivering woman. "I'll stay with her," Faith said, placing a hand on her shoulder.

Titus nodded. "I'll be chopping wood out back. Holler if you need me."

"I will." Faith pulled over a stool and sat next to her. She decided to wait for Olivia before determining the other woman's injuries. Ellen's eyes were closed, but Faith was certain she hadn't fallen asleep. Footsteps resonated through the floorboards from upstairs. The militia had returned. They would be expecting food. She wondered if Dorcas could manage until one of them returned. Ellen's hands looked tiny against the blanket. Faith rested her hand on top of one. Her fingers felt like ice. She wondered who had attacked her. Her thoughts turned toward the other women of color who had died and shuddered. Ellen was lucky to be alive.

Faith thought back to the crashing she had heard in the woods. Could that have been Ellen's attacker? What if she had come down the path earlier? Her heart chilled. What kind of animal roamed the woods attacking women?

Olivia came carrying a basket on one arm as well as a pitcher of steaming water. Setting them down on a nearby table, she retrieved the metal basin from the floor. "Dorcas and Titus are handling the meal. Between the two of them, they can serve what I have ready. We'll worry about cleanup later."

Faith nodded. She helped Olivia remove Ellen's torn clothing. Her jacket was ripped beyond repair. What remained of the pins that normally held it closed were bent and broken. Someone had forcefully ripped it apart. Faith removed her shoes and stockings, setting them down by the side of the bed. Other than being smeared with mud and having straw stuck to them, they were undamaged. Her skirt was dirty and wrinkled as well. Olivia undid the ties of both skirt and petticoats.

"Can you lift up a little?" Olivia said in a gentle tone. I want to get these filthy clothes off you so I can look at your injuries."

Ellen complied with a grunt. Together, the two women slid off the heavy woolen skirt and petticoats. They slid off the bed in a mass to join her shoes.

Ellen lay on the bed, shivering in her shift. Faith added wood to the already blazing fire. She suspected the shivering was not from cold. She looked over at Olivia. "I'm going to get a little brandy for her." Olivia shook her head. "I have laudanum. You never want to mix that with alcohol."

Faith nodded. She was aware of the danger. She watched as Olivia washed the cuts on Ellen's face. Her voice crooned as she wiped with a linen cloth.

"I'm steeping chamomile in the water. It should help with the cuts and bruises. Don't worry if the water looks yellow. It's from the flowers."

Ellen remained silent as Olivia continued her ministrations. As the mud streaks and dried blood left her face, patterns of swelling bruises were visible. Olivia shared an outraged look with Faith before returning to her work. "I need to check for other injuries," she said. "It won't take a moment." Her shift was stained with mud and grass, along with blood that had run down her chin from a cut lip. Olivia tried to lift the shift up.

"No!" Ellen cried, pulling it back down. She turned her face into her pillow and sobbed. "Leave me alone!"

Olivia exchanged glances with Faith. They waited until her sobs faded.

Faith spoke softly. "You have injuries that need tending, then you can rest." Ellen didn't speak but lay huddled in bed. She was still as a corpse, although the rough sound of her breathing could be heard.

"Let me tend her," Olivia said at last. "Go upstairs. I'm sure Dorcas needs you. We can talk later."

Faith started to protest. She glanced over at Ellen, shivering in the bed. It would be easier for her with fewer witnesses. She nodded and went back upstairs, her mind churning with unanswered questions. As she turned the corner of the house, she was nearly run down by Dorcas. The woman carried a tray full of bowls. Faith stepped aside just in time to avoid a calamity.

"We sure could use help feeding all these men," Dorcas said. Her face was flushed as she paused to adjust her load.

"Let me take that," Faith said. "I'm sorry you've been shorthanded." She took the tray with ease born of long practice. The weight made her pause to adjust her balance before she walked swiftly to the taproom, where the sound of male voices emanated.

Malachi stood at the bar filling a stein. He nodded as she entered the crowded room full of militia, boisterous from being called to action. Faith looked around the room and began serving bowls of pigeon pie. Once she emptied her tray, she turned toward the door to go get more. Titus entered, bearing more food. Their glances met as they passed. His face looked grim before he pasted on a neutral expression and continued serving.

Faith went back and forth a few times until all the men had bowls and thick slices of Olivia's fine bread, along with stewed turnips and a cobbler made with apples they had dried in the fall. There was no time to do anything but serve, even if her thoughts were elsewhere.

Captain Hoag sat by a window lit with afternoon sun. He had eaten quickly before setting his dishes to the side in order to leave room for a letter he was reading. Dark shadows circled his eyes, and his cheeks were covered with a faint haze of stubble. He glanced up as Faith took his stein.

"More cider?" she asked. He nodded his thanks and went back to reading. She set the sturdy redware tankard down where it would not disrupt him.

She wondered what was so urgent that he read it here and not in the room he had claimed as his office. The envelope lay crumpled at his elbow, its ink too faded for her to easily read.

"News from home?" she asked.

Hoag looked over his letter. "My mother passed away in her sleep." He folded the letter and put it in his pocket. "This news is two weeks old. The earth is already settling over her grave."

"I'm sorry," Faith said. "It must be hard to be far away from home."

He looked up at her. Dark lashes framed his eyes. "I haven't been home in some time. Sometimes I wonder if I ever will." His eyes had a faraway look. "Even when this war ends, nothing will be the same. Many of us will die or return maimed either in body or mind. Who knows what the future holds for any of us? All we can do is take each day as it comes and hope we survive."

"That is a remarkably grim outlook," Faith looked at him. "Surely your hopes extend beyond mere survival? We all have hopes and dreams. Isn't that why we are engaged in this war? In order that tomorrow will be better, if not for us then for our children?"

Hoag smiled. "You are an idealist, madam. I haven't been around one in a while. Forgive my mutterings. This job brings exhaustion and discouragement the longer it drags on." His expression changed. "My wife used to say such things. She knew how to drag me out of my dark moods better than anyone. You remind me of her in some ways."

"Maybe you will be able to see your loved ones again soon."

Hoag's eyes became distant. "I think we all dream of going back to the place we loved best, even if it no longer exists on this earth." He rose from his seat. "Thank you for the meal. I have work to do. The battle never ends whether within or without."

Faith watched him walk away. Even though he had been staying at her establishment many days, he remained a mystery. She wondered where his thoughts were and where he was heading. She shook her head as she gathered his dishes on a nearby tray to take back to the kitchen to wash. There were far more pressing matters to attend, ones she did not know how to mend, and that in itself was heartbreaking.

Chapter Seventeen

Will listened to the sound of rain on the roof. It was going to be a gray, miserable day, the kind he dreaded. He sharpened a quill before dipping it into an ink well. He didn't write many letters, but when he did, he wanted it to be as neat and elegant as possible. Writing remained a challenge for him. His mother had taught him his letters, and to make his name, but his formal education had been sporadic at best. Both his mistress, Georgia Clements, and his direct overhead in the Patriot spy network, Jeremy Butler, had spent time working with him so that he could communicate and send messages when needed. Figuring out how to use the codes associated with the spy network had been difficult, but he had mastered them. The key he kept hidden behind a board in the wall of the loft where he slept, a place unlikely for anyone to discover.

He blew gently on the page, encouraging it to dry. This was practice, a dry run on a new code. Once the ink dried, he folded the paper and placed it in an envelope before sealing it with a splash of wax from the candle he had lit. He pressed a seal on it that Butler had given him, an embellished letter that could be a monogram but wasn't. The letter M could be turned around to be a W, and no one would be the wiser.

He stuck the message into his vest pocket to leave at the new dead drop that Butler had told him to use. Standing up, he slipped back into the print shop to check on the drying sheets that formed the newspaper. His spirits lifted as he entered and took in the scents of ink and paper, along with beeswax from candles and the dusty odor of books. It was a place where he felt secure. He had mastered the skills of a printer, from making ink to laying type. Having these skills gave him both a sense of pride and security. Printers were in demand throughout the colonies. Once his term of indenture was complete, he could go anywhere. At one point, he had dreamed of setting up a home with Faith Clarke. Now, he had no idea what the future held.

Will's indenture kept him from joining the militia, although his mind turned to join the fight from time to time. The arsenic poisoning that had nearly killed him a few years ago had left a few residuals. He still tired more easily than he had, and his stomach bothered him from time to time. Athena encouraged him to drink peppermint tea for his bouts of indigestion. It had become a regular part of his diet.

The press creaked as Silas pressed it closed, printing another sheet of that week's edition. He grinned as he saw Will come in. "I was beginning to think you had left me to print the whole paper, mate." With the ease of long practice, he removed the newly printed page and handed it to Will to hang up to dry. Silas loaded the press with another sheet.

Will scanned the page as he hung it on the line that ran around the back of the print shop. Both eyebrows rose as he digested the information before him. "There are quite a few people refusing to take the Oath of Allegiance." He had sworn his oath late last year after word had reached Virginia that the Congress required it. The decision had been simple for him, but as he scanned the names of the men, he realized it remained a thorny issue for others. Will was honest enough to admit he had nothing to lose, whereas those who traded with Great Britain risked far more.

Silas looked over at him. "The militia will be going house to house to seize any armaments that those men possess. It's going to get messy."

Will nodded. "I can see that. I wonder if these men realized the consequences of their actions." He doubted it. Rich and privileged men rarely expected accountability. Having their homes raided would come as a nasty shock. It was a bold move on Governor Henry's part, given the number of powerful Tories in town. Nonetheless, Henry could not afford to let potential enemies of the revolution remain armed. If the British ever moved to take the town, they could join the battle behind enemy lines, inflicting terrible damage.

He and Silas worked through the morning printing the paper. Marcus came in halfway through and began assembling the dried sheets. Working together they had the next edition completed by dinner. By that time, the rain had dwindled down to nothing, and the clouds had left the sky a spectacular shade of cerulean.

Feigning an errand, Will slipped out of the shop. He wrapped a scarf tightly around his neck to keep out the wind and trotted down Duke of Gloucester Street past The Red Lion Tavern. As someone opened the door to leave, he could hear voices inside, along with the rich scent of roasted meat. It was a popular place for the working class. He was friends with the bartender, who was a Scotsman like himself. Jack was a good man. He kept an eye on the lads who swept and cleaned the tavern and intervened if anyone troubled them. Drunks who turned mean found themselves out the door and in the street. Of middle years, his stocky build indicated a man able to take care of himself. His face had seen its share of fights. All it took was a look, and people usually decided not to mess with him.

Will would have enjoyed sitting down for a pint of beer, but he had a job to do. Butler would be checking the dead drop to see if he had succeeded in dropping off the message. He would not be pleased if his time was wasted. Keeping that in mind, he turned down Queen Street and onto Nicholson before heading up the Palace green. He knew where the governor's mansion lay, even if he had never been there. Imposing brick walls surrounded the opulent grounds. The house looked quiet and still, although he could see smoke rising from the chimneys of the mansion as well as the nearby kitchen.

Will skirted the entrance and turned down to follow the outside wall. As he eyed all the uniformly laid brick that formed it, he snorted in disgust. This was going to be like finding a needle in a haystack. Butler had made it sound easy. "Go down the walls surrounding the palace toward the canal. Head around the corner and look for a loose brink about knee-high. It has a broken corner." He sketched out the mark on the brick so Will would know which one to pull out. "You should be in and out in a few minutes."

Will thought the location was a ridiculous choice and had told Butler as much. "What business would I have around the Governor's Mansion?"

Butler smiled. "Maybe you would be on the way to the theater. There is one down Scotland Street. The entertainments are pretty decent." Butler sat back and took a swallow from his tankard.

Will shot the other man an aggravated look. "Why would a man like me be there? The theatre is for an entirely different class."

"There are cheap seats, you know. All sorts of folk go there for a few hours distraction. You should try it."

Will snorted. "Not likely. Some of us work all day. Why would I waste the few free hours I have there?"

Butler chuckled. "Don't criticize what you haven't tried. Maybe you should take Faith there one night. I have friends, I could arrange for tickets."

"I doubt she would go with me." Faith barely spoke to him, and he didn't blame her.

Jeremy Butler shot him a sympathetic glance. "She doesn't strike me as a grudge holder. She knows you were trying to protect her. If she is that important to you, take some time to win back her trust."

Will sighed. He could only hope such a thing was possible. The theater lay a few streets down from the palace green, where the wealthy lived in their elegant homes, kept up by large numbers of slaves and indentured servants. Smoke rose from the chimneys of the tall buildings. Heating such enormous places must be an unending challenge.

He picked up his steps eager to be done with his errand and back in the relative warmth of the print shop. The footpath was quiet. Not even so much as a squirrel disturbed him, despite his misgivings, Will found the drop with little difficulty. After depositing his note, he shoved the brick back into the wall. It slid in smoothly, the brick lining up with its brethren with no obvious break in the mortar.

Convinced there were no watching eyes, he continued down the path until it met Scotland Street. This far from the center of town, it was not difficult to cut across yards until he was on the grounds of Bruton Parish church. The well-tended graveyard looked lonely. The cold stones stood out amidst the barren yard. A shot echoed through the air from soldiers drilling nearby. He watched a patrol pass by on Duke of Gloucester Street. They looked so young, not much more than boys. Georgia was right to be afraid that the militia would take Marcus. He was of a like age.

Will walked back toward the print shop, glad to see the sun. He wondered how Faith was handling her tavern full of militia. They could be a wild lot. He had watched groups of them leaving taverns late in the evening, some the worse for drink. He hated to think of her facing off against a group of raucous soldiers with only Titus to help.

As he passed the Market House, he spotted a pink bonnet paired with a blue shawl on the doorstep. Will froze and ducked behind a nearby tree. He had no desire to be accosted by Rebecca Clements. To his surprise, she looked around surreptitiously before walking swiftly to the back of Market Square Tavern. By the way, she looked about, it was plain she did not wish to be discovered, which only piqued his interest. Keeping the line of trees between them, he followed her from a distance, determined to find out what she was doing.

The back of the tavern was still this time of day. It was past the dinner hour, so most people were about their business inside out of the cold unless they were militia on patrol or drilling. Rebecca paused on the dirt path that had led her around the building. A shadow detached itself from the back porch. A young man in a militia uniform came forward and drew her into a nearby outbuilding, probably used as a smokehouse. Will slipped around to where he was against the outside wall. Soft murmurs resonated through the wall, followed by giggles. A sharp crackle from a fire let him know that the soldier had kindled a fire to warm his love nest. Will edged closer to the window and carefully looked in. He was not surprised to see them in each other's arms. Georgia Clements would not be pleased should she discover her daughter's activities, but it was none of Will's business. He had no desire to become entangled. He backed away, planning to slip back around and onto his business, until a branch snapped underneath his boot.

It was loud in the empty yard. Someone cursed in the shed, and Will darted behind the thick trunk of a tree as Rebecca's swain opened the door and looked about. His heart pounded in his chest as the other man stomped about looking for him. He carried his musket with its bayonet attached.

Will had no desire to connect with it in any fashion. He tried to temper his breathing as he waited.

Rebecca's voice called out. "Robbie, it was just the wind. Come back in. I don't have much time before my mother wonders where I am."

The young man looked about one more time. "I don't like it. If someone reports me to the Captain, I'll get sentry duty in the middle of the night.

There's no one else here," Rebecca folded her arms. "Come in, or I am going home."

Robbie went back to her. "You're too pretty to ignore."

She laughed and kissed his cheek as she led him in and shut the door firmly behind them.

Will waited. Just as he turned to go, he saw another man emerge from behind the shed and fade into the trees. Unrecognizable in the distance, dressed in the drab browns and tans of a frontiersman, Will wondered what business he had behind the tavern. There was no way to know.

Chapter Eighteen

Faith found it difficult to sleep. After closing up for the evening, she had gone down to check on Ellen and found her fast asleep. Cocooned in blankets, it was difficult to see much in the shadowy light. Olivia looked up. "I gave her something to help her sleep. It's the best thing for her now."

"Does she know who attacked her?" Faith looked down at the young woman's bruised face. She looked very young with her hair spread out on the pillow. One of her hands was wrapped up; the other was curled next to her cheek. An ache of protective tenderness washed over her, followed by anger that someone had dared hurt this young woman.

Olivia shook her head. "He took her from behind and threw a sack over her head. All she caught was a glimpse of homespun breeches like they all wear. They could have been blue or brown. She wasn't sure. She thought she was going to suffocate. His voice was a rough whisper; she hadn't heard it before." She looked up at Faith. "I think he would have killed her if you had not arrived."

Faith shuddered. "I had no idea anyone was out there." Her voice was hushed in the darkened room. "We're going to have to be more careful." Most of the militia wore blue or brown breeches.

Olivia's eyes gleamed in the darkness. "I always carry one of my knives."

Faith had no doubt she knew what to do with it either. She'd seen her use them in the kitchen. No one who attacked her would be unscathed. "We need more men around here."

"You don't trust the militia," Olivia said. "Good for you. Most of them are boys, but there are some that I don't like the looks of. I've caught one or two slipping around here up to no good. That Sergeant Phillips is not to be trusted. He came out here once when he'd had a few too many. He's nasty when he's drunk. Titus tossed him out by the fence and told him not to come back here again." She shook her head. "I've been meaning to tell that Captain about it. He needs to keep an eye on his men. I won't put up with them harassing anyone back here. I'll talk to Athena and see if Paul or Silas can stay awhile. They're good to have around in a pinch."

Faith nodded. She had seen the twins in town working at various odd jobs. She knew they were part of Jeremy Butler's information network, although they never reported to her. She presumed they shared their intelligence with their mother who Faith both respected and feared. Athena Wise was not someone to take lightly.

Faith went back up the stairs and into the main hallway of the tavern. This time of night, all was still. As she undressed, she heard the clinking of glass from the taproom. She peeked and spotted Malachi arranging bottles on the shelves behind the bar. "It's awfully late for that."

He turned and looked at her in her shift with a heavy shawl around her. "I don't sleep well at night, mistress. I prefer to keep busy rather than just lie abed staring at the ceiling." His voice was as deep and rich as molasses. His thick hair, streaked heavily with silver, shone in the irregular light provided by the fire. He would have been a very attractive man in his youth. As an older man, he was still distinguished enough to catch an eye.

Faith smiled. "I understand. I'm the same way myself. Do we need to get you a softer mattress? I could swap one of the ones upstairs—"

Malachi held up a hand. "The bed is fine, mistress. It's my thoughts that keep me awake some nights. Don't fret. I am grateful you saw fit to have me here. It's a good place for an old man like me."

"We are grateful for your presence," Faith said. "You are part of our family now." She looked at the bottles on the bar. "I appreciate all your hard work, Malachi, but try to rest some if you can. Tomorrow will be here soon enough." She turned to leave. He continued his work. Faith wondered about his past, where he had been before he had been sold to her in-laws. Did he have any family? She would have to ask Eugenia and see what she knew.

The blankets were cold when she turned them back. Dropping her shawl, she hurriedly pulled the blankets over her. Despite the heat provided by the tile stove, she shivered for a while until she was warm enough to drift off to sleep. It felt like only moments had passed before the crow of the rooster woke her.

Faith rose and quickly stirred the fire before throwing on as many warm clothes as she could. Placing the water basin close to the stove had kept it from icing, but it was still chilly as she cleaned her face. Spring could not arrive soon enough for her. Not even her heavy wool stockings kept her warm. Frost covered the glass, keeping her from seeing clearly outside. She wrapped a shawl around her as she went to make sure all the fires were blazing to warm the tavern before her guests came down for breakfast.

Titus had already lit the fire in the taproom so that it blazed heartily as she entered. Faith took a deep breath, enjoying the peace and quiet before the bustle of the day overtook her. Outside, the sky was dark, waiting for the sun to begin its sojourn across the sky. All was still except for those who rose before the sun to start the day. Taking down the metal lanterns that hung in the darker corners of the tap room, she began lighting them with a taper from the fire. Once the taproom was done, she moved to the hallway until a faint light glowed up and down the walkway. They would need it to negotiate the space with trays full of breakfast for the hungry men now slumbering upstairs.

Faith paused when she heard a faint creak overhead. Looking up, she saw nothing on the stairs or in the deep shadows of the hallway. The inn had its share of creaks and moans. Perhaps it felt the weather, too. She picked up her steps and headed out back, gasping as the outdoor air hit her, making her realize that her tavern was warmer than she had previously thought.

Stars glittered in the predawn sky as if someone had scattered diamonds across the cosmos. The moon was a pale crescent joined by the morning star nearby. To the east, the sky grew pale and gray as the sun made its presence known.

Faith went down the steps and gazed at the dormant yard as it lay quiet. A few dead weeds lingered in the garden. As she looked out, she saw a lantern enter the barn where the animals waited. That would be Titus taking care of their stock. Faith raised her own lantern and continued to the kitchen. She could smell smoke from the fire, along with faint hints of cooking food. As she opened the door, she heard the steady sound of Olivia's knife as she prepared the morning meal.

"Good morning," Olivia said as her large knife made short work of the onion on the cutting board before her. "Looks like it will be a beautiful day. The rain has left. There's not a cloud in the sky." She turned to add the onions to a pan, where they sizzled as they hit hot fat.

Faith nodded. Setting down the lantern on the windowsill, she turned to look at what Olivia had done. "How can I help?"

"Dorcas is checking the chickens. That rooster can be a cranky cuss sometimes. He's protective of his ladies. She took a broom just in case he acts up." Just then, they heard crowing out in the yard.

Faith grimaced as she listened to his lusty cry. "Well, no one will be sleeping now. I'd best get busy." She picked up a large wooden spoon and checked the porridge bubbling in the kettle. A jar of molasses stood waiting on the table she added a few spoons before stirring it into the mass of bubbling oats.

Olivia continued working on the hash she was making. "Athena sent word that Paul will come by later today to help out. Titus will show him what to do, not that he'll need much training. Those boys are sharp."

Olivia shrugged. "We do what we can, but we have an inn to run, and these men stay hungry."

"Yes, they do," Faith admitted. She stacked trays on the table to be loaded with bowls and platters. "Do I need to grind more coffee?" The grinder stood in a far corner of the room.

Olivia shook her head. "Ellen ground a lot before she went to market yesterday." They both fell silent, thinking of the young woman sleeping in her cellar room. Olivia continued. "Titus went down to stir the fire, but her room was quiet. I think it's best to let her sleep for a bit before I go check on her."

Faith nodded. "She needs her rest."

"When was the last time you practiced with that pistol Jeremy gave you?"

Faith sighed. "It's been a while." The thing made her nervous, although she knew how to load and fire it. Butler had made sure of that. Nonetheless, it was not the time for squeamishness. "I will get it out after our guests are fed," she promised.

Olivia nodded. "It's about time. There's a monster on the loose, and that gun could be the difference between life and death. You don't want to be caught at a man's mercy anytime."

Faith shuddered. She knew Olivia was right. Her own town was no longer safe, and she hated it. Walking about and doing her business was a freedom she had taken for granted.

The rooster crowed again. This time, there was a short burst before he ceased. His brethren within hearing distance took up his cry until echoes of crowing could be heard all around them.

Olivia glanced over to her. "You may want to check and see if any of the men are waiting for breakfast."

Faith nodded, and, wrapping her shawl around her, she picked up her lamp. As she opened the door, Dorcas burst in, bearing a basket and a broom.

"That rooster belongs in a pot! He went after my feet until I gave him a swat with the broom. That's when he decided to get on the henhouse and make all that noise." She shivered as she removed her own shawl, which was a dark shade of maroon. "There weren't too many eggs this morning. Luckily, we have some from yesterday as well."

Faith nodded. "Thank you for checking." She shut the door behind her and moved briskly down the path to the back door of the tavern. The sky turned gray as the stars faded away. Dark shadows covered the yard, making it difficult to see. A sudden crackling of branches caused her to look up sharply, but her eyes detected nothing. After a moment, she continued at a quicker pace. Even if it was an animal, she would feel safer inside.

In the main room, Malachi was setting up clean steins. He nodded in greeting as she entered.

"Go get breakfast before it gets busy," she told him. "It won't be long before this room is full of hungry men. You will need a full belly to handle them."

He nodded. "I'll do that, mistress. I've never turned down a hot heal." As he walked past, Faith realized his gait was a bit stiff whether from age or injury she didn't know. He was not a large man, but wiry with more strength than one might think at first glance.

Feeling eyes upon her, Faith looked up to see Captain Hoag on the stairs. She had not heard him approach. His gaze was mild as he continued down. "All is well this morning?" he inquired as his foot left the last step.

Faith returned his smile, "Well enough, Captain. I hope you slept well."

He shook his head. "I have no complaints, mistress. It is my thoughts that keep me awake, not the lodgings. That being said I would like to move a bed into the private room so my restlessness disturbs no one. The days of having nights to sleep may not last long. Even if the enemy has yet to arrive, they are coming, whether in a few days or a few months. We must be ready, and there is no greater fighting force in the world."

Faith nodded. "I will ask Titus to move a bed out here for you. I keep you and your men in my prayers."

"Please do," he said as he continued into the taproom. He stood before the blazing fire, holding his hands to its warmth.

"Can I get you anything?" Faith asked as she followed him in.

Hoag shook his head. "Go about your business, Mistress Clarke. I would enjoy a few moments with my thoughts before the men come down. I have no need of food or drink at the moment."

Faith nodded and went back to the kitchen to help Olivia. She wondered how Ellen had fared. She had hesitated to tell Hoag, although she recognized he would need to be informed of the violent attack at his doorstep. She wanted to protect Ellen from strangers. Troubled, she turned and went to the interior cellar door. She grabbed one of the hall's lanterns to light the way downstairs. She tiptoed across the floor and cracked open Ellen's door to where she lay inside, bundled up against the cold. The fire had been fed recently for which she mentally blessed Titus.

Faith turned to go back when Ellen spoke.

"Mistress?" Her voice was husky with sleep.

"Yes, Ellen. I'm right here. I didn't mean to wake you."

"You didn't," Ellen said. "I've been laying here a while. I'm used to getting up and feeding the chickens."

"Dorcas has taken care of that. You need to rest." Faith paused. "You are safe here. We are keeping watch."

Ellen sighed. "You have always been kind." She rose up slowly. "I need to visit the necessary then I would feel better with something to occupy my hands."

"There is a chamber pot here, but I am glad to walk you to the necessary if you prefer."

Ellen stood up. "I do not wish to smell piss in my bedroom. Please, Mistress Faith. Help me if you would."

Faith wrapped a blanket around her and helped her up the steps and out to the necessary. As she waited for her, she spotted a man come in through the gate. He was a stranger, dressed in the dull browns and greens of homespun with a wide-brimmed hat on his head. Looking about the yard, he spotted her and made his way to where she stood.

"Mistress Clarke, I presume?" His dusty brown hair was neatly tied behind his head. Slightly shorter than Faith, his wiry body looked able to tackle about anything.

"I am Faith Clarke," she acknowledged. Wondering what lay behind his clever brown eyes, she waited for him to proceed.

He smiled disarmingly. "I'm Cyrus Lovell. I've recently come to Williamsburg and am in need of work and lodging. I'm hoping you can supply both."

Faith hesitated. "I cannot deny needing an extra hand, although I'm not sure where I could put you. My tavern has been taken by the militia. In addition, I couldn't pay you much."

"I could sleep in the stable loft," he suggested. I've slept in worse places. Let's agree that I will work for my room and board. That will give me time to settle and seek other prospects."

Titus spoke from behind her. "He can share Malachi's room for now. He won't mind. I can move the bed down from the small room upstairs."

Faith. cringed. Her brother had been sleeping in that bed. It was long past time she went to the gaol to see him. "That is true. See to it."

Titus nodded and left with Cyrus Lovell in tow. Once they were gone. Ellen emerged, staring at the back of the stranger. Fear flashed in her eyes.

"Titus and Malachi will keep an eye on him," Faith said. "No one will bother you here."

"Olivia gave me one of her knives," Ellen said. "I keep it with me all the time."

Faith shot her a startled look. "Very well. Just be careful with it. Those things are wicked sharp."

"I'm well aware," Ellen replied. "And I know exactly where I will put it should someone attack me again."

Faith took her to the kitchen. "I'm sure Olivia will have some vegetables to peel or something where you can stay near the fire." As they walked together, Faith wondered how this all would end. Ellen would never be the same, and neither would anyone else. The safe, secure town she had come to know was gone. Her world was a place of secrets and unknown dangers waiting to come to light. She wasn't sure how any of them would emerge by the time the conflict was over.

Chapter Nineteen

livia held her market basket with her right arm, keeping her left arm ready to grab her knife if needed. Not many people realized she was left-handed, which had proven useful on occasion. Titus walked alongside her, whistling a merry tune. He had left the new man Cyrus chopping wood while Athena's son Paul added a latch to the room Ellen and Dorcas shared. The new man shared Malachi the bartender's room where the older man could keep an eye on him. Although he was hard-working and incredibly polite, Olivia didn't trust him. His arrival was all too convenient.

Gray mist drifted through the air as they walked toward the Market building. Even though it was just after breakfast, it was still considerably early. Not many people wandered up and down Duke of Gloucester Street at this hour, although she could see the lights of businesses as they prepared for the day. The heavy clang of a hammer on metal told her the blacksmith was already at work. She had seen the militia men leave the tavern en masse after eating. Captain Hoag liked his men up and out early to drill on the green. After they left, Olivia did her marketing, leaving Ellen and Dorcas to do the dishes. Ellen had been subdued but determined to work. Olivia felt better leaving her with the other woman. Dorcas asked no questions but put her to work sorting through the dried peas, a job where she could sit and not be disturbed. The compassion on her face told Olivia that the other woman knew something about what had happened. She was glad that Paul was nearby to help the women feel safer, although she hoped no one was bold enough to attack them within the bounds of their home.

She shivered and pulled her heavy woolen shawl around her more tightly. Olivia had never liked the cold. She had hated the long, cold winters of Pennsylvania, where she and Titus had gone after they had been gifted by Eugenia to her newly married son and his wife Faith. Joshua had been born there. She recalled the huge snows with a shudder. When Jon Clarke had decided to give up farming and return to Williamsburg, she had been overjoyed. She loved feeling the heat from the sun on her skin and working in the garden on a hot, muggy day. She would take every minute of it to avoid the bitterly cold winters that lay further north. Virginia could get cold, but not nearly as cold as Pennsylvania.

Now she was a free woman who earned an honest wage, it was a gift she never forgot. She longed for the day all her people would be free. In the distance, she could see a large group of figures moving away from the center of town. The militia was headed out to drill in the chilly weather. They frequently used the fields behind the armory, which made her wonder if one of them was responsible for the death of the woman she had found. She didn't like to think about it, how frightened she must have been. She looked over at Titus, grateful for his presence. His presence alone would keep most forms of trouble away.

Titus caught her glance. "What's on your mind, little bird?" He called her that from time to time. He had once said she was as quick as the small sparrows that nested near the barn. They frequently saw them flying about, looking for spilled seed from the grain they used. Olivia suspected that Titus tossed them a treat from time to time, although she couldn't prove it. He had a soft heart for any animal. Which was probably why she had noticed a stray cat about the barn, although Titus said the calico was there for the mice. Either way, it only went up to greet Titus. If she came near, it was nowhere to be found.

The market loomed ahead. A hum of human noise surrounded it. The sun had become a brilliant copper disk in the sky as it rose slowly, burning away the fog. Ice crunched beneath their feet from brittle spots of ice and frost-covered grass. As they drew close, Olivia could see more women like herself with baskets. Some men came too, likely shopping for whatever tavern employed them. The market doors opened and closed as they entered. No one was propping the doors open today. Everyone wanted to leave the cold outside, if only for a few hours.

Outside, someone had kindled a bonfire where a group of dark-colored servants like them stood to warm their hands. Some were children, wrapped and bundled against the winter's chill. As she looked at some of the enslaved, Olivia felt a wave of pity. Not all of them were dressed for the weather. Her anger burned against those who saw her people as property and not human beings deserving proper care. "They need warmer clothes,"

Titus touched her arm. "There's nothing you can do." By the way she stiffened, he knew she had noticed that some of the children lacked shoes. The frozen ground was cruel to bare feet and the rags they wore offered little protection.

Olivia bit her lips as she struggled to focus on the business that brought her here. This early, it was crowded with cooks and other servants who, like herself, sought the best possible offerings for their kitchens. Her nose informed her that men had been fishing in the cold waters of either the York or the James, both of which lay nearby. The strong smell of fish drew her down one side of the market where the day's catch lay on blocks of ice packed with straw. One of the fishmongers grinned as he saw her expression. "Fresh fish for you and your mistress?" he gestured to where they lay, still damp from the river. Their scales were bright silver, a good sign, as were the clear eyes of one she examined. She touched it with a gentle finger, delighted to see it spring back. Finally, she bent down to sniff the body. The scent was fishy but mild.

"These are acceptable," she said at last. "If the price is right." After a few brief moments of haggling, she was the owner of a nice parcel of the man's catch. Olivia loved trout. She planned to fry them and serve them with a batch of cornbread and potatoes. She let Titus pay the man and take the wrapped bundle, which he placed gently into the larger basket. Olivia kept a separate one for her vegetables.

One table held collard greens which she bought as well, leaving Titus to hold onto the fish. She happily checked through the broad green leaves in order to find the best ones. Finding greens in the dead of winter was a challenge. Having these on the table would round out the meal nicely. After she paid the woman, she turned to see Athena nearby.

Athena Wise was a good six feet tall. She towered over the crowd, her hair covered by a gold-covered cloth with white flowers printed on it. Looking into her basket, Olivia saw that she had scored some beautiful purple turnips, a side of bacon, and a small sack of dried beans.

When Athena saw Olivia's fish, she demanded to know where to find them. Olivia pointed to the corner where other cooks had begun to swarm. Athena used her long stride to get ahead of many of them. Olivia watched her go. She was not getting into that crowd again. She had no doubt that Athena could manage on her own. Once she had made her purchase and left the crowd, she rejoined them.

"I'm obliged. Mistress Georgia will enjoy these. That son of hers could out-eat a horse." She chuckled. "At least my folks aren't as particular as some." She nodded over to where Edith, the cook for Faith's mother-in-law, stood, looking aggrieved.

Olivia looked over at her, puzzled. "I don't recall that Eugenia was all that picky."

"She wants to impress her new gentleman friend. Monsieur Le Bon is French, so she's been asking for all kinds of fancy dishes with rich sauces and complicated ingredients. Apparently, she's forgotten it's the end of winter."

Olivia rolled her eyes sympathetically. "I know nothing of French food. If he's been in the colonies long, he will know that our ways are quite different."

"I don't think he's the problem. He's quite charming and has the prettiest little girl. His wife died after a sudden illness, so it's just them."

Olivia shot her an inquiring look. "So what is Edith planning to cook?"

Athena chuckled. "It will be interesting to find out." She nodded to where Edith had finished her business and turned about. "Edith is good at her job. I am sure she will fix a fine meal no matter whether it is French or not."

Olivia nodded. "I hope she can make Eugenia understand that she can only cook what is available at the market. Come spring, there will be more variety."

Athena nodded. "One would hope. I gave her some spices I had to fancy things up. I also had a receipt for beef cooked in wine that someone told me was French."

"Can she find beef?" Olivia pondered. A lot of cattle had gone to feed the militia. It was the wrong time of year for slaughtering cattle. Everyone would be tending their breeding stock for spring.

"I had a source," Athena replied. "We have to look out for each other. I won't see a woman punished for something she cannot help."

Olivia grimaced. Eugenia was better than most, but the fact was that the enslaved had no power against their owners. If Eugenia were angry over the meal, she could punish Edith. It wasn't fair, but it was how it had been for too many years. Olivia sighed. She was lucky to be free.

Olivia walked with Athena out of the market and into the chilly air. Within a few moments, Edith joined them. She looked tired. Olivia had always liked the quiet young woman. "What did you find today?" She leaned over to peer into the other woman's basket. She spotted potatoes and tiny pearl onions along with a few carrots along with a few other items. "I'm impressed you found carrots. I had no idea anyone still had them."

Edith rolled her eyes. "Making "Madame" happy takes a lot of work. I'm fortunate that I had a friend willing to share her largess. Mistress wants everything in the French way. You have no idea how hard it is to find mushrooms this time of year."

Olivia nodded sympathetically. "I gather her gentleman friend is particular about his food."

Edith snorted. "He's no trouble at all. Master Francis keeps telling her that anything is fine, that he doesn't require fancy food, but she insists. Hopefully, she'll settle down soon. I'm not cooking snails even if they can be found."

"Snails?" Athena looked started. "Who eats that?"

"Apparently, the French do, drowned in butter." Edith curled her lip. "I told her there were none to be found in Williamsburg, and unless she provided them, she would have to make do with normal food like can be found at the market in winter. Master Francis told her he didn't care for them and to respect her staff." She sniffed. "He appreciates a good cook. I can only pray he stays a while."

Olivia listened. She wondered what had brought the Frenchman to Williamsburg. It was an unusual time of year to travel, especially with a child. She wondered if Faith knew about her mother-in-law's gentleman friend. She bet not. Faith would have mentioned it. "I hope she will listen to Master Le Bon," she said. "I have plenty of herbs and pork so if you need something, let me know."

Edith smiled, revealing pearly white teeth. "Thanks. I have chicken cooking in red wine right now. She seemed pleased with that." A young man trotted up and took her basket. Olivia recognized him as Mistress Moore's coachman. He seemed smitten with Edith. She was an attractive woman, with flawless ebony skin and unusual green eyes with a delicate snub nose. A rose colored cloth covered her hair and complimented the colors of the dress visible under her apron. A dark brown shawl was wrapped about her to prevent the chill. She met the young man's eyes before breaking contact and turning toward home. 'I need to get back. I left one of the girls to watch the fire." She walked swiftly across the ground to where the town's walk lay. As she continued back toward the Moore home, a voice called out to her in French.

A little girl ran up to her, followed by the taller figure of a man. The man spoke briefly to the couple before continuing his walk, with the little girl skipping a few steps ahead of him.

Olivia raised her eyebrows in surprise. Most folks didn't acknowledge the enslaved, at least not in a social manner. "Is that him?"

Athena nodded. "That's Le Bon. Everyone likes him. They like he pays in European coins too. There's not a merchant in town who wouldn't like his business."

"And he's keeping company with Eugenia." Olivia's tone was thoughtful. Eugenia Moore had received a generous Widow's portion and the house. Ezra Moore's sons had decided that providing for her upkeep was better than letting her meddle in their father's interests once they realized she was not responsible for his death.

"Eugenia Clark Moore has money and connections in this town," Athena noted. "She would be quite a catch for a charming widower needing to start over. His little girl, Emily, is beautiful. She doesn't sound French at all, although she speaks it fluently with her pa. I'm willing to bet they didn't just come over from France. They're from somewhere else in these colonies. The question is, whose side is Master Le Bon on?"

Chapter Twenty

Jeremy Butler was enjoying a cup of coffee with his feet in front of Athena's cooking fire. He had finished a fine meal and was busy planning his afternoon. The sun had warmed the ground outside, making it almost pleasant for the dead of winter. He could check the new deaddrop and visit a few contacts while he was in town. He felt his time was wasted this far south and had told Washington as much when he'd received his orders to return to Williamsburg.

"The fight is here, General, in the mid-Atlantic colonies. I have no information that they have entered Virginia."

General Washington listened to him for a moment before raising a hand to stop him. "They have the most powerful navy in the world. They can sail and be in Virginia's capital within days. Don't underestimate them. They intend to destroy us and will use whatever means at their disposal. I need a set of eyes I trust to see what is happening there. I cannot afford to have the British military at my back as well as my front."

The retreat from New York continued to rankle. Butler knew it without asking. The specter of his own men fleeing the British regulars had caused the general to threaten to shoot his own troops. The humiliation, compounded with the brutal loss of the colony, must have been a nightmare. Butler was glad he had not been there to see it. As a spy, his work lay outside the field of battle. Right now, he worried that the enemy had Philadelphia in its sights where Hannah lived. It was also home to the Continental Congress, which made its capture a prize in British eyes.

Butler rubbed his eyes. He wished she would come south to join her sister.

Hannah was a stubborn woman. She fiercely loved the independence of having her own business. Philadelphia was home and she was not being driven off by threats of British invasion. They had talked long and hard before his sojourn south.

"You know this city is full of Tories who long for the return of British rule and will help them any way they can." He leaned up on one elbow from the bed they shared. He loved the way she looked, with her hair all tousled in a dark cloud around her pillow. She pushed it back out of her face. Her deep blue eyes blazed.

"I fail to see how this is any different from how it's been since the Revolution began. No matter what your leaders say, we are a divided country. Some want revolution, some want to remain a colony. Others want no more than to avoid any sort of conflict, so they pretend not to see what is happening around them." She sat up and started to get out of bed before he stopped her with a hand on her back.

"I meant no offense love, but I worry for your safety. You know, if anyone realizes you are married to a rebel spy, they will not deal kindly with you."

She turned back to him and tucked her feet back under the covers. "Everyone believes you are a surveyor. It provides an excellent explanation for your frequent absences."

Butler shrugged. "I have been a surveyor. When this war is over, I may be again." He drew in a breath as his eyes met hers. "I'm not going to change your mind—am I?"

She shook her head. "Philadelphia is my home. I have Nathan and Letitia to help in the shop. There is no reason for me to leave as long as people still want to purchase fine China. Although," she acknowledged. "the British are making it more difficult to receive new stock."

He nodded. The British had begun blockading the coast early last year, and it had made life difficult for those whose businesses, like Hannah's, that relied on European imports. She didn't admit it but he knew she worried about what would happen when she had no more stock to sell. Her clientele was dwindling as people struggled with the stranglehold the British had put on trade. Fewer people had money to spend on fine goods such as china and tea sets.

"How bad is it?" he asked gently.

Hannah bit her lip. "It's not good," she admitted. "Not many people come in to browse anymore. My storeroom is full of empty barrels. I have very little stock left. Letitia and Nathan haven't said anything, but I know they worry."

Hannah's former sister-in-law and her crippled son worked for Hannah. She provided a roof over their heads and income in exchange for their hard work and loyalty. Butler stroked her cheek. "I know you want to stay, but if circumstances force you to leave, I have a friend you can leave a message for at the Man Full of Troubles down near the docks."

Hannah shot him a look. "I remember the place." Her tone was dry.

He smiled ruefully. Yes, she would remember. That night had brought the two of them together in a way he would have never foreseen. Butler had never intended to remarry after the tragic death of his first wife. Then, against all odds, he and Hannah had found each other. He had no regrets.

Butler left the next day on his journey south to Virginia and Williamsburg. While he enjoyed catching up with his contacts, he saw no real reason for his purpose. Despite the scare over potential British Navy ships, nothing had occurred except for the murders of two young, enslaved women. The sheer brutality of the crimes troubled him.

He rose from the table. "I'm going for a walk. I may be a while."

Athena nodded. She knew it was better not to know too much about what he did, even if she did send coded reports north in his absence. She stewed a pot over the fire. "Be careful, Jeremy. I don't think things are as quiet as they might seem."

"Agreed," he answered as he closed the door behind him. The chilly air encouraged him to button his jacket and wrap his woolen scarf snugly around his neck. Winters were milder in the south, but they still packed a notable chill. Rather than stroll down Duke of Gloucester Street, he chose a footpath that would take him to the north end of town. Once he had crossed Nicholson Street he made his way to North England Street up toward the Governor's palace. The huge brick structure dominated the landscape.

His business did not lie within the grounds of that estate, however, but outside it. Nonetheless, he paused to take in the grandeur that had once been the seat of power for the Royally Appointed Governor. The last royal governor had fled the colonies two years ago. Now, the governor was a patriot, loyal to the Continental Congress. He wondered how Patrick Henry felt about living in such a grand residence. Despite the change of governors, people still went back and forth through the elaborate iron gates to conduct business.

Butler watched as militia men checked each man's business before allowing entrance inside. Catching movement from the corner of his eye, Butler's eyes looked toward the bare trees that lined the Palace Green. He was surprised to see a figure watching the entrance to the palace, hidden from most eyes by the wide trunks of trees that lined the area.

Curious Butler sank into the shadows of the brick walls that surrounded the palace. The other man was clever, his dull homespun blended in with the bare trunks. Nonetheless, he couldn't avoid the stir his presence caused birds nesting in the barren limbs. Their warning chitter alerted Butler to the whereabouts of the other man. Slipping into the trees himself, Butler followed the figure as he threaded his way south toward the palatial homes that lined the Palace Green.

Honest men didn't sneak through the trees. Butler's quarry was up to something. He wanted to know what. The man crossed to the walkway and walked with studied casualness until he reached the home of Robert Carter. Butler knew little of Carter other than he was one of the few nonpartisan men of influence in Williamsburg. Pausing at the white picket fence that separated the sideyard from the street, the man looked back at the governor's palace, revealing his face. Butler recognized it instantly; it was Cyrus Lovell, the Tory spy he had encountered once before in Philadelphia. His presence here raised the hair on the back of his neck. It was the proof he had been dreading. Washington was right, the British were planning on coming. The only question was when.

Butler stepped out of the shadows, revealing himself. As soon as Lovell laid eyes on him, he ran. Butler pursued, his boots thumping on the ground as he endeavored to overtake him. Lovell had a lead and longer legs, but there were limited places to hide. They continued down the walk until Lovell jumped a low fence.

Butler swore and hurried to where the man had disappeared. After clambering over the fence, he continued through the yard. A servant came out leading a horse. "Did you see a man run through here?" he called over to him.

The man shrugged. "No, sir. It's just been me and the stock here."

Butler scowled and trotted past. Surely the man could not have disappeared so quickly. But he had. Lovell had vanished, leaving no indication of his whereabouts. Butler slowed to a walk, his chest heaving from all the running. Leaving the yard, Butler retraced his steps to the governor's palace. He elicited a few stares from people who had probably watched him chase the other man. Butler ignored them. He drifted back into the shadows, hoping people would return to their business and forget about him. He had never enjoyed attention. Butler checked around to make sure no one, especially Lovell, was watching him. Within minutes, he found the loose brick in the wall surrounding the governor's residence. Removing it, he reached into the opening and withdrew the test message Will had placed inside.

He grunted in satisfaction. This one would work. Few people walked around the outside wall, especially in winter. If he could not connect with Will directly, this would serve as a safe spot for messages. Replacing the brick, he turned back to town, slipping down North England Street to avoid returning to any more staring eyes on the green.

Rather than enter a tavern to drench his woes, he ambled back to the small white building behind Georgia Clements' print shop where Athena would be cooking dinner. His stomach growled when he was greeted with the rich scent of roasting meat on the spit.

She looked up from where she was basting birds over the fire. "You always did have a nose for where to find a meal." She stepped back and surveyed her fire. As always, a large iron pot hung from a hook where something simmered. Small birds, possibly pigeons, rotated on the spit, browning in the intense heat. At the table were three loaves of bread that had come out of the oven recently, filling the air with a yeasty scent.

"I didn't come to disturb you," Butler protested, although he sat down where she gestured and accepted the cup of beer she poured. He took a long, thirsty pull, enjoying the fruity aftertaste of home-brewed beer. "I wanted to seek your advice." Athena ladled out a bowl of soup and set it before him. Pieces of pork floated on top. Never one to turn down a good meal, Butler thanked her and ate. Cutting into one of the warm loaves, she set a slice beside him. She continued working as he ate. As he pushed the empty bowl aside, she spoke.

"What did you want to talk about?" Athena asked as he stacked his dirty dishes in a tub to be washed later. She poured a cup of coffee for each of them and sat down.

She liked it black; he had more of a sweet tooth. She pushed the sugar over to him. watching as he broke off a lump to drop in his cup. Butler swirled it around before he blew on the boiling liquid. "We have a Tory spy in town."

"We probably have more than one." Athena took a sip of coffee and waited for him to continue.

He sighed and rubbed his brow with his fingers. She wasn't wrong, although her calm irritated him slightly. "I know him. He tried to recruit me in Philadelphia. If Cyrus Lovell is here, someone sent him."

Athena took a few sips of coffee. "What do you plan to do about it?"

Butler shrugged. "Nothing right now. I need to find out where he is staying and who he is connected with in this town."

Athena chuckled. "That's easier said than done. Where are you going to start? This town is full of new faces. That tavern keeper whose sister you wed has a house full of them. I hear she's even got someone sleeping in the cellar, doing chores for his keep."

"I hadn't heard that," he admitted. "She's got a bunch of militia sleeping there, I know. I've seen them hanging about when they're not drilling or patrolling the streets."

Athena nodded. "Paul has been lending a hand. They needed another man to keep an eye on things after Ellen was attacked."

Butler froze. "When did this happen?" He knew the young maid slightly.

"A few days ago. She was on her way to market when it happened. Fortunately, Mistress Clarke came down the path not much later. The brute ran off when he heard her."

"My God," Butler said, taking a deep breath. "Is she all right?"

"She was raped, but she is alive." Athena shot him a look. "One of my boys will be working at the tavern until this monster is caught."

Butler nodded. "Agreed. I can make rounds while I'm here, and Will can do more leg work now. He's mostly recovered." Rising, he ran his fingers through his hair. Strands were trying to escape the leather strap he was using to hold it back. "I'm going to start checking taverns and see if I can spot Lovell." It was not going to be easy. The man blended in like a shadow. He had no distinctive features to make him stand out from the crowd.

Butler left the comfort of Athena's kitchen and strode out from behind the print shop straight onto Duke of Gloucester Street. He had no idea how he was going to locate his quarry, but he had to try. Every day Lovell roamed the city, the patriot cause was threatened. There was too much at stake for Butler to allow a viper to roam free, striking whenever he chose.

Chapter Twenty-One

Faith was surprised to see Will McKay enter the tavern. Since their break-up a few years ago he had not entered the front door. He chose to conduct his business with Olivia or Titus out back. She was even more surprised to see his violin case with him. He avoided her glance as he walked into the taproom. When he took his fiddle out of the case, a cheer went up. After a few moments testing out the strings, he drew his bow across and broke into a jaunty tune. Within moments, the crowd were tapping their toes and clapping along. Bemused, she watched from the entryway. There had been a time when Will regularly played in her tavern, brightening her evenings with his music and his company. A bitter voice in her head reminded her that it had been his decision to end it, breaking her heart with a few swift words and the slam of a door. Faith might enjoy his music, but she wasn't trusting him again. The cost was too high.

Malachi continued pouring drinks as the concert continued. Titus brushed past her with a load of wood. He smiled as he fed the fire before moving to the bar, where he took a tray and served drinks to the men in the taproom. Not many filled the room, it was between dinner and supper where men were about their business in town. A few gathered at the tables in Clarke Tavern to talk, share news, or play a game of cards.

Afternoon sun streamed in the windows, revealing a few dust motes that swirled about restlessly in the air. On the surface, everything appeared well. Captain Hoag entered. When not training his men or on patrol, he spent most of his time in the private room that opened out back, meeting with his men and writing letters that he trusted no one to post but himself. "I didn't realize there was entertainment tonight."

"I didn't either," Faith replied wryly. Will McKay had not warned her, although she knew better than to consider it a whim. For whatever reason, Will McKay wanted her attention. Refusing to be drawn into his web, she went about her business, clearing away tables and making polite conversation. Once her tray was full, she walked back to the kitchen to deposit her load into the tub of dishes to be washed. Dorcas and the new man had made short work of the last load. Cyrus Lovell had blended in with her staff seamlessly. While she was grateful for his help, she wondered what had brought him to Williamsburg. Having an able-bodied man work for free troubled her even if she was feeding him and providing him a place to sleep. Something wasn't right, although she couldn't put her finger on it. Dropping her load outside the kitchen, Faith opened the door, feeling the warmth from the fire penetrate her skin.

Olivia was alone in the kitchen, putting the finishing touches on supper. There was leftover stew from dinner, fresh biscuits, and fried ham. The pigeon pie had disappeared, devoured by hungry men. She hummed as she worked, her rich contralto filling the space. Her sleeves were rolled up to the elbow. An old scar snaked around the muscles of her right forearm, remnants of a long-ago fire that Olivia never spoke of. She kneaded out her dough before rolling it out on an oak board that Titus had made just for her. The surface had been rubbed and smoothed until it was as soft as satin.

"Where is everyone?" Faith asked. No one had been in the yard chopping when she had come out. Nor was anyone in the kitchen except for Olivia.

Olivia looked over at her. "Dorcas and Ellen went to the smokehouse for meat. Titus went on an errand. I don't know where that new man is. He helped Titus and Paul with the stock, then took off. Why do you ask?"

Faith shrugged. "Just curious. What do you think of Lovell?"

Olivia continued her work. Her expression was thoughtful. "I haven't thought much about him at all. Lots of people are on the move these days. He's been no trouble, keeps to himself. He does whatever is asked of him. Lovell's a good hand with the stock. He's real fond of the horses.".

Faith shot her a look. "How fond of the horses is he?" She really did not want to lose another horse. Hoag had noticed that she kept some nice ones in the stable and had asked about her selling them to the militia. She'd refused, saying she was keeping them for a friend but suspected he was not going to let the matter rest.

Olivia's face turned serious. "Now, that is a very good question. I haven't really kept track of him. Titus says he's a good worker, does as he's told. But as to what he does or where he goes when he's not here. There is no telling."

Faith nodded. "Jeremy said to keep an eye on him."

"Then I suggest you do that. I have people to feed."

A pungent, somewhat familiar odor permeated the room, rich and faintly sweet. It made Faith think of autumn. "What is that?"

"Pumpkin," Olivia answered. "I found a few l that I'd gotten at the market. With all that went on, I had forgotten them, so now I'm stewing them to go with the ham."

Faith nodded as she walked over to look in the pot to see the deep orange flesh bubbling away. "It will be good." She liked having a colorful vegetable to go with the heartier fare they served during the colder months. Olivia brushed past her to add a pinch of salt to the pot.

Wiping her hands on her apron, Faith paused. "Did you know Will was coming to play his fiddle tonight?"

Olivia blinked in surprise before shaking her head. "He didn't mention it." Satisfied with the thickness to which she had rolled out the biscuits, she picked up a cup and began cutting them out and placing them into a Dutch oven she had placed next to her on the table. She didn't look at Faith as she worked. "He always asks after you when either Titus or I see him."

Faith sniffed. "I cannot imagine why."

Olivia shot her a look as she put a lid on the Dutch oven and set it aside. Biscuits cooked quickly. She would put them on the fire shortly before it was time for supper. That task accomplished, she swiftly wiped down her workspace to prepare for the next task. "He's a busy man. I don't imagine he has a great deal of time to drop by anymore."

Faith pursed her lips. "I'd best see why he's here." Her feet dragged as she returned to the tavern. As much as she did not want to admit it, she still cared. She hated herself for it, but her heart ignored what her mind knew. Caring for Will McKay was a pointless endeavor only bound to lead to heartache.

He was playing a ballad as she walked down the hall. Its mournful strains echoed through the walls as she approached. Will looked up as she came into the room. He played one last haunting strain before packing up his instrument.

The men in the tap room clapped loudly. Faith ignored him, leaving it to Malachi to decide whether or not to provide him with a drink, she was providing no reason for him to linger. To her surprise, Hoag paid for his drink. Malachi poured a large stein of her best short beer. Will leaned against the bar and took a deep swallow.

"My thanks," he said to the captain, who came over to join him at the bar.

Malachi already knew Hoag preferred wine. He pulled a bottle of deep red from under the bar and set down a glass before filling it for the captain.

"Thank you, Malachi, you are a good man," Hoag said before turning to McKay. "I appreciate the music. It's a welcome diversion from the responsibilities of the day. Please come again."

Will nodded as he looked over at Faith, who refused to meet his gaze. Titus poked the fire before adding a log, bringing it to a roaring blaze. She went and stood before it to warm her hands before she left. Will came beside her.

"We need to talk." His voice was soft so that only she could hear.

Faith shot him a sideways glance. "I believe you made yourself clear two summers ago."

He winced. "I was a fool, and I regret my actions, but regardless, we share an endeavor beyond personal affection."

Faith nodded reluctantly. "We do." She hadn't really wanted to become enmeshed in the rebellion but was now in it up to her neck. Her loyalties were firmly with the patriots. "Let's go to the kitchen then."

Will shook his head. "I don't want to disturb Olivia. I will meet you in the cellar. I can take a load of wood down for the fire. I know you've been keeping it stoked for Ellen's sake."

Faith nodded. She let him leave before exiting a few moments later.

Malachi watched her without comment. He spoke little; whatever went on in his mind stayed there.

Even with the fire in the hearth blazing, the cellar still smelled damp. She looked up the steps that led to the outside door. A crack was visible at the top of the frame. Titus would need to fix it before the spring rains started. It was quiet with the exception of the fire. Everyone who slept in the tiny rooms off the storeroom was upstairs working.

Will emerged from the shadows formed by a few barrels of salted fish. This late in winter, the cellar was becoming increasingly bare. "Thanks for meeting me."

Faith's tone was cool. "What is so important?"

"Athena warned me that Butler has spotted a Tory spy in town. He first ran into him in Philadelphia last year. It can only mean trouble." Will shook his head. "There's no telling when the British will move south, but I'm sure it's in their plans. Virginia has too many resources for them to ignore. They will be looking for allies to improve their chances." Butler's looking for him but hasn't had any luck. You need to keep your eyes open for any strangers."

Faith rolled her eyes. "The town is full of strangers: militia, government officials, and those who have come south to avoid the war. Does he have a name or a description?"

Will sighed, running his hand through his hair, making even more of it come loose from its tie. "According to Butler, he's pretty ordinary looking, brown hair, brown eyes, average build. Nothing distinctive."

"So, how will I recognize him?" Faith was exasperated. "There's likely over one hundred men in this town who look like that."

Will shrugged. "I'm not sure, but Butler says he's plenty dangerous. Lovell tried to recruit him once. What is it?" He said as he caught a look at her face.

"I have a new man staying here, called Lovell," Faith said slowly. "Cyrus Lovell. He's been helping out at the tavern in exchange for room and board."

Will drew in in breath. "It could be him. I'll tell Butler."

"What do I do?" Faith's mind whirled at the idea of a Tory spy in her home.

"Nothing," Will replied. "Let Butler figure it out. Just be careful what you say around him."

Faith nodded. She turned to go back upstairs.

"There's one more thing," Will said, putting a hand on her arm to stop her.

"What else has happened?"

Will was silent for a moment. "It's not what has happened, but what could." He paused. "There is a great deal of pressure for all able-bodied men to enlist for a year in the militia. The cause needs men."

Faith stared at him. "You can't enlist. It would violate the terms of your indenture."

"I could if I serve in someone's stead." He drew in a breath. "Georgia does not want Marcus to fight. He's her only son. She's willing to release me from the remaining time on my contract if I serve in his stead."

"You could be injured or killed. You are not a trained soldier."

Will shrugged. "Most of the patriots are not. That's why Washington is working so hard to train the men through the winter so they will be ready when the fighting resumes in spring." His expression was thoughtful. "I haven't answered yet, but if I do this, I could be free in a year's time. Free to start a life of my own."

"Are you well enough to do this?" Her tone was blunt. At one point, Will had despaired of every recovering from the near-fatal dose of arsenic he had gotten a few years past. It was the reason he had given for abandoning their courtship.

Will nodded. "I'm not as fast as I was, but I have pretty much recovered." His gaze turned pleading. "If I am to lay my life on the line for my country. I want to know you have forgiven me."

Faith stiffened. "In the blink of an eye, you went from wanting to marry me to slamming a door in my face. You became a stranger to me and have been ever since."

"I let fear rule my decisions, and I regret how I treated you." Will sighed. "I don't ask you to love me, but knowing you do not hate me would allow me to sleep at night."

Faith looked at him. "Hate only poisons the hater. I don't hate you, but I have no trust left. We serve a common cause, and I wish you no harm. If you choose to go join Washington, I will pray for your safety."

He nodded. "That's better than I expected. Thank you." Will trotted up the steps to the outside door of the cellar. "I need to return to work. Be careful. We live in a dangerous world."

"We do indeed," Faith said to herself. She held her hands to the fire, knowing that nothing was going to warm the chill inside. Tears burned in her eyes that she scrubbed away. Weeping served no useful purpose, and she was through with crying over lost causes.

She walked slowly up the steps that led to the main hallway of her tavern, not sure of where she was going or what lay ahead. Upstairs, the floorboards creaked as men moved around. The militia would be coming in for supper before long. Faith pondered what to do about Lovell. Titus had kept him busy chopping wood and tending stock. That was probably the best place for him. He had offered to help carry in the heavy trays of food and drink, now she knew why.

Faith knew how freely everyone talked over a meal and a drink. She had acquired quite a bit of useful information over the years. Lovell would have to be kept out of the taproom as much as possible without arousing his suspicions. Will may not have said it, but Faith knew she was in the best position to discover what he was up to. She would have to be careful. Spying on a spy could prove to be a deadly task.

Chapter Twenty-Two

Butler hadn't been to the tailor in a while. John Hancock had added to his wardrobe during his time in Philadelphia, and Butler didn't purchase things he didn't need. Nonetheless, the man who ran the business was an excellent source of information. It was well worth the time to drop in on him. He could always use a pair of leather breeches. He went through them at an alarming rate, given that he was constantly moving.

Traffic had slowed on Duke of Gloucester Street, and the afternoon sun rested on his back as he walked toward Nassau Street. The air was mild enough to make the journey pleasant. Within a matter of weeks, grass would be pushing up from the ground, and the worst of the cold would be over. The same could not be said of the colonies further north. His last letter from Hannah had talked about the snow and the challenges of keeping the walk to her shop clear. He worried about her alone in Philadelphia, where the British were undoubtedly casting a hungry eye. There was no telling when he would be heading north again or had time to do that which he desperately wanted, to stop to see her

A fine carriage was pulled up in the yard next door. The coachman, resplendent in livery, held the horse's reins with a resigned look. Butler nodded to him. "At least the wind's not blowing,"

The man nodded. "If it picks up, I'll take Nellie to the barn, but milady's gentleman friend swore he wouldn't be long."

Butler smiled sympathetically. "May it be so." He continued his journey to the shop, pausing to take in the display of a fine man's suit in the nearest window before continuing to the wide steps that formed a half circle beneath the entrance.

Butler entered via the front door. It was a small building filled with shelves of fabric. In one of the large front windows, an apprentice sat stitching on what looked like a fine linen shirt. The steel of his needle glinted as it slid back and forth through the fabric with the speed of long practice. Counters kept customers from laying dirty hands on the expensive fabrics, all the more dear after the British began blockading the coast.

Voices came from the back. The doorway was hidden by muslin curtains, which swayed gently as he shut the door behind him. Butler's ears perked up as he tried to identify who was being fitted in the back. Whoever it was knew how to curse in French.

Butler smiled in spite of himself. He knew from experience that sometimes the apprentices were less than delicate when pinning a garment. The chief tailor did little pinning these days. He claimed it was to provide experience to those he trained. Butler suspected it was due to arthritis creeping into his fingers. Age caught up with them all at some point, and Tremayne was well into middle age.

"Mon Dieu! Cochon Maladroit!" The man swore. "Are you trying to kill me by degrees?"

"My apologies, Master Le Bon, Charles is normally a steady hand." Isaac Tremayne was a familiar voice. He had run the tailor shop with his wife and son since Butler had started coming to Williamsburg.

Butler slipped around the counter, startling an apprentice who was showing a woman samples of buttons.

"Hey there!" The man gestured at Butler. "That's the fitting room. Master Tremayne is meeting with a client.'"

Butler smiled. "Isaac knows me. He won't mind." At least, he hoped not. Tremayne practiced a mellow demeanor calculated to put his customers at ease. But he had a temper when riled. Butler moved on cat feet to the dressing room, where he heard the tailor's silky tones soothing his latest victim.

"Now there, Charles has completed his work. See how the cut of the sleeves flows down your shoulders. The shimmer is from silk woven into the brocade. I was fortunate to receive this in a shipment from Italy before the blockade became so bad." Tremayne crooned as he drew the man into his web.

Butler recognized that tone. He had heard him use it time and again to convince men and ladies to part with their coins. Both men had their backs to him as he entered. Tremayne was fussing over a rich burgundy fabric while his hapless apprentice circled a man who faced an enormous gilt-edged mirror. Butler knew that mirror. It had been a complete nightmare to get off the ship and into town without breaking. But it had helped cement their friendship.

"I see you still offer the best textiles in the colonies," he commented as he moved toward them.

Tremayne spun around, his dark eyes startled, then relaxing in recognition. "Jeremy! It's been months since you last entered my shop. Someone told me you had gotten married."

Butler grinned. "Her name is Hannah. She has a sister here in town."

The other man turned more slowly, his face mostly in shadow, although his long beak-like nose stood out, strongly silhouetted by the light. Butler recognized him in a heartbeat from his time in Philadelphia. He had thought Fornier long gone, from the colonies. Before he could say a word, Tremayne stepped in.

"Allow me to introduce you to Francis Le Bon, of late from the New York Colony. He has come south for his daughter's health. The winters are far too harsh there. I am sure he will find Virginia far more congenial."

Butler nodded. "Welcome to Virginia, Master Le Bon. I see you have already managed to find the best tailor in Williamsburg."

Tremayne flushed at the praise. "My aim is to please my clients which includes some of the most noted men in Virginia."

Butler was aware of that, which is why he came here to receive information in exchange for things any good tailor would need, such as silk and fine needles. Tremayne appreciated him all the more since the blockade.

Le Bon bowed in greeting. "Williamsburg has been a most pleasant retreat from the rigors further north. My daughter and I are grateful for the hospitality of the fine people of this town."

Butler nodded. He intended to discover the man's business no matter what he was calling himself these days. He had little trust in anyone coming out of British-held New York, even if Britain and France had been at odds for centuries.

Le Bon changed back into his street clothes and left moments later promising to return for his suit in a week's time. Tremayne smiled as he left. "He is fortunate to find a widow eager to help him and his child settle in. Mistress Moore has been quite generous."

Butler raised an eyebrow. "Is he staying with her?"

Tremayne looked shocked. "Certainly not. That would be most improper. He is renting a fine tenement from General Washington. You passed it on the way here. Mistress Moore has been introducing him to society." He angled his head at Butler. "I am sure you didn't come here just for local gossip?"

Butler took the hint. "I need some new breeches, doeskin if you have it."

Tremayne smiled broadly. "I have the best skins in the colonies. The natives know I pay better than anyone around. They come to me first. "He went to a cabinet on the far side of the room and slid open a long drawer. As he pulled out an armload of hides, the scent of tanned leather permeated the room. He walked over to a long table and spread them out for Butler to inspect.

Butler ran his hands over them, marveling at the butter-soft hide. The tailor was correct. These were high quality, exquisitely prepared. Tremayne preferred trading directly with the natives. They had been hunting and tanning hides for ages. They knew better than anyone how to get a soft, durable product. "Has Le Bon been in Williamsburg long?"

Tremayne looked at him as Butler compared hides. "It was last year sometime." He paused for a moment. "My memory fails me."

Butler set aside some hides. "I would like two pairs of breeches."

Tremayne smiled like a crocodile. "It was November, just after the first big freeze. He joined us for a few of the harvest balls. He ordered the most elegant suit of navy wool."

Butler smiled. "I have some French Coins I can pay with." He paused as he pulled a pouch out of his pockets. "Have you seen or heard of someone called Cyrus Lovell? He's quite ordinary looking; taller than me, brown hair, brown eyes, perhaps a bit nosy."

Tremayne shot him a look. "No, I have not seen or heard of such a man. The nosiest man I've seen lately is you." He laughed. "But you keep me supplied in useful goods."

Butler smiled. "Indeed I do. He withdrew a small packet from his jacket. "I have some more needles for you, quite fine. I hope you find them useful."

Tremayne purred. "They will indeed, and if you find any lace, I would be happy to take them off your hands." He cast a proprietary glance at the hides. "We have not discussed a price."

After some haggling, Butler agreed to two pairs and selected the hides himself. He knew how to make them. He'd had to learn when he'd spent a few years surveying land over the mountains. He'd also learned the natives didn't care much for stray white men on their lands. After a particularly close call, Butler had decided to stay on the eastern side of the Appalachian Mountains.

He walked back slowly keeping an eye out for the house currently occupied by the man who now called himself Le Bon. Butler wondered if Faith knew that her mother-in-law was entertaining a gentleman. He was certain she did not. It was time for her to visit Eugenia and find out about Le Bon.

He stopped at the white picket fence that ran next to the house, pausing to take a look. It was a modest home, well-kept and elegant. It wasn't nearly as elaborate as the home he had lived in when he had been Francis Fornier, the toast of Philadelphia. He'd fled with his child after his wife's death and the revelation that she had traded goods and arms with both the British and Revolutionaries. He'd been wise to do so. Everyone would assume he'd had a hand in the business, and no one liked a turncoat.

"How in the hell did you end up here?" Butler wondered as he stared into the garden. He could see the sharp geometric pattern formed by intersecting gravel paths that crisscrossed the ground. In spring, the spaces in between would be filled with plants, both ornamental and useful. Further back, he could see a small kitchen where smoke rose lazily above the chimney. He had so many questions, but he dreaded the answers.

He had liked Fornier even if he had turned him down when the man had suggested a more intimate relationship. Butler's interests didn't run that way. He was guessing that Fornier enjoyed attraction wherever he found it. "Le Bon," he reminded himself. The man was now going by the name Francis Le Bon. He had better remember it.

Continuing his journey, Butler went up a short flight of steps where he paused to scrape and wipe his boots before knocking on the door. It was answered immediately by a maid with skin the color of coffee. Dark curls appeared under a snow-white cap adorned with a lavender ribbon. Her nose had a delicate Grecian arch to it and was complimented by enormous dark eyes that stared at him fearlessly.

"Greetings," Butler said, doffing his hat. "I'm here to see Master Le Bon."

She pursed her lips. "Master Le Bon said nothing about receiving callers."

"Who is it, Lenore?" A familiar baritone said from nearby. Le Bon stepped into the entry from a nearby room. He looked unsurprised. "Let Master Butler in. I will meet with him in the parlor. Come, we have much to discuss."

Bemused, Butler entered and the door shut firmly behind him as he followed the other man into the nearby room. Light streamed in from the windows, aided by the glow from a crackling fire in the marble-framed fireplace. Comfortable chairs were arranged close enough to warm whoever sat in them.

Le Bon gestured for him to sit in one while he took the other. "Emily has gone with Eugenia for a dress fitting." He grimaced. "To be a young lady in society requires quite the wardrobe. Lisette was always at the milliner's as well." He sighed, whether at the expense or in memory of his late wife was hard to say.

Butler accepted the drink he poured. He sniffed the liquid, giving the other man time to drink first. "It's been a while since I've had the pleasure of cognac." They sipped in silence before Butler spoke. "So what has happened since last year?"

Le Bon smiled, but his eyes held no humor. "That is quite a tale, mon ami." He shrugged and took a long sip. "But then, you already know part of it, so why not more?" His expression grew remote. "I left before the facts of my dear wife's activities became well known. Her death saved me trying to defend her from both irate patriots and British sympathizers that she toyed with." He sighed. "It was a mess. I had barely crossed into New Jersey when I heard the one ship, I had in Philadelphia had been burned. Given the acrimony I had thought either New Jersey or New York a better place to settle. I still had investments in the Indies, you see. I had hoped the British might be persuaded to let me trade, considering patriots had burned my assets."

"So you went to the British?" Butler found it hard to believe the Frenchman would dabble long on either side. He never seemed too interested in anything but growing his business empire.

Le Bon shook his head. "I went to negotiate with Admiral Howe. He's quite charming, but it was plain his only interest was in what intelligence I might have, not in freeing my ships for commerce." He paused to set down his goblet and adjust the ruffles at his wrist. "Since he was not willing to negotiate, I began making contacts in the city in hopes of finding someone of use. The Admiral was not amused. He sent soldiers to my home to arrest me on a charge of treason." Le Bon snorted. "I am not British. I am a simple man of trade, and I have no interest in rotting on a prison ship. I paid to be smuggled back into New Jersey where, thankfully, Emily was with her nurse, who declined to join us on our journey south." He sighed. "So here I am, unable to access my ships or my assets in the West Indies and hunted by the British on bogus charges."

Butler looked at the well-furnished room. "You don't appear to be suffering much." The house was in a respectable section of town. It was in excellent repair, and its yard was well cared for. Inside, the main room boasted a marble fireplace topped by a gilt-rimmed mirror. They sat in a pair of Baroque chairs that cost someone a pretty penny. Le Bon may have lost some assets, but he wasn't hurting financially.

Le Bon didn't comment but continued sipping his cognac as if he had nothing better to do on a late winter afternoon. "You didn't come here to inquire after my well being." His dark eyes flickered over to the other man. "I always suspected you were in the pay of either Howe or Washington. If you've come to recruit me, the answer is no. I'm too old, and I have a child to raise."

"How is Emily?' She was the daughter of Hannah and Faith's late half-sister. He imagined they both would take an interest in the child.

Le Bon's smile was genuine. "She is doing well. Her mother's passing was hard, but coming to Williamsburg has helped. Eugenia got her into a dame school, where she has made friends. We are gradually settling in here. It is good to be aware of all that is happening up north."

Butler nodded. "Rumor has it the British have their eyes on Philadelphia."

Le Bon swirled his drink, watching the dark amber liquid catch the light. "They plan to retake the entire colony. Washington's retreat from New York has emboldened them."

"He did very well at Trenton."

Le Bon nodded. "Indeed." He grinned. "You're a patriot. Good Luck. Your General Washington is facing the most powerful army in the world. Defeating them will take a miracle."

"You're staying in his house, you know."

Le Bon looked startled for a moment before roaring in laughter. "So I am. Eugenia found it for me. Lady Washington was happy to take my money. So it has worked out well for all of us."

"What brings you to Williamsburg?" Le Bon changed the topic quickly.

Butler shrugged. "I have family here." It was true enough. Faith was his sister-in-law now.

Le Bon looked skeptical. "Indeed."

"I am always interested in information," Butler added. "You've recently come from the New York colony. Given the state of your relationship with the British currently it would be in your best interest to help keep them north of here."

Le Bon shot him a considering look. "Information is a valuable commodity – is it not?"

"It can be. I imagine it would mean a great deal to you to have your ships returned to you and be able to conduct business in these waters."

Le Bon looked thoughtful. "Can Washington do this?"

"The General rewards loyalty. A word from him can open many doors."

Le Bon sighed. "Gold is preferable, but having access to my ships would be welcome. Right now, they are rotting in the harbor, despite my declarations of neutrality. Now that France is in the war, Howe trusts no one remotely French, so my shipping empire is at a standstill Nonetheless, I have no wish to aggravate them. When this is over, I will return to the West Indies. I can tell you this: a southern campaign is being planned. I do not know the details, but it is coming soon. There is a great desire to end this war. It is costing them in many ways."

Butler nodded. "My thanks." He finished his cognac.

The front door opened, and the sound of a young girl's voice echoed down the hall. "Papa? Papa!" A small figure raced into the parlor to hug Le Bon.

"Oomph." He gasped as they connected. "Easy, Emily. Your papa is not a young man anymore."

She released him and looked around the room. A young African American woman followed her in.

"I'm sorry, sir. She took off once I opened the door."

Le Bon shook his head at his daughter. "Emily, you need to remember that you are a young lady now." He looked over at the woman. "Do not worry, Sarah; I am glad you brought her home safely." He looked at Emily. "You need to get something to eat and prepare for your music lesson. Master Portman will be here in an hour."

Butler rose. "I should go. Thank you for the cognac."

"You are welcome." Le Bon walked him to the door. His voice was soft. "You will keep my daughter out of any of this." The threat in his tone was unmistakable.

Butler nodded. "Children have no place in war." The door shut behind him as he went down the steps and into the street. A curtain moved in the window as he passed warning him that Le Bon watched his direction.

Butler wondered if he would be able to keep such a promise. The revolution threatened to bleed into everyone's life, and the British, when they came, would show no mercy.

Chapter Twenty-Three

Faith walked down the path to market cautiously. She had not been able to sleep. Dreams plagued her through the night. Paul walked beside her, silent in the early morning mist. She had spotted Titus, and he was chopping wood as dawn streaked across the sky. When Titus spotted the basket on her arm, he shot the younger man a look, which made him put down his axe and join her.

She knew very little about Athena's twin boys, only that they were freedmen and worked a variety of odd jobs throughout the town. It was still difficult for her to tell them apart. Silas had a small scar on his lip that distinguished him from his brother, otherwise they were both light toned African American men somewhere in their twenties with medium length hair and wiry muscled frames that came from hard work. Freckles lightly scattered over both their faces and arms from exposure to the sun. They shared their mother's beautiful jet-black eyes and her somewhat crooked smile. The red tone in their hair had come from their father, whoever he might have been.

A rooster crowed in the distance. It wasn't Solomon, although she knew the stubborn banty would be delivering his reply before long. Wisps of fog drifted up wraith-like from where a nearby creek gurgled. Faith was familiar with it. She'd drawn water there before a well had been put in closer to the tavern. Some people still filled buckets from its rock-strewn banks or spent days scrubbing clothes when a warm day came.

Faith shivered. She wouldn't want to do that in the winter, even on a mild day. The cold water made her fingers cramp after a few minutes. She was more than happy to pay someone for laundry service. It saved both her hands and her back. The bush crackled nearby. Paul drew a nasty-looking knife from a leather sheath at his belt and stepped in front of her.

They both breathed a sigh of relief when a squirrel shot out and paused to glance at them before racing up a nearby tree, chattering at them for interrupting him. Paul sheathed the knife and fell in step with her. They were both on edge. Faith found herself searching the sides of the path, constantly wary of every little sound until she stumbled over a rock. Her basket went flying as she threw out both hands to catch herself as the hard ground raced to meet her. A strong brown arm caught her before she smacked the ground.

Faith found her footing and straightened up. She huffed in and out as she tried to catch her breath. Paul let her hold his arm until she found her balance. "Thanks," she said between breaths.

"The ground is pretty rough after all the rain last week. You may want to watch your step." He waited for Faith to retrieve her basket and start back down the path before falling in step beside her. "It would be quicker to go around the capitol and onto Duke of Gloucester," he noted.

Faith grimaced. "If you want to deal with everyone going in and out, being questioned by whatever militia is on sentry duty and the traffic that pools about that end of the road." She didn't add that some of the men who hung about liked to whistle and make comments about her. Faith's skirts tended to be around her ankles, which was more practical for her job of running a tavern. The men who loitered around the nearby taverns noticed and made comments about her showing a bit of ankle and calling for her to show more. Taking the footpath to Nicholson and cutting across was slightly longer but saved a great deal of grief.

They arrived at the market without further incident. Paul left her at the entrance, saying he wanted to see his Ma. Among the vendors and other people shopping, she felt safe. It was still early, but cooks, housewives, and working women like her crowded into the wooden building to find what was available. Someone had lit a fire in the fireplace that took up one end. The dancing orange flames broke up the shadows inside and cut the chill of the outside air to a degree. Someone was offering hot spiced cider while another walked about with a large basket of sweet rolls.

Faith's stomach growled. She'd grabbed a corn cake before she left, but it was by no means a full breakfast, and she longed for a large cup of coffee. Turning to where the vegetable sellers lay, she set about her task. By the time she had acquired some cabbages and some mushrooms someone was growing in their cellar, her head was pounding.

"Let me take that," a man said. Captain Hoag stood before her. He led her to a table where people were enjoying steaming mugs of various beverages. He offered her one. She drank gratefully. It was coffee, freshly roasted and sweetened.

"I took the liberty of getting us each a roll as well." He unwrapped a handkerchief and offered her a roll that gave off the scent of cinnamon and mace.

Ravenous, she tucked it in, noting the raisins that spotted the roll. Faith had no idea what she was eating, but it was sweet and warm. "Thanks." The captain had also made short work of his bun. He sipped his coffee as he watched her.

"What brings you to the market? It was early for most people to be about except those with business here.

"I couldn't sleep," he confessed. "I went for a walk and spotted you and that young man. When he left, I decided to ensure you were safe."

"No one is going to attack me in the midst of a crowd," Faith set down her cup. She wondered how long he had been following them. They had kept careful watch until they had hit town. Had he truly been idly wandering the street, or had he been engaged in something else in these early morning hours?

Faith rose and dusted off crumbs. She nodded as a woman came over and collected their mugs. It was time to go. "I need to return to the tavern." Picking up her basket, she headed for the door.

Hoag followed. "I've arranged for some salted fish and potatoes to be shipped there today. I hope that will help your stocks." He paused before saying. "Governor Henry has approved payment for food and board you have provided. You should receive that by the end of the month."

Money was always welcome even if it would be Virginia currency. Faith nodded, silently wishing that every colony didn't print its own money. It made for confusion and not everyone took another colony's money. "I need to return to the tavern. Olivia will need my assistance to feed everyone. She picked up her basket once more and headed out the door.

Paul was nowhere to be seen. Hoag came out behind her, taking a moment to slap his hat on as he exited. Faith looked about the yard. A pale lemon sun lit the sky, almost blinding her from where she stood facing it in the yard. Faint patches of mist still clung to the ground, waiting for the sun to burn it away. A handful of people warmed themselves over a fire built on where the grass had been removed. It was a clear winter day that appeared innocent of evil. She wasn't fooled. Evil lay everywhere, even in the bare light of day.

Her gun hit against her leg, reminding her of its presence in her pocket. Faith was taking no chances. Whether she had an escort or not, it was up to her to protect herself. She froze when she saw Will McKay drive up in a wagon. In the back were bundles of the Virginia Gazette, but it was far from full, beside him was Paul. Both men hopped down and strode toward her, their faces grim.

"Have you seen Rebecca this morning?" Will asked without preamble.

"No." Faith had never seen Georgia or her daughter at the market. They preferred to let Athena do all the marketing.

"Did you see her on your way here?"

Faith shook her head.

Hoag interrupted. "Has something happened to young Mistress Clements?" His eyes bored into both men.

Will ran ink-stained fingers through his hair. "No one has seen her this morning. My mistress says her bed has not been slept in. Needless to say, her family is in quite a state."

"I will rally my men to help search. Once I have put them on the task, I will speak with her mother to see what she knows." With that, the Captain strode off, leaving the others standing in the yard.

Will looked at Faith. "I will walk you home, Athena needs Paul to check with our contacts on the east side of town. Silas is already covering the west." Paul took off at a trot down the road. Will looked over at Faith. "Let's go. Once I get you home, you need to stay there. I can't worry about you while I'm looking for her."

Faith kept her silence. It was news to her that Will was worried. She started back down the main road, eager to get home. Will reached for her basket, but she shook her head. "I can manage for myself."

"So be it," His tone was short. Neither spoke as they walked down the road. He smelled of ink and soap and the leather of his apron. It looked as if he had been caught in the midst of his work. His jacket was misbuttoned, and his hat threatened to slide off his head. A smudge of ink lay across his chin as if he had absentmindedly touched it while printing.

"Do you think she has run off?"

Will sighed. "It's possible. She had a young man she liked to slip out and see. I think he was in the militia."

"Does Georgia know?" Faith looked at him. When Will looked away, she knew the answer before he said a word. "Why didn't you tell her?"

"Because I didn't want any trouble. Truth be told I was relieved when she quit looking at me" He ran his hands through his hair, knocking off his hat. It hit the ground on edge, rolling a few feet before Will could catch it and slap it back in place. "Georgia turns a blind eye to her daughter's behavior. She likes attention and has few compunctions on how to get it. I am tired of being blamed every time that girl sneaks into the shop to bother me."

Faith didn't reply, nor did she look at him. The capitol rapidly approached. Its brick enclosure was topped with a thin layer of ice that dripped on the ground below, leaving wet patches on the ground. Two militiamen stood at the entrance before them. These days, all the ways in and out of the governor's mansion and other government buildings were watched throughout the day and night.

As they passed the gate and made their way around, Will stopped underneath a tall, bare tree that stood out from a group of them that lined the dirt road they were on. He searched her face anxiously. "You cannot possibly believe I encouraged her. She is little more than a child."

"She's nearly seventeen. Many girls marry and have children at that age."

"I'm not interested in any girl that young and definitely not that spoiled. Her mother intends for her to marry well. She needs to, if only to ensure her husband can afford to keep her in ribbons and bows. That girl loves to shop."

Faith laughed humorlessly. "Most of us would like to be able to pay our debts." She looked at Will. "Do you remember what the man she stepped out with looked like? If she's as foolish as you say, she may be with him. Georgia will not be pleased if she's gone and destroyed her reputation."

Will looked exasperated. "Pray God she's not that foolish. There will be hell to pay if she's caught with a man." His expression turned troubled. "There are worse fates." Let's hope she's unharmed. There's been too much violence of late." They continued their journey around the huge brick building and walls that comprised the center of government in Williamsburg. The faint scent of tobacco lingered in the air. One of the soldiers at this gate held a pipe between his teeth. He nodded as they walked by. The other two with him said nothing, although their eyes followed them as they passed.

Faith didn't disagree. First, the two women enslaved to the Randolphs were murdered, then Ellen was attacked. She didn't feel safe anymore. Her pistol bumped in her pocket as her feet crunched on the cold ground. The chill penetrated her toes and ran up her spine, where it goose-pimpled her neck. The feeling of being watched was strong even though they had made it around the capitol and to the path that led to Clarke Tavern.

A low whistle drifted through the air. The eerie, high-pitched sound made Faith jump.

Will looked around warily. "What in hell was that?" The sound faded away leaving no clue of its origin. He looked back at the soldiers who stood at their post, oblivious.

The stand of trees nearby stood empty and bare of life. A few dead leaves crackled as a light wind sent them across the ground. No birds sang, nor was there anyone about either on foot or horseback.

"Perhaps it was the wind," Faith said, although she didn't believe it. The air was still,

"Or a squirrel searching for food," Will said. He squinted as he searched the area around them more than once. "No matter, let's get you home."

Faith fell in step beside him. The Tavern was within sight, but she still felt more secure having him walk her home. Fear nagged at her with every unexplained noise. Anger filled her. She shouldn't have to be afraid to step outside of her own home. No woman should have to live in that kind of fear. Fighting back her own nerves, Faith spoke. "The Tavern is only a stone's throw away. I should be fine."

Will glanced over at her. "Aye, but I will feel better if I see you to the door, and I need to speak to Olivia and Titus anyhow."

They walked toward the tavern. As they drew close, Faith noticed that the gate to the unoccupied tenement a few doors down was ajar. She frowned as she pointed it out to Will. "I've not heard that anyone was moving in."

Will paused, putting a hand on Faith's arm to stop her. "It may be nothing, but let me take a look." Leaving her on the gravel path, he went up to the tenement. Nothing stirred. The gate squeaked as he pushed it wide to enter. Tall weeds filled the tiny front yard. The house had been unoccupied all winter, and no one had come by to tend the lot. Will's feet crunched in the dead grass and leaves as he wandered toward the front steps.

Faith moved closer, curious about the place. It has been a tailor's at one time and then a mercantile, or so she'd been told. It had been occupied briefly when she had first come to Williamsburg, but that family had left some time ago. Will was up on the porch now. He looked through the dusty window "Someone's been here," he called. "I can see footprints in the dust." He pushed open the door and called out. "Is anyone there?" It echoed through the empty room.

As Will stepped over the threshold, a clatter arose in the back.

Swearing, Will took off in pursuit. "Stop," he called as someone disappeared from sight. The back door slammed as his boots clattered over the board floors.

Faith saw a figure emerge from the back, jumping from the porch and heading to the road. The man paused as he saw her. A broad-brimmed hat pulled down low kept her from seeing his face. All she could see was his dark-colored breeches and homespun shirt spilling underneath his jacket. The man turned sharply and leapt the fence separating the tenement from its neighbor, a small theatre. He disappeared behind the building before Will appeared around the side. "He went over the fence," she called.

Will ran and looked over into the other yard. Not seeing a connecting gate, he contemplated the fence before backing away, shaking his head. "There's no sight of the lighter, and he's more limber than I am these days." He walked over to her, a faint limp the only reminder of the poison that had nearly killed him. That was when she noticed the reddish smear on his hand.

Will's face was grim. "There's a body in the back, wearing a militia uniform. You'd better get Hoag here. Hopefully, he knows who the poor devil was."

Faith stared at him. "A dead man how…" she started before Will interrupted.

"Looks like he hit his head." He sighed tiredly. "Go get Hoag. We don't need to be discussing this in the street. I'll get help to guard the place until we know what to do." He walked her inside her tavern before heading to the back, where Olivia's kitchen lay.

Faith paused to get her breath before going into the taproom. Malachi looked up as she entered. His expression became concerned when he saw her expression.

"Trouble mistress?" His deep voice always made her think of thick molasses: rich, dark, and pleasant. As she approached the bar, he set a goblet down on the top and reached under the bar where they kept the finer stuff. Without asking, he poured her a glass of deep red wine that Faith recognized as coming from the last shipment they had been able to get in from France before the English blockade.

Raising the glass, she took a long sip, appreciating the deep, rich fruitiness of the vintage. Placing the glass back, she thanked him before asking. "Do you know the whereabouts of Captain Hoag?"

Malachi's shrewd eyes met hers. "This time of day, he's probably in that room he's taken over for his command center. He don't like to be bothered when he's in there."

Faith's expression turned grim. "This time, he needs to be. There's a dead militia man in the empty house next door."

Malachi's face turned expressionless, although his hand tightened on the bottle. "Do you need me to send for the sheriff?"

Faith shook her head. "I will after I speak with the captain. Thank you, though. Just manage the taproom, like you always do. I'm grateful to have it in trustworthy hands."

"Good luck, mistress." Light from the window picked out silver strands from the steel gray of his hair. It wouldn't be long before it was completely white. Despite this, he was wiry with muscle under his shirt.

She turned to go and then turned back. Malachi was busy wiping down the bar. He looked up when he realized she hadn't moved. "Thanks, Malachi, for all you do. I am fortunate to have you in my employ."

"You are welcome, mistress."

"If it ever comes into my power, you will be free."

He didn't reply. Faith didn't blame him. Promises were whispers in the air unless someone had the power and determination to see them through. She needed to find a way to convince Eugenia that it was the right thing to do. She just wasn't sure how.

She hurried down the hall and out back. The path to the private room was short, but she felt like she wasn't moving fast enough. Part of the path remained shadowed by the building, leaving the frost untouched by the warmth of the sun. As Faith hurried, she noticed the white rim of ice just before one of her feet slid out from under her. Flailing wildly, she fought to keep her balance before landing on the cold hard ground.

Her palms stung as they hit the ground while she struggled to catch herself. Rolling into a half-sitting position, she struggled to get her feet under her on the slick grass. Cold seeped through her skirts and burned against the exposed flesh of her legs.

"Are you alright?" Captain Hoag emerged from the entrance of the private room with one of his lieutenants in tow. He trotted over to where Faith lay sprawled on the ground and offered her his hand.

Faith took it and stood grateful for his solid footing when one of her feet started to slide on the grass. "My thanks." She took a moment to catch her breath, trying to ignore the various aching parts of her body. "I was coming to get you."

"Really, why? I was getting ready to see the blacksmith about some work he's been doing on my men's weapons." His sharp eyes bored a hole in hers. One booted foot tapped restlessly. He was not in the mood to be interrupted.

"One of your men is dead," Faith said bluntly. "You need to come with me." She turned and headed for the side gate without glancing to see if he followed. Ignoring the exclamation and the swearing that followed as he caught up to her.

She stopped when he put a hand on her shoulder. Faith turned to look at him. All impatience had been wiped from his face. Brushing his hand away, she repeated herself. "One of your men is dead. His body has just been found in the tenement next door. I thought you might want to come before I send for the sheriff."

"I would." He paused for a brief moment. "I apologize for misinterpreting the reason for your errand. It was rude. Please take me there."

They walked together to the tenement. Athena's son Paul stood on the porch, the axe from where he'd been chopping wood still in his hand. He nodded when he saw Faith. "Mistress," his dark eyes turned to Hoag. He said nothing but continued to stand in front of the doorway until Faith asked him to move aside. "Will has gone for the sheriff. It would be best not to disturb anything until they return."

"I agree," said Faith. "But I hope the captain can identify the poor man." She went to push open the door, which stood ajar. Paul put his hand on the knob, holding it shut.

"You don't want to go in there. It's not a fit sight for a lady."

"I've seen a dead body," Faith said gently, putting her hand on the door. "Let's see if the captain can identify him so we can inform his family.

Paul shook his head. "You don't understand. The back of his head is caved in. There is blood and brains all over the floor. It's not a place for any civilized soul."

Chapter Twenty-Four

Will said nothing as he watched the body being bundled out of the tenement. Faith had provided a sheet to wrap him in. It was now hopelessly stained with blood, but it kept others from seeing the carnage. One of the deputies tasked with loading the bundle into the wagon looked ready to puke. They dumped the shrouded corpse into the wagon. Will could hear the thump from where he stood in the Tavern yard. A crowd gathered outside the fence surrounding the tenement. Captain Hoag had stationed men along the fence to keep people out while he and the sheriff spoke.

Hoag had recognized the man, a boy just arrived from the backcountry of Virginia a few weeks ago. Private Robert Perkins had been young and eager to engage the British in battle. Will wondered what the captain would tell his family about their son's death.

Sheriff Johnson and Captain Hoag emerged from the house moments after the body had been taken away. Their voices were too low for him to hear, but he would wager they were deciding how to handle the matter. The sheriff ran the town, but the militia protected their own.

The sheriff mounted the horse he had ridden to the scene and headed back into town. Hoag turned back toward the tavern. While his back and shoulders were straight, his face was full of weariness. "I will write the boy's mother and let her know of his passing." He walked slowly around the side of the tavern to avoid attracting interest from the taproom. His boots made a soft crunch as they hit the shells that made up the walkway.

Faith stood next to Will as the crowd melted away. A pair of militiamen remained at the entrance to the tenement to keep the curious away. "What will happen now?" she wondered. Both Hoag and Johnson had asked them what the man had looked like. Neither had been able to provide many details beyond clothing, which was similar to what many men wore, including militia recruits.

"That depends on how they choose to handle it," Will said as he watched the wagon move out of sight. He knew where they were going. He'd overheard the sheriff giving them directions to a cellar used by one of the town's physicians. He wasn't telling Faith that. He was afraid she might decide to follow.

"What do you mean by that?" She stood eye to eye with him, eyebrows raised.

Will ran his fingers through his hair. He should have known she wouldn't let a comment like that pass. "It depends on whether they treat it as an accidental death or something else."

It took a moment for that to sink in. Faith shot him an incredulous expression. "They think that was an accident."

"He could have fallen back and hit his head," Will pointed out.

"Isn't that tenement unfurnished?" At his nod, she continued. "Then what, pray tell, was there to hit his head on?"

Will led her out of the front yard, gesturing for her to be quiet. Her voice was going up as she continued to speak. When they got to the relative privacy of the back, "You don't need to stir up your neighbors," he said in a low tone. "They're already upset about there being a body found so close to home."

"So am I!" she hissed, although her tone had dropped to where it was barely audible. "I fail to see how his skull could have been crushed on a pine floor."

He shot her a surprised look. "You've been in there before."

Faith nodded. "It's been a while. Ezra had me look at it for him. It's well built, and a decent location. It's a shame no one has lasted there. I don't know why. The owner lives in England. This war must be a trial for him."

Will nodded. He wasn't inclined to feel sympathy for a British landlord.

His experience with them had not left a good impression. "If you've been in there, you know the front room has a good-sized fireplace. It's quite beautiful except for the blood and brains splattered over one of the corners of the mantel."

Faith paled at the description. With her vivid imagination, Will had no doubt she could picture what he had seen. "Do you think he tripped and fell back?"

"It's possible," he allowed. "There was a half-empty bottle of liquor on the floor. If he drank heavily, his balance wouldn't have been good"

Faith shook her head, "So foolish to drink like that, but why was he in the tenement? And how did he get in? I imagine it is kept locked to keep vagrants out."

"I don't know," Will said. "He may have wanted to drink without sharing it with his mates." He had other questions about the dead man that he wasn't sharing with her. He was glad when Olivia stepped out of the kitchen and looked over at them.

"I thought I heard voices out here." She glanced over at them. "Come in and warm up and tell me what has happened.

Faith went to the kitchen door before looking back at Will. "Are you joining us?"

He shook his head. "I have to get back to looking for Rebecca. Georgia is out of her mind with worry. I need to return to the print shop." Once the door shut, Will slipped into the nearby yard. No militia men patrolled back here, so it was not difficult to slip in the back door, which was unlocked. Despite the light of the midday sun outside, the interior of the tenement lay in shadow. He stayed against the wall to avoid detection.

Dust covered the door and window frames as well as the floor. No one had lived here in quite a while. It was the perfect place to remain undetected. He squatted to look into the fireplace, taking care to avoid the blood-crusted side. Will avoided looking at it, although the scent of blood filled his nose, making him want to gag. The fireplace held partially burned wood from a fire. He used the poker to dig through the ash and wood fragments. All he could tell was that someone had built a fire not long ago. It had to have been at a time when few people would have been about to notice, such as at night when all sensible folk were abed. A brief cloud of ash tickled his nose. Will sneezed. The men standing outside at the gate didn't notice.

As he rose, he looked down at the floor. Footprints disturbed the dust on the floor. It was hard to say what belonged to the dead man or to the people who had come in afterwards to deal with his body. Moving carefully, Will looked up the narrow staircase. Footsteps were visible there, too, but only a few. Curious, he followed them up to the landing. One pair was large and heavy like a man's boots, the other was far smaller, like a child or a lady. He wasn't sure.

The wood floor echoed under his feet, making him uneasy. Will didn't want to find anyone up there. He turned to go back down when something caught his eye. A faint patch of white on the floor inside one of the smaller bedrooms. He stepped in and picked up a lady's handkerchief edged in knitted lace.

As his gaze circled the room, he spotted a pallet along an interior wall covered in heavy blankets. When he moved them aside, a musky odor tickled his nostrils. "You had a woman up here," he murmured. "Did she have anything to do with your death?" Moving the covers, back he rose. Coming up here had given him more questions than answers.

Will rolled his shoulders. He had responsibilities to the living to attend. Georgia needed her daughter found, and there was no telling where the rebellious Rebecca had gone. He put the handkerchief in his pocket, troubled. He hoped she had not gotten into anything foolish.

Slipping out the back, Will crossed over to the next yard and went down a path that took him to the east side of the Capitol building. Once on Duke of Gloucester Street, it was a relatively easy walk back to the print shop. He was surprised to see Silas at work printing the next edition of the Virginia Gazette.

"Shouldn't you be looking for Rebecca?" he asked as he entered, ducking to avoid the drying broadsides on a nearby line.

"She's back," Silas replied. "She walked right in here, full of apologies. She said she spent the night with a friend because by the time she noticed the hour, it was too dark to come home safely. Mistress Georgia was so relieved to see her she wept. They went upstairs over an hour ago."

Will nodded, relieved he didn't have to deal with the situation. "Let's get this paper printed then." He removed his hat and jacket and rolled up his sleeves, happy to be working on printing newspapers. By the time the sun had crossed the sky and settled on the western horizon, they had another edition ready to send out the next day. Will's neck and shoulders ached from running the press. He was happy to wash up and sit down to dinner with Athena and her sons.

After Paul offered grace, they began passing platters of food around. The Clements had eaten earlier, and they were settled for the evening. Mary, the maid, joined them at the long wooden table in the kitchen, sitting next to Athena. For the next several minutes, no one spoke as they filled their bellies with Athena's good food. It wasn't until they had settled with pie and coffee that Will felt the need to speak.

"Does anyone know what Georgia's daughter was doing that kept her out overnight?"

Athena shot him a glance. "She said she was with the Geddy girls."

"Do you believe her?" Will knew the silversmith slightly, but the man's family was a blur. He knew there were both boys and girls, but he didn't know their names or ages.

Athena snorted. "There is no telling. I'm sure she spent some time over there, but as to what else she did, we may never know. I hope Mistress Georgia keeps a better eye on that one, or eventually there's going to be trouble."

Mary broke her silence. "She's been seeing a man." She kept her head down as if afraid she would get into trouble.

"Who?" Athena asked softly. "Whatever you say will not leave this kitchen."

Mary looked up with fear in her eyes. "She threatened to sell me to a cotton plantation if I told."

Outraged, Will was silent for a moment before saying, "Rebecca is not in charge of that." What he wanted to say was that Georgia's daughter deserved to have her backside beaten for making such a threat.

Athena said, "Mistress Georgia and I will have a talk."

"Please don't!" Mary wailed. "I don't want any trouble. This place is so much nicer than the last one I was at. I don't want to be sent away."

"We'll do everything we can to protect you," Athena promised. "Do you know the name of the man she was seeing?"

"She called him Robbie; he was in the militia, or so I heard him say," Mary whispered. "I saw her sneak out one night when I was bringing in some wash. Mistress Rebecca and he were in the barn all cozy-like. I tried to be quiet, but she came to me the next morning when I was feeding the chickens and made her threats."

Athena bit her lip as she thought. "Go about your chores, child," she said at last. "Let me figure this out. If Mistress Georgia says anything, I'll say I saw them."

Mary nodded her head and left, scurrying back to the house.

"She's about Rose's age," Athena said. She had never forgotten the daughter taken and sold away from her before she had become a free woman.

Will said. "I saw her with someone once. I didn't get a good look at him."

Athena nodded. "I imagine everyone in this house knows but her mother."

"Are you going to tell her?" Will asked with a raised brow.

Athena shook her head. "Georgia doesn't know because she doesn't want to see her daughter as anything but a proper young lady. Telling her anything different would only stir up ill will."

"So what do we do?" Silas asked. He yawned. It had been a rough day between chores, printing the paper, and searching for Mistress Clément's' daughter. They were all exhausted.

"Nothing," Athena replied. "We're better off keeping an eye on the young miss so we're not searching the entire town the next time she takes off."

Will shook his head. "Georgia needs to rein her in before it's too late." It already was, in his opinion. Rebecca Clements was a badly spoiled child in a woman's body looking for a good time. The town was full of militia far from home and preparing for battle with the enemy. They would take their pleasure where they could, and to hell with the consequences.

He stretched out his legs, tired from all the walking all over town. There were still a few hours before sunset, and Will was exhausted. He was too young to feel this old. "Has there been any word from our friends?" Even in the security of Athena's kitchen, he knew better than to risk anyone overhearing them talk about the intelligence gathering they did for the patriot cause. One never knew who might overhear something and inform the enemy.

Athena glanced over at him. "We know they're coming the question is when."

Silas spoke. "Most everyone is waiting for better weather. Spring will be here in a few weeks. The last time I checked for news, no one had broken ground for a new crop." By that, he meant there had been no sighting of the British drilling or moving out of their winter quarters up north.

His twin commented. "Bees swarm when the weather warms. They'll be on the move once the roads become manageable."

Silas snorted. "You haven't been on The King's Highway much if you think it's manageable, particularly when it rains."

"None of these roads are any good in the rain, but they're all we've got." Paul pointed out. And they are better than tramping through the woods."

"Maybe," Silas didn't sound too sure, but they all knew he dreamed of heading west out into the wilderness. The only reason he didn't go was his mother. Athena wanted all her children close to home. She wasn't ready to let go.

Will let the boys talk, content just to sit and listen. With any luck, they would know before the British made it across either the James or York Rivers. Williamsburg's proximity to them made the town vulnerable to attack. He paid attention to ships coming up and down the rivers and checked in with his friends at taverns sailors favored when they came into town. Even if his indenture kept him from enlisting, he would fight to defend his home. He wondered if Marcus would enlist or if Georgia would let him go. They didn't talk like they used to, not since Rebecca had returned home.

When he left the kitchen, he cut around the side yard to avoid the residential side of the house. Entering the print shop through a side door, he spotted Georgia waiting on a gentleman at the counter where they sold stationery. She had recovered from her earlier fright. A dark blue bow decorated her cap and complimented the navy and rose pattern of her gown.

Her clear blue eyes were calm when she saw him enter the shop, and she returned his nod before returning her attention to her customer. Once she had completed the transaction, and the man left she turned to him. "I would like to speak with you in private."

Will nodded and turned to follow her. Paul entered from the back. He eyed them curiously as Georgia instructed him to mind the store for a few minutes. He nodded and went to the front, where he could see when anyone entered from the street. Will went through the door to the small sitting room where Georgia liked to serve tea. He hadn't been here in weeks.

"Take a seat, Will." Georgia sat in the upholstered chair nearest the fire, which held a small fire that burned low in the grate. The light softened her features and allowed him to imagine what a pretty young woman she had been, much like her daughter. The illusion didn't last long. Her piercing gaze reminded him that it was no girl that faced him. Her upright posture and serious expression spoke of years running a business in a world dominated by men. Georgia Clements was tough. "I have a proposition for you, William McKay, and I want you to take time to consider it before you give me an answer."

"As you wish, Mistress," Will said. He kept his gaze lowered. He was well aware that she held his life in her hands. She could sell his indenture to another if he became troublesome. He had never feared that until Georgia's daughter had returned home. Georgia Clements had been upset over Rebecca's interest in him even though he had been adamant that he was not interested in her.

"Before his death, my husband bought your indenture and trained you to be a printer. You've done well, and in time, you could have your own business."

Will nodded, wondering where this conversation was heading. The silence around them unnerved him. He didn't want to leave, not when he was well on his way to becoming a master printer. It was a dream just out of reach.

"I could cancel the remainder of your indenture if I chose, leaving you free to be a journeyman or open your own shop should the opportunity arise." She paused to gauge his reaction."

Will leaned forward, intent on her words.

Georgia's breathing became rough. "The militia wants a man from my house to join and serve for one year. They have spoken to me and to Marcus. I have no doubt they will continue to pressure me until I comply."

"Marcus is a young man," Will said. "I have seen young men in uniform that look to be about his age."

Georgia shook her head. "I'm not losing my son. Marcus and Rebecca are all I have. I will not risk him becoming a martyr to the Revolution." She shuddered before mastering her emotions and looking at Will. "You are older and more wise in the ways of the world. I have no doubt you would survive the rigors of the military and come out unscathed."

Will shot her a stunned glance. "I'm indentured for two more years."

Georgia offered him a tight smile. "Go in Marcus's place. Serve one year in Washington's army and I will release you from the remaining time of your indenture. You will return from the war a free man able to carve out your own future, run a business, marry the woman you want, and have a family who will grow and thrive in a free nation.

Will was speechless. He didn't know how to answer her. The war would be brutal and hard. He had seen the British, there were no better fighters in the world, but if he survived, he would be free. He took a deep breath and rose.

Georgia rose as well and motioned for him to be silent. "Think about it for a few days, then we will work it out." Before she left to go out front, she glanced back at him. "Don't make me wait too long, Will. I will do whatever I must to keep my son safe."

Will nodded. The door swung shut behind her as the bell tingled, indicating someone's arrival in the store. He went to the outside door and into the clean, cold air. The wind cut through his shirt sleeves, making him shiver. Will looked up to the sky, cloudless and blindingly blue. "Dear God, what do I do?" No answer came down, leaving him in the cold, torn between fear and hope, wondering what his future would be.

Chapter Twenty-Five

Jeremy Butler watched his quarry from behind a group of trees. Cyrus Lovell chopped wood in Faith Clarke's backyard just outside the kitchen. Smoke rose from the chimney, evidence that Olivia was busy inside. His stomach grumbled. He hadn't taken time to eat breakfast before leaving that morning. The scent of bacon drifted through the air. Butler knew it was sizzling in the big iron skillet on the iron spider near the front of the hearth.

When Lovell put down the axe, Butler came to attention. The man picked up a load of wood and took it to the kitchen before getting another load to take into the tavern. It was early. The predawn darkness made it easy to hide in the shadows. It also meant that the morning fires in the tavern would need to be lit, which took time. Perhaps time enough to grab some breakfast.

Butler kept an eye on the back door of Faith's tavern as he trotted into the yard and into the kitchen. Olivia jumped as he slipped into her domain.

"You're out early," she said before setting her knife back down on the table.

He gave her a moment to recover before sliding over to the table. He smiled at her. "Yes, it is. I missed breakfast this morning. Could you feed one more?" He shot her a hopeful look.

Olivia gestured toward the table. Her amused expression told him all was well. "Sit down. I'll get you a plate. Everyone else has eaten, but we've not served the men inside yet. There's plenty." She cracked two eggs in a skillet and let them fry while she loaded a plate with thick bacon, corn cakes, and biscuits. The eggs slid off the pan in one smooth move before appearing before him along with the rest.

Jeremy Butler sighed happily as he picked up his fork. "This is a feast. If you weren't already wed, I'd do the honor."

"As I recall, you already have a wife and I assume she feeds you when you're home." Olivia's tone was dry, although her face flushed with pleasure.

"She does," Butler said after he swallowed the first opulent bite. He took a swallow of the mug of coffee that appeared in front of him. "I wish she was here. Philadelphia is square in General Howe's crosshairs."

"Have you told her that?"

"I have." Butler sighed. "She doesn't want to abandon her business or her family. Although I'm sure her former sister-in-law and her son will manage fine without her." What he didn't add was that Letitia and Nathan faced less danger than Hannah. Neither of them was wed to one of Washington's spies. What could happen to her if the British found out gave him nightmares.

He wanted to see her so badly it hurt. Her letters, as delightful and detailed as they were, did not replace her presence. Hannah was too stubborn for her own good, although her last letter indicated that she also worried about the future.

Jeremy set down his cup. If he thought about Hannah much longer, he'd go mad. It would be better to focus on his mission. "What can you tell me about Lovell?"

Olivia snorted. "I haven't seen any British officers popping out of the bushes if that's what you mean. He does his chores pretty reliably. He does have an eye for horseflesh. He's brushed all of them and takes them treats when he thinks I'm not looking. He offered to take that black mare of yours to the blacksmith. He says she needs a new shoe. He's polite and helpful when someone's drunk more than he should. He's put a few of those boys to bed so they could sleep off their liquor."

Butler nodded. It was how he would behave if their roles were reversed. "He'd better not be planning to take Sheba. Someone already tried that once. I'd think it was him if he hadn't just arrived."

Olivia shot him a look. "Are you sure about that? We know when he came to this tavern. We don't know when he came to Williamsburg."

Butler blinked. "You're right. I had not thought of that. Have you seen him anywhere in town?"

Olivia shot him an aggravated glance. "When would I do that? I spend my days cooking. If I see him at the market in the early hours, I'll tell you, although all he's likely to find there is cabbage and salt pork."

"I apologize, Olivia. I know you're busy. I wasn't thinking." Jeremy shot her a regretful look.

"He normally takes off after he's finished helping Titus clean out stalls. He's likely doing that now that he's finished chopping the morning wood."

His meal finished, Butler picked up his dirty dishes and put them in the bin with the others waiting to be washed. He leaned over to kiss her cheek. "You are an amazing woman, Olivia York." He went to the door, buttoning his jacket before heading out into the chilly winter morning.

Olivia shook her head before getting back to fixing breakfast for the men in the tavern. "You need to keep your mind on your task, Jeremy Butler, so your Hannah has a husband when this war ends."

Butler trotted to the near side of the barn, out of sight of the doors. Inside, cows lowed, and someone, probably Titus, was whistling a happy tune. A horse whinnied, probably waiting for its breakfast. Inside, he could hear movement. Muffled voices, their words unintelligible, resounded through the heavy boards that made up the barn. It wasn't long before the door opened.

Butler leaned against the side of the barn, hoping the man would not come around this way. His luck held. Lovell exited and, after looking about, headed around the side of the house toward the side gate that opened near the street. Butler gave him a few scant minutes before slipping around to follow, just missing being hit by the barn door swinging open again.

Titus started before he identified Butler. He began to speak before Butler put a finger over his lips. Puzzled, the other man nodded, standing still as his friend darted around him to head around the side of the house. Titus shook his head before walking toward the warmth of his wife's kitchen.

Butler paused at the corner of the house. The side gate swung shut with a smack against the post. As he peeked around the corner, he saw Lovell heading up the street toward the capitol. He wore a dark green cap that covered his head and ears. The collar of his coat covered the back of his neck. But then Lovell had faced far greater cold in Philadelphia, he knew how to keep warm. He walked briskly up the graveled path around the brick wall surrounding the capitol, skirting the gates.

Butler glanced inside as he passed, noting a pair of soldiers warming themselves over a small fire in the courtyard. A few fingers of smoke drifted out, filling the air with the scent of damp wool and wood. His fingers tingled in their gloves. It would be nice to have the luxury of a warm fire. But that would have to come later unless Lovell decided to hang about in a tavern.

So far, the man continued until he was in the heart of Williamsburg. The sky remained a deep blue, with bands of gray forming on the eastern horizon as the sun began its journey across the sky. The moon formed a pale sliver, kept company by a few twinkling stars, in the trees behind Shields Tavern, an owl hooted, likely hunting for a meal before retiring from the light of day. Butler wondered what creatures were out in the early morning cold.

A horse clopped by. The rider a dark silhouette hunched over the saddle. Like Butler, he headed north toward the market unless the rider's business was elsewhere. Small groups of women walked toward the market. No one spoke. They were all eager to get their errands done and return home. Olivia was cooking so Butler suspected Faith was at the market if not on her way. He had not spotted her, although he hoped she had enough sense to take someone with her.

As he approached the blacksmith, the steady ring of the hammer distracted him. Flames from the forge flared shades of orange, red, and gold from the open shed. Both the smith and his two apprentices were already hard at work. Butler turned his head to realize Lovell had disappeared from the street. Butler hurried to see where he had gone. He had only looked away for a second. He peered down a narrow alley but saw no movement. Butler moved forward, berating his stupidity for looking away. Looking down a side street, he spotted a flash of green.

Butler breathed a prayer of thanks as he continued his pursuit, taking care to stay in the shadows as the sun continued its ascent. Lovell idled near the coopers, which had not yet opened. It made no sense until another figure joined him. Either a slave or freedman, Butler didn't know which, but the young dark-skinned man spoke with the spy briefly before heading back inside. Nothing exchanged hands, but literacy remained a gift for the lucky and the wealthier classes. Butler would have been surprised if he had been handed a note.

Lovell continued on his way over to Nicholson Street. A rooster crowed in a nearby yard, followed by challengers to his cry of dominance. It continued on steadily for a few minutes not dying down until they reached the edges of the Governor's mansion.

Butler followed his quarry as he circled the walls, keeping trees and brush between them. The dead drop he had created for Will and a few others was on the opposite side. He hoped it had not been discovered. Thankfully Lovell did not continue over to that side. He remained on the eastern side. He disappeared into one of the brick buildings that faced the front garden. Butler paused. There was no place he could move closer without being seen, and the governor's slaves and servants were up and about doing their chores.

Lovell had to be meeting someone—but who? Butler didn't like the notion of a British informant in the governor's household. It was too close for comfort. As a loyal and dedicated patriot, Patrick Henry was privy to all sorts of information. None of which needed to fall into the enemy's hands.

Butler looked about, wondering what to do. The clop of horse hooves told him that someone was on the road that encircled the palace green. The soldiers that kept watch over the gate to the mansion called out to the rider in friendly greeting before granting him access.

The horse nickered as the man dismounted, and it was led away to the well-appointed barn. Butler felt a stab of envy. That horse would be in a warm comfortable space, its every need tended to while he froze his backside off in the winter cold.

"Hey!" Butler whirled around. A man on a cart approached. Mentally swearing, he went up to him as if he had nothing better to do. The man leaned forward. "Do ye know where the market is in this town? I came in place of my brother, who knows the way. I'm recently from the North

Carolina colony."

Butler pointed behind him. "Go back to the main road through town and turn left. You'll spot it soon enough."

The man tipped his hat before turning to cluck at the mule pulling his cart. "Maggie, Let's go. We've got business in town."

Butler sighed. He looked back at where Lovell had disappeared. There was no sign of him. He walked closer, hoping to see a familiar green hat.

"Hey, you!" A man in a militia uniform trotted over, a shiny bayonet at his side. "What business do you have here?"

Butler offered him an easy-going smile. "I'm out for a walk. I've not seen much of Williamsburg so I thought I would look around while my wife is at the market." He rolled his eyes.

The other man grinned. "Women. Both my mom and my sister spend way too much time at the market when they come to town. Thankfully, that's not often." His smile faded. "You'd best move along. There have been some women killed recently, slaves. It's got the town on edge. My captain wants us to watch out for any suspicious activity, especially around places like the governor's residence."

Butler looked shocked. "Murders, you say. That's terrible. I'd best get back to my family. This does not sound like a safe place to be."

The soldier nodded. "Not in these times. Be careful."

Butler turned and headed down the green, aware of the guard's eyes on his back as he made his way to Duke of Gloucester Street. Whatever business Lovell had in the Governor's Mansion, Butler would have to investigate it later. There was no way he could slip back without causing trouble.

Fortunately, he wasn't far from Athena's kitchen. He entered the door and took a seat by the fire, stretching out his boots to its steady heat. For the moment, it was quiet. The crackle of flames from the fire soothed him. Before long, he was nodding as the world faded out. He awoke to the crash of pans. Startled, he jumped to his feet, looking about wildly.

Athena laughed from the table where she had dropped a couple of her iron pots.

"Now you're awake. It's a good thing I'm not an enemy. You were sleeping like a small child."

Butler glared at her for a moment before letting out a huff. "It's been a long cold morning. Can a man get a cup of coffee?"

Athena snickered. "You're lucky I roasted and ground some beans last night. You can have some peppermint tea while I get it ready. It will be good for you. I make it for Will every day."

Butler sipped it cautiously. He respected Athena's cookery and her healing skills, but he knew that when she said something was good for him it didn't always mean it tasted good. The tea, sweetened with honey, was very good. He wouldn't have chosen it but had no complaints. Nor did he have any objection to the hot biscuit that came with his coffee a little while later.

Athena listened as he told her about his morning. "He's been talking to some of the enslaved out there. The British have been promising to free whoever helps them."

"Do they believe that will happen?"

"It's more than the American Congress is offering,' she pointed out. "Everyone wants to be free." She sighed. "But I also know the British have great plantations on the islands they possess, and those have slaves, too. I think this is a ploy meant to cause trouble."

Butler nodded. It was his belief as well. "Do we know who Lovell may have swayed?"

"I'll ask the boys to keep their ears open." Athena waited a moment. "Lovell does spend a decent amount of time at Jane Vobe's tavern. You could stick your head in there."

Butler knew the establishment. He had met her enslaved man Gowan Pamphlet a few years ago. The man pastored a church for freed and enslaved people when he was not working for Mistress Vobe. He also kept a finger on happenings in town that impacted his flock.

"I will go see what I can discover." He rose from the table and went back out. The sun blazed in the brilliant cobalt sky. The streets were now busy with people conducting their business. Butler felt restless, so he walked the length of Duke of Gloucester Street, stretching his legs and taking in the town. Everything would change if the British broke through and captured the town. He hoped it never happened even as he acknowledged it could. Williamsburg lay between the James and York Rivers, both of which were navigable by British warships. It was a notion that made him shudder. As Virginia's capital, it was a prize worth taking. He had no doubt it was in the sights of the British military. He prayed Washington could keep them at bay.

Williamsburg hummed with activity. A wagon unloaded barrels outside of Greenhow's store. A pair of men worked to get everything off the street and inside while an apprentice held the door and watched the men work with a nervous eye. One barrel fell on its side and began rolling. It traveled several yards until it came to rest against the side of a cobbler who ran outside and yelled at them to come get it.

A pair of ladies went by in a carriage. If Butler were a betting man, he would lay odds they were on their way to visit a milliner. Not even a war could stop the desire of the wealthy for nice things. He watched a skinny apprentice come out and sweep the walk outside the shoemakers. The youth was probably not much more than twelve and already used to a hard day's work.

It was close to dinner time by the time Butler made it to Mistress Vobe's tavern. A few years ago, it had been known as the Kings Arms. The war changed that. He couldn't remember what it was called now, but references to the king tended to be taken the wrong way. Business didn't seem to be hurting. He watched a couple of gentlemen enter the door, chattering about the price of tobacco.

Across the street, the Raleigh Tavern pulsated with life. It was the unrepentant home of patriots, and they had no hesitation proclaiming it. Jane Vobe's establishment was quieter and a little less peopled. Butler cut around back through the gate on the pretty white fence and around to the back yard where the steady sound of an axe could be heard.

Gowan Pamphlet stood before the chopping block, splitting wood. He wore no jacket, and the sleeves of his shirt were rolled up, revealing muscular forearms. Judging by the pile of stacked wood, Pamphlet had been working a while. The yard smelled of wood shavings and sweat. When he spotted Butler, he paused and set the axe down.

Butler looked at him and the enormous stack of split firewood. "You've been busy."

Pamphlet nodded. "It takes a lot of wood to keep the fires going this time of year. That, and Sadie stays busy in the kitchen, keeping everyone fed. He sniffed. "I think I smell Chicken. We thinned out the flock of some of the old birds. I bet she's making a stew." He leaned over and began stacking wood to carry inside.

"Sounds tasty," Butler said. He helped the other man stack the wood. "I was wondering if you have seen any strangers in the tavern?'

Pamphlet glanced at him, his shrewd dark eyes assessing. "There's been a few. Not many travel when the weather's cold, but with the militia in town, there are a good number of men I haven't seen before." He headed toward the outdoor kitchen with a load. "It's been a few years since I've seen you around."

"I've been away on business," Butler admitted. Even though Pamphlet was a man of God, he wasn't about to admit the work that kept him on the colonies' roads day and night. He had no way of knowing the man's leanings. And the offer of freedom to the enslaved was like honey to a bee, not that he blamed them. He just knew better than to believe it.

Pamphlet deposited his load in the firebox next to the kitchen door. Butler followed his lead. The older man walked back to the wood yard and picked up his axe. Pamphlet had a broad, stocky build and not an ounce of fat on him. He was hard muscle through and through from a life of hard work. To look at him, one would not think of him as a minister, but Butler knew he was devout and did all he could to help his flock.

"I'm looking for a man who may have come into town before the killings started." Butler described him. "Can you tell me if you have seen him?'

Pamphlet straightened when Butler mentioned the murders. His voice was soft. "Do you think he did it? I have grieving families that would like to know." Huge hands gripped the axe. His forearms were thick with muscle. He would be formidable in a fight.

Butler respected the minister too much to deceive him. "I don't know. He came here to spy for the British. What else he does, I cannot say."

Pamphlet looked at him. "This town is filled with people who still feel a bond with that country as well as others who talk of freedom."

Butler flushed. He couldn't deny the irony that many who supported the revolution also owned slaves. It wasn't right, and there was nothing he could do about it. "Everyone desires to be free," he said.

Pamphlet's face lost expression. "Mistress Vobe says she will set me free when she no longer needs me. I pray for that day." He lifted the axe. "Until then, I serve her as I serve my God, faithfully."

Butler had no answers for that. As he turned to go, Pamphlet spoke again.

"I believe your man may be inside talking to one of the barkeeps. He keeps a horse in the stable, too."

Butler flashed him a smile. "I'll go find out."

Pamphlet spoke softly. "If you find he had anything to do with those killings, tell me."

Butler looked at him. "I will, " He promised before going around to enter by the front door of the tavern. He entered the taproom behind a group of men, sliding off to the side to a table in the corner. Lovell was also in a corner. He was near the fire, but he faced the doorway. A middle-aged man with dark hair sat across from him that Butler recognized as Robert Carter. They were engaged in quiet conversation. Butler drummed his fingers restlessly. At least he wasn't cold. A servant came by with a stein of beer. Butler looked up. "I didn't order anything."

"It's paid for," The servant told him before he moved away.

Butler looked up. Lovell smiled at him and raised a stein to his own lips. After concluding his business with Carter, who left, Lovell walked over.

"If you want to talk to me, you just need to leave a message with Chester. I won't be here much longer, so don't dally about it." With that, he left the tap room and headed upstairs.

Frustrated, Butler watched him go up. His beer wasn't bad, but he was no closer to finding out what Lovell was up to or who was helping him. It worried him more than he wanted to admit. After finishing his beer, he left and slipped around the building. He wanted to know what the man's horse looked like and if anything interesting was hiding in his saddle. Then he would visit Lovell.

The contrast from the bright sun to the shadow-covered interior of the barn blinded him. As he waited for his eyes to adjust, he listened to the animals moving about in their stalls. The barn smelled of hay and manure, as well as the faint scent of leather. Light beaming in through a few cracks illuminated dust fairies that danced in the air.

This time of day, the animals had been fed, and their stalls mucked out. Butler moved slowly down the row of stalls, looking for a likely animal. Mistress Vobe kept a few horses for her use, but Butler had seen them before and knew to pass them by. A fine gray stomped his foot in a big corner stall. He was a handsome beast with long legs and a solid body. This was a horse built for traveling fast. "Hello, my beauty," Butler crooned as he reached out to rub the animal's nose. Liquid eyes gazed at him before flickering left. Warned by the animal, Butler entered the stall and crouched down as footsteps approached.

To his relief, the footfalls stopped short of his hiding place. Butler didn't fancy a confrontation in the stall. Horse hooves could do a wicked amount of damage.

Lovell's voice was low. "Hide up in the loft until nightfall. It will be easier to get you out of town then. I have a friend with a sloop who can take you across the York River. You'll be safe once you reach the British Lines in the New Jersey Colony."

The other voice spoke. "New Jersey. That seems so far. The Randolphs will be hunting for us. How can we be sure..."

Lovell's voice was impatient. "Nothing is certain in these times. If you want to be free to live with the woman you love, your future lies with Great Britain. The King will manumit her as a gift for your loyalty to him."

A woman sobbed. "I'm afraid."

The man spoke. "It's the only way, Tabby. We have to run."

Lovell's voice was sympathetic. "I'll get you out of town. Here is some food. Lay low until I return."

The ladder up to the hayloft creaked as it was climbed. Butler peeked out through a crack in the stall. Two figures climbed the ladder, a man and a woman. Puzzled, he watched them, trying to figure out what he had witnessed.

The shuffle of footsteps warned him that Lovell was still in the barn and coming closer. "Let's see how you are doing, Socrates." A hand reached over and rubbed the horse's nose lovingly. "I've been with you longer than any woman. You are far easier to keep happy." The horse nickered and danced around a bit. "What's got you so restless?"

Butler crouched by the door, waiting for the inevitable. When the door opened, he leapt, knocking the other man to the ground. Not taking time to look back, Butler ran.

Lovell shouted. "Come back, you bastard. How dare you disturb my horse!"

Feet pounded behind Butler. He skidded on a horse pile unseen in the dark. He grabbed a stall door to keep from falling as it swung open. He froze at the vision of a body sprawled across the hay. Long blonde hair was spread over a blanket. She would have been beautiful if her head had not been in such an unnatural position. Butler spun as footsteps came behind him.

Lovell paused when he caught Butler's expression before he, too, looked inside the stall. "God almighty!"

"Did you do this?" Butler asked hollowly. He turned to face the other man while keeping a hand at his side where he had unsheathed one of his knives.

Lovell looked sick. "I had nothing to do with this. I'm interested in information, not death." His expression turned sad. "She looks young."

"Sixteen," Butler said. "Her name was Rebecca."

Lovell shook his head. "There's nothing we can do about this, and you have questions to answer." He moved toward Butler before a whoosh warned them that someone else was about.

A lantern rolled on the floor before shattering and releasing both fuel and flame. Fire roared to life. All around them, horses screamed in terror. It was shared by the two men trapped inside. Up in the loft, someone screamed.

"Get out," Butler yelled. "The barn's on fire!" Two figures stared down at him. Seth Payne and Tabitha. "You need to hurry unless you want to burn."

They scrambled down as Butler looked in the smoke-filled barn for a way out.

Lovell had disappeared. Butler spotted him wrapping his shirt around his horse. "Come, Socrates, follow me." The horse reared in terror. Butler opened stalls as he went, hoping the animals would escape. He came alongside Lovell.

They both were coughing. "Is he worth it?"

"Yes!"

"Then let's get him out." They passed other men running in to retrieve their animals. Butler thought he saw Gowan Pamphlet but wasn't sure in all the smoke and flame. They stumbled out into the cold, clean air. Men were pumping water from a nearby well and throwing it on the blaze. A few threw buckets of earth as well. Butler's head whirled as he struggled to put one foot in front of the other. His knees gave way and tumbled to the ground just as the fire wagon pulled into the yard. Grey fog filled his vision as consciousness left.

Chapter Twenty-Six

Butler woke to a pounding head and the sound of someone saying. "He's not dead."

"No, I'm not," he moaned as he tried to sit up. It was a bad move. His stomach heaved, and he had to fight not to retch. He blinked and opened his eyes. Cold air chilled him to the bone.

"Let's get you off the ground." Gowan Pamphlet knelt next to him putting an arm around his shoulders, half supporting him as Butler struggled to sit up. "Take it slow, lean on me."

Butler complied. A grey fog misted his vision for a moment before clearing away. It wasn't an illusion. Smoke drifted around them. Butler coughed as it filled his burning lungs. Memory flooded back. He squinted to try to bring his world into focus, staggering slightly as he rose and tried to walk to the barn.

Pamphlet held him fast. "Let the fire crew do its work. You need to be looked at. You took quite a pummeling. You're lucky to be alive."

Butler stared at the smoldering barn. "Someone tried to roast me alive," he rasped. Two men pumped water on the fire from the engine, dousing the flames. The barn was still largely intact, although one side was blackened. He was relieved to see horses in the adjoining corral. He hoped they all got out.

Pamphlet continued to lead him toward the tavern. "Lucinda takes care of all of our injuries here. She can take a look at you and bandage those burns."

Butler only half heard the other man. He stared at the barn, trying to figure out who had set it ablaze. He looked about. Lovell was nowhere to be seen, neither did he see Seth Payne. "Did everyone get out?" he asked.

Pamphlet looked down at him. "That other man left after he dragged you out."

Butler started to ask about the couple in the loft, then closed his mouth. If he revealed them, someone would start hunting for the young fugitives. He bit his lip in frustration.

Pamphlet's expression softened. "You need not worry. Everyone got out." He looked at Butler his eyes dark with understanding. "All you need to focus on is you. The good Lord will manage the rest."

"I pray he will," Butler muttered leaving himself to the care of the other man. Pamphlet took him in the back, down a hall to a room obviously used by staff. Sparsely furnished with a table and chairs, it was warmed by a small brick fireplace that blazed merrily. A woman waited for them. From the mugs on the table, Butler inferred that someone had been drinking before the fire broke out.

"Lucinda, can you take a look at his man? he was in the barn." Pamphlet helped Butler to a chair. His legs buckled slightly as he sat.

Butler said nothing. He was beginning to feel where he had gotten too close to the flames, along with all the aches and pains he had acquired.

The woman stood before him. Their eyes met before she dropped her gaze. "If you permit, sir, I will tend your injuries as best as I can."

"Please," Butler replied. "I would be grateful." He let her check his head, running her fingers through his hair. He winched when she hit a tender spot.

"So sorry," she said, pausing.

"It's not your fault," he said. His voice rasped from all the smoke he'd inhaled. He breathed in and out slowly, trying to clear his lungs. His throat tickled, causing a hacking cough.

"Here," she said, "Drink."

Butler took a swallow with her help. It was cider, cool and sweet. It eased his throat. "Thank you."

Lucinda bathed his head and arms before cleaning and wrapping a scrape on his arm. She coated his burns with ointment but left them unwrapped.

"You're fortunate that you escaped." She said as she stepped back.

Butler nodded. He owed Lovell for that. He could have left him to roast. Memory returned. "I thought I saw a woman's body in a stall," he said.

Pamphlet nodded. "We found her. The fire didn't get that far. Mistress Vobe sent someone to tell the family."

"Who was she?' Butler asked, although he knew the answer.

Pamphlet sighed. "She's the daughter of one of the printers, Mistress Clements. Although I do not know how she ended up in our barn." He looked at Butler. "The sheriff is coming. He'll want to speak with you."

Butler nodded tiredly. He would have to watch his words. There were some things that did not need to be shared.

The sheriff arrived before Butler had a chance to slip away. His headache had reduced to a dull thud, which did nothing to lighten his mood. The sheriff's questions were blunt and to the point.

"I don't know who threw the lantern," he said once again. "I didn't see who did it. I was focused on a horse I had admired."

"You mentioned that," Johnson said. "A big black? Yes?"

Butler shook his head, then regretted it as the throbbing amplified. "He was gray, a big brute. I was hoping to buy him, but his owner wouldn't part with him."

"And where did this horse and his owner go? I didn't see any horse like that when I arrived."

"I have no idea," Butler said. "I was unconscious for a while." He rubbed his head. The knot was tender to the touch.

Johnson glared at him. "You don't seem to recall much of anything, Master Butler. I may call on you later once you've had time to clear your head." He turned and stomped out back.

Butler had no desire to talk to the man again. He got up, checking his balance carefully. "I need to go," he said.

"I'll walk you home," Pamphlet said, rising from the chair he'd been occupying.

Butler shook his head. "I'll make it. I don't want to take you away from your work."

Pamphlet offered a tight smile. "Mistress Vobe knows where I am. She's got Amos minding the bar while I tend to you."

"Please give her my thanks," Butler walked slowly out the door and around toward Duke of Gloucester Street with Pamphlet at this side. Even though there were few people about, all the surrounding noise felt amplified. He stood contemplating his direction before pivoting and turning toward the capitol. The minister looked at him but said nothing as he walked alongside him. Butler spoke. "I'm heading to Clarke Tavern. I know the way from here. I plan to get a drink and rest my head." Now was not the time to impose on Athena. Her hands would be full, helping the family deal with an incredible loss.

Once he made it around the Capitol building, the noises of town quieted, much to his relief. A few birds flew overhead, calling out to each other as they searched for food. The path was so quiet he could hear the gravel crunching underneath his boots.

A lone militia man stood guard on the porch of the abandoned tenement. He looked chilly with a scarf wrapped tightly around his neck and face. Only his eyes were visible underneath his wool-felt hat. Dark gloves protected his hands but would make shooting awkward, but then there was always the bayonet lashed to his musket. Butler avoided his glance as he passed before entering the gate that led to the side yard of the tavern.

Pamphlet paused. "I think you can make it from here."

Butler nodded. "I'm good. Thanks." He watched as the other man turned and walked back to the capitol, his back straight, his steps steady. "In another time or place, my friend, you could have been one of our leaders." Then he paused, thinking. Gowan Pamphlet was a leader. He pastored people others overlooked, and that perhaps made him a better man than many others considered to be in power.

Linens billowed on a line from where they were airing in the sun. Butler eased around them before the kitchen came into view. White smoke floated out of the chimney in a steady stream, promising warmth. Butler quickened his steps. Just before he reached the door, Titus stepped out. He paused before stepping aside to let the other man in.

The warmth hit Butler like a wall, penetrating his skin and melting both the physical and emotional pain of the past few hours. He breathed deeply, taking in the scents of pine, beef stew, and coffee.

"I guess you better take a seat," Titus spoke from behind. "You look like you have a story to tell.

Butler didn't argue. He hadn't been sure he would make it all the way here. Weariness engulfed him as he shifted. Leaning forward, he placed his head in his hands and took a moment to breathe.

"Your clothes are singed," Olivia said. "I'm guessing you were in that fire at Mistress Vobe's."

Butler nodded wearily. "So was Lovell. It wasn't an accident. Somebody tried to kill one or both of us." Lifting his head, he saw a basket on the table partially full of foodstuffs. He glanced at Olivia.

"It was supposed to be for Seth. Faith found out when she arrived that he was gone."

"Gone?"

Olivia tightened her lips. "Someone let him out. Men were swarming all over those cells looking for him and trying to figure out who left the door unlatched. He escaped along with the other men in that cell with him. The gaoler is fit to be tied."

"Did Faith have any idea this was going to happen?"

Olivia shook her head. "No. She's been trying to get George Wythe to defend him, but he's been out of town. Faith's worried sick about what will happen when they catch up with him."

Butler didn't blame her. There was little patience these days, and quite a few in town thought he was a killer. He could end up dead by any number of hands in town if he was stupid enough to hang about. He fervently hoped both Seth and Tabitha were long gone from Williamsburg. It was the only hope they had.

A hard knock sounded on the door. Silas came in before anyone could open it. He breathed in and out at a rapid clip, indicative of his hurry. "Rebecca is dead. They found her in Mistress Vobe's barn. Somebody broke her neck. It's a wonder the fire didn't destroy her."

"Good God," Titus said. "When will this end? Another woman dead." His hands closed into fists as he stared at Silas, his eyes hard.

"Seth escaped right before she was found," Olivia said. "The sheriff will not miss that."

Titus met his wife's gaze. "You don't really believe that boy had anything to do with all this?"

Olivia had no opportunity to answer as Faith entered without knocking. Tears glittered in her eyes. A few streaked down her cheeks. "The sheriff and his men are here searching for Seth." Her voice turned hoarse. "They think he killed Rebecca." Trembling, she stopped to wipe her eyes. "I don't know where he is. I don't know what he's done." A sob tore out of her throat. "I don't know what to believe anymore."

Titus pulled a chair out, which Faith collapsed into. Her shoulder hunched over as she strove to control her emotions. No one spoke. Butler silently handed her his handkerchief. It smelled smoky, but it was clean. Faith didn't seem to notice as she wiped her face and eyes. She drew in a few choking breaths. "I told them he wouldn't come here." Her smile was bitter. "They're tearing the tavern apart anyway. The sheriff isn't even trying to restrain them. He wants to send a message. Since he can't find Seth, I'm the next best target."

Butler spoke. "He's with Tabitha." The other three stared at him. Butler continued. "I heard them come into the barn with Lovell. Seth's been feeding him information in return for a chance to free her. He may be a traitor, but he's not a killer. Rebecca was already dead by then. We just didn't know her body was there until the fire broke out."

Faith sat still as a stone. "All this time, I thought he believed in the patriot cause. He never said anything to make me wonder."

Butler's tone was light although he worried about what Seth might have shared. "I don't think it was about ideology. The British have been promising to manumit slaves who help them. Lovell must have seen how desperate he was and offered to help for a price."

Olivia shot him an angry look. "Why didn't you tell us about Lovell? We could have watched him had we known."

"I should have," Butler admitted. "But I was hoping if he roamed free, he would lead me to his allies in Williamsburg. I prefer to know my enemies so I can plan for what they might do."

"Now we have nothing," Faith said. "Both Lovell and Seth are gone. I don't know what either of them know."

Titus spoke. "Not much. We've had very few messages this winter. He commented about how fine the horses were, but I don't think he realized what we use them for when the weather warms."

Butler shook his head. "Don't count on it. He knows we have committees of correspondence that send messages from colony to colony. Lovell is perfectly capable of putting the pieces together. I'm sure he suspects, but without proof, that's all he has. We'll have to be more careful. There's no telling what that boy shared."

"Not much," Titus said. "We didn't tell him anything. I was waiting to get to know him better."

"I'm grateful for your caution," Butler said. His head was beginning to clear. With the exception of his minor scrapes and burns, he was feeling better.

"Do you think they will get away?" Faith asked softly. Her eyes were dry, although her face remained puffy.

"I don't know," Butler hesitated. He didn't believe in offering false hope. "They have as good a chance as anyone. Lovell was going to see them over the York River and to a contact that would help them find their way north to the British lines."

Faith rubbed her eyes. "I hope the British keep their word. Seth will have no way back to any of his family now. He's cut off by his own choices."

Silas went to the door. "I have to get back. Will is running the print shop on his own. The Clements have gone to bring Rebecca home."

"Poor Georgia," Faith said. "She must be devastated." She looked over at Olivia. "Do you think we should take some food?"

"I'm sure Athena will take care of that," Olivia said. "Although they might enjoy some of your strawberry preserves. I think we have a jar or two left. They could use some kindness right now."

Faith stood. "There is nothing I can do about my brother. Let me see if the sheriff is through in the Tavern, and then I will go.

Someone pounded on the door. "This is the sheriff. I'm coming in to search the premises." The door was shoved wide open before anyone could respond.

Three men entered the room, their faces grim. "We have orders from the sheriff to search the premises."

Faith made to rise until she saw the bayonet pointed at her. She sank back into the upright wooden chair without a word.

"Stay where you are, Mistress Clarke. I know Payne is your brother, but in my eyes, he's a ruthless killer. I won't let you warn him."

Butler doubted that any warning was needed. The half dozen men sent by the sheriff had all the subtlety of a herd of cattle. If Seth had been anywhere near, he would have seen them swarming over the property. He resigned himself to being trapped in the kitchen until the men had satisfied themselves that their fugitive was not to be found here. Upstairs he could hear the men bumping around. A dull crash told them something had been destroyed.

Olivia's voice was flat. "I liked that vase." She went back to the fire to stir whatever she was cooking in the black iron pot. When one of the men protested, she shot him a look. "Unless you think your man is up the chimney, I suggest you let me finish preparing dinner for the militia we house here. They will be returning from their morning drill soon and will expect a hot meal."

The man subsided, although his hands were far too restless. They tapped the bayonet strapped to his musket. It had only been minutes, but it felt like hours waiting in the kitchen, trapped by the sheriff's men. As the door opened, a long low whistle sounded.

"Let's go," a man said, sticking his head in the door. 'That's the signal. The sheriff wants us to move off, to search the barns on this side of town. No telling where that rascal is hiding."

The door slammed behind them, leaving a blast of cold air. Butler didn't care. He was glad they were gone. He rose to leave, eager to be out of the confines of the kitchen, when Faith stopped him with a hand on his arm.

"Tell me if you hear anything."

Butler put his hand over hers. "I will." Although he hoped that he would never have cause to tell her the fate of her brother. No news he had access to would be good.

Chapter Twenty-Seven

Faith had waited a few days before venturing over to Georgia Clements' home. On her arm was a basket containing her last jar of strawberry preserves and some fresh biscuits. She wasn't sure how to approach Georgia. They had grown close over the past few years, sharing sentiments about the war and the struggles to raise children without a father present. She had never cared much for Rebecca. Faith admitted that in their few meetings, she had thought the girl incredibly spoiled and willful. But to Georgia, she was a reminder of her long-dead husband. She had to be devastated.

Faith thought about how she had been found murdered in the barn of a local tavern far from her mother's watchful eyes. What had Rebeca been up to? She had to have been meeting someone. But why so far away from her home? It made no sense.

The print shop came into view all too quickly. Faith already knew that the shop had been closed for the past two days although Will and Athena's son had continued with printing the paper. Rebecca's charred body had been buried in the graveyard by Burton Parish. It had been done before Faith had realized. It was past time to pay her respects.

She entered through the side gate, pausing briefly to see if anyone was out in the yard. It was empty of life. A breeze moaned through the bare trees, adding to the eerie feeling of abandonment. A woodpecker broke the silence, tapping on a distant tree.

Faith rapped on the side door, which led to the family's living quarters. No one answered at first then Athena approached and let her in. Dark shadows lined her eyes. She looked tired and sad. Deep grooves ran down from the corners of her nose to her lips. She stared at Faith and said nothing.

Faith uncovered her basket. "I brought some strawberry preserves." She wasn't sure what to say. Athena was normally more voluble. The silence unnerved her.

Athena paused. "I know you mean well, Mistress Clarke, but now is not a good time. I will tell her you came by." She started to take the basket when another voice was heard.

"Who is it, Athena?" Georgia Clements stepped into the room, looking pale and tired. She froze when she saw Faith. "What are you doing here?" she whispered.

"I came to pay my respects. I am so sorry about your daughter." She offered the basket. "I thought you might enjoy some strawberry preserves."

Georgia Clements took the jar out of Faith's basket and looked at it. "It takes time and attention to keep fruit over a long winter." She threw the jar across the room, where it exploded against a wall, staining it deep red with the released fruit. "A pity you didn't take the time to keep an eye on that brother of yours. My daughter might still be alive."

Faith stared at her, stunned. "Seth had nothing to do with this."

Georgia's voice was bitter. "So you say. Yet no one was killed while he remained in the gaol. What did you do, bribe a guard to leave the door unlatched so he could slip out?" She stepped toward Faith with an upraised hand. Athena stepped between them.

"She means you no harm," she said as she took the other woman's hand and lowered it down. "This is pain talking. You need to rest. This is too much for you."

Georgia's voice cracked. "My baby is in the ground. She should be here, choosing ribbons for her gowns, planning her future, but I had to put her in a box and watch as they shoveled earth over her."

"I know," Athena crooned. "Let me take you to your room where you can lie down. I'll bring you some chamomile tea. It will help." She looked around at Faith, who stood frozen in place. With her head, Athena gestured to the door before turning away to lead Georgia Clements to her room.

Sobs sounded down the hall as they walked away, shadows shrouding their figures.

Faith took deep breaths of the chilly outside air once she left the room. Georgia had shocked her. Her pain had manifested itself into anger against her and her family. She wondered if it would ever end. She stumbled as she stepped off the wooden stoop and onto the uneven ground. She would have fallen if someone had not reached out to catch her.

"Easy now," Will said. "I've got you. He held her for a moment before setting her back on her feet. He looked at her. Seeing her tear-streaked face, he used his thumb to wipe away the tears. "What is this now? What has happened?" He drew her away from the windows to the side of the building where they could not be seen.

Faith let him lead her away. She took a few deep breaths to calm herself. It didn't do a lot of good. Sobs kept bubbling up despite her best attempts to quell them. After a few moments, she managed to regain some composure.

Will found a handkerchief in a pocket that was not ink-stained. He handed it to her and said nothing as she wiped her face. It took a few moments before she could speak.

"Thank you," she whispered, handing the crumpled fabric back.

He stuffed it into a back pocket. His eyes showed a concern she had thought long since dead. Will asked no questions but waited, sheltering her from the wind with his own body. His ink-stained apron revealed he had not planned to step outside.

She trembled at the unexpected kindness. "Georgia thinks Seth killed her daughter. She is very upset."

Comprehension flooded Will's face. "Yes, she is. We heard he escaped with that enslaved girl. The Randolphs are doing all they can to find them. I hope they are far away. It will be ugly if they are caught."

Faith sniffed. "I should have listened to what he was trying to tell me. Seth can be so impulsive. I didn't realize he felt that strongly about her. That family will never let her go."

Will sighed. "You're right about that." His glance was rueful. "But love finds a way even when it seems impossible. Color should not be a reason to keep them apart. They deserve the same chance as anyone else."

Faith shot him a look as a suspicion took root. "She said Seth's cell door had been left open. How could that have happened?"

Will's face lost all expression. "I'm not the gaoler, so I'm not familiar with their practices. Though I imagine it's like many things in this life. Where there is a will, there's a way." He wrapped an arm over her shoulders. "Let's get you home. You'll get sick standing out in the chill." He took the basket off her arm, seeing the forlorn bread that had not been touched.

"I'll drop this off in the kitchen. When Georgia recovers, she will appreciate your kindness."

Faith doubted Georgia Clements would want to see her anytime. She didn't object to Will's company and let him lead her to the white-painted outbuilding where Athena worked to feed the Clements family and their staff. It was quiet, although a pot bubbled on the fire. Will removed the loaf and placed it on the table gently.

"Athena now has an assistant who helps her in the kitchen. I don't see her, but I imagine she's close by. Either one of them will take care of the bread." He glanced at Faith. "Please thank Olivia for providing it."

Faith nodded. She didn't feel like talking. Will took her hand and led her back to the main street.

"I'll see you home, then I have to return to the press. Silas and Marcus are printing as quickly as they can. Eduard and Henrik have been helping where they can. Tomorrow we will reopen the shop. We can run it until Georgia feels able to come out." He paused. "Please forgive her. Rebecca was her blind spot. In her eyes, that girl could do no wrong. I don't know if she will ever accept the truth."

Faith shot him a sideways look. "What is the truth?" She had heard of her pestering Will. She wondered what else she had done.

Will didn't answer. "Let's get through town. This is too public a place for that sort of conversation." He dropped her hand as they moved down the walkway toward the capitol behind which lay Faith's tavern. The mild weather had brought people out. Shopkeepers cleaned their windows with rags and vinegar, leaving a sharp scent in the air. A few wagons rumbled down the street, their drivers headed to buy goods while the roads were dry. A pair of boys shouted as they ran chasing a hoop in the open field in front of the armory. It was a beautiful day for those not in mourning.

Faith was eager to get home. Nothing suited her more than going home to Clarke Tavern, where she knew the routine, and there were no unwelcome surprises. She shied away from thinking about Seth. She didn't know what to tell their father. Anger and hurt flooded her emotions, both at him and herself. Faith had done nothing to help him, but then what was there to do? Elizabeth Randolph ruled her home with an iron fist. She would never have agreed to free Tabitha.

Faith swallowed a knot in her throat. Seth was too young to get into so much trouble. He'd come here to make a new start; instead, he had been accused of two, now three gruesome murders and had run away with an enslaved woman he'd fallen in love with. Where would it all end? She would never know. All she could do was hope and pray they escaped to somewhere that their enemies would never find them.

All too soon, the sturdy brick walls surrounding the capitol came into view. About a dozen militia lay ahead of them, released from drill and eager to go get a drink. They watched them sprint around the capitol, laughing with each other.

"They're no more than boys," Will said suddenly. "I wonder how many will come home when this war is over?"

Faith glanced over at him. He was older than a good number of them, although she was certain he was not much over thirty. He had faint crinkles at the corners of his eyes and a few worry lines on his brow. None of which took away from his appearance.

Will smiled at her ruefully. "You're giving me the eye. Have I grown old to you?"

"You never will to me," she said. "A good man ages like fine wine."

He was quiet for a moment, and Faith wondered if she had spoken out of turn. They turned to go around the wide expanse that formed the grounds of the capitol. "I'm glad to hear that. There is no guarantee that this war will leave any of us unscathed. I would like to know that there is peace between us in case I should be called to leave."

Faith stopped and grabbed his arm. "What are you talking about? You are indentured. You can't go anywhere unless Georgia says so."

Will's expression was serious. "She's made me an offer. If I go and serve in Marcus' place for a year, she will release me."

Faith paled. "You are considering joining the militia?"

He nodded. "I've been thinking about it since she first suggested it. Now that she's already lost a child, she can't lose the only one she has left."

"So you would choose to risk your life for his?" Faith couldn't believe it. She had seen the men drilling constantly, waiting for the British to come. Hoag had told her that some units had already been called north to join Washington. Now Will was telling her he would be joining the fight as well. "Does Jeremy know about this?"

"It's not his decision, it's mine." Will watched the men guarding the south entrance to the capitol building. "All of us will have a part in this war. I at least know what I'm facing. I've seen the army in action in Scotland. They know how to fight."

Faith closed her eyes. She wasn't prepared to deal with this. "You could die."

"Aye. A lot of men will, but with any luck, I will come out of this in one piece with my freedom." His voice was soft. "I need to be free, Faith. I came to this land to be my own man, not to serve another until I'm old and gray. It's time."

A rising flood of panic filled Faith. "No," she breathed. "There has to be another way." She gripped his arm hard. "Think about what you are saying. The winters are brutal up north and you don't know anyone up there. Where will you turn when you are hurt or sick?" She swallowed hard. "How will we know if something happens to you?"

Will looked at her. "I've already agreed to go. I'm training Georgia's new indentured men to run the press. I've worked there for four years. With my freedom, I have the skills to run my own press. I can save my pay towards that. We could have a life together where you wouldn't have to wait on people all day long."

Faith stiffened. "I run a business. I am proud of that. I have kept a roof over my family's head and fed and clothed my son and my employees. I am not a servant."

Will raised a hand in surrender. "I didn't mean it like that. You have done well. Many widows do not balance the burdens of work and family well." He shrugged. "I've always wanted to take care of you, allow you to have some time to yourself. I've loved you since we first met. Nothing has changed about that."

"You're the one who changed that," Faith reminded him. "You dropped me like a bad piece of fruit with no warning."

Will ran his hands through his hair. "I nearly died of arsenic poisoning. I thought I was going to be an invalid. I still have some issues from it. I could not burden you like that."

"We should have discussed it." Faith shot him a pointed glance. "Wherever life leads us, we should discuss important decisions. I will not tolerate that sort of behavior again."

"I apologize," Will said. He shot her a hopeful look. "Does that mean you've forgiven me?"

Faith didn't answer at first. She hadn't planned on saying that. She hadn't wanted to admit that the sight of him still made her heart quicken no matter how many times she called herself a fool. "I'm no longer angry, but I don't feel comfortable trusting you yet."

"That's something," His tone was subdued. "I suppose I deserve that even though my goal was to protect you. Will you accept my letters after I go?"

Faith nodded. "I will write to you until you return safely to Williamsburg." They had nearly reached Faith's home. Titus was sweeping the porch. Next door, the soldiers had cleared away from the abandoned tenement. In the back Olivia would be working hard to make sure all was ready for dinner in a few hours. She paused at the bottom of the steps. "I need to go help Olivia. We will have a lot of hungry men coming back from their morning drill."

Will nodded. "I will leave you to it. I'm needed at the press." He turned and walked back through the gate without looking back. The wind blew his tricorn hat, He put up a hand to keep it in place as he moved swiftly away, back to his side of town.

Faith went up the steps and into her tavern. Titus had returned inside. The broom rested in a corner. The faint rattle of crockery turned her attention to the taproom. Malachi was putting clean steins on the shelves behind the bar. He turned as she entered, his sharp ears alerting him to her presence.

"Mistress Clarke," he said. "Good morning. I trust you are well."

Faith smiled as she lied. "I am fine—and yourself?"

He nodded. "A good night's rest is a blessing." He rolled his shoulders. "I appreciate such things more and more as I grow older."

"I think we all appreciate the gift of rest." She turned and left him to his work. Since his arrival she had not had to worry much about the taproom. Malachi knew how to settle men with a soft word or a quickly poured drink. Titus helped with those who overindulged which left her time to work on other things.

She was unsurprised to find Titus in the yard. This time of year, the fires needed constant replenishment. Since Lovell had apparently taken off, there was one less hand to tend to things. He had been very helpful even if he was also a spy. Butler should have told her. It still irritated her that he had chosen not to.

When she opened the kitchen door, a billow of smoke came out. Olivia ran out with a smoking pan and dumped the contents on the ground. The black smoldering lump was unrecognizable. A heavy cloth was wrapped around the pan's handle as Olivia continued to shake it before letting it fall on the ground, where it hissed.

"Are you alright?" Faith stared at the mess and at Olivia, whose breath was going in and out at a rapid rate.

"Grease fire," she huffed. "Stupid of me to look away. It could have burned the kitchen down." Her hands shook as she wiped them on her apron, part of which was charred on the edges.

Spotting the blackened edges, Faith approached. "Are you hurt?" Running her eyes down the other woman's clothing, she couldn't see anything besides the apron. But she was worried. She turned Olivia's palms over and checked them.

"I know not to pick up a hot pan bare-handed," Olivia said, taking her hands back. "I'm not burnt, just aggravated. I was going to use that fat back in some beans."

Faith shrugged. "At least it's not any worse than a bit of burned meat." She eyed the other woman curiously. "You always pay attention to the fire. What had you so distracted?"

Olivia gestured. "Come and see. I need to salvage dinner before all those boys in the militia get here." She propped the door open with a rock to air out the place. Smoke lingered strong enough to irritate eyes and nose.

Faith used her sleeve to wipe her stinging eyes. She didn't object when Olivia propped open a window as well. The air was cold, but it was breathable. Stepping inside cautiously, she looked about to make sure no stray sparks remained to cause trouble. The room looked untouched, with the exception of the bare spider that leaned at an angle in the fire and the acrid air.

Dorcas entered behind them. "I smelled smoke. I came as soon as I could. Is everything alright?" She looked about the room as well. Her apron was full of turnips from the root cellar. She took a wooden bowl and placed them inside it. When she moved the bowl, a scrap of paper flew up. Caught by the breeze, it fluttered through the air until Faith grabbed an edge, ending its flight.

"What is this?" she said, looking at the torn paper in puzzlement.

"Titus brought it here. He helped the other men take Rebecca's body home to her mother a few days ago. That scrap fell on the ground when they put her in the wagon. Titus stuck it in his pocket and forgot all about it until he found it again this morning."

Faith walked over to the window for better light. The scrap was a little bigger than the palm of her hand. One edge was jagged from being torn. Whoever had written it had a strong, bold hand. All she could read was *"Vobe barn, 9 am. Come."* The rest was torn off. She turned over the other side, to see a few figures written down for food and drink. The handwriting on this side was her own.

"This is from the ledger I keep." Faith turned to the other side. "I don't know who wrote this or how they tore it from my ledger." People went in and out of the tavern all day. She frequently kept the ledger on her desk for when she had a moment to tally accounts and take payment although the governor had been very good at reimbursing her for expenses related to feeding and housing the militia. Outside, the steady chop of the axe continued as Titus worked to provide fuel for both the kitchen and tavern.

Olivia turned to face Faith. "That girl was seeing a boy from the militia, the same one that turned up dead next door. Now she's dead. I think whoever did it is staying with us." Her words floated across the air, carrying a chill all their own.

Faith stared back at her. "I think you're right." What she didn't say was she had no idea what to do about it.

Chapter Twenty-Eight

Jeremy Butler trudged through town, weary and cold. Despite searching in every hiding spot he could think of, Cyrus Lovell remained elusive. It troubled him. But then he was no longer sure what he would do once he located him. The man had saved his life. Dragging him out of the fire had been a risk Lovell didn't have to take. It would have been far more convenient to let his nemesis die in the blaze. As grateful as he was to be alive, Butler was both surprised and confused by the other man's actions. He hoped he would have done the same had their roles been reversed.

Loud cursing startled him out of his reverie. A stray dog ran out of the market, a large sausage in its teeth. He was pursued by a man intent on its demise, given the violence of his threats. The dog knew how to evade an enemy. It dodged around groups of people and wagons, making it difficult to follow. Amused, Butler watched the shaggy beast negotiate the street before disappearing down an alley. It would find a safe place to hide before devouring it ill-gotten meal. Butler remembered being a hungry street rat himself long ago. He walked over to the irate vendor and gave him a few coins to cover the dog's meal.

"You need to keep a better eye on your dog," the man muttered before trotting back to the market. The door slammed behind him, just in front of a group going in. Early morning was the busiest time. Cooks and wives, along with other servants, came to get the best choices of items. Or to get something before vendors ran out.

Butler didn't correct him. In his line of work, he had no place to keep a pet, although he wondered what Hannah would say if he showed up with the creature in tow. They'd never discussed a dog. He didn't know if she liked them or not, although, being raised on a farm, she undoubtedly knew how to care for animals.

For lack of a better idea, he turned down the alley where the dog had gone, wondering where the creature had taken refuge. It was probably long gone. Nonetheless, Butler looked around for a sign of its shaggy hide.

The alley appeared deserted. It was a narrow space between a tavern and another business, possibly a cooper, by all the scraps of wood lying about. A few barrels stood outside of the buildings, holding rags and other items. One lay in pieces on the ground, several of its staves broken and splintered.

His nose wrinkled as he picked up the scents of urine and stale beer. Apparently, someone had used a corner as a privy as well as a spot to finish off a drink. He spotted a few broken steins outside a door. Likely from the tavern that faced Duke of Gloucester Street. A faint rustle from a rubbish heap made him jump until he spotted a rat scurrying away with something in its jaws. He suppressed a shudder. Butler hated rats. They reminded him of the ship that had brought him and his family from Ireland so many years ago when he'd been little more than a skinny child. Being shut in that hold with the vermin had nearly driven him mad.

The buildings surrounding him cast the narrow alleyway into shadow, making it hard to see what was hidden behind the piles of rubbish. He picked up his pace, desiring to get back on a regular street and away from whatever lurked beyond view. A sudden thump made him spin around, only to see a cat run out across the alley in pursuit of prey. He wished it happy hunting.

A wave of relief swept over him as he spotted a street just ahead. Butler broke into a trot, eager to feel the sun on his face and breathe fresh air. He wanted the sun on his face and bright light to chase away all the shadows. His ear barely caught a whisper of steps before an arm locked around his throat. Terror flooded him as his airway was choked off. Butler thrashed, trying to break his assailant's hold. He stomped the other man's instep, causing him to curse. His elbow went back, trying to connect with his ribs. No luck. The other man stayed out of reach. Butler clawed desperately as he tried to throw his assailant off.

The grip on Butler's throat tightened, cutting off his air. The strain of trying to breathe was overwhelming. Spots rose over his eyes as he felt consciousness leave. His last desperate thought was of Hannah waiting for him in Philadelphia. Would she ever know what had happened to him?

He awoke to the smell of hay and horses. As he lifted his head, it bumped into something hard. As his eyes opened, he realized he was tied to a pole in a barn, sitting on hay-strewn ground. Butler took in a deep breath, glad to be alive.

"It's about time you awoke." Lovell walked into view before squatting down where they were eye to eye. "You've been out for over an hour."

Butler glared at him. "Maybe you should have tried talking to me instead of trying to kill me." He tried to knock the other man over with his legs. The other man scuttled back just out of reach.

Lovell chuckled. "If I wanted you dead, we wouldn't be having this conversation. You're still pretty lively, which is good. You need to pay attention. We need to talk, and I prefer to do it where I don't have to worry about you turning me in to your patriot friends. I'm too pretty to hang."

Butler shot him a look. "That's not why I was looking for you. Although once we win this war, you will be a hunted man. I was wanting news on young Payne. I assume he made it out of Williamsburg?'

"He did," Lovell said. "He and his lady love made it over the river and made contact with a friend of mine. Beyond that, I have no idea where they are." He quirked an eyebrow at Butler. "I didn't think you were the romantic type." He wrapped his arms around his legs as he sat back looking as if he hadn't a care in the world.

"Look who's talking," Butler snapped. "You're the one who broke him out of the gaol."

Lovell shook a finger. "That was business. I didn't want him revealing my whereabouts to anyone. His sister or her cook visited him nearly every day with food or something. I knew it wouldn't be long before that boy slipped up." Lovell sighed. "I would have liked to have kept him here a while. He was useful. "He looked over at Butler. "He may be a lovesick puppy, but he's no killer."

Butler's throat hurt. His voice rasped. "How would you know?"

Lovell smiled. "When he wasn't at the tavern, he was either working for me or sneaking off to see that girl. He was nowhere near where those two enslaved women were. I've kept my eyes on him. I wanted to make sure he wasn't playing both sides."

Butler tried to swallow, but the knot in his throat was too hard. He glared at Lovell as he tried to find a way to loosen the ropes that held him fast.

"Here," Lovell offered him a sip from a flask. When Butler jerked back, Lovell took a long pull before offering again. This time, Butler took it, enjoying the cooling taste of cider. He bet it was some of Faith Clarke's. She brewed some of the best beverages in town. He gulped down another swallow before Lovell took it away.

"I don't have a lot of that left, thanks to you." Lovell took another sip. "I'm leaving tonight, so we need to complete our business.'

"I'm not holding you up,' Butler said. "I might feel more like talking if you'd loosen these ropes."

Lovell snorted. "I'm not that stupid, mate. You'll get loose when I'm out of range. You're a little too good at tracking, as I recall." At Butler's surprised look, Lovell grinned. "We were once on the same side, years ago. I was a mere foot soldier, fresh to the frontier. You were there with your master, helping scout the area for Colonel Washington. He took a shine to you. It's little wonder you decided to rebel when he did."

"You fought the French?" Butler racked his brain but couldn't recall the man.

"I did and when I got home, I decided I wanted nothing more of army life." He shrugged. "Now, here I am."

Butler eyed him. "You've had experience killing people."

Lovell squatted near Butler. "In war. I didn't care for it much. I still don't. The Quakers have a point with their philosophy of nonviolence although I don't agree with all of it. I don't know who is killing women around here, but it's not me. You need to cast your eyes elsewhere unless it's been you."

"Hell no," Butler snapped. "Those dead women have spooked people. They're afraid to go out alone."

"They should be," Lovell said. "These are dangerous times. Your killer has made it impossible for a stranger to go unnoticed. People watch me and follow me about. They want blood, and I'm not giving them mine."

Butler looked at him. "So why are we having this conversation? I doubt you really felt the need to assure me of your innocence." He rested his head back against the beam that held him. If he leaned close enough back, it gave him a slight amount of give in the rope wrapped around his wrists. It was rough and cut into his skin. Butler bit his lip as he tried to find a way to distract his captor.

Lovell rose and began pacing back and forth. He wore well-made boots of deep brown leather that had been polished to a high gloss, a military man's boots. Hay crunched underneath his soles. "We're not very different, you and me. We chose different masters, but we both work towards the end of peace in these colonies. Once the British squash this rebellion, we may become allies once more."

Butler stared at him for a moment. "You're not trying to recruit me again, are you? I was born Irish. I would prefer the British go back to their little island and leave other countries alone."

Lovell snorted. "Then you should know how futile fighting is. I know you are too stubborn to admit you're fighting a losing cause, and I will mourn if you're caught behind enemy lines. But I have a more practical reason for our little meeting."

He took a folded piece of paper out of his vest pocket. "Seth wanted to leave a message for his sister, and I agreed to deliver it. Please make sure she gets it. It is likely the last she will ever hear from him." He leaned over and placed it in Butler's hat, which rested on the ground nearby. "They got married, by the way. That pastor for the slaves, Pamphlet, wed them before they left town."

Butler blinked. He knew Gowan Pamphlet. It really didn't surprise him that he had performed a marriage for the young couple. He was probably the only minister they could ask, given their situation. "I'll give her the letter. Will you let me go now?"

Cyrus Lovell shook his head. "Not yet, my friend, although I'm sure you are already working your way out of that rope. One more thing before I go. I saw Rebeca Clements sneak out of her house the other night. I was curious, so I followed her. Imagine my surprise when she slipped through the gate of the abandoned tenement next to Clarke Tavern. Her lover had kindled a fire in one of the rooms. They had blankets spread on the floor and a bottle of wine. She'd brought a basket of goodies with her, so they dined together before becoming intimate.

Butler stared at him. "She was meeting a lover?" Somehow, it didn't surprise him, although he wondered what else Lovell had to share.

Lovell nodded. "She also brought some coins and jewelry she'd taken from home. I believe they were planning on running away which would have made her young man a deserter, he was a militia recruit."

Butler stared at him. "A young militia man was found dead in that house."

"I'm aware." Lovell's face was serious. "He and she were very much alive when I left. I don't know who found them, but I think your killer is close by. The tavern is full of militia, and I'm pretty sure he was one of them. I'm sure some of his mates knew something. It makes me wonder if someone got jealous and decided to confront him."

"Did you see anyone else around the tenement?" Butler could feel a knot starting to loosen. He could also feel blood from his abraded wrists running down his hands.

Lovell shook his head. "No. That worries me. I'm pretty good at keeping an eye out. Not many men can sneak up on me. If anyone was there, they would have to be skilled at going undetected."

"Or someone who hunts regularly," Butler said. One knot slipped loose. There were at least two more before he could be free. "Who do you think found him? Rebecca didn't die until a day or two later."

"That is the mystery," Lovell admitted. "She had to have left before the young man met his killer. There's no way he would have let a witness escape to report his crime. Those militia officers have been working on discipline. They would have executed someone who killed one of their own."

Butler didn't disagree. He wiggled the loose end of the rope, hoping to find where he could slip it through another knot. He shot Lovell a glance.

"Why have you been meeting Robert Carter?"

Lovell shot him a glance. "Carter is an influential man. He's accepted by everyone regardless of their stand. He is a useful man to know."

Butler leaned against the pole, trying to get more slack in the rope. "Playing politics now?"

Lovell laughed. "Wouldn't you like to know?" Outside, a low whistle sounded.

"Well, there's my ride. I doubt we will meet again this side of a victory. Good luck, Irishman. I hope you find your killer before he strikes again." He picked up his black felt hat, which had been lying on top of a trough. "I imagine you'll get loose sometime before dark." He laughed as he slipped out the door.

Butler heard the horses trot away as he was left alone in the shadowed barn. A faint rustle in the corner warned him that something else was there besides the mule he could see in its stall. "Can anyone hear me?" he shouted desperately as he tried to break free. The rope held fast. He twisted to try to get another knot loose.

"Help!" No one responded. Butler kicked the ground in frustration. From the back, a low creak caught his attention. "Hello? Can you hear me?" The soft sound of feet drew close. He twisted around to try to see who or what approached. Nothing emerged from the shadows. He slumped back against the post and focused on trying to untie the knots that held him prisoner.

Butler jumped when he felt a wet tongue on his hand, followed by the pants of an animal. He twisted about to see the shaggy stray he had seen at the market. "Good boy," he crooned. "Good boy." The dog looked at him. Its eyes were a clear blue. It bore close resemblance to a wolf despite its doggy friendliness. A wave of relief swept over Butler when he felt its paws and teeth dig into the rope that held him. Somehow, he had found a friend when he needed one most. As he felt the rope break, he spoke to the animal. "Come on, friend, let's go home."

Chapter Twenty-Nine

Faith served the men gathered for supper. She was beginning to get used to the crowded tap room, full of young militiamen and their officers. Though often boisterous, they were not disruptive. By the end of the day, they were just tired and hungry. She wondered if they wrote to their wives and mothers. She hoped so. The idea of waiting for word and never knowing unnerved her. They reminded her of her brothers although she had not heard if any had joined the fight. Her older brother, Caleb, was a staunch Quaker who didn't believe in war. He also had a son born six months ago. Faith had sent them some things which she hoped they had received. Mail delivery had become more uncertain with the conflict. She, like so many others, would have to learn to deal with it. Faith pushed the idea out of her mind. There was plenty here to keep her busy.

Thanks to the governor she had just received a shipment of foodstuffs to help feed them. Olivia had put Ellen and Dorcas to sorting the barrels of turnips and salt fish, among other things, so that she could plan meals later. Both she and Faith focused on feeding the men the evening meal. Thankfully, it was far less complex than dinner.

The men took their bowls of food with no complaint, happy to be out of the cold and have a hot meal before them. There wasn't an empty seat to be had, so many had crowded inside. Faith wondered where so many men had come from. Her inn only held so many although she had noticed some men sleeping on pallets in the hall upstairs. She would need to ask Captain Hoag about the added men.

The fire crackled as Titus fed it, making the flames flare as they received more fuel. Something about the warmth of the hearth comforted her. She went to stand before it for a moment, warming her arms and legs. Already shadows gathered outside. It would be dark within a few hours. Faith shivered. She was glad to be out of the cold and dark. From the cloud cover, she suspected there would be rain overnight. It would not be a time for anyone to be out and about.

Titus whispered to her as he passed. "When you get a moment, go see Olivia."

Faith nodded, puzzled. They had already served the men, and it was too early to gather dirty dishes. But then it could be anything. Olivia was the voice for the rest of the staff as well as a contact for the messengers who rode in from other colonies. Whatever it was, she'd best find out quickly. As she passed by the bar, Malachi's coffee-colored eyes rested on her. She wondered what thoughts went on inside his head. He had a whole lifetime of memories she knew nothing about.

Faith stopped by the bar, where he had picked up a cloth to wipe down the table. "Can you watch the taproom for a moment? I need to see Olivia."

He nodded to her. "Yes, Ma'am. Everything will be fine." He continued his work, pausing to take a stein from a waiting man and refill it.

Faith moved to the door. It was then she realized she had not seen Captain Hoag in the dining room. She wondered if he had chosen to take his meal in the private room. He tended to eat with the men, but it wasn't impossible. After a day of drills, he probably longed for a private moment. She would ask Olivia if someone had served him supper.

Once she was outside, she took a deep breath of the cool air. A few stars had become visible on the edge of the eastern horizon, which had already turned dusky blue. The sun rested on the other side of the horizon beyond her view, blocked by trees and buildings. Her nose took in the faint, smoky scent of the air from all the fires that burned this time of year.

Faith walked swiftly to the entry of the kitchen. The door stayed shut this time of year to keep out the cold. The bench next to the entry was stacked with pots waiting to be washed. As she approached, Dorcas popped out carrying a loaded tray. She nodded to Faith before moving swiftly to the back entrance of the tavern. From the window, Faith watched Olivia moving about inside. She knocked before entering.

Olivia pointed to the table. "There's a letter for you." She watched Faith come over and stare at the folded note, a red wax seal covered where the edges folded together to keep it from unwelcome eyes. "I'm going to the root cellar for some herbs. I'll be back in a few minutes." With that, she left, closing the door firmly behind her.

The kitchen felt empty without Olivia there. Normally the room pulsed with energy as women worked to prepare meals for all the people under their care. Faith was grateful for the privacy. She recognized the neat scrawl immediately. All the Payne children had learned to write from their father's sister, who had been a stern task mistress. Sloppy writing had to be redone until it met her standards. Seth, being left-handed, had struggled more than the others. She had worked with him so that he could write with either hand so he wouldn't get into trouble, although she thought her aunt's stubbornness both ridiculous and cruel. He'd struggled with reversing letters as well. For some reason, he just didn't see things the way others did. It wasn't his fault. Faith knew how hard he'd tried. It was no wonder Seth was drawn to those bullied and oppressed. Her heart ached over her little brother. He deserved some happiness. She'd never met Tabitha, but she hoped she was a person who could love Seth as he was and not try to mold him into something different. Whatever might happen, their fates were now bound together. She hoped they would evade capture wherever they were bound.

Faith sat down and broke the seal. Emotions washed over her as she read his words.

Dearest Sister Faith,

I don't believe we shall meet again this side of Heaven. Do not worry about me. I am with the one I love. While I am grateful for all you have done, it is time for me to strike out on my own. We are going where no one will find us, and we can live a life of our own choosing. Perhaps the wilderness will prove a kinder place than what we have experienced in the colonies. Pray for God's providence on our new adventure.

You were the one who fought for me when I was small. Now, it's time for me to fight for myself and my family. We wish you well.
   Seth & Tabitha Payne

Faith laid the letter aside. Would they really find a place where they could be together? She hoped so, but it would not be within the colonies, not even under British control. Slavery was too widespread. They would have to go out far beyond the reaches of civilization. Tears rolled down her face as she contemplated their future. Her nose dripped onto the page, blurring a word. She grabbed a handkerchief out of her pocket and dried her face. Foolish tears, they helped no one. But the ache welled up inside, refusing to be vanquished. There was nothing she could do but pray for their safety, which she did with painful fervency.

The fire hissed. It was the only sound in the kitchen beyond the air moving in and out of her lungs. She rose and stuck the letter in the fire. The flames devoured it within seconds, destroying any evidence that she had heard from her little brother. It was the only thing she could do to help keep him safe. Faith watched as the last edge turned to ash. Her brother was truly gone, far from any member of his family. It was up to her to inform her father. Faith dreaded composing that letter. She couldn't bear thinking about it.

Olivia returned, bringing the faint scents of rosemary and garlic. The herbs rested in her hands before she put them on the table. Her glance slid over to Faith standing over the fire. "Everything alright?"

Faith nodded. "He's gone as far away as he can from this place. I don't blame him, but" her voice choked. "I will never see him again."

Olivia said. "That was his choice."

Faith nodded. "I guess it was the only one he had. He loved that girl enough to leave all he's ever known."

"He loved her enough to want her to be free." Olivia looked at Faith. "No place in these colonies will see beyond her skin color—you know that."

"I know. I hate it. I hate that this had to happen." Faith moved out of the other woman's way. She was still thinking. "The only place they could go is into the wilderness." She shuddered. "There's no telling what is out there."

"The natives have no interest in capturing escaped slaves," Olivia said. "Or so I hear. Although they're pretty tired of white folks going out there and taking their land."

"I guess so," Faith said. "I thought the British had negotiated for lands out west."

Olivia snorted. "I've traded with some of the natives. Negotiate is not the word they use when describing all the folks staking claim to lands they've had for hundreds of years."

Faith had no answer for that although she was sure Olivia was right. Land or anything of value had a way of going to those in power. It was a disturbing thought. She turned from the fire, eager for a task to distract her. "Has Captain Hoag eaten yet?"

Olivia shook her head. "I haven't seen him today. I fixed a tray for him, but none of his men have come to take it to him." She pointed to a tray near the end of the long table she used to prepare meals. A bowl of stew, along with a healthy slice of bread, sat there along with a slice of pie. A napkin contained a spoon. Steam still rose from the bowl.

"I'll do it," Faith said as she lifted the tray. "He needs to eat like anyone else. There is no point in letting it get cold."

Olivia raised an eyebrow. "You know he doesn't like to be disturbed."

"I'll leave it just inside the door," Faith waited for Olivia to open the kitchen door so she could step outside. It was a short walk down the path to the private room. Grass had long since worn away from the well-used path. Every now and then, she could see bootprints where someone had stepped into the soil after a rain. Within seconds, she stood just outside the small window. No light burned except for the fire, which looked like it had been stirred recently. She frowned, then went to knock on the door.

To her surprise, it was ajar and swung open easily at the touch. Faith walked inside and looked for a place to rest the tray. A small square table stood near the fire. Only a few items rested on one side: papers, a quill, and a pot of ink. He must have been dealing with his correspondence before he stepped out. A small knife rested by the quill, useful for keeping it sharp.

She approached and set the tray on the other side, away from his work. Faith was careful not to disturb his papers. She had no right to pry, but she wondered what he did when he was not drilling men.

The scent of smoke caught her attention. Her eyes searched for signs of fire, remembering a few short years ago when this very room had burned to ash and nearly destroyed everything else with it. Her nightmares had faded with time, but it took very little to bring that fear to the surface. Her eyes searched for the source. Within moments, she saw a candle smoldering in a sconce on the wall. It had not been out long. Faith circled the room to make sure nothing else was about to burst into flame. Relieved, she headed for the door only to stop when a bright pop of color caught her eyes.

Curiosity aroused she turned back to seek the source. Hoag didn't seem the type to indulge in bright colors, even the deep blues and scarlets of his uniform were somewhat subdued. Faith turned to the table next to the bed. A piece of bright pink silk spilled out of it. A token of affection? Hoag was a widower who had shown little interest in female attention despite the best efforts of many of society's mammas. A flash of memory niggled in her brain. Not many wore that bright shade of pink. Faith couldn't remember where she had seen such a bright ribbon before. The memory would not return to her. Pink spilled over the side and toward the floor, shimmering in the shadowed room. She paused for a moment, feeling like an intruder. This was his private refuge where none but a selected few were allowed to intrude. Given how much time he spent drilling his men, she imagined his private moments were few and far between. A wave of guilt washed over her at her own intrusion. The poor man deserved a little time to himself.

To assuage her conscience, she decided to do a brief tidying of the room. She would then leave his room so he could return in peace from wherever he had gone. The coverlet was rumpled as if he had suddenly been disturbed from his rest. Smiling, she plumped the pillow and smoothed the blankets. He needed a good night's rest as badly as his men, if not more so.

As she went around the bed, her skirts brushed by the troublesome drawer. As she bumped into it, the ribbon unfurled, spilling over the side. Faith grabbed to keep it from hitting the floor. In her hand lay a pink rosette, its edges gathered prettily together with thread to form a flower. Edges of the ribbon trailed out from the drawer, pulling it up on edge. Reaching out a hand, Faith tucked the ends back inside. Her hand brushed by something else. She was surprised to see a brightly printed headcloth, much like the ones Olivia wore. This one was a brilliant shade of scarlet. "What in the world?" She murmured. This was getting stranger and stranger. More ribbons lined the drawer, along with a delicate handkerchief edged in lace, all gathered together as if a magpie had started a collection. Faith stared down, puzzled, wondering what Hoag could possibly want with such things.

The floor creaked behind her warning her she was not alone. Faith looked up to see Captain Hoag entering the room. Heart pounding, she pushed the drawer closed. Faith could feel her face flush with embarrassment as she offered an apologetic smile. "I didn't mean to pry. I brought your dinner and saw the ribbon falling out of the drawer. It would be a shame for such a pretty thing to fall onto the floor."

Hoag's eyes appeared dark in the shadowed room. He didn't respond as he walked toward her, ignoring the tray of food. The slow tap of his boots echoed across the floorboards. Hoag stopped a few feet from her. His gaze never left her face.

Flustered, Faith stammered. "I'm sorry if my presence upsets you. I meant no harm." She gestured to the drawer. "I can see that you have been shopping for your daughter. Rosettes are very popular this year. I've seen them on a number of young ladies." That was a lie. She'd only see one, and she couldn't recall who had been wearing it.

He made her nervous as he stood there without speaking. Faith heard herself babbling but couldn't stop. "You haven't said a lot about your daughter. I don't think you've shared her name or her age with me. Children grow up so fast. I know it seems like yesterday my son Andrew was rolling a hoop in the yard."

Hoag nodded, breaking his frozen pose. "Amelia is growing into a lovely young lady. My sister keeps me informed on her growth. My responsibilities keep me from seeing her often. Letters suffice for now." A shadow crossed his face. "I wish her mother could have lived to see her turn into a young lady."

Faith nodded sympathetically. "There are times I think of Jon and how he would have enjoyed watching Andrew mature. It's our responsibility to share the memory of those who have passed so that they are not forgotten."

Hoag was quiet for a moment. "I can never forget Margaret. She passed too soon. There is no greater loss than to lose your heart's desire. It is difficult to continue once that is lost." His knuckles cracked as he clenched one hand in the other.

Faith shot him a concerned look. How long had it been since he had lost his wife? "I'm so sorry," she said at last. "She must have been a remarkable woman."

Hoag moved by the fire, looking at the flames. "There was no one else like her."

Feeling like an intruder, Faith edged toward the door. "I will leave you to eat in peace," she said, gesturing toward the tray.

Hoag looked at the bowl of stew and its accompaniments. "It was kind of you to bring it. My mind has been busy. I had forgotten the time." He gestured toward the chair opposite the tray. "Please join me. It has been a long time since I have enjoyed the company of a lady. Being in command leaves one without many friends, I'm afraid."

Faith hesitated. There was nothing untoward in his demeanor, yet she couldn't shake the feeling she should escape and leave the man to whatever demons disturbed him.

Hoag's gaze caught hers again. In the darkness, his eyes black and unfathomable. He smiled disarmingly. "Surely you can spare a few moments. It would mean a great deal not to eat alone. Since my wife's passing, I've had little respite from my duties."

"Very well." Faith pulled out the chair across from him and sat down uneasily. It was a small request. They were at the end of the evening meal so there was little left to do beyond gather the dirty dishes and make sure everything was ready for the morning.

Hoag took a sip of cider before digging into Olivia's stew. "You're fortunate to have a fine cook. I imagine there are many who would pay a fine penny to have her at their home. I imagine she's quite valuable."

Faith stiffened. Olivia was a person, not property. "She is a free woman in my employ. She chooses to work here at the tavern with her husband, who is also free."

Hoag set down his spoon. "I meant no insult. You are fortunate to have her and her husband. Titus—isn't it? He looks to be a strong man. Have they been with you long?"

"They joined our family after my marriage. They have been with me a long time." She chose not to say that Olivia and Titus had been slaves gifted to them by her mother-in-law. Freeing them had been a difficult task. He didn't need to know.

Hoag nodded. "You are fortunate. Having a loyal staff is a blessing." He paused to blow on his stew before taking another bite. "I brought more help into our house after the birth of our child. Margaret had a hard time recovering from the birth."

Faith nodded. "Most women need some time to recover. I am sure she appreciated your thoughtfulness." She wondered where this conversation was going. In the weeks since his arrival, he had shared very little of himself. Now, he was freely discussing his family. She watched him chewing quietly. Hoag had excellent table manners. Wherever he had come from, he had been taught well. The fire crackled as he continued to work on his meal. Faith looked about the room. He'd done nothing to personalize the space. She knew everything that was in it, even the bed had come from one of the upstairs rooms. With the exception of the ribbons in the drawer, there was nothing of a revealing nature present. The papers stacked on the table listed goods and men, notes of a commander managing his responsibilities. She wondered if he wrote to his daughter or those who cared for her in his absence.

Hoag set down his spoon. His expression grew distant. "Margaret struggled for weeks after our daughter was born. Some days, she stayed in bed. It was as if neither I nor the babe existed for her. I bought Marianna to help her around the house. She took over most of the housekeeping chores so Margaret could focus on the baby. She showed little interest in the wee thing. I thought maybe if she could rest, things would improve." He paused and set down the roll he had bitten into. "She was no longer the woman I'd married. It was as if a stranger had taken her body." He rubbed his head. "I didn't know what to do."

"Marianna found a wet nurse and took charge of the household. She began serving my meals." He rubbed his forehead. "I was lonely, and she listened to me." He looked down at the table. "She was kind to Margaret. At first, I saw her as an angel, a gift from heaven to rescue us in our time of need. I didn't see her beauty for what it was until it was too late. She lured me to her bed, and before I knew it, I was trapped." He shot her a frank gaze. "Men have needs. We suffer when denied what was once taken for granted. Marianna filled an emptiness in my soul." He sighed. "I could be more patient with Margaret, give her the time she needed to recover. A year went by, and all was well. Margaret was beginning to act like she had before the baby. She was getting dressed and smiling at Amelia as she played.

Then Marianna became greedy." His tone remained low but filled with rage. "She started asking for clothing, trinkets, and money, all for her silence. If I didn't provide it, Margaret would be told of my perfidy."

He sighed. "I decided to get rid of her before disaster struck. I had a friend with family down in the Georgia Colony willing to purchase a house slave at a good price. Marianna would have gone too far to cause any trouble. But she found out and made sure my wife knew every detail. By the time her new owner came to collect her, it was too late."

His fingers went around the band around his finger. "Two days after Marianna was sold, I found my daughter sitting on the side of a riverbank alone on a blanket with a note pinned to her frock. My wife had left her and waded out into the river. She said she couldn't live with lies."

Faith drew in a sharp breath. "I'm sorry. That must have been terrible."

Hoag scrubbed his face. His voice cracked as he continued. "It was. I searched up and down the river, hoping to find her before it was too late." He slammed a fist on the table, making Faith jump. "Two days later, her body washed up. I told all our friends it was an accident that she had fallen in, but I don't think they believed me. After the funeral, I left Amelia with my sister and joined the militia. I wasn't fit to be a father. I failed her mother. I thought a life of service was the only way I could redeem myself." His face changed, "Then I saw her in Williamsburg. The witch who destroyed my life."

Faith rose from the table. She knew who he meant, had known it when he first mentioned his former slave's name. She struggled to keep the knowledge from her face. "You have worked very hard to train your men. You're exhausted. Let me leave you to your meal and a good night's sleep. You will need it for the morning." She stepped back, intent on getting out the door as swiftly as possible, but she wasn't fast enough. Hoag reached out and held her wrist in an iron grip.

"You're not going anywhere."

Chapter Thirty

"Let me go." Faith tried to twist free, but his grip was too tight. "Olivia expects me back in the kitchen any moment now. She knows where I have gone."

Hoag stared at her, his eyes glittering. "You'll talk. Women always do. All Marianna had to do was stay quiet and do her job, but she couldn't do that. Why should I believe you would be any different? There is only one way to ensure you won't tell."

"You took advantage of an enslaved woman and sold her off to try to hide what you had done." His sense of entitlement outraged her. She let her anger rise to the surface; it was better than terror. No one would check on her for a while. There was no time to wait for rescue.

"Sit down." He pulled her arm until she fell back into the chair she had just left. The hard wood dug into her back. She stared at him, showing all the disgust she felt. "I liked you. I really did, but you had to pry in matters that didn't concern you, and I have no choice." He sighed. "I had hoped that since your brother's escape, everything would die down until we received our orders to join Washington, but you had to meddle." He frowned thoughtfully. "I can't afford any attention to be drawn to our quarters. It was bad enough when one of my privates set up a love nest next door. It was a dishonor to the unit."

Faith stared at him. "You killed Marianna because of what happened to your wife, but what about the others? Joanna, Rebecca—one of your own men. Why?"

Hoag was silent for a moment before shrugging. "I may as well tell you.

You're not going to live to let anyone else know. Joanna saw me with Marianna. I wasn't in uniform, but she was hell-bent on finding out who killed her friend, so I made it easy for her. I waylaid her on her way home from church and broke her neck. Hiding her in that old barn was easy. I was going to drop her in the river once it got dark, but someone found her first." He grinned at her ruefully. "Killing is easy. Hiding a body is not." His smile faded. "Marianna tried to run. I caught her and killed her before I'd really thought about it. When your cook came along, I hid in the woods. I was going to silence her, but there were too many people around. Luckily, you had a horse in the barn I could use to haul her away. I didn't have time to do it properly. If that printer hadn't been nosing about the old coffeehouse, I would have simply made her disappear. No one really cares about what happens to a slave."

Faith stared at him in disbelief. "Their lives mattered. All lives do."

"Killing Perkins was a favor to everyone. He dishonored my unit." Hoag looked tired. "My men were under orders to leave your staff in peace, but he got drunk one night and attacked one of your servants. That's forbidden. I confronted him, and he attacked me. He hit his head on the mantle, and that was it." His hands shook. "It should have been the end of the matter except for that girl. I had no idea she was there until I received her note."

"The ribbon isn't for Amelia, is it?" Faith remembered where she had seen the rosette. It had been on Georgia Clements' daughter one time when they had crossed paths in town.

He shook his head. "I should have burned it and the other bits, but I wanted to remember how they tried to take my honor, all that I have left." Hoag walked to the dresser and picked up the rosette. "She wanted money for her silence so she could live the life she wanted without her mother ruling over her. Foolish child. Everything has a price."

The ribbon dropped to the floor as he bent to pick it up. Faith ran for the door. Her hand covered the handle before he slammed into her, pinning her against the rough wood.

"I will be missed soon," She gasped as she tried to catch her breath. "People know I am here. Someone will check on me. You won't get away with this.

Too many people know where I am."

Hoag spoke into her ear. "Then we'd better go before anyone gets suspicious." Lifting away, he twisted an arm behind her back at a painful angle. "Be still unless you want me to break it. I could shatter that elbow with ease." He slid the door open and looked out into the yard.

It was quiet. The sun was an orange glimmer on the horizon, while the sky had turned a deep blue. The trees had become dark silhouettes on the landscape. Not even a breeze moved the dead weeds on the edges of the yard. It was as if the back of the house had been abandoned.

Faith glanced about frantically as she tried to find a way to escape. The kitchen door was closed to keep out the cold, as was the back door to the tavern. The light glowing in the windows felt miles away. She opened her mouth to scream only to feel Hoag jerk her arm up so hard she cried out.

"I did warn you," Hoag forced her to walk across the yard to the path that ran out the back. The cold that made her shiver didn't seem to impact him, but his military coat was made to withstand the weather. Noticing her shiver, he said, "Fear not, you won't feel the cold long, I promise."

If she left the yard, she would die. Faith knew it beyond a doubt. The only way to survive was to save herself. Seeking to distract him, she said. "What would Margaret say about this? Surely, she didn't expect you to be a murderer?"

Hoag didn't answer for a moment. "Margaret is beyond caring what I do. She died believing I no longer loved her. There is no forgiveness for that. All I have left is my honor. They threatened to besmirch it. They all deserved to die."

"There is no honor in killing innocent women," Faith said. "None. God himself knows what you have done. It is his justice you face."

Hoag continued dragging her over the yard. "What God allows a good woman to drown herself?" He stumbled over a piece of rough ground, giving Faith a chance.

She wrenched herself free and slugged him as hard as she could. As he recoiled from the blow, she ran for all she was worth, screaming into the black night, praying someone, anyone, would hear. Faith raced over the field to the safety of the kitchen. In the darkness, she could see the axe resting near the kitchen door. It was only a few yards away. Behind her, she could hear the hard breathing of her pursuer. Hoag reached and grabbed the top of her cap, pulling it loose and leaving her hair to trail behind as the pins fell out. Faith screamed as she felt him grab her once again, imprisoning her in his arms. She stomped his foot as hard as she could and threw her weight against him, causing him to stagger.

They fell hard to the ground as a man's voice called out. "What's happening?"

"Will!" Faith wrestled to get away from Hoag, stumbling through the rough ground of what had been the garden. Hoag grabbed her ankle, sending them both into the weeds and dirt. Her fists pounded against his body, trying to break free. She caught a glimpse of his enraged face before his hands wrapped around her throat.

She couldn't breathe. Faith clawed at him, trying to break his grip, but he would not let go. Crushing pain surrounded her neck as spots danced in front of her eyes. Her lungs burned. All she could think of was breathing. She needed air. Kicking blindly, she heard curses as her foot connected with something. A weight fell off her as consciousness faded. Air rushed into her lungs as she lay on the cold, hard earth.

In the background, Olivia screamed. "Dear God, he's killed her."

Nearby, Faith heard the sounds of grunting and cursing. Dimly, she realized a fight was happening nearby. Two figures wrestled on the ground. She struggled to sit up.

Olivia grabbed Faith's arms and began dragging her toward the kitchen, away from the battle. Titus lifted her to her feet and picked her up like a potato sack. She looked up to watch, her head still spinning.

Two men fought in the twilight. As they separated, Hoag drew his saber and slashed at his enemy. Will jumped back and grabbed a long branch from the ground, using it to block. Hoag thrust again, catching the edge of Will's shirt tail and ripping it.

Will jumped back, blood trickling from where the blade had nicked him. He circled Hoag warily, watching for his next move.

"Let me deal with him, Will." Butler joined, holding a long hunting knife. Will backed away, still holding the branch. Metal blades clanged as each tried to force a way in. Hoag's blade was longer than Butlers', but the shorter man was lighter on his feet and danced out of the way. Will stood back, watching, blocking any chance of escape.

Hoag feinted before thrusting with his blade. Butler blocked, barely avoiding a sideswipe. As Hoag turned, he stumbled on the rough ground of the garden. His foot went out from under him. As he fought to regain his footing, Butler slapped his sword arm with the flat of his blade. The saber hit the ground, bouncing off the churned-up earth. Will ran in and grabbed it, taking it out of reach.

Hoag crouched, waiting to be attacked.

Butler's weapon was ready, but he did not advance. "Surrender now. You will face justice like any other soldier."

Hoag laughed. Spinning on his heels, he turned to flee. Throwing the saber to the side, Will tackled him. Despite his desperate attempts, Hoag could not shake the other man off of him. Butler knelt next to his head and put the edge of his knife against the side of his throat. "Yield."

Hoag looked up at him for a brief moment before opening his hands in surrender.

"Get some rope," Butler yelled.

Titus ran over with a length of rope. Together, they tied his wrists behind his back.

"You have my word," Hoag complained. "There's no need for that."

Butler shot him a look as the other men hauled him up. "I'm not taking any chances. You nearly burned me alive a few days ago."

Hoag shrugged. "You picked the wrong time to enter the barn. It was deserted when I put her there." With the exception of his torn and dirty uniform he looked much as he always did. He stood upright and proud, an illusion of a leader of men with a demon hiding inside.

Faith looked up from where she sat on the bench by the kitchen. When his gaze caught hers, she shivered. Her throat hurt terribly. Her eyes burned as she stared back at him, refusing to back down. She got to her feet, using the back of the bench for support.

"Get the sheriff," Butler called out to Paul, who had just exited from the back of the tavern. "Tell him we have his killer."

"I'm a captain in the militia," Hoag said stiffly. "Civilians have no authority over me."

"The jail will still hold you until a superior officer arrives," Butler replied. "You can explain to him why you killed three young women and one of your own."

Will looked over at them. "I'm getting a few of his men. They can escort him to the gaol. This town is safer with him behind iron bars."

Faith's head buzzed. She didn't want to look weak in front of Hoag, but dizziness overwhelmed her. Olivia tucked an arm around her and turned toward the kitchen door.

"Let's get you inside."

She collapsed on a chair and put her head on the table. Olivia moved around in the background, stirring up the fire. "I'm putting the kettle on. You need something to chase away the chill and settle the shock you've had."

Faith didn't disagree. Outside, she could hear the murmur of men's voices. She presumed they were taking Captain Hoag away. "What will happen now?" she croaked. Her voice rasped. She could barely hear it herself.

Olivia came closer. "Don't try to talk. Your neck is really swollen. I need to make you a poultice."

Faith pointed at the door and raised her eyebrows.

Olivia looked out the window where the faint glimmer of a lantern could be seen. "They're taking him to the gaol."

Faith frowned and tried to speak again, but all that came out was a painful croak.

Olivia turned back to her. "Don't worry," she said grimly. "He'll hang."

Chapter Thirty-One

A soft, warm breeze blew across the yard, bringing a hint of spring. Faith paused from her sweeping to take it in. She knew when the sun set, the temperature would drop again, but she decided to enjoy the break while she could. Andrew was coming down the road. His law teacher was away on business and had sent him home for a break. Having her son near helped put her mind at rest.

A week had passed since Hoag had gone to the gaol. Faith wished the nightmares would go away as well. The sensation of having the life crushed out of her woke her many nights, leaving her in a cold sweat. Her gun now rested on a table next to her, and a stout hunting knife stayed within easy reach under the mattress. Neither helped, but she kept them close at hand.

Shading her eyes with her hand, she peered down the road. Aside from a few wagons headed to the market, there was no activity. Still, she knew time was passing too swiftly. Day by day, the newly trained militia troops were being called north to join the battle against the British. This time Will McKay would be going with them. Faith didn't tell him how frightened she was. Outgunned and out-manned, Washington's soldiers fought a brutal war against the most powerful army in the world.

Will had told her after he had enlisted in place of Marcus Clements. "It's one year of service. After that, I will be a free man. She may even hire me as a journeyman so I can save for my own shop." She had already supplied him with sturdy boots and a new set of clothes. Faith prayed it would be enough.

Faith had nodded. It was too late to object. He had come by regularly to check on her after Hoag's attack. She'd been grateful for his company. It was as if they were starting over again. They could, if he survived the war.

A horse trotted up. She recognized the fine black from her stable. Jeremy Butler peered down at her. She had never seen him in uniform before. The reds and blues reminded her of Hoag until she brushed the disturbing memory away "Are you heading north, too?"

"I will soon," he replied. "Washington needs every man he can muster. I'm an officer, so I've been tasked with keeping these boys in hand until their new commanding officer arrives." He sighed. "Drills are necessary, but quite tiresome. Most of them have little idea of what they are supposed to be doing."

Faith shivered. "When will they deal with their former officer?"

Butler's expression tightened. "His trial will be soon. We've received a warrant from General Washington. We now have enough officers to proceed. The officer representing him is visiting him this morning. We will convene in a matter of days." He tipped his hat to her. "I have troops to drill, so I must be off." He smiled before he left. "Private McKay is doing well. I predict he will drop by to see you around supper time." With that, he set off at a trot down a path that led to Nicholson Street.

Faith wasn't fooled in the least. He was off to the gaol seeing if there was any useful information to be gotten from Hoag. It was a futile gesture. He hadn't spoken since he had entered the prison. She wasn't sure she wanted to hear anything he had to say.

The day passed quietly enough. She helped Malachi in the taproom after the evening meal was served until Titus tapped her on the shoulder and told her someone waited for her out back. She needed no encouragement to go. Her feet flew down the hall and out the back toward the kitchen.

Not bothering to knock, Faith swung open the door and stared. "Where is he?"

Olivia shot her a cross look. "Come in and shut the door. We don't need all that cold air in here. "

Faith complied even as disappointment filled her.

'Don't' start looking like that," Olivia said. "You need to learn to be patient. I sent him to the cellar for a bottle of wine." She put two glasses on the table, along with two bowls of the apple tart she had made for supper. Somehow, she had managed to keep them hidden during the supper rush.

The door creaked open. Faith started to rise as Will entered carrying a dusty bottle of her much-horded French wine. He gestured for her to stay seated. She complied, waiting for what he would do next. She wasn't used to seeing him dressed in the long hunting shirt and breeches of a militia man. He looked older somehow and a bit dangerous. The feeling in his eyes when he looked at her told her all she needed to know.

Olivia gave him a cloth to wipe off the bottle before discreetly exiting her domain. Faith was grateful for her sensitivity. The door creaked as it shut behind her, leaving them in peace. The fire popped as it burned down in the grate, bathing them in its warm glow.

Will poured the wine, filling each of their glasses with ruby red wine. He looked down at the glasses before meeting her eyes. "We leave in the morning."

Faith tried to push down all the emotions colliding inside her. "I knew it would be soon. Where will you go?"

Will shrugged. "They don't tell us foot soldiers the details. All I know is we will head north to join other troops. I suspect at some point we will meet up with the General himself."

"Washington? He's in Pennsylvania—or so I've heard."

"Aye, but armies travel more swiftly than news—or so I hear." He looked at her. "I will write when I can. Butler tells me I can also send a letter with him, and he'll get it down here."

"That's kind of him," Faith said. "He's got worries of his own."

"Your sister?" Will guessed.

"Hannah lives in Philadelphia. The Continental Congress has been there since New York fell. The British will come before long"

Will took her hand. "We have no way of knowing when or if the British will come, or where for that matter. I pray they never enter Virginia, but who knows? Please be careful. I couldn't bear it if something happened to you."

Faith gripped his hand. "You are the one going into battle, not me. I pray for your health and safe return."

"I pray for a short war," Will said. "But I don't think that is our fate." He released her hand and dug into his pocket, bringing out a long strand of wooden beads. "I would like you to keep this safe for me. It was my mother's."

Faith fingered the dark wooden beads down to the ivory cross at the end. It was a beautiful piece. "It's a rosary, isn't it?"

He nodded. The light reflected off his auburn curls, catching red and gold hairs and making them glisten. His eyes were dark. "It's all I have of her. I know you are not Catholic—"

"It doesn't matter," Faith said. "This is your mother's memory. I will keep it safe."

"I would like something in return."

Faith raised an eyebrow. "What?"

"A lock of your hair, so I can have a piece of you with me no matter where I am."

Faith rose and picked up one of Olivia's small knives. It cut through the hair easily. "Take it. I hope it comforts you."

Will rose to join her. He took the lock and wrapped it in a handkerchief. "I've treated you badly in the past, not been the man you deserve. I regret those actions more than I can say."

"Hush," Faith said, putting a finger to his lips. "The past is done. All we have is this moment and the dreams we share for tomorrow." She reached up and took his face into her hands. "I love you. I always have. I always will. That is all that matters." Her lips touched his. He startled before wrapping his arms around her. They might not see one another for months, but the memory would remain, keeping them going through all they could not know but was bound to come.

A Note from the Author

Historical events never happen in a vacuum. Amidst conflicts such as the American Revolution, ordinary people lived out their lives the best they could. The British Blockade of the colonies caused economic hardship for everyone, not just those desiring to part from Great Britain. Williamsburg, Virginia, the original capital, was particularly vulnerable given that it lay between the James and York Rivers, allowing easy access by ship. This was one of the main reasons Jefferson later relocated the capital to Richmond. Working class people—tavern keepers, blacksmiths, and printers, among others—couldn't afford to move to avoid the conflict. They had to endure both economic hardship and the constant threat of invasion. The enslaved population could not flee either. They were bound by their owners to stay, regardless of the danger. Rarely noted, the war had a profound impact on those on the homefront. Those are the people whose lives I wanted to acknowledge.

Acknowledgements

Colonial Williamsburg remains a treasure trove of information regarding this time period. The restored buildings, gardens, and, most of all, the many interpreters who bring historic people to life. The reference staff at the Rockefeller Library have always been willing to answer questions regarding the minutia of life during the 18th century. Lastly, the team at Level Best is the reason these books exist. Verena, Shawn, and Deb—you are the best.

About the Author

Julie Bates' first novel, *Cry of the Innocent*, premiered in June 2021. The eight-book Faith Clarke series is set in the American Colonies during the Revolutionary War. Needless to say, Julie is an avid history buff—some would say nut. She is a member of Sisters in Crime, Triangle Sisters in Crime, Mystery Writers of America, Southeastern Mystery Writers of America (SEMWA), and The Historical Novel Society. She enjoys doing crafts, working in her garden, and experimenting in the kitchen. When not plotting her next story, she spends time with her husband and son, as well as a number of dogs and cats who have shown up on her doorstep and never left.

AUTHOR WEBSITE:
https://juliebates.weebly.com/

SOCIAL MEDIA HANDLES:
Facebook: https://www.facebook.com/JulieBates.author/
X (Twitter): @JulieBates03
Instagram: juliebates72

Also by Julie Bates

Cry of the Innocent

A Taste of Betrayal

Rise to Rebellion